ALL
FOR THE
GAME

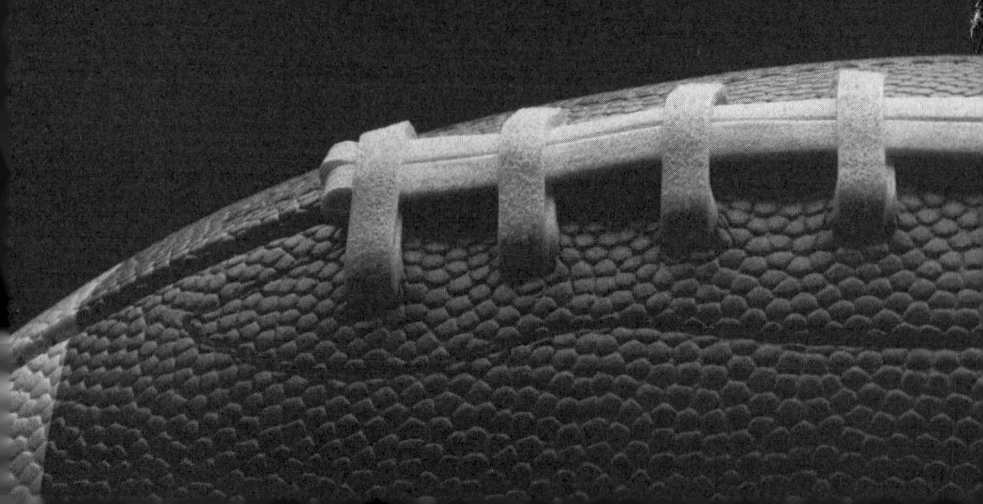

THE GAME

Heather Buchta

Penguin Workshop

For Vanessa Hernandez, I'd sever an appendage for you—thankfully, you've never asked. You're my ride-or-die, beyond words. Think Ruth from the Bible, but cooler. And if you hate this dedication . . . then Jesus made me do it.

PENGUIN WORKSHOP
An imprint of Penguin Random House LLC
1745 Broadway, New York, New York 10019

First published in the United States of America by Penguin Workshop,
an imprint of Penguin Random House LLC, 2025

Text copyright © 2025 by Heather Buchta

Photo credit: ii–iii: courtneyk/E+/Getty Images

PENGUIN is a registered trademark and PENGUIN WORKSHOP
is a trademark of Penguin Books Ltd, and the W colophon is a registered
trademark of Penguin Random House LLC.

Visit us online at penguinrandomhouse.com.

Library of Congress Cataloging-in-Publication Data is available.

Printed in the United States of America

ISBN 9780593384985

1st Printing

LSCC

Design by Mary Claire Cruz

The authorized representative in the EU for product safety and compliance is
Penguin Random House Ireland, Morrison Chambers, 32 Nassau Street,
Dublin D02 YH68, Ireland, https://eu-contact.penguin.ie.

Spencer Collins, driving south down East Pages Highway, watched his speedometer. Britney knew why. No more than five miles above the limit. Not at this hour.

"Make a wish," Britney said through a lipstick smile, her shoulders back like riding shotgun was her place in life.

It was, at least with everyone at her high school. Well, shoot, everyone except Spencer. But that was on him, always growling at anyone who looked at him, even head cheerleaders.

Especially head cheerleaders.

"Eleven eleven," she continued, pointing to the car clock. "It's good luck."

His eyes darted to her and then returned to the dark road. He half laughed, then cut it short. "No such thing."

"Sure there is." She punched him in the shoulder.

"Brit." He looked at the sleeve of his hoodie where she'd touched him. "Don't. I only agreed to let you ride with me because you showed up at my house."

She ignored his tone and checked her makeup in the visor mirror. She'd opted for the smoky palette tonight, more dramatic against her light skin, highlighting her hazel eyes and the smattering of freckles across her nose. "FYI, I showed up to take your sister."

"To an upperclassmen party? She's fourteen."

"Still. If Leah was invited—"

"She wasn't."

Ugh. So uptight. It was no wonder he didn't have a girlfriend. She could've sworn Tammy told her Spencer's sister, Leah, was invited. *And since when did Spencer get invited?* She reached for the radio dial and turned it on. A man's voice, scratchy through the old speakers, leapt into the car with his deep southern drawl: "—rigorous running and passing game of this squad. Which brings me to—and no surprise, because who isn't talking about eleventh-grade running back Finn Geringer, new to East Pages High just this summer"—Brit smiled, hearing Finn's name—"and I'll tell y'all, I'll tell y'all that he does not have the history, does not have the two years' backbone of practice, does not have—"

Spencer turned the dial down.

Brit shifted in her seat and flipped the volume back up. "—first transfer in eleven years to be brought on as a starter to the varsity squad of EastPay, which begs the question of recruitment, but coaches insist on a high moral code of—"

His palm extending like he was stiff-arming the announcer, Spencer slammed the radio off. Brit jumped, but then turned to him, narrowing her eyes. *So dramatic.* She could match it, and she did, staring at him with unblinking eyes, turning away slow and exaggerated until she again faced the windshield.

Strung from one side of the highway to the other, a huge banner flapped from the warm Texas wind. It read "FIGHT ON, EAST PAGES HIGH!" with a picture of a red football helmet on each side, framing the letters. She and the other cheerleaders had put up all the signs just last week. Already the town was filled with the energy that came at the start of every football season. Electric.

Proud. After all, football kept the businesses alive in this small town. Pastor Mike would say it was the good Lord. But Brit would bet her pom-poms he'd miss a Sunday morning before he'd miss a Friday night.

"So whatdya think of the new guy?" Brit said, following the sign with her eyes as they drove under it. "Finn Geringer."

"You mean your cousin?"

Well, dang. She chewed on her lip. Guess everybody knew by now. She'd only admitted it to a couple cheerleaders. She fidgeted for her lipstick in her pockets. "That's irrelevant."

"Is it? Finn Geringer hands us our only loss last season, and our head cheerleader is *related* to him?"

"So? It's not like I was trying to keep it secret."

"Sure you were. You'd be dumb not to."

She hated that he was right. "Anyway, he plays for us now, so who cares?"

"You do. People would've eventually dug it up—you being cousins. But lucky you. The enemy *transferred* to our team. Britney Wallace still gets to be queen."

She threw her head against the headrest, annoyed he hadn't answered about Finn. She flipped up the visor like she wanted a better view of the stars, only she never looked. She flipped it down again. Up, down. Up, down.

"Brit."

She stopped midflip. Lolled her head to the side window and tried to sound casual. "You been practicing with him all summer." She pressed her forehead against the glass. "He got what it takes?"

She immediately felt him step harder on the gas pedal, but she wasn't sure if it was to drown her out or because they were already late to the party.

"You don't scare me," Britney continued, absently drawing on the glass with her finger. She'd tutored Spencer in math back in ninth grade. Neither of them would admit that now, but they would've even called themselves friends. That is, until the day she noticed a pattern in the school's football stats—how EastPay's scores were higher against teams with better records. She'd confided in him—told him how the magic of Dante's Ravine was helping them win—but he said there was no such thing. Then he went and blabbed it. Thank God no one found out it was her idea. She saw the backlash he got. He shut up real quick, but that's also when he became ugly—acting mean and moody with everyone. But he never snitched, and secretly, she loved him for that. "The other kids at school might be scared. But I've seen the way you look at your little sister. Like you're a human. Like you look after the ones who—"

"Do you want a ride or not?"

"I'm in the car with you, ain't I?" A semi drove by in the other direction, shaking Spencer's 1998 Chevy Blazer. Everyone in this part of Texas had a light accent, but Brit made sure hers was thick, like she'd swum in it. "Horror movies don't freak me out. I seen 'em all."

"This isn't a movie."

She rolled her eyes back toward her blond curls. "Exactly. It's a party, Spence. Don't act like we're heading to war. It's beer and music and—"

"At Dante's Ravine."

"Not scared, are you? It's been years."

"Doesn't change what happened there."

His words unnerved her, but she shook it off. "It's a *river*. We're hanging out with friends on the river. Lighten up."

She played with the #39 key chain hanging from his rearview mirror. Behind her, the two Spartan helmets in the back seat knocked against each other and rolled around. Not football helmets. Spartan armor. The kind warriors wore with nose plates cascading down from the forehead and cheek plates that wrapped forward. "Invitation helmets," they were called. Tickets into the preseason party. They were just the cheap plastic versions, spraypainted brass, but they still felt powerful to Brit. They were numbered, and everyone knew that not just anyone was asked to these parties. Definitely not students like Spencer, who kept himself outside the team's social circle.

"Hey, how in the name of Texas did you get invited, anyway? When you're not on the football field, you just brood around school glarin' at people like they run over your cat and spit in your cornflakes."

Spencer didn't reply.

They passed a speed limit sign. Above it, a marquee flashed the words "FIRST GAME FRIDAY! EAST PAGES HIGH FOOTBALL. BEAT THE PIONEERS!"

"Look at you," Britney scoffed, pulling out her lipstick tube and applying it. "Why'nt you just stay home? Not gonna be enough alcohol tonight to make up for your buzzkill."

Spencer swerved into the shoulder, jarring Brit's lipstick across her cheek. He skidded to a stop, and the wheels spun under them, a cloud of dust billowing behind the back window. Britney's arms flew forward and slammed against the dashboard, the lipstick flying out of her hand.

"Jesus, Spencer!"

He threw the Blazer into park and looked at her. She kept her chin high, pretending that she hadn't just taken the Lord's name in vain, that she didn't have a red painted line that now went from her lips to her ear. He gripped her by the forearm, but she noticed it wasn't rough. "You listen close, Britney, because I'm saying this once, you got it?" He paused, and she saw again that glimmer of *human*. He didn't let go of his hold on her, but he opened his mouth and then shook his head and breathed through his nose, like he was struggling to find words or debating what to say.

She waited, letting him hold her by the forearm, instead focusing on how her beige-pink skin contrasted with his, those hours of practicing football in the Texas sun toasting his arms to a golden brown. Bronzed skin. Hair the color of sand. He was an earth tones palette. She had one at home called Vintage Garden. Eucalyptus. Moss. Caramel. She stifled a grin, envisioning his broody glare softened with eyeshadow.

He finally spoke, but it was quiet, like the outside might hear. "Why'd you say Leah was invited?"

"Your sister? Heck if I know. Tammy just said—"

"Leah's *boyfriend* plays football. Eli. *Not* Leah. She's not in band. Not a cheerleader. Why the hell would you think that?"

She licked her lips. She hadn't thought about that. "Whatever, I was wrong."

"You think I want to be here? It's a party for football players."

"Yeah?"

"*Players*, Brit." That human look was gone, replaced by steel. "I'm on the bench, remember?"

She ignored his grip, looked into the mirror above her, and with her free hand, rubbed to blend the lipstick line, a dark rouge but only on one side, high on her cheek like a bruise. "Then play better."

Spencer shoved her arm away and ripped his car into drive again, peeling out onto the highway, his #39 key chain swinging back and forth.

She continued, "Maybe you could do some suicides, you know, running back and forth on the field touching the ground, like each time you go farther—"

"I know what suicides are."

"Well, your running game don't. Maybe if you showed up on a Sunday, did some bleachers, built up your quads. My mom has one of those thigh machines you can borrow." She hiccupped and held in her giggle.

He inhaled deeply, blew it out slowly. "You about done?"

She slapped her hand on the dash and laughed. "Just stop already! You walking around bitter like you play with a bunch a Plano princesses, but this is EastPay High football. You wanna play, then you gotta perform, so why don't you stop talkin' crap the way other towns do about us, like we can't possibly be just good at football. No, if we're winning, there's gotta be more, gotta be the cheatin' devil involved, or some abracadabra on the field, rabbits up our sleeves or hopping around in our jockstraps and making us win championships, and meanwhile, we're makin' out and drinking beer and dancing our asses off at Dante's Ra— Spencer!"

She screamed, matching the squealing of Spencer's tires as he slammed the brakes. In the middle of the highway, a guy at a dead sprint turned at the sound, eyes wild with fear, holding up a hand as if that alone could stop Spencer's SUV. Spencer stopped at a sideways skid, grazing the guy's shoulder and sending him tumbling across the bike lane and into the drainage ditch.

Chapter 1

MEGAN

It was early Sunday morning. Megan Kaufman, toes up on *relevé* with the grace she once exuded during dance recitals, was tapping on Finn Geringer's window. Finn, already wearing his practice jersey minus the shoulder pads, opened it and leaned out for a kiss. With a single movement, he wrapped an arm around her and lifted her up and into his room.

"Stop," she joked. "I'm late to my boyfriend's."

Finn grinned. "Better not tell him you stopped here first."

She ducked back through the window and hopped down to the dewy grass, then jogged past the garden, across the lawn where the "Just Sold!" sign still stood firmly staked, and made her way back to his front door. She had knocked only once when Finn answered, flinging the door open.

"Hey!" he said, faking surprise. "You're here!"

She suppressed a laugh as he scooped her up and swung her inside. "Sorry I'm late," she whispered into his ear. "This sexy football player kept trying to kiss me."

"Did you tell him you had a boyfriend?" he whispered back, his long eyelashes tickling her cheek. His father, whom he'd never met, had strong genes, Meg reasoned, because he looked nothing like his mom. Middle Eastern, most likely, from Finn's olive skin and curly hair.

He pulled back and looked at her. His large dark eyes—the color of midnight, she'd always said—had a way of climbing inside her, and today they twinkled, and she grinned. "I keep forgetting," she joked, "now that he doesn't go to my school anymore."

"Oh, really?" He tickled her side, and she burst into laughter. "Grandma, look who's here!"

Megan waved at Finn's grandma on the couch. "Hello, Mrs. Callahan. Thought I'd help with some of the unpacking."

Mrs. Callahan set her tea down on one of the moving boxes littering the living room. "You gonna work that poor girl to death, Finn."

Megan wished her parents had heard that. For them, there was no such thing. It was ballet, and cotillion, and piano, and *Oh, you must join us for dinner with our colleague from Columbia*, some politician or financial adviser—she could hardly keep track, but it was always somebody she absolutely *must* rub shoulders with—because *connections are everything, Megan.* When her ballet career ended, every free hour was filled with church and volunteer work, which by definition should be voluntary, not penciled into her calendar by her parents. Her dad was a lawyer and as white as the star on the Texas flag, but since her mom was Black, and "only thirteen percent of this state," as she loved to remind Meg, "*and* a woman," Meg should understand why it was so important to never say no to an opportunity. She understood that as a Black woman, her mother needed to work twice as hard for half as much. She knew in many ways, this would apply to her, too, but sometimes she just wanted to have fun and be a normal teenager. But bringing that up was akin to blasphemy. Her mother didn't gain the city's respect through "fun" or by wishing and hoping—no, she had worked relentlessly for it. Meg had heard the speeches countless times, and when the speeches finished, the Bible verses continued. *"In all toil there is profit, but mere talk tends only to poverty." "Whoever is slack in his work is a brother to him who destroys." "Slothfulness casts into a deep sleep, and an idle person will suffer hunger."* Meg loved the Bible but marveled at how her mom could narrow the focus of such a large book every time Meg asked to hang out with Finn.

Finn's grandmother's words echoed in her mind. *"You gonna work that poor girl to death."* How she wished she could bottle up those words in one of her mom's empty vodka handles hidden throughout the house. Pour it out on her parents' plate of caviar at the luxury hotel in Austin where they'd stayed last night for a benefit. Megan smiled at Mrs. Callahan. "No ma'am, I love helping y'all unpack."

"Should be done by now. My new garden is done. It's more lived in than this place."

"And it looks great! Love the vines on the trellis," Megan added, but Mrs. Callahan wasn't derailed.

"We been here since June, but they been keeping Finn at the field like a full-time job."

"I know, I know," Finn said. "There's a lotta plays to memorize, Grandma. Got two years to make up in two months."

Megan leaned down to the couch and hugged Mrs. Callahan. "Came early to help out for an hour," Meg said. "Then we'll head out."

"East Pages Parade, Grandma." Finn handed her two pills. "Remember?"

"'Course I do," she said. "Got arthritis, not Alzheimer's. Only Sunday of the year East Pages churches add evening services. Well, outside of Good Friday and Christmas Eve. I'm goin' to the parade with you, remember? But why in Sam's heaven *you* goin'?" She pointed a crooked finger at Megan.

"You mean because my boyfriend's playing for the enemy now?" Megan poked Finn in the ribs, pretending it would be no big deal not seeing her boyfriend anymore during passing period at West Oak High. It wasn't so much that he'd be attending their rival school. It was that they'd gone to school together since they were six. In fifth grade, he found her in the hall crying because she had to miss a birthday party for a ballet recital. That night, Finn and his grandma showed up with balloons and flowers, and he told her the recital was way better than a silly birthday party.

They'd been friends ever since.

In middle school, she'd complain to him how hard her parents pushed, and he'd remind her how lucky she was to have parents who cared—to have parents at all—always bringing sanity to her world of right angles and tucked-in shirts. In ninth grade, when she went down with two stress fractures that left her in a wheel-chair for three months, he was the first to push her through the hallways, popping wheelies and making her laugh. He was a well-known football player by then—varsity as a freshman—and one day she jokingly asked him why he didn't have ten girlfriends by now. He got quiet and said he had to hurry to class. When the bell rang to end the day, he rolled her down the school hallway and there, next to her locker, was a giant piece of butcher paper, his sloppy writing painted across it: "WHEEL you be my girlfriend?" She leapt up on her wobbly ankles, and they embraced. Nothing had felt so perfect. They heard a lot of "Finally" and "It's about time" from their friends.

And now the everyday presence that she'd come to love since first grade wasn't going to be there. No more ballet, which was fine by her. But no more Finn? She knew he felt it, too. But the chance to play for EastPay was too good to pass up.

Meg smiled warmly at Mrs. Callahan. "I'll wear sunglasses and a beard so my school won't hear about it."

"She's too good for you," Mrs. Callahan hollered to them as they walked toward Finn's bedroom. "Better marry her before you get hit in the helmet too much!"

Chapter 2
FINN

Thirty minutes later Finn was breaking down his fifth box with an X-Acto knife. He knew his girlfriend. Every movement was gentle but calculated. As if even her personality wore ballet slippers. Delicate, sure. But powerful and purposeful. She smiled whenever he mentioned his new school. Always supportive. But sometimes, he noticed her fists tighten and release. Eighteen months had taught him to look beyond her smile.

"Megs," he said, the nickname he gave her because she was so efficient and organized, it always seemed like there were two of her getting things done. She looked up. "You really okay with East-Pay now?"

"Sure," Megan said, but Finn noticed her slicing open another box with more force than it needed. "I mean, I get it. You're Finn Geringer. Why wouldn't you transfer to the best football school? Even Jamal understands."

Finn tensed.

Meg set the knife down and added, "He *does*. Just give him time."

Finn and his best friend, Jamal, had planned their entire football careers together. They swore they'd both head to community college in two years—play locally—and then both transfer to a big school. Always together. However, after Finn decided to play for EastPay, Jamal had stopped texting—even before the move. Finn hadn't exactly tried hard, either. It was that way with guys. You didn't have to have some big falling-out. Sometimes you just faded into the background. He blamed the busy schedule. But really, they both knew it wasn't that.

"He'll come around," Meg said, like she knew what Finn was thinking. Her arm disappeared inside the box, pulled out something wrapped in newspaper. "You had to go."

"But?"

"But nothing." She unwrapped it to reveal a trophy, set it on Finn's dresser. "It's just— It's gonna feel different. I've been watching for you at my locker since ninth grade."

"I'd been watching *you* long before that."

"Stop it," she said, but blushed.

"You know you're the whole reason I'm any good at this sport." He thought of his mom—wherever she was—and knew his life could've gone in a far worse direction.

Meg gave him a friendly shove.

"It's true," he said. "You'd get to school early to change out of your workout clothes—"

"I had ballet practice before school—"

"You were nine!"

Meg shrugged.

He remembered how she'd study during lunch and then change into her leotard and sweats right after the bell rang, so her parents could take her straight to rehearsal. It got in his head—made him want to work hard at things, too. He'd tell his grandma about her all the time. After he got home that day in fifth grade, he was telling his grandma about Meg crying in the hall when a knock on the door interrupted him. Back then, his mom would show up maybe five times a year—always for money or groceries—and always with the same vacant look in her eyes from years of addiction. It was like any other time, but this time, she hadn't acknowledged Finn. Not a word.

After she left, Grandma pulled him into a hug. He didn't know why the tears came so quickly. "Is that how I'm gonna end up?" he'd croaked. He'd thought it before, but never voiced it.

Grandma sighed. She started to answer, but then said, "I have an idea. How about you and I go to Meg's recital?" He nodded, even though he couldn't quite shake the sadness, and got ready.

Meg was magic on stage.

Afterward, Grandma said, "See? You focus on the right things, it'll keep you out of the wrong things."

She looked hard at him, and he understood, even back then, even in fifth grade.

He would never become his mom.

He started waking up early, just like Meg. Practicing football more. Practicing runs. Fakes. Moves. Watching tape. He said it was for the sport. But it was also for Meg, the girl who'd captivated him with her hard work and her ballet slippers.

"Anyway," Meg said, waking him from the memory, "I'll be fine. You have to go. It's East Pages High."

"Your rival school." He threw a ball of newspaper at Megan, and she ducked. "And *East Pages High*?" No one called it by its formal name, the town's name. It was simply EastPay. She was clearly bothered.

"It was *your* rival school just four months ago!" She reached into the box and put another trophy on his dresser. "It's not the football, Finn." She stopped and looked up, wrinkling her nose. Then she said, "No. It is. It is the football. I just don't want you to get sucked in . . ." She trailed off, fishing around in the box for another trophy.

"To what?"

She shrugged, but she didn't need to say more. EastPay had a rep for cheating, for cutting corners, for going for injuries rather than clean tackles.

"Look," he said, "every school in this county—heck, this *state*—is crazy about the game. EastPay's no different. I've been playing with them all summer, and, and hey." He waited for her to look up at him. "Hey, c'mere." He pulled her to the bed, where they lay down on pillows facing each other. Stripes of morning sunlight peeked in on them. He laced his fingers in hers. "So you've heard weird shit about East Pages—"

"*We've* heard—"

"Okay, *we've* heard. But that was *our* school sayin' it. *Your* school. Do you think it's possible that— Meg, I've been at two-a-days, three-a-days all summer with football players, and band members, and cheerleaders—and half the school in the stands watching—but I haven't seen anything 'weird.' And Brit's been there since ninth grade."

Meg lifted an eyebrow. That eyebrow lift, *similar to her father's*, Finn thought, *the way her father looks at me when he shakes my hand.*

"Okay," he said, chuckling. "So maybe my cousin isn't the best example of normal. Look, what I'm saying is maybe people need a reason to hate East Pages. And if they can't think of one, well, then . . ."

"So you think our school—*my* school—made it up?" She absently played with the drawstring of his football pants. He could tell she was trying to accept it but was having a hard time. Just four months ago, he believed those rumors, too.

He pulled her fingers from his drawstring and linked his index finger with hers. "I think I'm here to play football. That's it. I don't care about rumors. Football—this school—it's my best shot."

There was no way he was letting Grandma end up in a "facility." She wasn't senile. Still, he knew eventually she'd need one-on-one care, something neither of them could afford. That would put her in the hands of the state.

A nursing home.

Maybe community college had been the original plan—take care of Grandma by becoming a physician's assistant. But it would be seven years of school and a load of debt before he became a PA, or . . .

Or.

He could get drafted in four. Rookie NFL players pulled in 705K last season, and with annual 45K salary bumps until 2030, a shot at that was everything. If EastPay could get him a D1 scholarship straight out of high school, he had to try. It was his best chance at getting drafted. Even Jamal knew that.

So, yes, he'd risk leaving his girlfriend. Moving to another town. Breaking promises to his best friend.

Meg spoke gently. "I told you we can talk to my parents."

This again? He pulled away from her. "No. Look, I'm not a charity case. I can do this on my own. I don't need rescuing. How do you think that'll look to your dad? On top of how he already feels."

Megan threw her head back on the pillow. "Finn, my dad's not gonna change. No one will ever be good enough for his daughter. Meanwhile, you're going to wait until you get to the pros to provide for your grandma? You haven't even gotten to college! Just let my parents—"

"No!" Finn sat up and squinted out his window into the morning brightness. He knew the pressure he felt shouldn't be taken out on Meg. His voice was quiet but lined with steel. "I don't need any charity checks from your father. This school is my chance. Think of all the scouts who check out EastPay." Still, she was right. It *was* going to be different not seeing her in the halls every day. He dropped his head, softened his voice. "I need you to believe I can do this."

He heard her movement behind him as she sat up. Felt both of her arms as they reached around him, her lips as they brushed his collarbone. His muscles flexed under her touch.

"I've always believed that," she murmured. He turned to look at her, and she kissed him again, this time on the lips. "But okay. I'm all in. I'll even cheer for you when you're playing against my school."

He could feel her muscular back as his hands pulled her in. He loved how athletic she was, how hard she worked to maintain strength even when she'd been injured. He smiled, speaking into their kiss. "You better."

"Oh really?" He let her pull him back down on the bed. "I can take you, Mr. All-State Running Back." She climbed atop his stomach, pinned his shoulders to the pillow.

"We'll have to see about th—" Their wrestling was interrupted by a vibrating phone on his nightstand. Megan reached for it. Finn saw the caller ID: *Britney.*

"Your cousin," she said, handing him the cell.

"Hey," he answered.

"You on your way?" He noticed again how much thicker Brit's accent had become over the last few years.

"We're about to head out."

"Who's *we?* You and Grandma?" She paused. "Meg?"

His eyebrow crinkled. "Yes, Megs too."

Brit offered only sound effects, a sort of whistle-inhale.

"She'll be fine." He chuckled. "She's a big girl."

"Hmph. Can I talk to her?"

"Sure." He handed the phone to Megan.

"Hey, Brit," Meg said. He loved how close Meg was to his family. "Can't wait to watch you in action today!" She listened, and then, "Of course I'll be there. Because he's my boyfriend, not a terrorist. Of course I'm okay. You okay? Yeah, no, you sound fine. Just . . . I dunno. Yeah, we're on our way."

Finn knelt to tie his cleats.

Meg set the phone down. "That was strange."

"Can we take your car?" He stood. "What was strange?"

"Why'd she call?"

Finn grabbed his helmet. "Who knows? Pregame jitters?"

"First game isn't till next week. When has she ever called to check on you? On me?"

Finn shrugged. "She's head cheerleader. Probably wanted to make sure I wasn't late for the charity game. Big show for the media today."

"It's just football." She grinned, knowing her words were blasphemy.

He put his arm around her and ushered her out of his bedroom. "Don't let Texas hear you say that."

Chapter 3
BRITNEY

Down on seven. Pop on eight. Her blond hair whipping across her face and music blaring through the speakers, Brit led the cheerleaders through choreography on the sidelines. The counts drowned out the images of last night. As the song ended, her co-captain, Tammy, bounded her way.

"Whole town's here." Tammy motioned to the overflowing stands.

The parade had finished, and the boys from the group home were suited up in their donated football gear and playing against the famous EastPay High District Champions.

A scrawny preteen boy crouched and glowered at Finn. The front of his oversize #42 jersey touched the grass.

"So adorable, right?" Brit whispered to Tammy.

"If you mean your cousin, then yes."

The football was snapped. The eleven-year-old charged, galloping at Finn with his skinny legs. Finn, instead of spinning out of the boy's grasp, let himself be pushed. Brit knew Finn wouldn't fall—that would be too obvious—but he faked a stumble, and the play was dead four yards down the field.

For this game, there was only one rule: Make sure the kids had fun.

The emcee shouted through the loudspeaker, ". . . and All-City transfer Finn Geringer could *not* break free for the pass!" Finn pulled the young boy up off the grass by the back of his jersey, then hit him on the side of the helmet. "Nice play, forty-two." The kid stood tall, a big cantaloupe smile across his face. He quickly hid it, nodded once, and ran back into position.

Brit looked up at the crowds, who were chanting, "FORTY-TWO! FORTY-TWO!"

She loved this school.

She'd been worried about her cousin transferring. People at her school knew Finn. How could they not? West Oak's Finn Geringer broke EastPay's perfect record last season. His touchdowns—four in the same game—brought the EastPay Spartans to a shocking one-point loss to their crosstown rivals. And the talk in the halls afterward. Asking each other where he lived. What car he drove. Who his friends were. She knew her classmates were angry, just talking smack. Still, only her good friends Jalisa and Dalisa Powell knew, and they kept her secret the way only twins could.

No one knew they were related until he hugged her at the first practice, and two JV cheerleaders accused her of kissing the enemy. "Ew," she blurted. "Gross. He's my cousin." Silence followed, and she immediately wished she could take it back. When she turned around, the girls were gone, but for the next two weeks, she got the silent treatment. She swore she could hear the whispers—above the players' grunts and tackles, the band yelling out formations, drums banging, varsity cheer clapping—whispers as loud as the cicadas about how dare she and did you know and why'd she hide that he was her cousin and is it her fault we lost?

Even her co-captain, Tammy Shaw, said as they dressed in the locker room, "Can't believe you kept that one under wraps for this long. I knew, by the way. Why do you think they didn't trust you to be captain on your own?" Brit hadn't told a soul, but she wasn't surprised that Tammy knew. That was the thing about small towns. People sometimes just *knew*.

She was pretty sure he was aware of the lion's den he had entered back in June, but by August, he was like Daniel—and the lions? Kittens. She sighed in relief at that. How quickly talent could make people forget. *Did you see him practice this summer? Geringer? He could bring us to State. Who said they hated him? It wasn't me. Not me not me.*

Everyone at school loved Finn, and according to them, always had. Still, every time Finn made a good play, she'd see faces smile at her, as if the play was her ticket to keeping her captain armband.

"Heard you rode with Spencer last night," Tammy said, pulling her from her thoughts.

"Not my fault." Brit tightened her ponytail. "Thought you said I was driving Leah. I showed up, and Spence was all, 'What are you, my chaperone?' So I just figured he had an invite." Head cheerleaders got to deliver the invitations, but it was the football captains who were in charge of who was invited.

"I'm pretty sure it was *Leah's* invite. But whatevs. 'Bout time he showed some school spirit. Can't believe you hit someone."

She felt the panic rising. How had Tammy heard? "I wasn't driving!"

"Would've been amazing if you were." Tammy pushed a pompom in Brit's face as if powdering her nose. "Asshole deserved it for trespassing. *And* walking into oncoming traffic."

Brit could still hardly believe it had happened. They'd called 911.

"Do we look?" she'd croaked to Spencer, peering into the drainage ditch, only seeing darkness.

"We wait," he'd said.

In less than ten minutes, a patrol car had arrived. "Never you mind, miss," the cop had said. "My partner spotted the gentleman off the turnout where Lamar Lane cuts the highway. He's fine. With him now." No mention of the hour she and Spencer were out. Just a tip of the hat and then back in his car, blue lights fading down the highway.

Shaken and confused, she'd wobbled behind Spencer through the dark, across dead leaves and knotted roots, keeping the water tower slightly left and the rush of water ahead. Halfway there, they met up with Zach Johnson and Malik Taylor, two defensive linemen, and they all put on their invitation helmets and headed to the party. She swallowed the alcohol and soon lost herself in giggling and playful flirting, loving the camaraderie of her football family. But the look on the guy's face, like they had hit him on purpose—

Brit shook off the memory and threw herself into three handsprings and a back tuck. She wiped the sweat off her forehead and scanned the packed bleachers, spotting her grandmother in the third row. Mrs. Callahan returned Brit's wave with a thumbs-up.

"Hey." A friendly arm wrapped around Brit's waist.

Brit turned and hugged Meg. "There you are!"

It wasn't until Meg said, "You okay?" that Brit realized she was still holding on to Meg. Brit pulled away, tried to cover.

"Of course! Just impressed you're in one piece. I mean, you are walkin' on enemy ter'tory." Brit giggled, motioning to the spongy track under their feet, the white lines that divided the racing lanes. "Watch out for land mines."

"Shh!" Meg motioned to her red shirt. "I'm wearing your colors so I camouflage. I wish West Oak's home games never conflicted with EastPay's."

Beyond the color guard preparing for their eleven a.m. performance—their flags bobbing like giant floating toothpicks—Brit noticed a policeman following her with his eyes.

"Oh, it's okay," Brit said. "You're allowed to miss games."

There was a short pause. "No, I just mean I wish I could support Finn every game."

Brit nodded absently, her eyes still on the policeman. "Yeah, I'm sure the coaches would love that. Having you around more often." The words came out more sardonic than she'd intended. She quickly added, "For team spirit and all that. Anyway, they're fine with you dating. Not thrilled, but whatever."

He was still watching her. *There were supposed to be cops today*, she reminded herself. Every EastPay Day, they strolled in their starched and stiff uniforms, filtering through the crowds, tapping their batons and winking at children, keeping East Pages *All-American*. She waved, and he tipped his hat to her. Like the cop did before he left last night.

"What do you mean?" Meg asked, but Brit forgot what she'd said.

"Wanna join the cheerleaders?" She noticed her voice was louder than necessary. Steadied it. "We're doing makeovers."

"Sure, but—" Brit grabbed her hand, and they walked over to the visitors' side of the field, where the rest of the squad had set up their cheer boxes for the foster girls. The cheerleaders were painting the girls' faces with designs, glitter, stars, unicorns. Dalisa and Jalisa were helping the girls into fancy clothes from boxes spilling over with costumes.

"Brit," Meg said, stopping Brit with an arm. "You been acting jumpy, even for you. You okay?"

"'Course!" Brit chirped. Too much. Meg's eyebrows lifted, and Brit pretended not to notice. Instead, she turned to a girl with lopsided ponytails. "Guess what?" she said. "Miss Megan here is a professional ballerina!"

Meg opened her mouth to protest, but Brit squeezed her arm. These girls didn't need to learn about quitting. Meg's mouth closed into a big smile. "What's your name?" Meg asked.

"Tawny," the girl whispered.

"Would you like to learn how to do a pirouette?"

Tawny nodded.

"Okay, arms up!"

Tawny mirrored Meg's body movements, and as they spun away, Brit relaxed. She was making everything bigger than it needed to be.

"That Finn's girl?" Tammy said, sidling up beside Brit.

Meg—who must've overheard—waved. "I'm Megan!" she called to them, then resumed twirling.

Tammy smiled without showing her teeth. Britney knew that smile. Not friendly at all.

"Well, aren't you the happy family," Tammy muttered. "Sweet kid." She nodded at Tawny. "Remember when *you* were a nobody?"

Brit's stomach curled. She could hear what Tammy was really

saying: *Watch yourself. You could be a nobody again.* She didn't think anyone remembered her middle school days when she first moved here. Her math teacher, who was also the cybersecurity club adviser, had recruited her for the team on the first day of sixth grade. Something about her high scores in the placement exam, but when he announced it to the whole class, she heard someone snicker and someone else mutter, "Nerd alert." She turned to see who said it and came face-to-face with a cute girl in a high ponytail smirking at her. Tammy Shaw.

No one talked to her after that, even during passing period, when huddles of giggly girls never once said hi. She joined the team, hoping she'd find friends there, but there were only three other students in the cybersecurity club, and their noses never left their screens. She did the same until her mom enrolled her in gymnastics to counteract the endless hours of screen time. She'd grown up tumbling, but this was a new gym with none of her old friends. Every day after school—walking to gymnastics, losing herself in tumbling and balancing and flipping. Such an individual and isolating sport, the loneliest three years of her life. Until everything changed: the day Ms. Ricky, the East Pages cheer coach, walked into the gym to pick up her daughter from the toddler tumblers class. "You trying out for EastPay cheer? We could use a new flyer."

"Of course," Brit had answered, not even knowing what it meant to be a flyer. But auditions for the fall squad were in two weeks, and she gave herself a YouTube and TikTok cram session every day leading up to it.

Tryouts were intoxicating. She'd learned the dance easily— like she was built for it—and when her number was called, the music pulsed through her veins in perfect sync with her movements.

She'd never looked back. She'd forgotten that she'd ever eaten lunch alone, ever walked through the halls with her chin tucked down. Her national award in cybersecurity stayed tucked away deep in her closet. But everything resurfaced with one sentence: *"Remember when you were a nobody?"*

Brit shook her pom-pom in Tammy's face like Tammy had done earlier. "Remember when I made varsity flyer as a freshman?"

Tammy's mouth clamped shut. Brit was the only freshman to make varsity squad. Tammy had made the frosh/soph squad that year. Not even JV. Brit couldn't believe it when she saw her name on the list by the juniors and seniors. Britney Wallace. The youngest one. The tiniest one. The new favorite of every eleventh- and twelfth-grade cheer girl. She'd gotten her Cinderella story, and the clock never struck midnight. She stepped onto EastPay's campus and went from zero to goddess. EastPay was home. Family. Everything. And girls like Tammy were all talk, she had to remind herself. Tammy was just being Tammy, and later today, she'd text Brit a pic of her new nail color or questions about Physics notes.

Sure enough, Tammy snapped to a smile. "'Course I remember! You were the Fearless Flyer!"

Brit smoothed down her cheerleading skirt with shaky hands.

Tammy wasn't smiling with her teeth.

Chapter 4
MEGAN

When the referee blew the whistle an hour later to end the game, Megan was helping Britney zip an eight-year-old named Cassie into a Snow White dress.

Finn jogged their way, and Meg sighed. She'd been dying to talk to him all morning. Brit had said some strange things. Earlier, Meg texted her best friend, Kylie, about it, who wrote,

What's Finn's take?

Dunno. He's on the field.

Pay you five bucks to get his attention by flashing him.

Meg laughed and sent a response.

I'd prob get banned from EastPay.

Surprised that hasn't happened already.

"Hey, superstar," Britney greeted Finn.

"Hey, Brit," Finn said. He leaned around Brit and gave Megan a quick kiss. "You okay?"

"I'm perfect!" Meg lied. She twirled the little girl. "I'm dancing with a *princess!*"

Cassie beamed and spun in her dress. Another girl tapped Cassie with a wand and said, "Tag! You're it!" The two girls chased each other in and out of the cheer boxes.

"You got a minute?" Meg said to Finn.

"Sure."

She led Finn away from the cheerleading squad and into the mass of booths. Between two bounce houses, their voices muted by the generators, Finn said, "You having fun?"

She thought for a moment, then answered truthfully, "Yeah." It really *had* been a fun day. "I can see why you love this place."

He tilted his head. "But?" He squeezed her hand gently.

She squeezed back, thankful he could read her so well. "It's just . . . something's off. Today, when Brit saw me, she hugged me, like, forever long."

"Sounds like Brit."

"No, it was like she was glad I was safe or something." His eyebrow reached up, and she knew he didn't buy it. "You wanna hear what she said to me?" He waited. "Because I go to a different school, I'd be *allowed* to miss games."

"So?"

"Since when are games mandatory?"

"It's just an expression, Megs. No one misses football games here. Especially not the starters' girlfriends." He swung his arm around her shoulders, but she pulled back.

"And that's another thing. Brit said the coaches would be fine with us dating."

Finn chuckled. "Well, I'm glad they approve."

"I'm not kidding, Finn. What the heck? Your coaches are *discussing* me?"

"You're right," Finn said, and started undoing the drawstring of his football pants. "I need to return this uniform. Can't play for a team like this. Bastards."

"Okay, okay." He was making her feel ridiculous. Maybe she *was* being ridiculous. "It's just weird. When do coaches talk about their players' relationships?"

Finn held her softly by the shoulders. "When they want their top players to focus on winning a championship and not be distracted by relationship drama, that's when." Oh, that look. How quickly it disarmed her. "Come on, Meg. You're reading into things that aren't there. West Oak is just as obsessed with football."

"Not like this."

"No. You're right. Because EastPay does it better. Loving football's not a crime, not in this state. That's all these people are doing. That's all my team's doin'. Look around."

She looked at the football players helping the young boys push the sleds. The cheerleaders putting makeup on the little girls, taking selfies with their phones. Across the field, the mayor, *the mayor* of the town with his thinning hair gelled to his scalp, shaking hands with folks in the popcorn lines. It felt a bit much, for sure, but there wasn't anything wrong with pure devotion. She'd given the same to her ballet career before it ended.

"Okay." She relented. "Okay."

She noticed Britney talking to a policeman in uniform as they returned to the field.

"—said something was chasing him," they overheard the officer saying. "You have any idea what that something was?"

"Wild animal?" Britney offered. "I dunno. He just ran into the street 'fore we could—"

The officer glanced at Meg and Finn over Britney's shoulder. Brit turned and noticed them, too. She stiffened, her usually flexible body now locked at the joints.

"He was pretty sure it was a person." The officer continued like he was discussing last night's TV show. "You got any ideas?"

"We were just driving's all." Meg noticed Brit's accent was heavier than usual. It usually lessened when Brit was around Finn. "No idea what made him run inna the highway at that hour."

"After eleven, I recall." He stroked his chin with one thumb, letting the statement hang. Meg had heard about their town's ten p.m. curfew for minors. They cracked down on teens loitering, but drivers were usually exempt. Still, he pressed, "There a reason you were out that late traveling south on East Pages Highway?"

"Just getting a ride home from Spencer after studying at the library."

"Before the school year started?"

"I'm an honors student, sir. I don't wait for the school year to learn."

"Atta girl," he said, which struck Meg as odd, as if he was proud of her answers, an attorney preparing her for a case. "Don't you worry about nothin', Miss Britney. Just covering protocol. Had to ask. We issued him a ticket for being out after hours. Kid by the name of Ryan Quaid. Football player, but not one of ours. Ain't from this school, this neighborhood, no reason he should be racing around on the highway at that hour, no matter what was chasin' him. Coulda made you two get in one hell of an accident. Up to no good, that one. But we took care of it. That pricey fine'll keep him from visitin' this side for a while."

"Yikes." Brit smiled, big bright teeth that shouted Crest Whitestrips every day and coffee through a straw. "Why, thank you for lookin' out. 'Preciate it. Gotta get back to my squad." She bounded off without a backward glance.

The cop looked at Megan. "Miss Kaufman," he greeted her.

"Sir." Her chest tightened. *How'd he know her name?*

He offered Finn his hand. "Looking forward to seeing what you can do for us, Geringer." Of course. Meg suddenly felt dumb. Everyone here knew Finn. Meg was "the girlfriend." Therefore, everyone knew her. Even cops. Because in this town, even the cops supported EastPay High football.

"Thank you, sir," Finn said, shaking the policeman's hand. Meg saw Finn's hand blur white where the cop gripped him, tighter than a handshake should be. Finn didn't flinch. "Looking forward to making this city proud."

"Let's hope you do," the officer said, releasing his hand. As he walked away, he repeated his words. "Let's hope you do."

In the distance, the band started, indicating the start of the parade, the drum line echoing all the way to the lot. "You should go," Meg said. "I'll take your grandma home after lunch. Give her time to nap and get ready for church."

Finn kissed her. "I can hitch a ride with one of the guys. I don't want your parents to start in on you."

"They're not back till tonight." She'd make sure to be playing her latest piano piece when they walked in the door, as if she'd worked all day on it.

She pulled him close. "For now, I'm gonna enjoy every minute with you till Monday." Monday it would be real. They'd officially be at different schools. She kissed him once more, then shooed him off.

She took her time walking back to the track, wandering through the maze of booths. *West Oak loves football, too*, she thought as she walked by Pete's Dogs and their striped tent where they were handing out mini deep-fried dogs. She turned left at the local car dealership booth with their free key chains in the shape of goalposts. *But this is next level.* Rows and rows of booths. Pollyanna's Homemade Jewelry Shop on Fifth Street. Honor Society. Key Club. Veterans of East Pages.

"Spencer Collins!" a voice called out. "A word, sir." The cop again, this time talking with a football player who stood next to a girl a couple of years younger. Definitely his sister, by the resemblance. They were standing by the fire truck on display, the doors open for families to explore and take photos. The girl glanced Meg's way, but Spencer and the cop couldn't see Meg from where they stood.

"Officer Clarke," Spencer announced. "Working on the Lord's day?"

Officer Clarke squinted at the sun, then back at him. "We found the guy you hit last night." He let the sentence hang. Meg could see the tension—the way the cop stood stiffer, the way Spencer folded his arms tighter—and she couldn't look away.

"That so," was all Spencer said. Meg saw his sister shift from one foot to the other.

"Cited him for curfew," Officer Clarke continued. He tipped his hat to Spencer's sister. "Miss Leah." She glanced his direction but said nothing. "Heard you and Eli are dating. Great football player."

"Thank you, sir," she mumbled.

Officer Clarke turned his attention back to Spencer. "Britney Wallace claims the two of you were driving home from the library."

Spencer nodded. Officer Clarke waited. Spencer didn't say more.

"Heard you don't attend the parties at Dante's Ravine."

"No time," Spencer said. "Need to focus on football and my future."

"That so," the policeman said, mimicking Spencer's words. "I heard it was because you've never been invited."

"And good thing, now that I know you cite for curfew. Haven't heard any EastPay students getting curfew tickets. Funny—seeing how you know about these parties."

Officer Clarke opened his mouth to speak, but nothing came out.

Spencer smiled. "Now if you'll excuse me, I gotta get back to my team. Don't want to be late." With a hand on Leah's shoulder, he led his sister away.

"Doubt they'll notice," Officer Clarke said.

Meg saw Spencer pause, muscles taut, but then he called over his shoulder, "Have a blessed day."

Chapter 5

FINN

After driving Finn's grandma home after lunch, Meg returned to the field, though Finn had told her he'd find a ride. He knew she was trying to soak up their last moments together, and he didn't mind, not a bit. It was going to be hard on both of them to go to different schools. He just wished she'd say that, instead of trying to make the football program out to be shady.

He couldn't imagine a better choice for him than EastPay. In the early afternoon, the defense and offense scrimmaged, showing off their readiness to dominate next week's game. The team jumped in unison to hype themselves up, the coaches raised their fists at the offense's completions, the defense chest-bumped anytime they stopped a first down. The band played the fight song while the cheerleaders danced, the flags twirled, and the crowd stomped. You could hear them blocks away.

As the festivities concluded, the local news station filmed an interview with Finn and the head coach, Cedric Wilkins, while a more regional reporter interviewed quarterback Thomas White. Finn smiled at Meg while being interviewed, saw her eyes say, *I love you*, but he knew Meg, and as she looked away, her eyes said, *This is a circus*. As he was shaking hands with the sportscaster, she waved and grabbed his duffel bag. He ran to catch up, helmet in hand.

Most of the spectators' cars had cleared the parking lot, leaving the cleanup crew and a scattering of students. "Thank you," Finn said. "Seriously. For all of this. I know you're not—"

"—coulda killed him!" It was Britney's voice, from behind a car.

"But we didn't. Not even close." The male voice, unidentified, was tight and low.

Finn jogged around the car, Meg close behind.

Spencer Collins was holding Britney by the wrist. Finn knew Spencer, knew him mostly because he was the only player on the football team who hadn't spoken to him since Finn joined the team in June. He thought it was because he'd taken Spencer's position. Now he wondered if it had to do with his cousin.

"What the hell, Spencer," he said, eyeing Spencer's grip on Brit. Spencer let go, smirking.

"Something funny?" Finn stepped closer.

"Finny . . ." Brit said, using her childhood nickname for him, as if that would calm him.

"Well, hello," Spencer said. *"Finny."*

"Let it go, Finn," Brit said. "It ain't nothin'." She puffed her cheeks out, then exhaled loudly. "Last night, Spencer and I hit a guy on the road."

What? Finn's mind whirled.

"Just tapped him, really," Spencer said. "And what the hell, Brit?"

"They already seen me talkin' to the cop. Anyway, the guy's fiiiine. Just spooked me is all."

No wonder Meg had said Brit was acting strange. "You okay?" Finn said.

"Absolutely!" Brit's voice sounded squeaky. She was so bad at lying. Since they were kids, she'd overdo it, then switch subjects. Sure enough, she turned to Spencer. "Where's Leah?"

"Who?" Finn asked.

"His sister," Meg answered, and all three of them turned to Meg. Finn was thrown. Did she know Spencer? Spencer's face was unreadable, but she had his attention. "Sorry," she added. "I saw you guys talking to the cop."

Spencer's eyes narrowed, but he kept his voice even. "She got a ride home with her boyfriend."

"Right," Meg said. "Eli. *'Great football player.'* It was weird—right?—that the cop knew they were dating?"

"And who are you?" Spencer stepped forward. "Don't think I've seen you around. Would've remembered a pretty face, especially one who likes to get in my business."

Before Meg could speak, Finn inched closer to Spencer. He spoke through clenched teeth, like his mouth guard was still in. "Doesn't go to school here. She's my girlfriend."

"Ah." Spencer stepped around Finn. Held out his hand. Meg took it respectfully. Instead of shaking it, he kissed the inside of her wrist softly, smiling at Finn as he did so. "Pleasure. Megan, is it? At least, that's the rumor."

Megan pulled her hand away and rubbed her wrist. Finn steadied his breathing. It was one thing for Spencer to ignore him at practice. But this felt personal. *Ineligibility*, he reminded himself. *You punch him, and you're ineligible.*

"Don't be gross, Spencer." Brit rolled her eyes.

Without a word, Spencer got into his car and started the engine.

He lowered the window and tapped the edge of his cigarette box. *Spencer smokes?* Finn couldn't help but wonder if this was a new habit, a middle finger to the team who had demoted him.

"Students here love to win, Finny," he said, flicking on his lighter. "But they're not the only ones. This town expects to win like they expect to breathe. In fact"—he lit a cigarette, the end crackling as he inhaled. He blew the smoke out the window, and it dissipated into the twilight—"that's why I'm on the bench and you're starting. So I'm fine with your *distractions*." He winked at Megan. "It might help me get some playing time. But the town"— he took another drag—"they aren't so forgiving." Even though he was speaking to Finn, he looked at Meg the whole time. "You be careful to play real good."

Finn's adrenaline pumped through his arms, reaching into his hands and closing his fists for the fight he wanted as he replayed Spencer's grip on Britney, the kiss to Megan's wrist, the sound of Spencer's voice cooing "Finny." *"You be careful to play real good."* The way he purposely changed his light accent to a drawl, like a threat from the whole state of Texas.

As if Spencer knew, he blew the smoke out slowly, smiled into his side mirror, and floored the gas pedal, screeching the tires as he sped off.

Chapter 6
BRITNEY

Brit was bugged. She'd tried telling Finn and Meg that she'd seen way scarier movies and wasn't bothered by the cop or Spencer or his car hitting a pedestrian, but Finn had insisted on driving her home. He'd already sent Jalisa and Dalisa out of the parking lot with a wave of the hand. Brit's ride.

Now she was being chauffeured by Finn as he drove Megan's Audi north on East Pages Lane, the seven-mile artery of two-lane highway that cut through the various parts of the town, from square office buildings to the houses spaced out on small plots of farmland about two or three first downs apart.

Brit leaned her head out of the passenger window to feel the summer air, and that was the only reason. Not to avoid Megan's question from the back seat.

"Britney," Meg repeated.

"I heard you." Brit brought her head back inside. She looked into the sun visor mirror. Her curls were frizzy from the wind. "I told you already. We were drivin' home from the library."

"Really," Meg said, and the slow way she said it made Brit nervous. "He doesn't seem like your typical study buddy."

"Look, I know it looked bad, him holdin' me like that, but Spencer's no harm. He only flirted with you to get a rise outta Finn."

And it worked. Brit could tell by Finn's white knuckles around the steering wheel, his exaggerated exhales. But Meg seemed prickly, which was surprising. Megan Kaufman, so agreeable. She interacted with everyone the way she danced on stage, with grace and poise. Brit had known Meg since Finn started dating her two years ago, and she was convinced Meg was the reason her cousin stayed so level-headed. Finn was the stubborn one, the one still having a Lamaze breathing session to recover from Spencer. "Spence is just on edge from hittin' that guy last night with his car," Brit continued. "Real scary. Even for a guy like Spence."

"*A guy like Spence,*" Meg echoed.

Brit nodded.

"Same guy you study with."

Britney licked her lips. "So? Just 'cause he's an ass doesn't make him a *dumb*ass."

All three of them cracked up, the tension broken. Finn finally spoke. "Let up already, Meg. Give her a break." To Britney, he said, "She's convinced our school is up to no good."

Brit thought of the guy they'd hit, the fear in his eyes as he ran from them. She laughed, but it came out forced—a snort through her powdered nose. "Hogwash. You're high, Megs."

"Maybe," Meg said. "Or maybe the cop was high."

"The cop?" Now Brit was lost.

"He's the one who placed you driving on East Pages over an hour after the library closed."

The words hung in the air. Brit's stomach dropped somewhere below her white tennis shoes and pom-pom socks. She hadn't thought about that. The Crestview Library was open until nine—except on Saturdays, when it stayed open one extra hour. Ten p.m. It's not like Meg would judge her if she knew the truth. Dante's

Ravine wasn't a crime. But Meg went to West Oak. Rules were rules. No talk of Dante's with outsiders.

Britney riffled through her purse. "Where are my house keys," she mumbled. She set her phone down and fished around some more. She found her lipstick tube instead and opened it, rubbed it on her lips, bright red against her pale face. She stopped suddenly, remembering she was going home. She put the tube away, hoping Finn and Meg didn't notice, then licked her teeth.

Finn tilted his head. "You hook up with Spencer in the library parking lot?"

Britney scrunched her lips like she'd tasted a lemon. "No!" She'd known Spencer since her freshman year. Tutored him, even. They traveled on buses together. Spent every Friday on the same field. But she'd worked too hard to become who she was. She wouldn't let someone like Spencer taint that. She couldn't bear the thought of dropping, of becoming less important, becoming a nobody again. Never again.

"She wasn't at the library," Meg said to Finn.

Brit jumped at Meg's words and opened her mouth to argue, but Meg placed a hand on her shoulder.

"Brit," she murmured, barely over the hum of her Audi's engine, "the cop said you were traveling south on East Pages. Your house is north of the library. North on East Pages. Not south. I'm south. West Oak is south."

Britney pulled her hand away and opened her lipstick. Twisted it all the way up, a long finger of dark red jutting out, an exclamation point in a dark car. She stared at it, then twisted the lipstick down and snapped the lid shut. "Let's just say there was a party."

She needed to make sure she didn't reveal too much. "There wasn't. Just hypothetically."

Finn turned into her tract housing complex. "Nobody in this car cares if you drink." Finn's voice was flat. She couldn't read his face, but Meg was making her uncomfortable—the way she was scrutinizing her. Brit turned the lipstick case like she was wringing out a dripping sponge. She hated lying, especially to them.

"No one's supposed to know," she blurted, "except the people invited." And then she hastily added, "Hypothetically." She could feel her fear rising, how it strangled her volume. "And if you tell anyone I told you, they'll find out. They always find out if you talk."

"Who?"

Brit didn't know who. But she'd seen enough to know the river had power over things. Maybe even people.

"Them," she whispered.

Chapter 7

At the word *them,* Finn hit his blinker and pulled into Brit's driveway. He killed the engine, leaned back, and blew out an exaggerated breath. Meg knew that face, that "here we go again" look every time Brit brought up her superstitions. But Meg heard something different in Brit's voice. This wasn't her childhood fear of mirrors in the dark or trains after midnight. This was the real thing. At least to Brit.

"Do you feel Finn's in danger because of them?" Meg asked.

Britney shook her head aggressively. "Oh no. He plays football."

A chill shot through Meg, but Finn laughed.

Brit glared, undone. "Look," she said, smashing down her frizzy hair with sweaty hands. "Here's it straight. Somebody died there." She lowered her voice to a whisper. Lowered her head, too. "At Dante's Ravine."

"Everyone knows that, Brit," Finn said, his full volume making Brit flinch. "Back when we were in elementary school. Sean Lloyd, some football player from another school. Drunk and stupid. So?"

Brit sank deeper into her seat, her eyes level with the dashboard. "So he talked garbage 'bout Spartans last time anyone saw him alive."

"If that were true, every student at *my* school would be dead by now," Meg joked.

"No, not like that, Megs. They said he got all worked up, at a restaurant, curse words and spit flying so people felt it next table over. Said something about how he'd figured it out. That what he knew would '*end*' us. Following day, they found him. Downstream from Dante's."

Meg noticed Brit dropping her accent. That happened sometimes around family, according to Finn. But rarely around Meg. Brit must've noticed, too, because she cleared her throat, and her next words pulled out such a strong drawl, it was almost comical. "Don't matter if he were drunk. River got him."

"Strained?" Meg asked, all humor gone from her voice, and she shivered at the word. The currents were strong in that area—could shove you under and press you against a tangle of twigs and branches. The rushing water kept you pressed against the river debris until you drowned. People in this area had a name for that kind of drowning: *strained*.

Brit nodded solemnly. "Some think Sean's still there, you know, in the river, trying to make up for what he did. But it's Dante's Ravine that's protectin' us. There's something there. Spirits, maybe."

"So . . ." Finn started, the end of his mouth turned up slightly. "The river . . . is . . . a Spartan football fan?"

Brit jutted out her chin. "Go on, make fun. But Spartans been going there first and third Saturdays every season for eight years. I been there the past three. You know, pay tribute. And since we been going, we've made it to Regional finals four times and State twice. Whatever's helping, I ain't chancing missing a party at Dante's."

Meg wanted to hear more, but if Finn kept this up, Brit was going to clam up again.

"That what you were doing last night?" Meg pried, making sure to sound reverent. "Paying tribute?"

"Tryin', only we got held up a minute." Brit jumped from a noise outside. A raccoon, ballooned from a trash can diet, skittered across her driveway and into the shadows of the front lawn.

Meg tried to say it plainly, tried to hide her doubt. "And Spencer likes these parties?"

Brit looked out the window as if the raccoon might hear. "No matter. You get invited, you gotta show. You don't, you risk ruining the whole season."

"Bullshit," Finn said.

Britney threw her head against the headrest. "There's rules. Like you gotta be invited. You gotta be on time. Things like that. You can't break 'em."

"Otherwise what?" Finn challenged.

"Otherwise I dunno! Otherwise we might not win, that's what. And they're watchin'."

"Who's watching?" Meg asked, hoping her soft volume would calm Finn. "Who's this *they*?"

Britney's eyes searched outside the car windows. It was dark. No movement. "Not sure. But they watch. They know. And they can help you out. Get you things."

It was creepy, and she didn't trust EastPay, but the more Meg pressed, the more ridiculous it sounded. Spirits? Sean Lloyd? River power? Meg shook her head. "You don't need anything."

"Not anymore," Brit muttered, fiddling with her lipstick tube. She put it back in her purse and pulled out her keys.

Not anymore? Meg wondered.

She opened her mouth to ask, but Brit rushed on. "Anyway, they can't hold nothin' against me. I got there late, but that guy got in our way. They can't make us lose a game for that."

"Lose?" Meg giggled. She couldn't help it. "River spirits are gonna make you lose?" She looked over at Finn, who just stared over the steering wheel at the garage door. "Finn, you wanna back me up on this one? Finn?"

Is he even listening to the conversation? She looked up into the rearview mirror and tried to catch his attention. His eyes were zoned in, trained on an unseen defender he would tackle at all costs.

"I'm here to play football," he said. "That's it. I don't care about some party I wasn't invited to. You figured out the secret, Meg. My cousin is offering sacrifices to a river because of some drunk, dead guy. End of story."

"Sheesh, Finn," Brit said, giggling, but at least she looked less scared. "When you say it out loud, now *I* sound like the dumbass."

"So there's some superstitions running high," he continued. Meg could tell by the dead calm in his voice that he was trying to be reasonable, but he'd reached his breaking point. "That's probably what all the rumors are. Superstitions. I only have time for one type of game this fall, and I'm not letting anything get in the way of that, ya hear me?"

"Loud and clear, Coach," Brit answered, rolling her eyes. On the center console, her phone vibrated. All three looked down at the notification lighting up the car. "You think they know?" Brit whispered, widening her eyes. "I'm not allowed to talk about Dante's Ravine. It's the rules." She reached for her phone and unlocked it with shaky fingers.

Megan wasn't sure how to navigate this. She wanted to get back to the reality of things—the cop's strange behavior, the fact that she was *allowed* to miss games—but Brit was talking spirits and dead people. "Who's it from?" she asked.

Britney chewed on her bottom lip, her teeth gnawing off a stripe of lipstick. "Tammy," she said, then clarified for Meg. "The cheerleader you met." She scanned the text. "The QB playing us this Friday?" She spoke in shallow breaths. "Just deemed ineligible for two games." Relief and awe came out of Brit in short gasps. "It was Dante's Ravine."

Meg resisted the urge to mimic Brit's signature eye roll.

"Well," Finn said. "Looks like the river didn't mind you were late. When we play Meg's team, I'm gonna need you to take out the whole D-line. Maybe offer a goat?"

"Hilarious, Finn," Brit said, exiting the car and slamming the door behind her.

Chapter 8
BRITNEY

That night, as Brit hugged her covers, she recalled the first time she went to Dante's Ravine. She'd made the squad back in May of eighth grade, practiced with them all summer, but Caitlin didn't invite her to a private party until the first week of high school. With knees that wobbled on the uneven ground, she'd walked by the light of her phone toward the party sounds, gripping the invitation and the plastic Spartan mask with clammy hands.

"Britness!" Caitlin, a senior cheerleader, had linked fingers with her in the dark and pulled her into the clearing. "Welcome to Dante's Ravine."

A sea of plastic masks turned to look at her like something out of a nightmare. Caitlin wore one too. You didn't dare enter without one, and only fifty people had them. It was an honor, but it still looked like a sea of monsters in the dark. She shuddered and pulled on her own mask, her face slippery with sweat.

Brit remembered looking down at the river, the fierce way it cut through itself in braids and tangles of white water that reflected the moon, the echoing of the rushing force that made her swallow and take a step back. It was beautiful.

And terrifying.

"Dark as dark. And if you honor the river . . ." Caitlin handed Brit a rock the size and weight of a brick. "State champions past two years. So tell them. Anything you want."

Brit closed her eyes, let the sound of water flood her mind as she offered her plea. She hurled the rock, and the river devoured it in a gulp, splashing her calf. Caitlin offered her a drink of something in a water bottle, the smell so strong that Brit recoiled. She shook her head politely.

Caitlin said, "Now you have to show your devotion back. It's shallow here."

She could hear the murmurs of "newbie" from the football players and cheerleaders who'd gathered, and felt the masks closing in on her. Caitlin handed Brit a knotted rope that was looped around a tree and motioned to the rapids. She didn't know what possessed her, but she lifted her mask and took a swig from the water bottle, the burning filling her throat as she swallowed. She knew it was a test.

She plunged in, choked against the force that tried to rip her grip on the rope. She couldn't pull herself out against the water's strength, and just as she started to panic, as the river water threatened to flood her lungs, as the world started to turn wavy and dark and she felt herself letting go, five or six strong hands reached down and lifted her out. She sputtered and coughed, looked at the concerned but proud faces observing her.

"Girl," Caitlin said, lifting her mask. "You're legit. Doubt we'll lose one game now." Everyone clapped, and Brit offered a weak smile, warmth coursing through her despite her shivering. The sophomore twins, Jalisa and Dalisa, pulled off their masks to hug her, identical smiles shining bright in the dark night.

A guy knelt next to her, broad shoulders and twinkling eyes, and returned her mask. A few raven-black ringlets hung loosely across his forehead. She smiled shyly. The yellow flecks in his eyes made them look almost golden. "Damn," he said. "Most cheerleaders don't go through with it." He touched her cheek. "I'm Walker. *Terrance* Walker, but at EastPay, just Walker." Brit drank from the water bottle he handed her. "Mad respect. You're fearless."

"Fearless Flyer," Caitlin echoed. Brit remembered her plea to the river. Begging to be somebody.

It answered. The river had spoken her new identity. Fearless Flyer. *Fearless.*

Chapter 9
FINN

On Monday morning, the moon was still visible enough to light the beads of sweat on the grass when Finn left his house, backpack around one shoulder, equipment bag slung over the other. The scent from his grandma's garden flowers awakened his senses, his mind, his tired body, and he drank it in before getting into his car. He drove quietly, no radio, no commentators doubting him a week before his first game. Just steady breath and a mind focused on football.

Once at school, he parked in the empty lot and headed for the field. The air was thick and warm, the front of his shirt sticking to him even before he jogged a lap. He imagined the empty stands flooded with stadium lights and people. Come Friday, they'd be shoulder to shoulder, an army of black and red, shouting and cheering, loving him until he messed up, missed a catch, fumbled a play, and they once again remembered that they shouldn't support transfers. At EastPay, you started as a freshman and paid your dues, earned the right to play. And in East Pages it started even before that. It began with peewee and Pop Warner. It began with parents who moved to this town to groom their boys into young men who bled football.

But all rules had exceptions, and Finn Geringer knew he was theirs.

Still, he had a lot to prove this Friday. No surprise when Brit spilled that he hadn't been invited to their secret party at Dante's

Ravine. Last year, he'd blown through their defense. And now he wore their jersey?

The gray light was just enough for him to read his playbook. After reviewing a few pages, he palmed his football and ran through some routes—the spins, the screens, the sprints to open space—as if his guards and tackles were protecting QB Thomas White to make the perfect pass. Handoff. Lateral.

Forty-five minutes later, he was soaked in sweat when a single hand clap echoed from the stands. Finn turned and spotted a familiar face. His light eyes shone brightly against his dark brown skin, piercing the dusky hues of early morning. Number 62, Terrance Walker, senior defensive back. Captain. With a first name no one ever used.

"Hey, Walker."

Walker continued applauding as he descended, then hopped down from the bleachers to the field, over six feet of muscle and as agile as a rabbit. "You tryin' to make us all look bad?" He slapped Geringer on the shoulder.

"If I were that good, then yeah." Finn gave him a friendly shove. "Just practicing the plays. A lot's riding on this first game."

"Just follow the protocol, you'll be fine. Your QB is solid. He'll find you."

"Yeah."

Walker looked at his watch—an expensive one. "Why don't you shower up and I'll give you the walk-through. Tell you what's what and who's who at EastPay. Make sure you're not flying solo first day."

Back in the locker room, Finn grabbed his towel. He noticed

an orange notebook left on a bench, and he flipped through it. Other teams' names were tabbed. Opponents and positions, some highlighted. Lots of scribbles and different handwriting like a yearbook that had been passed around.

He spotted Coach Goode and Coach Wilkins in the adjoining office, their personalities as different as their looks. One warm, the other distant, pale-skinned versus dark, freckled versus pock-marked. Together they worked perfectly. Only six losses regionally in eight years. The team had qualified for State every year since they'd been hired, clinching a title for their division twice. There were two other hired coaches, Hart and Stockton, as well as various coaches from the middle school who volunteered at practices and games, but everyone knew they were backup dancers, extras to fill positions.

Goode wasn't the head coach, but he'd been a significant part of Finn's recruitment, though nobody would dare call it that. He never told him to transfer, but last season when Finn ran into him at a grocery store, Goode introduced himself, the fluorescent lights reflecting off his chalky skin, and congratulated him on dealing EastPay their only defeat. He asked if Finn knew the rules about transferring, how students were allowed one transfer without a zone permit. He smiled, said how unfortunate it was to waste Finn's talent at West Oak, when colleges like A&M, Bama, and Ole Miss had their eyes on EastPay. He left it at that. No need to say more.

The week before their run-in had been weird; his grandmother had gotten food poisoning bad enough to send her to the hospital— the same food that Finn would have eaten had Megan not shown up with a surprise anniversary dinner. Granted, his age may have protected him from being hospitalized, but it would have laid him flat on his back. As it was, Finn almost didn't make the game, but his grandmother insisted that visiting hours were over and he better go play or he'd be grounded for a month.

He'd had the game of his life. Somehow his school, the West Oak Brahmas, took down undefeated East Pages by a score of 29–28. West Oak's secondary had allowed four easy touchdowns, but for each touchdown EastPay scored, Finn's offense had countered. Four touchdowns to four touchdowns. Finn scored all four. The last one came in the final minute, and rather than tie the game as Coach instructed, Finn persuaded his QB with one look to go for the two-point conversion. Finn took the snap and sold the sweep. As EastPay scrambled to shut him down, he lobbed it to the kicker, alone in the end zone. Game over.

East Pages' only loss of last season.

Now, ten months later, at six in the morning on a Monday, Finn was the ally, not the enemy, standing less than twenty feet from them. Coach Goode was on the phone, slouched over his swivel chair, raking his fingers through spiky gray hair. Behind him, Coach Wilkins was pacing, as if the tiny, windowed office had room for a man his size to pace; he stopped when he saw Finn across the locker room, nodded curtly, then closed the blinds and shut the door, sending a wave of cold air in Finn's direction.

A smile crept across his lips. He loved how important football was at this school. Coaches were blowing the AC at six a.m., making phone calls, shutting doors to discuss strategies. Plays. Opponents. Special teams. It needed to be this important if he was ever going to have a future in it.

A urinal flushed and Walker appeared, slapping the Spartan painted on the locker room wall for good luck. "You gonna shower this century?"

"Gimme five." He showed Walker the notebook. "This yours?"

Walker took it. "Nah, that's Coach's notebook. Always lying around. I'll get it to him when he's not busy."

Finn tossed his cleats into his gym locker. "Meet you in the cafeteria?"

"Just 'caf,' rookie. We call it the caf. All right." He slapped the Spartan open-palmed once more as he headed out the double doors.

Chapter 10
BRITNEY

The first bell rang, and Brit bounded to her locker. She loved the feeling of her cheerleading skirt as she skipped, how it flapped like a bird taking flight.

Droves of high schoolers entered the hallways. No one missed the first day of school, not with this Friday on the horizon. Brit spotted Finn and Walker leaving the caf, the crowds parting for them as they headed her way. That first night at Dante's—her freshman year—when she'd dunked in the river, she and Walker had ended up kissing, but they were both drunk at that point, and by the way he acted the following Monday, she was pretty sure he never remembered it. Neither of them had ever mentioned it again. She approached as Walker was midtour. "—two main hallways, one stairwell. Upstairs, same layout. Math and science, second floor. English, history, electives, down below." Finn had stopped walking. Mouth agape, he turned slowly in a full circle, and she beamed. Butcher paper covered the halls, fall colors, twisted brown paper wrapping the pillars and transforming the posts into autumn trees, orange leaves taped to the paper branches, stapled and hanging from the ceiling.

"What the—"

"And each hallway's different," Brit bragged. She'd been here for weeks with the squad and student council transforming the school into a wonderland utopia.

"Unreal," Finn breathed out.

"Hell yeah," Walker said. "No school with more pride." He leaned against the wall and patted a straw-stuffed paper scarecrow wearing a flannel shirt. "In every single thing we do. Don't forget that."

"What's your schedule?" Brit asked. Finn held out the paper, and Brit unfolded it.

"Your first period's next to mine," she said. "I'll walk you there. Football, band, and cheer have electives first and last period." Walker scanned the schedule over her shoulder.

"Yup, just what I thought," he said. "You're fine, teacher-wise. Toughest one will be Mrs. Ingham. Still, just flash a smile and wear your jersey—you'll pull a B."

They continued to his locker, only three down from hers.

Two football players flanked him as he twirled the lock. "Hey, Geringer."

"What's up, guys?"

Cornerback Jake Smith and linebacker Reggie Curtis gave him a welcome nudge on the shoulder. The guys nodded at Walker, who nodded back. Brit knew how tight these players were. Finn wouldn't be alone or looking for friends his first day.

Suddenly, Finn froze. Brit ducked her head into the group to see what had caught his eye. The inside of his locker was covered with wrapping paper and a written note: "Good luck, Finn!" She recognized Tammy's loopy writing, the same hand that painted the banners the boys would charge through before games.

"Hope you like it," came a cheery voice from behind. Tammy, with her freckles and bouncy red hair, crowded in to admire her handiwork.

"Hi, uh—" Finn said.

"Tammy! Tammy Shaw. I'm the lucky one who got assigned your locker."

Brit thought back to the time when Tammy first found out that Finn was her cousin. How Brit got the silent treatment for two weeks, until the gossip tidal-waved across the bleachers: *He's transferring here! Can you believe it? So talented, so unstoppable, so . . . hot.*

"Gotta run to class," Tammy chirped. "Looking forward to Friday. Everyone's talkin' Finn Geringer these days."

"I'll bet," Brit piped in, and there was a flash of something in Tammy's eyes before the twinkle returned, and she smiled and flounced away.

All of his textbooks were neatly stacked. Usually books were assigned on the first day when students stood in line at the school library. She wondered if Tammy had pulled some strings, but then Reggie said to Finn, "Football players' priority. All books are assigned before the first day. We got bigger things to focus on."

Wow. Brit didn't even know about that privilege.

Finn reached in and removed a red wristband, made of plastic and metal but shiny as glass. *Number 25* was written on the inside. Jake held up his wrist, already donning one. "Free gift. All the football players wear 'em. Monitor your health, your sleep. How many steps you're takin' during the day. It's all online. Pretty sweet."

"Plus," Walker added, "chicks see the band, know you're on the team, and, well, you know—" He gave a knowing smile and added, "Right, Brit?"

The boys chuckled. Embarrassment torpedoed through her, so

much worse because it was right in front of her cousin. Guess Walker did remember their kiss at Dante's after all.

"Starting next week," Walker continued, "we watch tape every Monday, first period. It's your elective. Players are excused. No need to check in. Head straight to 203. It's reserved for viewing. Afterward, report to B105—Coaches' office in the locker room—for one-on-ones. First-string players meet weekly with coaches. I think your time's eight forty. It's posted in the locker room."

Finn slipped his wristband on. "So I've got the books, the privileges, the full tour. When do I get the invite to dunk my head in Dante's holy water?" Brit felt her eyes might pop out, wide as golf balls. She watched the guys side-eyeing one another. "Oh, come on," he said. "I'm kidding."

"You wanna lose the season for us?" Walker spoke behind him, directly in his ear, but it was loud enough for Britney to hear. Loud enough for the boys to nod once in agreement. "One: Don't mention that place by name. What we do there. Out loud. Ever." There was venom in his words. Brit saw the hairs on the back of Finn's neck move with Walker's breath. He looked at Brit accusingly as he spoke again. "Two: You weren't invited. Not yet. Who told you—"

"No one. Everyone." Finn grabbed his trig and physics books. Turned to face Walker. "I used to go to your rival school. You think they didn't dig up dirt on you?"

No one spoke. They looked at each other, shoulders taut like before the snap. Would they buy it? Walker looked at Brit again, and she lifted her shoulders and shook her head. *It wasn't me, please don't think it was me.*

"What is this—*Fight Club*?" Finn joked. "What does it matter? I'm on the team now, yeah?"

Reggie spoke first, clapping Finn on the shoulder. "He's right, Walker. Relax. No harm, no foul. I'm sure an invite's coming your way. Let's see how Friday plays out."

Brit noticed all of them collectively relax, and she realized she'd been holding her breath. She hiccupped a gasp of air, but thankfully no one noticed. Finn slammed his locker shut.

"Look, if we win," Finn added, "I'll take a dip in my birthday suit." This time they all laughed.

Walker threw an arm around his shoulder, corralling him toward first period. "For real, though, no more talk of it."

"Processed and filed, bro," Brit heard him say as the boys walked away.

If Finn was bothered that he hadn't been invited, he didn't show it. He was in the starting lineup, so he should've been, but who knows. Maybe they wanted to make sure he didn't choke first. Maybe they were worried who he'd tell—aka Megan.

Brit looked over the heads of milling students. Spencer, standing next to his sister, Leah, glared from across the hall, arms crossed. He may not have been part of the football clique, but Brit noticed he wore the red wristband. Even Spencer knew the perks of this team. She stuck her tongue out and waved, which took him off guard. He turned away, but Brit swore she saw him grin.

She turned her back and sprinted to Finn. The boys had just parted ways at the English and electives wing.

"Hey, thanks," Brit mumbled. She knew Finn would know she meant *thanks for not snitching.*

He slapped her on the back. A text lit up his Android as they walked.

"Meg," he said, showing the text to Brit.

U ok?

He texted as he walked, speaking the words aloud so Brit could hear.

Better than ok.

His phone vibrated again as they arrived at their neighboring classrooms. Brit could see Megan's question light up his screen.

Yeah?

He typed a response, then showed it to Brit.

Best decision I ever made.

They smiled at each other, a new bond between them that was more than just family. She'd always known it, but now he did, too. EastPay was everything.

Chapter 11
FINN

It was only practice, but there were at least a hundred people in the stands.

Finn could hear the shouts: "Let's see some yards, Geringer!" "Bring 'er home Friday, will ya?" "All bets on you!" "It better get ugly out there! Not gon' be happy till it's ugly."

They ran a quick route up the middle, and after only one play, Coach Goode whistled and waved Finn over. He subbed in an unknown—was his name Chance? Lance?—and Finn jogged up to Coach.

"You ready for Friday, Geringer?" Coach Goode asked.

"Gettin' there, Coach. Gettin' there."

"Nice. That's what I'm looking to hear."

Spencer, sitting on the bench, grunted. Both Finn and Coach turned to look at him, but he busied himself with his mouth guard. "Got somethin' for you in the locker room," Coach Goode continued. "Why don't you head there now with Collins." Spencer whipped his head at Goode, but Goode ignored him. "Coach Wilkins's waiting for you both."

Finn looked around, realized for the first time Wilkins wasn't out here. Goode was only the offensive coordinator. Wilkins was the head coach, the one who should be out here watching every snap. Must be important.

"Yes, Coach."

Tammy Shaw distracted him momentarily with a wave. He

waved back. She'd been near his locker a lot today, checking in, making sure he had everything. He smiled cordially, careful not to show that he noticed how much she was staring.

Spencer didn't wait for Finn to remove his helmet, just started walking. Finn caught up at the edge of the track.

Neither of them spoke.

The sound of their cleats echoed off the concrete floors as they entered. Coach Wilkins was waiting, standing erect like some badass LeBron James. Of course, a foot shorter. But his presence made him seem just as tall.

"What's up, Coach?" Finn asked. Wordlessly, he handed Finn a binder. Finn absently flipped through it. A playbook, only it couldn't be theirs. Finn had already memorized their plays, worked the sweat out of them all summer long.

"You've done well, Geringer. You're the real deal. We had to make sure you were in, not just practicing with us." He motioned to the playbook in Finn's hands. "There's about twenty-five plays in there," Coach Wilkins continued.

Finn thumbed through the book. "But these aren't the plays I learned."

"'Course not. Still usable, those plays, but those were *summer* plays. We hold open practices. People come watch, Geringer, not just fans. They take notes. We have talkers. You get me?"

Finn nodded, but it took great effort, the last rep of the last set. He looked to Spencer, but Spencer's face was unreadable.

"Sir," Finn said, "the first game is this Friday."

"Well, I'll be sure to attend then." Coach Wilkins's voice was crisp.

"It's just— And the others? You giving them this book, too?"

"Don't need to," Coach Wilkins said. "The seniors have the fall playbook at the start of the summer."

Spencer folded his arms, like he loved watching Finn squirm. But he also looked uneasy. His eyes darted toward the exit and then back at Coach, probably wondering the same thing Finn was wondering: If Spencer knew these plays, why'd Coach ask for both of them?

"Some of the juniors, too," Coach added. "Just not you. Well, until now."

"But," Finn said, shaking his head. "The runs. The"—he was at a loss—"the structure. Autonomy. I mean, with all due respect, Coach, how do you expect these to go smoothly? It doesn't—"

"You do your job, Geringer, we'll do ours. You have three days. We'll light the fields at four forty-five a.m. and have a couple players meet you to work the routes. That's why Collins is here."

Spencer's arms dropped, his smugness evaporating. "Hell no." Coach looked at him like he forgot his manners. "Hell no, *Coach*," Spencer amended. Coach chuckled, pretended not to notice. In fact, he completely disregarded Spencer, directing everything at Finn.

"He'll be there in the morning, won't you, Collins." Coach didn't wait for an answer. "Most of the plays are 'summer book' this Friday. We're playing Prescott. They won't have done their research. It's like a warm-up. We're not playin' you full speed this Friday. Might even sub in Collins a bit." He motioned to Spencer with his chin, as if Spencer was an afterthought, not the person they'd depended on for the past two years. It concerned Finn how quickly a player could be replaced. "McGeever, too. Maybe roll in third string for a few plays. But in two weeks it's the Chargers. They need the wind knocked outta them—not know who blind-sided them—you get me?"

Wilkins handed Finn two SD cards. Finn cocked an eyebrow.

"Last season." Wilkins pointed to one of the SD cards. "All the Pioneers' games." He pointed to the other. "All the Chargers' games."

"How did you—"

"Study the D. Figure out your toughest matchups. Let me know Wednesday."

Finn let the playbook dangle in his hands. "Wait, Wednesday? This is twenty games."

"Twenty-two with the Chargers' postseason. If you can't, I'm sure someone on the bench is willing to do some research." He looked at Spencer, who apparently existed again.

Finn jogged his jaw side to side, trying to make sense of it all. He was better than Spencer—supposedly, that's why he had been recruited—but with this deep squad, they could chance benching Finn to make a point. "No problem at all, Coach," Finn said squarely. "I got this."

Coach Wilkins slapped him on the shoulder. "'Course you do. Now, get back out there."

Finn trotted for the door, but paused when Coach added, "And Geringer?"

He turned.

"No one knows about that book."

"I get you."

"You still in touch with your teammates at West Oak? Or your coaches?"

He remembered the anger in Coach Cooper's face when he'd told him he was transferring. He wanted to explain it was for his grandma, but he never got the chance. "Get the hell outta my office," his old coach had said. And that was that.

As for his friends, if he hadn't felt so guilty for transferring, maybe he would've shown up for the West Oak summer parties. Met them at the lake. Hung out on Kylie's roof.

Who was he kidding? He would've been too tired from the two-a-days—sometimes three-a-days—to hang out, anyway. So did it matter that he never called them? He shook off the guilt.

"Not really," he said, which was mostly true. It was weird how he'd taken himself from well-known to obsolete status at West Oak in less than three months.

"You and Jones, thick as thieves as I recall." Finn Geringer and Jamal Jones—they were like a single unit. Meg always joked that you had to be willing to date Jamal if you wanted to date Finn. Of course Coach knew about Finn's life at West Oak if he'd been on their radar. People talked big in small towns. Jamal's face burned in Finn's memory. The look of betrayal when he told him he was going to play for EastPay.

"Not anymore," Finn clipped. "Haven't talked since . . ." He trailed off. "Long enough."

"Good, good."

Was it?

"Hear you got yourself a girlfriend over at West Oak."

Finn stiffened. "That's the rumor, sir."

"You know her, Collins?"

"Not in the biblical sense," Spencer piped up.

Finn breathed through his nose, quelling his rage. Coach Wilkins chuckled. "Easy, Collins." He addressed Finn again. "We play your old school, week after homecoming. Which side is she sitting on?"

"Whichever side she wants."

It was a knee-jerk response and the wrong one. He could see Coach hiding his anger, moving his tongue around like there was something stuck in his teeth.

"That's good," Coach Wilkins said. "Had myself a girlfriend in high school. She came to the games. Never talked much football except what color her favorite jerseys were. Great girl."

He stared at Finn unblinking, the silence shooting a message like a bullet pass to the chest: Meg wasn't to know of this book. Of anything in the huddle. Of any football word, conversation, or cleat on the Spartan field. Not that she would understand it, anyway, because according to Coach, all girls were idiots.

Finally, Finn broke the silence. Kept his voice calm. "That all, Coach?"

Coach Wilkins smiled at Finn, then rubbed a pock on his cheek. "Lookin' forward to Friday, Geringer."

Chapter 12
MEGAN

The following evening, Meg walked into Finn's empty locker room. Spotting the coaches through the glass window of the adjoining office, she approached tentatively. The door was ajar, maybe for circulation, as the four coaches crowded together on folding chairs watching a flatscreen, their backs to her. They held clipboards and legal pads and Styrofoam cups of coffee. She stood behind them as they stared up at the screen. *The Pioneers*, Megan recognized. EastPay's matchup this week. Realizing they hadn't seen her, she lingered in the doorway, waiting for a break in their meeting.

"There's the hole. Left side." One of the coaches, a Black man with rich, weathered skin, was pointing at the paused screen. Meg remembered him from EastPay Day—Cedric Wilkins—the one doing the interviews. Must be the head coach. "How's our line, Goode? Injuries?"

"Healthy as of this morning," Coach Goode said. "We'll use the corners. Load up three receivers on the right." Meg thought he looked like a taller, older Ron Weasley. Red hair that had turned gray. Friendly eyes. His shoulders said he could've gone pro but didn't because of timing or injuries. She could tell by his stature—though slightly sagged with age—that he was built for football. His exposed calves below his shorts were white, ashy, and freckled, but sculpted. *Probably still lifts three times a week*, Meg thought. "Or bubble screen. Bubble screen might actually work with this team."

"We'll adjust," Coach Wilkins answered. "And find out what you can on forty-nine defense. He's their playmaker."

"Six interceptions last year," Coach Goode answered, thumbing through an orange notebook. "I hear he hasn't been feeling well this week." The two other coaches chuckled.

Coach Wilkins smacked his clipboard on the desk, and they stopped. "Not my player. Not my problem."

The third coach cleared his throat. His fake tan looked rusted. "If we can move to the secondary, Jake's hamstring—"

"Keep the D as is, Stockton," Coach Wilkins ordered.

Coach Stockton and his fake tan shook his head. He licked his lips, thoroughly displeased. "And Damarius?"

"You let Goode be the offensive coordinator," Wilkins said.

Goode said, "I'll deal with Damarius. We have Collins to fill in for him. I'll even pull out McGeever." He paused, then said under his breath, "If it comes to that."

Coach Stockton nodded and scribbled on his legal pad.

"What the hell?" yelled the fourth coach, a short, squat man whose scrunched face swallowed up his beady eyes. Meg jumped when she realized he was staring at her.

She walked into the office, the freezing room causing her to inadvertently shiver. She spoke lightly. "I'm sorry. The locker room was propped open. I knocked. Then I saw you in the office. Finn said—"

"Easy, Hart," Coach Wilkins said to the short man, then

addressed Meg. "Geringer's girl—Meg, isn't it? Thought you went to West Oak." He snapped off the screen. The other coaches leaned in, suspicion crinkling their faces.

"I got a note at school." She held up the school stationery as proof.

Coach Wilkins eyed the note doubtfully. "Finn wrote that?"

"No. An office aide," she said. "I'm guessing he called." Finn knew Tuesdays were her Future Business Leaders meeting. "It said since practice would be long, I could meet him here after my meeting. But . . . the parking lot's empty."

Coach Stockton took the note from her hand and dropped it into the garbage can. "Practice ended hours ago, sweetheart," he said. "Four thirty today."

"But"—her eyes pinballing between all of them—"did you cancel early?"

Coach Wilkins said, "Don't usually discuss our practice schedules with other schools."

Her parents would expect her to say, *I'm sorry, sir,* and curtsy out of there. She'd been taught to never question authority. *Respect your elders.* But she was also taught to follow through with what she started. She looked at her note in the trash can. Her words tiptoed out of her mouth. "But he said you had late practice."

"Did he now?" Coach Hart interjected, doubt dripping through his voice. "You called him?"

"N-No," she stammered. He was incredibly intimidating for being so short. "His phone's off." She gestured at the trash can. "But the note."

Coach Hart crossed his arms, but it was Coach Goode who

spoke. "Lemme take this one." Meg was used to interacting with important people. Why did she feel so rattled? "Saw you and Geringer at EastPay Day. Must be tough going to different schools."

"It's okay. We're fine."

Coach Hart added, "For now."

"Pardon?"

"Is this about the cheerleader?" Coach Stockton said.

"Cheerleader?" Meg stopped, then, "Oh, that's his cousin. They're super close. We're fine, really. This isn't about—"

"No, not that one." Coach Stockton slurped his coffee. "I know the cousin. A different one."

"Stockton," Coach Wilkins said, holding out a hand to silence him.

Coach Stockton stayed quiet, but a smile crept over half of his rusty orange face. Instead, the beady-eyed guy, Hart, spoke up. "Well, I mean, he could have his pick. You see all the swooning in the hallways?"

Coach Stockton nodded, snickering. "Only so much a guy can resist." They grinned at each other.

"That's enough, you two," Coach Goode said. At least *someone* was standing up for her. Coach Wilkins was still watching her, his expression unreadable on his weathered face.

They were trying to stir something up. She steadied her anger. "I wasn't trying to spy on your meeting."

"'Course you weren't." Coach Stockton patted her shoulder.

They didn't believe her. She could tell in the way they looked at her, arms folded, eyes unblinking.

"Appreciate you stoppin' in," Coach Hart said in a way that she knew he most certainly didn't. She backed out of the office, and he slammed the door and lowered the blinds. No one said goodbye.

•　•　•

Back home, she sat alone at the dinner table, piecing their words together while nibbling on a casserole that had been left on the stovetop. Something felt off. The suspicion of all four coaches as they looked at her. Why would she lie? She thought about Finn's note, crumpled in the coaches' trash can. If Finn didn't make that call to school, who did? She texted Finn again for the thousandth time today, but he had an Android, so she could never tell if it was delivered. When she called, it went straight to voicemail. She knew the coaches had him watching an insane amount of game footage, so he probably had his phone off. Still, it was frustrating.

After washing her dishes, she flopped on the living room couch, exhausted, and looked around at the tall ceilings and over-size pillows, the limited-edition paintings in jewel-encrusted frames. Too much of everything. Her mother rounded a corner, ripping at an envelope. She stopped when she saw her daughter.

"Meg."

"Mom."

A piece of the envelope escaped from her mother's fists and fluttered to the ground. Meg picked it up, noticed the return address: East Pages Community Church. *East Pages?*

They went to church every Sunday without fail, but they attended West Oak Baptist.

"Does the Lord know about this?" Meg said jokingly.

"Junk mail," her mom said, not even cracking a smile. Then she crumpled the envelope as if to prove it. "You missed dinner."

"Sorry. I ate some. Thank you."

"Where were you?"

"Errands."

Meg marveled at how they could talk without communicating.

Her mom surprisingly didn't press it, but shuffled away into one of the house's wings, pouring herself a cocktail. Her mom had always loved a drink or two, but over the summer, the daily one or two had evolved to four or five. Meg wasn't sure what had spurred this on—maybe her father working late hours on a big DUI case?—but no way she'd point out the irony. Questioning her parents? It was "yes, ma'am," "no, ma'am," and "thank you" as long as she could remember.

Meg scanned her awards—volunteer, leadership, piano—lining the walls, and paused at the space where her ballet honors stopped. The day the pain started in her right foot. The physician made it sound like a six-course meal: "multiple transverse fatigue fractures of the anterior margin of the tibia in association with diffuse anterior cortical thickening."

Stress fracture.

If she stayed off her leg for three months, she could start slow, and in six months be back to the traveling ballet company. Her parents were hopeful, so hopeful they didn't even chance crutches. They bought her a wheelchair, and despite the humility of navigating the school hallways on wheels, she did it to please them.

However, as she spent those three months in the wheelchair, it was like whatever had been squeezing her heart and lungs her whole life suddenly released. She never wanted to lace up a ballet slipper again. And although she was released from the wheelchair in three months, she never recovered from her limp, which baffled the doctors and left her parents heartbroken. The company released her and signed a twelve-year-old ingenue in her place, ending her ballet career.

Her parents comforted her, their words laced with disappointment. "You did what you could. Did everything they said. We watched." They didn't, however, see her in her room in the months after her wheelchair, how she'd set her alarm nightly and practice *relevés* and *entrechats* and anything else that would exacerbate the fracture, keep it from healing. And now, a year later, the pain was gone, but she kept up the limp, just in case.

She sometimes wondered if her mom started drinking more to call her bluff. She knew that wasn't true, but those were the horrible thoughts that rattled her mind whenever she felt guilty for lying.

She turned in a slow circle, her eyes drawn to the blemish of empty wall space where New York and England ballet pictures were never hung, and she suddenly couldn't breathe. She walked out her front door and sat on her porch swing. The creaking of the swing at twilight calmed her, and she called her best friend, Kylie, on speaker.

"Hey, sis," Kylie answered. "How's the traitor?"

Meg smiled. "He's good, I guess. I wouldn't know."

"Oh no. You get in a fight? I told him not to wear Crocs with socks around you."

Meg laughed. "No. He wasn't there. Nobody was."

"But the note—"

Her father drove up in his BMW.

"Shoot, gotta go. I'll call later and fill you in." No phone before homework, and Meg never broke her parents' rules. At least not in front of them.

"Wait, don't you dare—" But Meg had clicked off her phone before her dad exited the car. She looked at her watch. Another day at the law office ending probably two hours ago, but there was always more work or a drink with an associate.

"Megan," he said as he stepped up the porch. "You eat already?"

"Casserole. More on the stove for you."

"Homework?"

She nodded and continued swinging. "Soon."

"Your mom called. Said you came home late."

It bothered her that he referred to his wife as "your mom" as if she were only attached to Meg and not him. Of course she didn't say it, though. "I went to meet Finn after practice."

"Couldn't wait till the weekend?"

Here we go. She plastered a light smile on her face. She'd perfected this dance.

"My meeting was close by. Anyway, I didn't see him. He was gone when I got there."

"He didn't text you?"

Please don't start, she wanted to say, but instead: "My fault. Phone was off." She didn't say *whose* phone. She stood and said, "Homework." The swing's creaking suddenly sounded noisy, broken.

"Good, good. You need help with pre-calc, just holler."

"I will!" She wouldn't. With a quick hug, she left him on the porch and headed inside. He kept talking, something about being good in math, and the value of being well-rounded. She took the steps two at a time up to her room, making sure to limp on her healed right foot.

Chapter 13
FINN

By eight p.m., Finn's eyes were bleary from watching tape at the Crestview Library, scrolling back, note-taking, and rewatching. Yesterday, when Coach Wilkins had handed him the SD cards and threatened that others could replace him, Finn didn't point out *he* was the one they had recruited. They did hold the power to bench him, after all, and he didn't want to test their pride. He needed playing time. Exposure.

"Geringer."

Finn only heard his name the second time. He removed his earbuds and looked up. Walker's six-foot-three frame was towering over him.

"C'mon, let's get out."

"Can't, man." He motioned to the computer screen playing tape of the Prescott Pioneers. "Coach has me studying the next two matchups. Still taking notes on Prescott. Fifth game but skipping around."

"Do 'em at home later."

"It's Tuesday, no time. And too distracting." He felt a pang of guilt that he'd ditched most of his classes today to study tape. The wild part was that Coach Wilkins actually wrote a note excusing him—on the condition that he turn off his phone for the day. With a quick *Miss you* text to Meg, he'd done just that. He looked around at the library, at Walker. "Besides, nobody'll find me here." He cocked an eyebrow at Walker. "Well, not usually. What the hell you doing at the library?"

Walker put a hand on his chest. "I just so happen to be widening the doors of my intellectual future. I'm hurt that you don't think I spend countless hours here. We're the children of tomorrow, Finn."

"No, really."

"Okay, you didn't answer my texts, so I dropped by your house." Walker picked up the legal pad, slid it into Finn's backpack, zipped it closed. "Your gram said you were here. Now let's go. I'm starving."

"No money." But he was closing his laptop. He stood and turned on his phone.

"Who said anything about money? School'll cover it. Booster Fund. We'll call it a team dinner." As Walker ushered him through the exit, he could feel his pocket blowing up with texts. "Minus the team," Walker added.

• • •

Once in his car, Finn saw the multiple missed calls from Meg and scanned through her texts. Something about the coaches. *She showed up at EastPay?* He called her and she answered on the first ring.

"There you are," she answered, sounding relieved.

"You okay? What happened?" He followed behind Walker's Mustang into the sports bar parking lot. The outdoor lights blinked on in the darkening sky, flashing the blue neon of Fourth and Goal.

"Did you call West Oak today?" Her voice sounded strained.

"West Oak *High*? Why?"

He heard her exhale. "That's what I thought. Someone called the school pretending to be you. Told me to meet you at EastPay after my meeting."

What? That made no sense. "Your meeting's not over till six."

"Exactly." She was silent for a moment, and then she said, "The note said practice would be late. And I got there, and the coaches—they were so mean. They thought I was there to spy on them."

"You explain the misunderstanding?"

"Tried. They didn't buy it. It's just—if it wasn't you, then whoever it was knew my schedule. That takes effort."

He was interrupted by Walker rapping on his driver's-side window. "Come on, man!"

"Hey, can I call you later? I'm so sorry." He felt his anger rising. He remembered the dismissive way Coach Wilkins had spoken of Megan. He could only picture how they must've treated her. "I'll talk to the coaches."

"No, it's fine." She sounded tired. "I'm sure it was some student from your school messing with me. Just—poor timing with your coaches." She laughed softly. "Walked right in on them. They were so mad! Anyway, I don't want to mess it up for you with them. First game Friday, and all."

He held one finger up to Walker, who was waving at him impatiently. "Love you."

"Love you back."

He followed Walker inside, but the conversation gnawed at him. Who would set her up like that? Should he say something to the coaches? They couldn't bench him for that, could they? He knew attending different schools would be hard on him and Meg. But he never imagined others would get involved.

Walker handed Finn a menu as they slid into seats away from the bar. "Just so you know, coaches have a zero tolerance policy on drugs and alcohol."

Finn shifted in his seat. *Did Walker know about his mom?* "Never touched a drug. And I'm dry. Don't even have a fake ID."

"Me neither." Walker stood and stepped away for a minute. Finn looked around, his mind still on Meg. All the local sports teams' photographs littered the walls, from baseball to football to volleyball, from six-year-old teams to adult leagues.

Walker weaved between the pool tables and returned with two Coronas. Finn took the beer apprehensively. "Zero tolerance policy?"

"Cheers," Walker said, clinking Finn's bottle. Finn watched him take a long swig, then cautiously brought the bottle to his lips. Pretended to sip. His friends at his old school knew why he didn't drink. Walker didn't need to know. Not yet, anyway.

"Got something for you." Walker pulled a brass-colored Spartan helmet out of his backpack. It looked like the real armor, nose plate coming down and the sides wrapping forward, revealing only the eyes and mouth. "Only fifty of these. Your invitation to any weekend party at Dante's. Every first and third Saturday of the month during the season."

"Can't people buy their own?" Finn set down his beer. Took the helmet.

"They're numbered."

He turned the helmet in his hands, surprisingly lightweight.

On the back in Sharpie was a large "XIX," the Roman numeral for 19. "Seems like you can still see the mouth and eyes."

"Some wear a bandana underneath. Covers up the rest."

"That's not creepy."

Walker laughed. "You can do whatever the hell you want. It's dark. I've taken mine off plenty of times. Kissing ain't happening otherwise, you feel me."

Finn laughed nervously and picked up his water glass.

Walker smirked. "Besides, I like letting people see me. Let 'em know, of course I'm here. Of course I'm invited." He shrugged. "You're kinda like that, too. Legends don't need an invitation."

It sounded like a compliment, so he didn't press Walker about why he was only getting the helmet now.

"Most guys keep it on, though," Walker added, leaning back. "Snitches, you know. If the party ever gets broken up, no faces, no witnesses."

Finn kept his expression neutral, letting the words settle. He wasn't sure what to make of them. A text buzzed on his phone. Megan.

Xo. Be careful, kk? ♥

So like Megan. Worried about him while she was the one being messed with. Finn noticed Walker reading the text, so he turned his phone over. Drank his water. Walker eyed him, then set his beer down. "So what do you want, Geringer?"

Finn stopped midsip. "I'm sorry?"

"This. All this. You transferring. Leaving your girl. Moving your grandma. Joining your *rival* school. Comin' to the dark side. What do you want?"

He remembered his mom, the vacant stare. Thought of his grandmother's kind eyes, felt her hand on his, calloused with dryness and age. *You focus on the right things, it'll keep you out of the wrong things.*

He took another drink of water. His voice was steady but fierce as a blitz. "I wanna play."

"You better. Everybody on EastPay wants to play. But what *drives* you? What keeps you up at night, makes you better'n you were yesterday?"

Finn shrugged. "Pure love of it, I guess. You?"

"For me, it's the tender feel of the pigskin in my hands. The romantic rush of the wind as I run a forty." Walker paused, then mimicked Finn's voice. "'*Pure love of it, I guess.*' C'mon, Finn. I'm a better bullshitter'n you. That ain't what keeps you pacing all hours. What keeps you up at night?"

Finn shrugged. No way he was going to share his fear about ending up like his mom.

A waitress came by, set two hamburgers down. "On the house, boys. Good luck Friday." Walker nodded thanks and then returned to Finn, waited for him to continue.

Only Finn didn't.

Walker took a long swallow of his beer, let his lips roll off the rim slowly. "Fine. You wanna know what drives me? It ain't the sport, that's for damn sure." He fixed his amber eyes on a pool stick leaning against the wall. "I hate my dad. Beat the shit out of me. Just once, but s'all it took. I was six."

Finn looked down at the table, uncomfortable. Walker hadn't seemed like the vulnerable type. They barely knew each other.

Walker took another drink. "The Rams were on TV behind where he stood over me, gettin' the shit beat outta them, too. But when I was cryin' on the carpet, still bein' kicked, I saw the TV sideways-like. QB got sacked hard. But he got up again. Next play threw a completion. Didn't win, but made no diff. I wanted to be big someday. Big enough to get up again. When I told the old man I wanted to sign up, he told me *girls couldn't never play*. What a guy."

Finn could hardly swallow his water. He thought about this kid laid out on the carpet, being pummeled by someone who was supposed to do the opposite. He'd never known his own dad, but he knew how dads should be. He looked down at his beer, still out of sorts from Walker's brutal honesty. What was the best thing to say? *I'm sorry? That sucks? Good for you?*

"I don't know my dad," Finn blurted, taking the beer in his hand. Looked up, eye to eye with Walker. "Mom didn't either."

Walker whistled low under his breath.

"Yeah," Finn agreed.

Finn only knew about his dad from the few clues left behind in the mirror—his height already at six feet by eighth grade, the way his olive skin would darken in the sun so quickly, the large almond shape of his eyes. Thick eyelashes. Strong chin. Even in the few times he'd seen his mother he knew these traits weren't hers. "And as for Mom—who knows." He sighed. Turned the bottle in his hand, picked the corner of the label with a fingernail. "She shows up here and there when the government stops givin' her money.

But I haven't seen her in three-plus years. My grandma, she started all over again with me. Didn't do a bad job first time around, with my mom. But. It's meth, ya know. Fuckin' beast, that drug."

Walker lifted his beer to that. Finn lifted his, then set it down.

"So she's got arthritis. My gram. Just eating away at her. Still early, no big deal now, but it's comin'." Finn bit into his burger, wiped his face with his napkin as he chewed. "She's straight in the head, though. Just needs someone to look out for her."

"And that's you."

"Which is fine, I owe her everything. But I wanna give her more than an apartment and minimum wage supporting us." He pushed the fries around on his plate, positioning them like players on a field. "I play my cards right, get a full ride, six years I could have her in her own house, own care, get her places she could see her friends. Ya know. Normal life, like she gave me."

"Big gamble. Makin' the pros."

"Damn straight." He drained the water in one swallow. Set it down and wiped his mouth with the back of his hand. "Keeps me up at night."

Chapter 14
BRITNEY

Brit was waiting at her cousin's house when he came home that night, excitement pulsing through her fingers. As soon as she saw the headlights turning off the dark two-lane highway, she whipped open the screen door and pranced outside. Walker's Mustang pulled in behind Finn, the gravel under the tires crunching in protest. Finn got out of the car.

"You escorting me home?" he joked, but his gaze landed on Brit and the van in front of their house. "What's going on?" His tone was suspicious. She hadn't stopped to think how it must look, his house lit up like a stadium, an unknown van parked out front.

He blew past her.

"Wait!" Brit chased after him through the wide-open front door.

"Gram?" he called.

"In here!" she hollered from his room.

Mrs. Callahan, her arms crossed against her robe and nightgown, stood behind Tammy and Amy Jane as they hung something on Finn's wall.

"What the hell—" he started.

Brit grinned. She loved this part.

The two girls were hanging a framed 49ers jersey. Finn gaped at the number 16, white against red, looking back at him.

Walker appeared behind Brit at Finn's doorway. "Had to get

you out of the house. Couldn't chance you leaving the library early and ruining your surprise."

Finn lifted a shaky hand and pressed his fingers against the glass frame, less than an inch from Joe Montana's autograph across his number. His fingers still touching the glass, he looked over his shoulder.

"I know, right?" Brit squealed. She'd installed a shelf near his bedside, where a football rested in a square case.

Mrs. Callahan huffed. "They made quite a racket with all their drilling."

Amy Jane apologized with a curtsy. "Sorry, ma'am. Gotta be careful hanging the important stuff."

Finn bent closer to the square case, reading the signatures strewn across the ball in black ink. "Denver Broncos, 1999," Brit proclaimed, beaming. "Super Bowl champs." She'd read the placard as they were hanging it. But Finn added—

"For the second year in a row." He spoke with reverence as if the signatures were the actual players standing in front of him. "They won their first thirteen games that season."

Walker leaned against the wall, arms crossed, eyebrows up. "*Bo knows football!* That's right, best start since the '72 Dolphins."

"Come on," Brit said. "You ran right by the best one."

Brit led Finn into the living room. Above the couch, a four-foot-by-two-foot black-and-white headshot of Gale Sayers wearing his #40 jersey smiled down on them. She nudged Finn. "There's your running back to chase."

"What the— How'd you know?"

Brit rolled her eyes. "I grew up with you. He's all you talked about."

Walker nodded at the portrait. "Heard Sayers had something like twenty touchdowns in his '65 rookie year."

"Twenty-two," Finn corrected. "His kickoff return average? Thirty-point-five-six yards."

"Insane."

"Unbroken."

Brit left them to gawk and helped Amy Jane and Tammy zip up their duffels of power tools. They walked past Finn and headed through the front door. Brit noticed how Tammy brushed up against Finn even though there was plenty of room to walk around. "Glad to be of service, Geringer," Tammy said, a playfulness in her words. She dipped toward him when she said it, one tank top strap falling off her shoulder. Brit was sure Meg wouldn't be so glad for Tammy's service.

With her strap still dangling, Tammy said, "You coming, Brit?"

She really didn't want to sit in a car with Tammy gushing about her cousin's hotness. "Finn, you wanna drive me home later?"

"I'll take her," Walker said. "She's on my way."

"Perf." She hugged the girls, and Tammy hesitated, probably wishing she could stay, too.

Brit and Walker helped carry the tools out, then returned to the living room. As the van engine faded in the distance, Finn was still staring at the signed photograph of Sayers, his Bears uniform tucked in neatly. "What— I don't— Why—"

Walker added, "Every starter gets this in their home—different players, different teams, of course."

Brit added, "But it's just on loan till you leave."

"Thank the Lord," Mrs. Callahan mumbled from the kitchen.

Walker looked at Sayers and spoke like a patriot reciting the Pledge of Allegiance. "We get to come home to this, every day. Remind us of the heroes who went before us. Paving the way. Setting the records for us to chase."

Brit had heard Walker give this speech every time she decorated a player's house, but each time, it gave her chills. His words were a prayer.

"They were once our age, ya know," Finn mused. "Same dreams as us."

Mrs. Callahan plopped onto the couch. "Hope they were taught how to fill in holes, too. Because that's what y'all are doing when Finn goes to college and you come pick up these pictures."

"Yes, Grandma," Brit said, kissing her forehead. "We'll get every last one."

"Come on," Finn told Walker. "I'll walk you out."

Autumn hadn't quite reached East Pages, and the night air was warm and sticky as Brit followed the two guys outside. The night jasmine from the garden wafted around them. Finn reached into his car, fumbling around, and Brit figured it was to retrieve his backpack or phone, but instead his hand emerged gripping a Spartan warrior mask. Brit's heart warmed at the sight.

"'Bout time," she said, indicating the plastic helmet, his invitation to Dante's Ravine.

Finn turned the helmet in his hands. "Meg stopped by the school after practice. Ran into the coaches."

"She just misses you," Brit said, unsure what this had to do with anything. "It's like football's your new girlfriend."

"Nah, she gets sacrifice. Look at her athletic career. I wish it was that simple," Finn said, turning to Walker. "Someone called my old school today pretending to be me. Telling Meg to head to EastPay."

Walker shrugged, but Brit said, "You sure?"

"Yeah," Finn said. "And they sent her there late. Like, after everyone had left."

"That's a mean prank," Brit said, but she wasn't surprised. She couldn't imagine anyone from EastPay being happy that someone from West Oak was dating their star player. She remembered the way they used to talk about Finn back when he went to West Oak—back when they lost to him last year. A chill shot through her. "Any idea who?"

"I dunno. They knew her schedule." He leaned against his car. "Walker, you can be straight with me, yeah?"

Walker twirled his keys in his hand. "'Course."

"Who's messing with her?"

"Hell if I know," Walker said. "Kids at our school are obsessed with football, yeah. But come on, who isn't?"

"So the rumors about EastPay?"

"How they go after people?" Brit laughed. "Hogwash, Finn. I woulda seen or heard something."

"No one's gonna do anything to your girlfriend," Walker said.

"You should know. You were our biggest threat last two years. And nothin' ever happened to *you*."

Finn held the Spartan mask up. "How come I wasn't invited to the first party?"

What was wrong with him? She picked at a fingernail, annoyed that instead of appreciating their hard work, he was questioning everything.

"Tradition," Walker said. "Only returners."

"How long's everyone been going?"

"Does it matter?" Brit interjected. "All schools have rituals."

"Who does the inviting?"

"Seniors," Walker said. "The ones who are in. Look, I'm giving it to you straight. We play football. We play *good* football. Other schools talk shit and you're surprised by that?"

The screaming of the cicadas filled the air. Brit watched Finn move his jaw side to side the way he did when something bothered him.

Finally he said, "I can't imagine how much these signed photographs, jerseys, and footballs are worth. What gives, Walker?"

Walker sat down on the front hood of his car like he was sacked by the weight of the question. "Your girlfriend been putting thoughts in your head? Someone pranks her, and now everyone's a suspect?"

"Nah, man. It's just— Never heard of a football team decorating a house. I—" He turned the plastic helmet over in his hands.

Walker leaned back, and the hood of the car made a hollow tin sound.

Brit didn't like the shift in Finn. At school, he was all in. And now, so quickly, he was doubting the integrity of EastPay? The beauty of Dante's Ravine? She wanted to wring the neck of whoever had pranked Megan that way. She broke the silence. "It's not the football team. It's the cheer squad. We have a collection. From a beneficiary."

"Benefactor," Walker corrected.

"That's what I said. Anyway, oil business. 'Bout ten years ago, his girlfriend was on our squad. So he donated that"—she waved loosely toward the house—"and poof! We get to give it to all of you. On loan, of course. Been doing it since 'fore I came. But I'm pretty pro with power tools after three years."

Walker hopped off the hood and patted Finn on the back. "Haters gonna hate." He climbed into his Mustang, started the engine, rolled down the window. "I'll take Miss Cheerleader home. You got Gale Sayers's record to beat."

"Twenty-three touchdowns," Finn said, fist-bumping Walker.

Brit slid into the passenger seat and watched Finn through the side mirror as they drove away. He was looking down at the mask, turning it over slowly. *Ugh.* He was still unsettled about Meg.

Back on the highway, Walker grinned at Brit. "Thanks for saving my ass back there."

Brit hid her confusion with a broad smile. "Of course."

He offered that deep knowing look, one that said they shared a secret. "You know more than you let on. Me too."

He placed his hand on her leg and squeezed a silent thank-you. His hand was calloused and strong, but his touch was soft. For a moment, all she could think was that Terrance Walker, captain of the football team, had his hand on her leg, and she instantly felt small and in eighth grade again.

"Makes us more connected somehow," he continued. "At our school, that's everything. You feel me?"

Then she remembered she wasn't in eighth grade; she was *somebody*, and he knew it. She put her hand on his leg, too, and squeezed. "Yeah. I get you."

Terrance Walker had made varsity as a freshman, and a year later, she'd made varsity cheer as a freshman, both unprecedented feats. It made her feel a bond, even though he was one year older.

Walker moved his hand back to the steering wheel. "How'd you figure it all out? I was told they decided not to tell you back freshman year. Makes sense now. Someone must've known you were related to Finn. Too close to the enemy and all—well, before he transferred."

Huh? Brit's mind reeled. Figure *what* out? And *who* decided to keep her out? Of *what*?

"I pay attention," she said, feigning confidence, but she felt her accent grow thick. "Don't take a genius."

"Yeah, it does. But that's why I thought they didn't want you in. Heard you *are* a genius."

Her stomach both fluttered and dropped. It was a compliment, but who was talking about her past? Cybersecurity club was social suicide. Who would throw her under the bus like that? She laughed, but by Walker's strange look, she knew it sounded forced. She threw her hands up. "Guilty," she said. "But I ain't telling you shit." The cursing was overkill, but she couldn't take it back. Luckily he didn't know she only cussed when she was nervous or really riled.

"Ha!" He slapped the dashboard. "Don't worry. I won't tell anyone. Better that way anyway, right?" He tapped the steering wheel to a silent beat.

Brit smiled. "For sure." He looked at her then—*really* looked—his eyes off the road, studying her. Could he tell she was lying? Then he relaxed and laughed.

"Britney Wallace," he said. "Keeping a secret from the secret keepers. You *are* a genius."

Brit fumbled in her purse for her lipstick. She didn't know any secrets.

Chapter 15
FINN

It was Friday night, and Finn scanned the locker room. The sounds were familiar—players tightening their laces, adjusting shoulder pads, wrapping ankles and knees in athletic tape—a symphony that amped his teammates as they prepped for the game.

Cleats *click-clack*ed like tap shoes against concrete as everyone mentally and physically suited up. Lockers slammed. Players paced. No one talked except under their breath, angry words, hopeful words, muttering conversations to themselves that outside of a locker room would raise a few eyebrows. Finn could feel the pulse of the whole team beating as one, calling to him to embrace this group energy that shouted what he knew already: Football was everything, and all of it—this moment—was right.

Once he was outside, his adrenaline amplified. The stadium was a curtain of red, thousands of bodies pressed against each other and drunk in the pulsing heartbeat of football that ran this town. The East Pages Stadium, or EastPay Stay, as it was commonly called, seated eighty-five hundred, and at any home game, there were no less than five thousand Spartan fans in attendance. Usually the opponents from a neighboring city would bring in half of that, and the vacant lot across the street made twenty dollars a spot for the Booster Club.

The Spartans had the district's best record for the past seven years, and superstitions were as high as expectations. Furniture was never rearranged during the fall. If the team was down a touchdown, the patrons would switch to a different soda, shift their weight to their other foot, uncross their arms, turn their hats backward, even send a quick online donation to the local church—anything and everything until the game's momentum changed. If a business had a lit sign with a letter that burned out on the night of an EastPay win, the bulb would not be replaced all season. Consequently, although the *S* was finally replaced last December, Super Shoes Outlet would forever be known as Super Hoes by the locals.

Finn felt the stadium cheers echo in his chest, the volume of the crowd bellowing until they were hoarse and lightheaded, as if the future of businesses, marriages, and retirement rode on the victory of this one game. By kickoff, an intoxication infected every person within earshot.

Adrenaline coursed through him—there was nothing better than the beginning of a game. No fumbles yet. No incomplete passes. He was perfect in this moment. As his team shouted and pushed each other and lifted their hands to the fans, he knew they felt it, too. The invincibility. The beauty of the game. The choreography. The plays and the runs culminating on the turf in a perfectly executed dance. His heart bled for this.

This was football.

Less than two minutes into the first drive, Finn had scored the Spartans' first touchdown. The plays were simple, all "summer plays" like Coach said they'd be, despite what was run at 4:30 a.m. practices. Nothing had changed Coach's plan of "quick action, quick handoffs, bubble screen them to the end zone."

"Folks, it's Friday night, and football has returned to East

Pages," the announcer rang. "This Spartan blast offense has been unstoppable, as the left-side O-line's providing everything but the red carpet for Finn Geringer."

In the second quarter, Coach subbed out a slot receiver and put Spencer Collins in with Finn. Finn could see the whole bench shifting uncomfortably, players looking at one another, but Spencer sprinted on as if he expected it. This was wrong. It should have been Damarius for the play. Finn didn't know much about Damarius Davis, except that he always waved at Finn in the hallways, and he hung out with Eli McGeever—Spencer's little sister's boyfriend.

And that he was *thick*, a fullback who doubled as a tree trunk. A fast one.

Instead, Collins was in there—Collins who was lean and fast, who was perfect for tailback. Not fullback. But at the Pioneer twenty-two, it was Collins who blocked, allowing Finn to catch a short lateral from White and squirrel his way into the end zone. It was a textbook summer play, but it had only been run with Damarius. Never Collins.

Finn didn't feel the elation of the touchdown. He was shook. What did Damarius do? If coaches could bench a key fullback like Damarius, how secure was his own spot?

As they jogged off for special teams, Finn approached him. Damarius Davis, the one who'd smile when most guys would just offer a head nod. He was sitting on the bench, elbows on his knees, head tipped down. "You okay?" Finn said.

Damarius didn't look at him, but Spencer walked by, muttering, "Leave it alone. Not the time. Not the place." Finn glared, but

Spencer was already at the far bench. He offered Finn an almost imperceptible head shake. Finn lifted his hands like, *What's your problem?* But the look in Spencer's eyes gave Finn pause. Spencer wasn't being pissy.

He was concerned.

Chapter 16

BRITNEY

Brit knew football positions and plays more than she let on. But she didn't like people knowing. It was too close to who she used to be. Plus, since her last conversation with Walker, she was on edge, watching for anything that would clue her in on what she was being kept out of. She did her best to blend in, be part of the crowd she had *thought* she led. She made a point to giggle with Amy Jane, her fellow cheer team member, about how she'd lose track of the score if it weren't for the scoreboard. "How many times is this?" Brit had asked as they danced their fight song and ran to the goalposts for the extra point. Amy Jane lifted a pom-pom and mouthed, "Who knows?"

Six.

Six times exactly, Amy Jane. No missed PATs. *Points after touchdown, Amy Jane. Not Ponytail Adjustment Time.* They won 42–7, a slaughter and a statement for their first home game. Spencer was in and out for the rest of the game—not that she noticed. She didn't. Of course she didn't. She also *didn't* notice Spencer switching with the slot receiver or the tight end, and that Damarius Davis usually ran that play.

She was last to grab her bag off the field after the game. People were filing out of the parking lot, celebrating with one another, good spirits and good moods. Winning was such a high, and she liked being the last to enjoy it under the stadium lights. In the distance, she saw Spencer exiting the locker room. Of course, he was dragging his feet. Party pooper. She waved. He looked at her like she'd been waving to the wrong person. His sister, Leah, approached him with her boyfriend, Eli. They talked for a minute—most likely Eli was asking to drive Leah home—and then they jogged off to the parking lot, leaving Spencer. No one else was around, so she walked over to him, meeting him at the blacktop basketball courts.

"Look at you, fancy pants," Brit said. "Someone's getting some playing time again."

"Shut up, Britney," he said, but she could tell there wasn't a lot of venom attached. He sounded almost disheartened. He didn't look at her.

"Now you're mad about it?" She slung her duffel over her shoulder. "You're something else, Collins. You get benched, you whine. You get on the field, you whine. That wasn't even your play, second to last of the half. Damarius Davis should've run that."

He smirked, still looking away, and she knew there was a little part of him that was impressed. She also knew there was a part of her that loved he was impressed, but it was short-lived. He sobered quickly.

"Yeah, well, Davis sure as hell ain't playing anytime soon. Speaking of Davis, tell your cousin to keep his head out of other people's asses. He's gonna get himself in trouble if he starts asking questions."

"That a threat?"

"Not from me."

She threw her head back and her pom-poms up. "Gah! Why do you still hate Finn? No one else does. That was so two months ago," she joked. He didn't laugh. The single light from the basketball courts was directly over him, casting an ominous light.

"You wanna know why I hate him?"

Brit stood still, shocked that he offered to share.

"It's because he's a fucking mirror of how stupid I was in ninth grade. He runs around with stars in his eyes like he's part of something Mother Teresa started. Just like you do. Just like I did, freshman year." Brit could see Spencer's muscles flexing, like he was ready to pull a swing. "Only I admitted the truth when I saw it."

She groaned. Just when she thought she was getting somewhere with him. "You are so dramatic. I think it's because he took your position."

"There ain't a position to take! Don't act dumb with me, because I know you're one step below genius. There's always two backs on the field. Sometimes three. So why aren't we both out there? Finn's more talked about. But he's not faster."

Brit snorted. "Maybe he's just better than you."

"Keep drinking the Kool-Aid. Or as you think, the river water."

"Look, you got on the field tonight."

Spencer narrowed his eyes, but his anger didn't seem directed at Brit. "Yeah, well, he has me by the balls. He can do whatever the hell he wants."

"Who, Coach? Of course he can. He's the *coach*."

He scoffed—actually scoffed—at her. She was undone. He licked his lips and shook his head, then looked back at her when he said, "No, not Coach. For being so smart, I don't know how you can keep being so dumb."

He walked away, leaving her stunned, before she finally found the nerve and shouted after him, "Good chat as always, Spence! You're a ray of sunshine!"

In the darkness, his back silhouetted by the streetlights, she could still make out his raised middle finger. She stayed there under the yellow light of the basketball court until he was gone, fiddling with her jacket zipper. Spencer—*who was he, anyway?*—hinting that she wasn't clued in on something. Just like Walker had. She stared at the glitter on her arms, adjusted her striped Captain armband. What did it matter? She was the Fearless Flyer. She blew out her breath and tried to relax.

"I'm fearless," she said aloud, but her voice came out small and wavering. She suddenly felt very alone in the darkness, and she ran to her car as fast as she could.

On the drive home, Meg in the back seat and his grandma riding shotgun, Finn noticed neither of them were saying much.

The win had been sweet. He spotted Meg climbing over the front railing of the bleachers. She ran to him and jumped, throwing her legs around his waist. They hadn't spoken much this week, but as soon as he saw her, he knew she hadn't held it against him. She squeezed him and whispered, "That was amazing. You were amazing." He kissed her, then walked to the bleachers and found his grandma.

"Well? How'd I do, Grandma?"

She bobbed her head side to side. "Eh. Average."

He had laughed and hugged her. But now in the car, with everyone silent, Finn smiled at his grandma. "So just average?"

"I wasn't joking with you. I was there with you watching your tapes."

She'd been up a lot of the nights this week when he'd streamed his laptop to their TV to study the footage of this week's and next week's opponent. He reached into his center console and held up two SD cards. "You mean these?" He'd meant to return them at school today, but coaches weren't around in the morning. He'd bring them Monday. "I studied the plays, Grams. You saw that. Talked to Coach about their weak lines down the left."

"Then you got lucky because you were facing a different guy. Maybe the guy we watched on tape was a senior and graduated."

"Nah, I watched the film. Met with Coach about how to get around that corner, make him misread the play. It was only their QB that was out. Ineligibility. Maybe that's who you're thinking of."

"You think I don't know the difference between a quarterback and a corner? That guy on the film was big. This guy wasn't. You were charging through a toothpick tonight."

Finn grinned. "That so, Grandma?"

She nodded. "Toothpick."

Meg's eyes found Finn's in the mirror. He looked away.

· · ·

Back at his house, he walked Megan to her car. "No texts from your parents tonight?"

She lifted a shoulder. "Dad has an early flight. He'll be packing. Mom's probably passed out on the couch."

He hated hearing how broken Meg's family seemed and how they worked so hard to make it look the opposite. Megan had told Finn everything: how gregarious her father was at bigwig functions, how her mother's laugh trilled at jokes, how they mingled only with groups wearing suits and designer dresses. They loved bringing Megan to these functions, presenting her as their trophy who played concert piano and started nonprofits and, until recently, traveled with a professional ballet company.

He recalled Sunday morning when Megan had offered her father's financial help. He'd seen Mr. Kaufman with his own family, and no thank you. Finn wanted nothing to do with this man helping him, buying Finn's future in some way that would make Finn owe him later. He circled Megan with both arms, drew her in deeply.

She rested her head against his chest. "Finn?"

"Mmm?"

"You flirting with anyone?"

He stepped back.

"I never thought that," she said. "It's just when I was at your school, your coaches—"

Finn sighed. "Look, I'm sorry. I'm sure they were assholes. I don't know who called and set you up like that. But—"

"And you heard your grandma tonight—"

"Yeah." His fists clenched. He'd left the field on such a high. "I thought I had a great game."

"You did! But something feels off, doesn't it?"

What felt off was Damarius sitting out. He wanted to know what got a starter benched so he'd be sure not to do it. He *had* to play. His grandma's future rode on how well he did, and the thought of that made it hard to breathe.

Meg opened Finn's car door, which was parked alongside hers, and reached into his center console and pulled out the two SD cards.

"What are you doing?" Finn asked.

"Can I look at these?"

"No."

"No?"

"I need them." That wasn't true. He'd already copied them onto his laptop, but something about handing them over felt traitorous. "Meg, those are EastPay's."

"So? They're Prescott's games, right? Tonight's team? If you already played them, why does it matter? Isn't this last season?"

Finn thought of Coach and his words about the playbook: *"No one knows about that book."* He definitely wouldn't be okay with Finn sharing information with anyone at West Oak, girlfriend or not.

"They're Coach's property."

"And I'm your girlfriend. You afraid I'll find something?"

"No!" He raised his hands in surrender, but his jaw tensed. "Fine. Have at it. Here's what I think. I think Grandma was wrong about the corner. I think the coaches are jerks to you because you go to West Oak. And I think someone—*a person,* not an organization or the Mafia or some Area 51 conspiracy—called you at school to mess with you. And I hate that, but we knew this wouldn't be easy for us. We *knew."*

She nodded, tightened a fist around the SD cards, and climbed into her car without hugging him.

"Hey," he said, softening. "I'm not mad at you. I'm mad that all this is messing with us." She didn't answer. "You okay?" he asked through the closed door. She started the car and lowered the window.

"Finn—" She locked eyes with him, waiting, but he wasn't sure what he was supposed to say. When he didn't say anything, she looked up, wrinkling her nose like she was thinking hard. "You never answered my question."

He shook his head, not remembering, but then she added, "I asked about the flirting."

I shouldn't have to, he thought. The annoyance came back. "No, I'm not flirting with any cheerleaders. I have a girlfriend, remember? One who supports me and trusts me."

She put her car in reverse but kept her foot on the brake. "I didn't say cheerleaders, Finn."

"What?"

"I asked if you were flirting with anyone. I never said cheerleaders."

Finn was struck silent. Why had he said that? An image of Tammy Shaw flashed across his mind, the way she batted her eyes, how she dipped her shoulder so her tank top strap would fall loose. "I, I just assumed—"

"Apparently, so did your coaches."

Finn swallowed.

She dipped her chin, her eyes a little shiny. "I never did, though. I've never doubted you." She gave him a sad smile. "Night, Finn."

"Megs—"

But she backed up and drove away, tires crunching over gravel in the wet summer night. He stood there, unmoving, guilt heavy in his chest. The night fell silent, but the weight remained.

Chapter 18
MEGAN

Meg parked in her driveway and pushed the screen door with unnecessary force, taking the stairs two at a time. She wiped from her cheeks the few tears that had escaped on the way home.

Her bedroom didn't make her feel much better. This place her parents thought described her perfectly hadn't been "her" in a long time. Canopy bed, mattress higher than her waist. White bedspread and a mountain of white pillows, with a lavender one in the back for, as her mom said, "a soothing pop of color." Drapes hanging from the window like wedding gowns cascading down to two bows on either side. Finn called her room "fluffy."

Finn.

She needed to take a step back and look at the whole picture. Finn's team was good. Sure, there were rumors. But what were the facts? Britney Wallace—well, technically, Spencer—had struck a guy while driving to a party. Finn's grandma said the opposing team's top defender hadn't played tonight. Did either of those things mean the school was part of a conspiracy to take down every other school so they'd dominate football? No. Those were rumors she'd heard from people at *her* school. West Oak. The enemy of East Pages High.

Yes, the coaches had been mean to her. But why wouldn't they be? She *did* go to West Oak. She *was* still dating Finn.

She pulled out her phone and texted, *Sorry.* There was so much more to say, but that seemed to be the best word right now. Her phone vibrated in response.

Me too. You're my everything. You believe me?

Her smile cracked the dried stickiness of tears on her face. *Always*, she wrote.

On her dresser, a porcelain ballerina figurine stood atop a circular base. As a child, she'd danced around the room with it every day. She lifted it now, and it stuck slightly to the finish before pulling away, leaving a circular ring on the dresser from the years of heat and humidity. She didn't remember when she'd last picked it up. It wasn't her anymore. She set it down, making sure to place it where it had sat for years, hiding the ring, and then stared into the mirror. Who was she now?

Her gut still churned. It wasn't the fake phone message. Or that someone lured her into a confrontation with Finn's coaches. It was one word.

Toothpick.

Finn's grandma—no stranger to football—had dismissed the guy Finn played against.

Emphatically.

If Mrs. Callahan was right, then Prescott didn't match their best against Finn tonight. Which would make no sense. Schools knew Finn Geringer. Meg wanted to look at the SD card, but not here. Too much "fluff." Plus, her laptop didn't even have an SD slot. She texted Kylie.

> You have an adapter for an SD card?

An immediate response popped up.

Yep. Why

Wanna play detective w me

Ooh who are we spying on

Long story. Meet at Jaybees?

Gimme 10. At Tara's

Meg smirked. Tara, the infamous player on Kylie's volleyball team who was "terribly annoying" because she never shut up about her girlfriend. Then they broke up, and suddenly, Kylie was spending all her free time with this "terribly annoying" Tara. Meg grabbed her laptop and raced down the steps, blowing past her mom, who was walking from the kitchen to the den to retrieve an extra wineglass. Murmurs of a few ladies' voices came from the kitchen.

"Where are you—"

"Study group!" Meg slammed the screen door.

Outside, a darting light caught her eye, and she skidded to a stop. A flashlight was shining into Meg's car from the opposite side.

"Hello?" she called out, but the light had gone out, and with a faint sound like an animal through the bushes, it was suddenly silent and dark. Her heart pulsed in her throat. "Hello?"

Nothing. Had she seen a flashlight? It was a light, wasn't it? She examined the driver's side. No signs of attempted entry. No cicadas sounded in her neighborhood, just quiet. She unlocked her car and climbed in, locking the doors. Her eyes searched the rearview mirrors as she drove away, but nothing stirred.

• • •

Five minutes later, she pulled into a twenty-four-hour diner near the West Oak truck stop whose Friday night crowd consisted of a couple of travelers, three or four truck drivers, and some older ladies wearing either too much leather or all-matching denim. Finn and Meg had often come here for late-night dessert back when he lived in West Oak.

People ate pie and sipped their coffee, the atmosphere hazy and thick, interrupted by the bright flashing sign outside the front window: "Jaybee's." In the back booth below a no-smoking sign, a truck driver sucked on a cigarette. He exhaled as the waitress passed, a cloud encompassing her black skirt.

Meg was ordering pancakes and two coffees when Kylie flopped into the seat next to her. Kylie was still wearing her volleyball uniform, her dreadlocks tied back into a ponytail, which meant she hadn't changed since her game. "Sorry I'm late. Had to swing by the house to grab it." She held out the adapter.

"You're a lifesaver," Meg said. She opened her laptop, connected the adapter, and slid the SD card in.

"What dinosaur gave you an SD card?"

"EastPay football coaches."

"Uh-huh, that's cute," Kylie said. She'd told Kylie about her confrontation with them the other day.

When Meg didn't say anything, Kylie sucked in her breath and gripped Meg's arm.

"You steal these?"

Meg understood Kylie's fear. Whether you believed the rumors or not, you steered clear of anything East Pages if you were from West Oak. "No! Relax. They gave Finn some games to study."

"Finn . . . Do I know a Finn?"

Meg could detect a little edge behind Kylie's playfulness. "I'm sure he'll come around to calling you guys."

Kylie snorted. "He hardly responds to texts. You think he's gonna call?"

"He told you guys it was gonna be like this. He's busy."

"That why you're doing his homework for him?" Kylie motioned to the SD cards.

Meg looked around. No one seemed to be paying attention to them. Quietly, she told Kylie about the game and what Finn's grandma had said afterward. Then she told her about the light near her car right before she came here. Kylie tugged on one of her locs.

"So someone's after you. And now we're snooping. Sounds totally safe." She motioned to the laptop. "What happens if you find something?"

Meg shook her head. "I haven't thought that far."

"You better hope no one finds you digging." Then she added, "You sure you don't want to break up with Finn and date Scott?"

Scott was in the school band with Kylie. He'd had a crush on Meg in middle school when she played piano for all the accompaniments.

"Come on." Kylie nudged her shoulder. "He plays the oboe. It's a very sexy instrument."

Meg giggled. "I'm good, thanks."

"Your loss." She woke up Meg's laptop. "Your funeral."

The card held the Pioneers' whole season. Meg clicked on the first game. It was against the Greenville Bengals.

"How'd *we* do against the Bengals last year?" Kylie asked, leaning in toward the screen. Meg loved how her best friend immediately was all in.

"Lost." Meg remembered that game because afterward, Finn had canceled their date and driven home. He hated losing, and West Oak had lost to the Bengals by a field goal. She toggled through the first quarter, watched a couple plays. Thanks to growing up in Texas and dating a football star, she knew the game. She could tell Prescott's secondary was weaker than Greenville's offense, but there were a few standouts, their corner being one of them. It wasn't an easy victory for Greenville. She pushed pause on her computer and took a snapshot of a Prescott player, then zoomed in.

"Was that the guy tonight?" Kylie asked.

Something dropped in the pit of Meg's stomach. "No."

This guy's legs were stocky compared with Finn's. In fact, he was stacked all over, legs, arms, and neck like a brick wall. She pushed play and recited Mrs. Callahan's word to Kylie.

"Toothpick."

"Ha!" Kylie said. This guy, their strongest corner, was *not* a toothpick. He kept pivoting, like a pick and roll in basketball, trying to trick the quarterback or throw off the runner. That seemed like his token move. If he'd played tonight, he would've tried it at least once. He hadn't.

"You trying to learn that play?"

Meg and Kylie jumped.

A man stood behind them, looking at her laptop screen. "It's not that great. I know a lot of better fakes for a corner."

"No— I was—um—" Meg tried to calm her nerves, tried to reason that maybe this man was just being friendly, maybe he knew her from one of her parents' soirees. Did she recognize him? Nothing registered, but she was tired. "Do we know you?"

"No, just saw you studying so intently, made me curious. You girls Pioneers fans?"

"Oh." She looked at Kylie. "No, actually. We go to West Oak."

"So who's the Pioneer? Boyfriend?"

Kylie laughed. "One could only hope. Her boyfriend's EastPay."

Seriously? Meg kicked Kylie under the table.

"Ow!"

The stranger widened his eyes at Meg. "And you're West Oak? Ooh. House divided."

Megan smirked. "Yeah. More than you know."

"Strong victory tonight. Helluva team he has this year. Spartans." The man sipped his coffee. Slurped it loudly and swallowed slowly as he stood over them. "So why you studying your boyfriend's opponents?"

Kylie shifted uncomfortably. She tore off a piece of pancake with her fingers and popped it in her mouth. Meg wondered who this guy was. He wore a vest over a tucked-in dress shirt, like he should be on Wall Street. He was almost retirement age, she guessed, eyeing his silver hair that glistened like an oil stain. Too old to be curious about what two young girls were doing.

Meg revealed nothing. "Thought I'd give him some pointers. They're great this year. I think they have a shot."

"Mmm." The man slurped his coffee again. "You sure that's why you're watching?"

He let that hang as if it would trigger a response in her. *Did he know something?*

"I'm sorry, who are you?" she asked.

"No one of consequence. However, you are. Lotta people asking why you're still with Finn Geringer. Rumor has it he hasn't mentioned you to anyone. That doesn't bother you? Make you think he's embarrassed by you?"

Meg was stunned.

"How do you know who her boyfriend is?" Kylie cut in, a tinge of pink appearing under her tawny brown skin. Meg knew the look. It only happened when Kylie ran during PE.

Or got angry.

"Did you follow her here?"

"Oh, I doubt I'm the only one following her." He lifted his mug to his lips. Finished his coffee in one gulp, then looked directly at Meg. "You best take care no one feels you're holding him back. Finn's moving on. I suggest you think of doing the same." The man tucked the back of his shirt in and twirled his car key around his fingers. "A little yeast works through the whole batch of dough."

He scanned the smoky room like he was taking a panoramic pic, slow, steady, while he repeated the same words, "A little yeast works through the whole batch of dough."

"What's that supposed to mean?" Kylie snapped.

He smiled down at Kylie like she was a child. Like he'd follow it by patting her on the head. With his eyes on Kylie's uniform, he said, "Stick to volleyball, girls. Good night to you, Meg. I'm sure I'll see you again."

The two girls sat in silence, even after he was gone. Meg knew the Bible verse, understood his underlying threat that she was the problem—the yeast that infected the whole batch.

Finally, Kylie squeezed Meg's arm. "You sure you're not into oboes?"

Meg smiled faintly.

Kylie gestured toward the exit where the man disappeared. "Listen, ignore him. He was all hat, no cattle. It's just the EastPay way. Bunch of bullies, that whole town." She helped Meg pack up her stuff. "Did you hear about the oboist who played in tune?"

Meg shook her head.

"Neither did I," Kylie said. She grinned, and Meg laughed. They walked out to their cars together, and Kylie made Meg promise to text when she got home.

Rattled, Meg didn't remember much of the drive, except that she kept checking her mirrors. No headlights followed, and she was soon back in her *fluffy* room, which made her think of Finn. She called him, and he immediately answered.

"You were right," he said instead of hello. "Grandma was right. I watched the footage. It was some other corner."

"What?" She was calling to tell him about the strange man, and she'd completely forgotten their earlier talk. "Oh. Yeah, I know. Kylie and I watched it, too."

"You showed *Kylie?*"

She didn't have the energy for another argument. "Finn, listen. It doesn't matter. This guy at Jaybee's tonight . . ." And she launched into a recap of the man with the slicked-back hair who'd approached them. The threats. The implication that she was being followed. Using the Bible—something she loved—to send her a message. Even through the phone, she could feel Finn's anger toward the guy—his quiet murmurs of disgust as she explained what had happened.

"It's him, I bet," Finn said. "The one who called West Oak and set you up. You didn't get a name?" She could hear his voice quiver with anger.

"Doubt he would've told me," Meg said.

"You're home now?" he asked.

"Back in my fluffy room," she joked, "protecting me from the outside. Guarded by ballerinas and an obscene amount of pillows."

Finn chuckled.

Pillows.

Meg thought—no, *knew*—that earlier tonight, the violet pillow had been against her headboard, underneath the piles of white pillows. Now it was propped in front, and her duvet was ruffled. Or had it been that way when she left? She looked at her ballerina figure on her dresser. Next to it was the faint ring it had left on the varnish. *Next* to it. Not under it. Her heart lurched.

"Finn, I gotta go. I need to ask my mom something." She kept her voice steady through their *I love you*s and then hung up. She hurried downstairs and into the den, where her mother dozed in an oversize chair, a glass in hand.

She nudged her awake. "Have you been in my room?"

Her mom looked at her, bleary-eyed.

"Have you been in my room?" she repeated. "My pillows are different. Did you move my ballerina?"

Her mother's eyes narrowed in a way that said, *Really? You woke me up for this?*

"One, I haven't been upstairs since this morning. Two, if you have an issue with your pillows, then maybe you should make your own bed before school."

"Who was here tonight?" Her mom stiffened at this new clipped tone that never came from Meg. It surprised Meg, too. It felt scary. Exhilarating. But mostly scary.

"No one went into your room." She peered into her empty glass. "So this is the first discussion you want to have today?"

Of course this was Meg's fault, this lack of communication, even though Mom never asked how Meg was. As long as Meg could remember, her mother's words were only plans or advice. Still, Meg heard the reproachful tone at her impolite behavior. This wasn't how to speak to adults. "Sorry," she mumbled. "How was your day?"

"Good, thank you." Her mother's voice was cold. "I haven't heard you practice piano today."

Her insides squeezed, a tightening in her rib cage to hold down the swirling frustration. It used to be so easy. Why did her parents' words grate on her lately?

"I'll practice double tomorrow."

Meg limped up the stairs and down the hallway to her parents' bedroom. There, her father stood over a suitcase, zipping up a garment bag. He glanced up. "Megan."

"Dad."

He paused, waiting.

"You weren't in my room tonight by chance, were you?" she asked carefully.

He didn't answer, but she could tell by his eyes he was curious, not guilty. He hadn't been in there. She looked away, not sure where to begin.

"Your mother," he started. "She said you ran down the stairs tonight and out the door."

"Study group."

He shook his head. "It wasn't that. It was the running. She said you weren't limping."

Meg stood still. Chose her words carefully. "It's improving. The leg."

"Mmm." He eyed her. "From limping to running. In a day."

Meg stayed silent.

"You sure you're not elongating your injury to spend more time with that boyfriend of yours?"

The night had gotten to her. Everything boiled up to the surface and her body shook in frustration, down in her fingertips.

"His name's Finn," she growled. "My boyfriend's name is Finn Geringer, and I'm *elongating* my injury because I don't want to do ballet anymore. You and Mom want that. Not me." She could feel her volume rising. "And Finn's the only one who truly gets who I am, not who I was when I was seven and twirled till my toes bled.

That's *your* version of me. And dammit, I'm sorry if that disappoints the people at your parties. But right now, nobody—not one person at my school, his school, coaches, strangers—wants me to be with Finn. And I need you, for once—*for once*—to be on my side with this! Because nobody else is."

Her father stood there for too many seconds. She shifted the weight onto her supposed bad leg, didn't care that he saw. She stared at her hands, vibrating from the adrenaline, the pent-up feelings of two years—two years? Had it been stirring that long?

Her dad sat down on the bed, exhaling.

Megan's thoughts raced. *What had she done?* She chewed on her bitten-down fingernail. "Dad, I—"

"Finn Geringer," he began. She tensed at her father saying the name, unsure what would follow. "What position does he play?"

It was the closest he'd ever come to an apology. She softened and sat down next to him. "Running back," she said. *He's good. Really good,* she wanted to say. But instead, she told him about fifth grade, about how she cried when a ballet recital conflicted with a birthday party, and how Finn skipped the birthday party and attended her ballet recital instead, just to cheer her up, to make sure she didn't feel alone.

Chapter 19

BRITNEY

Sunday morning after church, Brit was at Finn's, scooping her second helping of Grandma's egg soufflé onto her plate. She was nervous eating. By the way Finn grinned at her across the table, he knew it, too.

She shoveled in another mouthful, trying to squash the uneasy feeling that hadn't left her since her conversation with Walker. That night, she'd texted on her group chat with five members of the cheer team.

> If you think idk then udk what ik ;)

A few friends wrote back question marks, but Jamie Lynn put words to it.

> Know what?

Somebody sent a gif of a toddler scrunching his face in confusion.

Jalisa left the group chat.

Tammy sent a private text.

> Then you should know better

Another private text came through, this one from Amy Jane.

Amy Jane never yelled.

Brit hadn't slept much after that. And then Spencer, telling her she was clueless about what was *really* going on.

"Spill, Brit," Finn said, jarring her back. "You in love with a guy? You worried about a cheer competition?"

"I don't know what you're talking about." He smiled wider, which made her more bugged.

"Brit, you can't lie, so don't go trying. If you don't wanna talk about it, just say so."

Of *course* she wanted to. "I don't wanna talk about it."

Finn nodded an okay, but it was a game they'd played since they were kids, a tug-of-war of who'd give in first. It was always Brit. It infuriated her how he could sip his orange juice like he was scrolling through Instagram, pretending they weren't in a life-or-death situation. After all, she did almost die of shock that night in the car with Walker, so it was basically the same. Suddenly she felt like she might explode if she didn't tell him. She looked out the kitchen window. Grandma was busy in the garden.

"You know when Walker took me home the other night?"

Finn stopped drinking his juice and looked at her. She loved that about her cousin, how he'd give her his full attention no matter the subject.

Once she started, she couldn't get the words out fast enough. "He was like, thanks for covering my"—she lowered her voice and whispered—"ass." She cursed here and there, but she never felt right about it, especially on Sunday. "He implied I'd figured something out. That I was in on *the secret*."

She watched Finn's face change. What had she triggered? Did he know? Was she the only one who didn't know? She considered telling him the other part—what Spencer said after the game—but that'd probably make Finn angry.

"What secret, Finn? Why would they keep me out? I'm cheer *captain*."

He set his jaw. "I don't know."

Finn drummed three fingers against his chin and mouth, the way he did when he was running something through his head. He slapped his hand to the table and jumped up, his chair clattering backward, startling her.

"Finn?" she said, but he was already rushing out the door.

"Grandma!" he called out. "I'm heading out. Taking Brit home."

From the garden, Grandma waved, and Brit was climbing into his car before she knew what was happening. "Finn?" she asked, but he started the car and clicked on his seat belt.

• • •

On the drive, he was quiet. They were traveling the opposite direction of East Pages, thank the Lord. For a minute, she thought Finn was heading to Walker's to figure out what he'd kept from Finn that night. If so, Walker would know she'd snitched, and she for sure wouldn't learn this "secret" Walker thought she already knew.

"Are we heading to Meg's?" Brit asked. "You're not sharing what I said, right? Anyway, she's at church till one. Do we need to go to West Oak *today*? Like right now? You wanna drop me off first? Finn?"

He was in one of his contemplative moods. He'd get this way when he had a plan. She'd eventually hear it, but he needed to work it out first. Fine by her. There wasn't anything on her agenda, and she probably would've ended up on the couch all day with Grandma, watching Game Show Network and replaying her convo with Walker. She busied herself on her phone, thumbing through Tik-Tok. "I'm so happy to be on this Sunday drive with you, Finn. Thought you'd never ask. Love our talks. Riveting."

He chuckled, momentarily brought out of his stupor. "Sorry, Brit. You made me remember something. I gotta do this before I lose my nerve. You can wait in the car. I'll tell you more. I just . . . I need to think."

"I know, I know. Gawd, you been the same since we were kids. Do your Jedi focus. I'll be here in the scroll hole." She went back to TikTok and searched the newest dances.

They parked next to a chain-link fence on the edge of a run-down park, weeds shooting through cracks in the concrete. Beyond the fence, six high school guys were playing pickup basketball. Probably a weekly ritual. Brit spotted Jamal, Finn's old best friend from West Oak. Great.

Finn removed the keys and was on his way before Brit could unlock her door.

"I thought you two broke up," Brit joked, speed walking behind him.

"Told you to wait in the car," Finn said.

"And miss this?" Brit quickened her pace.

Instead of going through the gate, Finn stopped at the fence and shoved his hands into his pockets. Ten minutes of silent thinking had only gotten him this far. Brit rolled her eyes. "Hi, Jamal!" she called.

Jamal glanced over, mid-dribble, looked oddly at Brit, and then saw Finn. The ball bounced out of his hand and was picked up by another guy, who made his way to the basket, followed by everyone except Jamal. His feet were still planted. She waved more aggressively, and that woke him up. Jamal walked over until only the chain-link separated them. He gripped the fence. Finn's hands stayed in his pockets.

They stared at each other, and whether they wanted to hug or punch each other, Brit couldn't tell.

"Well, well, well," was all Jamal said.

"That's a deep subject," Brit said, trying to loosen them up.

They didn't break their gaze from each other.

"Wells are deep," Brit explained. "You said 'well, well, well.' I said 'deep subject.'"

Finn looked thoughtful. "I should've . . ." But he couldn't seem to finish the sentence. "It's been a minute."

"Nah, man. It's all good." But it sounded like something guys say, not what they mean.

"How's the team?" Finn asked.

Jamal shrugged. "Yours?"

It was a small cut, even Brit recognized that. How's *your* team, meaning Finn wasn't part of West Oak anymore. He'd drawn the line. Finn jogged his jaw. "I had to transfer. I had to try."

Jamal knew why, but didn't answer. Like he needed to convince himself first. Behind Jamal, the basketball game continued. "How is she?" he finally said.

"Grandma? Good. Opinionated."

Jamal smirked. "And your mom? She know you moved?"

"She'll find us when she needs money."

Brit marveled at how casually Finn spoke of his mom's addiction, but she knew it didn't faze him. It's not like he'd lost his mom. He never really had her. Grandma had been his guardian since birth.

"What gives, Geringer?" Jamal said, folding his arms. Brit fidgeted, looked around to see who was watching. She was begging Finn with her eyes not to tell Jamal what she'd said about Walker.

"Someone at school is keeping Brit on the outside," Finn started.

"Finn!" Brit shoved him, but he barely budged. The two boys were zoned in on each other.

"Supposedly there's some secret she's not in on," Finn continued, and she hated hearing that out loud. Brit wasn't supposed to be on the outside. Not anymore. Not ever again.

"Great, Finn. Let's just spread the gossip to the next school," she said. "Brit's a loser. Maybe start a state campaign."

"Made me think about last Friday," Finn said. *Did he even hear what she'd said?* "One of our starters didn't play."

"Injury?" Jamal asked.

"Healthy," Finn said. "We ran plays with him at practice."

Jamal nodded, taking it in. "Coaches switch things up?"

"Maybe." Finn lifted a shoulder. "I tried to ask, but this guy Spencer stopped me."

Brit guffawed. "Spencer-who-hates-you Spencer?"

Finn didn't even flinch. It was like she was on mute. Maybe she was being oversensitive. But ever since Walker had told her she'd been kept out of something, she kept seeing middle school in her mind on repeat. The other girls giggling as they brushed by her. Bumping her shoulder like they didn't see her. *Invisible.*

Jamal said, "This Spencer—he has it out for you?"

"Yeah, I thought so," Finn said. "But this moment, it was almost like he was"—Finn dug his hands deeper in his pockets—"looking out for me."

Brit considered her postgame conversation with Spencer. "Impossible. He told me after the game you should keep your head out of other people's"—she searched for a less curse-y word than *asses*—"business. Said you'd get in trouble for asking questions."

"What's that mean?" Jamal asked. "Some gang gonna jump you?"

"Like an EastPay mafia?" Brit said, cackling. "Are you off your bull?"

"What?" Finn's eyes flickered to her.

"It means are you crazy," she said. "It's a saying."

"No, I don't think it is," Finn said.

"Definitely not," Jamal added.

She glared at them. "Well, glad to see you two have kissed and made up."

Jamal craned his neck to look back at the court. "What's Meg think?"

Finn sighed. "I haven't run this by her yet. She's already leery."

"Why." Jamal said it like a statement, not a question.

Brit didn't like his flat tone, and she matched it. "Because we win."

Finn ignored her. "Coaches gave Meg shit the other day when she showed up unannounced. And she's heard rumors. Same ones we've all heard. How EastPay wins because of shady tactics. So it didn't help that the corner I was supposed to play against was out. She noticed."

Jamal said, "Heard their QB was out, too."

"Maybe we're just lucky that way," Brit said, louder this time, thinking of Dante's Ravine. No other teams had a place quite like it. Once she'd dunked in the river, her life had been transformed.

"So you think the coaches—" Jamal went on, ignoring her.

"No way," Finn said. "They'd be risking too much. I think the players missing was just a fluke. But somebody's messing around, and it's making all this other shit look suspicious. Meg had her run-in with the coaches because someone set her up. And some prick threatened her and Kylie at Jaybee's."

Jamal bristled. "What the hell?"

"Yeah. I think this player set that up, too. Maybe that's why he was benched, ya know? Maybe the coaches found out he was doing bad shit. If I can find who's behind it and stop them before they mess up our football program . . ."

"Then you still get to play football." Jamal sounded resigned, as if this wasn't what they'd talked about their whole lives, like it wasn't *both* of their dreams to go pro. Brit had heard them rehash their plans ad nauseam since grade school.

Someone on the blacktop shouted for Jamal. Ignoring them, he kicked the toe of his sneaker at the concrete, which reminded Brit of the way Finn drummed his fingers against his face before making a decision.

In a quiet voice, Jamal said, "There's a guy on your team you should talk to. Good guy. Heard he's trying to transfer to our team."

"Why?" Brit blurted. "I mean, no offense."

"He won't say. Least not to us. But I never heard of anyone trying to get out of EastPay once they play for them. Maybe he can help you dig. Name's Davis."

Finn's hands shot out of his pockets and raked through his hair. Brit didn't realize she'd stopped breathing until her body convulsed in a cough.

"What'd you say?" she asked hoarsely. And then she spoke the name, sounding out each syllable, as if by the last syllable, he'd shake his head and take it back. "Da-mar-i-us." When he didn't take it back, she said the name again, this time rushing through it in a whooshing exhale. "Damarius Davis."

Jamal's eyes pinballed between Brit and Finn. "What's going on?"

"He's the player who was benched," Brit said when Finn couldn't find words.

Jamal whistled low. Brit saw it happen in an instant. Finn stiffened.

"Never mind, man," Finn said. "I'll figure this out."

"Hey," Jamal said, before Finn could back away. "Why'd you come here?"

Finn lifted and dropped a shoulder. Brit rolled her eyes. "Because he missed you," she said, feeling satisfied that she could snitch on him, too. Finn looked past Jamal's shoulder at the guys playing ball, but he didn't disagree.

"Because I don't know what's going on," Finn muttered. "You always see the field. You anticipate. You read the opponents."

"And I don't have as much to lose."

"Stop," Finn said, the guilt clouding his face.

Jamal shook his head. "Don't beat yourself up. You're nothing you haven't always been. I think you're looking for answers you don't have. But are you ready for them? I think you came here hoping that I'd tell you that no matter what, you gotta play. It's football. It's your future, all that."

"I just need to find out who's behind it."

Jamal nodded understandingly. "What happens if you find out it's not just one person?"

"It has to be." Finn's jaw was set.

"If Damarius did something bad, it's on him. But if he didn't . . ." He let that hang, but Finn didn't respond.

Brit understood the implication, and she didn't like it. "Maybe coaches benched him because they heard he was thinking of transferring. Wanted to start prepping for the game without him."

The coaches were an extension of the football program she loved. But so was Walker—Walker, who said she was kept out of some "secret." So were the cheerleaders who acted weird when she texted. She remembered Spencer's words: *For being so smart, I don't know how you can keep being so dumb.* No. She balled her hands into fists. It had to lead back to Damarius. Or somebody who hated EastPay. Dante's Ravine was real. She knew firsthand. The blessings that came from there onto the football team were magical. Jamal would never understand. Or Meg.

One of the guys on the blacktop shouted, "Jones!"

Jamal looked over his shoulder. "I gotta get back to my game. Lemme talk to Damarius. See what I can find. In the meantime, keep your head down. Don't let anyone see you talking to Damarius. I'll do that, okay? And keep an eye on Meg. You sure there were only two opponents out that game?"

Finn nodded. "Positive."

"Let's hope that doesn't become a pattern." Jamal slapped the chain-link fence with an open hand. "Don't be a stranger. We're cool." And he grinned and jogged off.

Chapter 20
FINN

Finn had lain low all week—kept his head down in practice—but on Friday during the forty-five-minute bus ride to Liberty Ranch, he found himself staring at the back of Terrance Walker's head, wondering if Walker was the one messing with Meg. He'd originally thought Damarius Davis was behind the harassment, but after talking to Jamal, he wasn't so sure.

Brit had made Finn swear on his football jersey that he wouldn't tell Walker what she confessed. What "secret" did Walker think Brit was in on? He knew Walker's history—how Walker wanted to make it big just as much as Finn did. Did Walker think Meg was a distraction, too? The coaches had made it clear they already thought that. Would Walker try to sabotage Finn and Meg's relationship just to help himself? It seemed petty, but not when Finn thought about how much Walker hated his dad and wanted to prove him wrong.

• • •

An hour later, Finn was tearing through Liberty Ranch's secondary, and all thoughts of Damarius or Walker had been left behind. The Spartans were on fire. Finn had scored twice in the first quarter, and the defense intercepted on a first and long, returning it for a touchdown. On the sidelines during a defensive play in the second quarter, Damarius Davis approached Finn. "Looks like someone did their homework this week."

Finn didn't look at Damarius. He kept his focus on the play

and said, "Every night. Got through the Chargers' whole last season."

"You get any sleep?"

"Some." The defense dropped the Chargers' halfback at the thirty-yard line, only a two-yard gain. Finn glanced sidelong to make sure no one on the bench was within earshot. He spotted Walker on the far side of six players, stretching out his quad, before he said to Damarius, "So Jamal talked to you?"

"Yeah." They both kept their eyes on the field. Manny Hernandez, a linebacker, made a tackle. Damarius clapped, then said, "You notice anything?"

Finn switched his helmet to his other hand, kept his voice low. "Someone called my girlfriend at school pretending to be me. Another harassed her at a coffee shop."

"I meant on the field tonight."

Finn paused. Of course he'd noticed. He'd watched the footage this week, but part of him wanted to believe it didn't matter who they matched him with. He could've torn through anyone tonight.

Before he could admit anything, Damarius said, "Two of their backs aren't on you."

"Three," Spencer corrected, appearing from seemingly nowhere. He stood behind them, close to Finn's ear. "Three of their best defenders aren't here."

Finn shifted his weight from one foot to the other. He glanced back at Spencer. "So?" But even as he said it, he thought back to Prescott's missing players. Jamal's words echoed in his head: *"Let's hope that doesn't become a pattern."*

Spencer smirked. "So."

Over Spencer's shoulder, Finn searched the crowded stands, the thousands watching. He looked over at the coaches, their heads in the playbooks or eyes on the field, focused.

Impossible.

At halftime, Finn approached Coach Wilkins on the way to the locker room and asked about the absent players. From behind, he heard someone barreling his way. "Geringer!" It was Spencer, and he tugged on the back of his jersey. Finn swatted at his hand.

Wilkins made a sucking noise like he was pulling a piece of food out of his cigarette-stained teeth. "Nice job studying the tape."

"But you don't know?" Finn pressed. "You didn't hear anything?" In his mind, he was pleading with Coach Wilkins to come through. End the rumors.

Other players walked by them, but Coach Wilkins hung back. Waited for the team to pass.

"Hey, Finn," Spencer repeated, reaching for his elbow, but Finn shook him off.

Coach Wilkins moved his lips in a puckered circle. "One on ineligibility. The two others sick."

"Sick?" Finn asked.

"Food poisoning? Flu? Who knows. Didn't you come to me Monday morning saying these were your three biggest threats?" He held out the orange notebook, the one coaches left out for the players to take notes, share their findings from studying tape. "They're all out—you're luckier than a leprechaun with a horseshoe up his ass and you're *complaining*, Geringer?"

"No, sir."

"Don't waste my halftime."

"No, sir."

Wilkins stomped off, and Spencer muttered, "Keep your mouth shut. Maybe I wasn't clear about that. You're better off not questioning things you shouldn't."

Finn turned to Spencer and shoved him. "You don't give a shit about me. So what're you trying to do? What's your angle?"

Spencer licked his lips. "Let's just say I owe your cousin one."

"Britney?"

"She's your cousin so she likes you. I don't. So I'll say this. Watch yourself. They haven't found anything to hold over you yet—and they *will*, eventually—to keep you from snitching." Spencer turned and continued toward the locker room.

Finn jogged to catch up. "Who? Our coaches?"

The rest of the team was disappearing through the tunnel. Spencer kept walking but muttered, "You think our coaches would get caught taking other players out? They keep their hands clean. But you ever notice how much they leave that orange notebook lying around? The one *everybody else* writes in? Notes on players. Tabbed and highlighted. The coaches know something's going on."

"You think Walker's involved?"

Spencer eyed Finn curiously. "What makes you say Walker?"

Finn remembered his promise and held his tongue about Brit. "He wants to go pro as bad as I do."

Spencer rolled his eyes, and it made Finn want to punch him. "Here's all I know," Spencer said. "Someone bigger's pulling strings. Bigger than a football player. Maybe a teacher. Someone's feeding information, and players aren't showing up to play against us. Good players. Walker—he acts like he's tough shit. But no way he's big enough to do what's being done out there."

"Then who?"

"Hell if I know."

Spencer continued toward the locker room, but Finn's feet stayed planted. Was it true? Was someone out there getting information on EastPay's opponents? Was someone finding ways to remove them from the lineup against EastPay?

Impossible.

Coach said tonight's matchups were all different reasons. Ineligibility. Sickness. Did Spencer actually think there was some guy out there injecting players with the flu? Making sure they failed tests? He shook his head, quietly laughing. Spencer had gotten to him. Put the fear in him that other teams did with rumors. He needed to focus on football. It's all he'd come here to do. That feeling swelled in him—his love for his grandma, his fear of his mom's addiction, his desire to go pro that consumed every part of him—and it pushed out all doubts.

He sprinted for the locker rooms, shoving past Spencer without a backward glance.

• • •

They destroyed the Chargers 46–14. It was supposed to be close. The Chargers had the third-best record in the conference. Spencer played in Damarius's position, and although Finn got most of the plays, Spencer received four handoffs, one of which he ran for forty yards. Finn watched as Spencer slowed slightly midrun, until the D-back was pounding after him—his panting breath on Spencer's neck—and he was taken down. He tucked the ball in, Finn noted, but he didn't score, and Finn knew he could've.

As they walked off the field with the final seconds ticking off, Finn caught up to him. He didn't try to hide his anger, his loud breathing, the way he stood too close to Spencer, shoulders brushing even though there wasn't a crowd pressing them together.

He didn't look at Spencer when he said, "I wanna win State."

Spencer snorted derisively. "Don't talk to me."

"I wasn't. Wouldn't waste my time. Just thinking aloud. Thinking that if you played like you could, we might have a better chance. The more we win, the more I get seen. The more recruiters start looking. I don't know what's going on behind the scenes. I only know one thing. I love this sport. And I don't need you ruining my future by playing like garbage."

Or my grandma's future, he wanted to add.

Spencer whipped around to face Finn, blocking him from moving. He spoke so only Finn could hear. "So that's it, huh? You learn the truth, and you ignore it."

Finn gritted his teeth. "Someone harassed my girlfriend. I'm trying to get to the bottom of it, but in the meantime, I gotta play."

Spencer half laughed. "Yeah, okay. Keep telling yourself that." He left Finn and jogged for the bus.

Finn called out, "Don't fuck with my chances!"

Spencer responded with a middle finger high in the air.

Chapter 21
MEGAN

Meg's piano lesson Saturday morning started at ten fifteen, which left just enough time to grab a coffee on the way.

Her mother was waiting at the front door like a bellhop, a thick envelope in her hand. "Do you have all your music?"

Meg never left her music at home, but this was as close to a "good morning" as she'd get.

"Yes."

Mrs. Kaufman slid the envelope into Meg's hands. Meg turned it over. The Harvard insignia was stamped on the outside.

"I sent for it," her mother continued. "Thought you might want to do some research beforehand."

"Research?"

"I've arranged a luncheon for you with a colleague I met at the lymphoma benefit." Her mother beamed as if Meg was being introduced to an A-list celebrity. "Dr. Florence Strohman."

Meg had no desire to attend Harvard. She didn't know where she wanted to go, but *indecision* was a four-letter word in their household, and this was her quickest exit without an argument. She pulled out her phone and added it to her calendar. A text from Kylie appeared.

Yo!

She ignored it. Texting while her mother was speaking would be a whole other argument.

"Saturday, September twenty-third. Café République." Mrs. Kaufman spoke slowly so Meg could type. "The French restaurant just outside West Oak. The edge of Trussels. It's off of—"

"I'll GPS it," Meg answered. And then, "Thanks."

"Your piano lesson is that day."

"I'll reschedule."

"Good." Her mother kneaded her hands together, which meant there was more. Meg waited. Finally, her mother said, "Dr. Strohman isn't from here."

Meg nodded.

"No ties to anything here."

"Okay."

"I simply mean she doesn't know about the setbacks you never overcame." She glanced down at Meg's leg. *Oh.* This was about Meg's ballet career. The investment that had amounted to nothing. "You're still fairly accomplished at piano."

Fairly. Nothing like ballet, of course, is what she really meant.

"And you have quite a résumé in academics and service," she finished.

"I do," Meg agreed.

"Well, then."

"Well, then."

She waited to see if there was more or if that was code for goodbye. After a few awkward beats, Mrs. Kaufman stepped away from the door to let Meg pass.

• • •

Once on the highway, she called Kylie. As usual, Kylie didn't even say hello.

"Remember what you told me about that guy? The one the cheerleader and the football player ran over?"

Meg thought back to the East Pages Parade. How the cop talked with Britney about hitting someone with their car. About the ticket issued to the guy for the curfew violation. "Spencer was driving. But yeah. They hit a guy named Ryan Quaid. Didn't run him *over*. I mean, he was okay."

"Maybe. But people at school are saying they hit him on purpose."

"What people?" Meg asked, but Kylie kept going.

"Like, they were aiming for him, and Ryan just got a lucky break."

"False." Meg shook her head. The rumors were dizzying. How could she figure out what was true when there was so much garbage mixed in? "We're talking about Finn's cousin, Kylie! You've *met* Brit!"

"Well, I heard Ryan Quaid works at John's Hardware."

"So?"

"So maybe this Ryan Quaid knows something. We could pretend we're, like, buying a hammer or whatever. See if he'll talk."

Meg laughed. "No. We're not buying hammers."

"Come on, Meg! After all that at Jaybee's?"

Meg recalled how the guy with slicked-back gray hair had spoken to her. The Bible verse about contamination, aimed at her. *A little yeast works through the whole batch of dough.* "That still makes me mad, too. But Ryan was just in the wrong place at the wrong time."

"What if they're related?"

"They're not." There was an exaggerated groan on the other end. "Listen," Meg said, "I'll come by after my piano lesson. We'll grab lunch."

"Hammers."

"Bye, Kylie."

"Fine."

• • •

Meg didn't mind piano; for an hour she could get lost in the arpeggios and crescendos and forget about questions she had no answers to, problems with no solutions. But today, as she played, it hit her how all the notes were so different, but it was still one song.

That made her wonder.

Ryan Quaid, cited for curfew after getting hit by a car. The forged note to her school. The coaches. The corner absent at the game. The man at Jaybee's. Her ballerina figurine moved on her dresser. They weren't related. They couldn't be. So why did they feel like they were?

She couldn't risk talking to anyone at Finn's school. She'd witnessed their school spirit, the unity behind the painted faces in the stands, the blind devotion men had fought wars with. But there had to be a chink in their armor. Was there anyone on the outside who knew more than they let on?

She left her piano lesson and beelined for the car, where she stared at the packet of Harvard materials. She should head home. Research universities. Focus on homework and her future. Her parents had paved the way for so many doors to open. She started to call Kylie to cancel lunch, then stopped. She sent a text before she could second-guess it.

> Pick you up in ten. Turns out I'm completely out of hammers.

> YES!

John's Hardware was on Main Street, tucked between Lynn's Antiques and Dollar Fluff and Fold. Kylie and Meg walked five aisles before they spotted a guy their age in an orange apron and a name tag that read "Ryan." She noticed the yellow of a leftover bruise under his right eye.

"Hi. Can I talk to you about the incident that happened in East Pages?" Meg said.

It took a moment to register, but when it did, Ryan turned on his heel and walked away.

"Way to be subtle," Kylie grumbled, and then called after him, "Actually, can you direct us to the hammers?"

They caught up to him on another aisle. He was reorganizing a shelf. "Please," Meg said. "I'm not with a newspaper." No response. "I'm not from East Pages." He walked to another aisle, where there was a cart of flowerpots waiting to be shelved. They followed. "I go to West Oak High."

He ignored her and began stacking pots.

"I heard something happened to you," she whispered.

"How'd you find me?" His voice was suspicious.

Meg said, "Come on, you know small towns."

Ryan turned to them, his eyes wary. "Or you're a narc for EastPay."

"She's Megan Kaufman," Kylie said. "Junior class president, West Oak High. Look her up."

He looked from Kylie to Meg as he fumbled in his pocket to pull out his phone. He turned his back on them again and searched on his phone.

Kylie stood on her tiptoes and looked over his shoulder. "West Oak High dot com. Look up student officers. Kaufman. *K-A-U-F—*"

Meg elbowed Kylie to stop.

"Here's the truth," Megan said. "I go to West Oak. I'm dating EastPay's star running back. I heard about what happened to you, and now weird stuff is happening to me, so I thought we should talk."

Ryan turned to them again, slid his phone back into his pocket. "Not surprising. You being followed?"

She was shocked. No one had asked her that before, and this guy acted like it was a given. "No one believes me, but, yeah, I think so. Pretty sure they've been in my house, too. One night, in my *own* town—West Oak—some guy came up to me."

"Us," Kylie interrupted. "He came up to us. I was there."

"What'd he look like?"

"Silver hair," Meg said.

"Slicked back like he just swam," Kylie added.

Meg thought. "Wore glasses."

"And a sweater vest even though it was ninety out."

He offered a half smile. "President of the NRA? Republican Club? Sounds like half the old people in East Pages."

"Exactly!" Kylie said. "He said something about yeast working through a whole batch of dough. Like a Shakespeare quote."

"It's a Bible verse," Meg said just as Ryan said, "Sounds like it's from the Bible."

"Really?" Kylie asked. "Huh."

"That all he said?" Ryan asked. "Most people around here quote the Bible."

"Not like this," Meg said. "It was meant as an insult. Pretty sure he wanted to scare me."

"That town's messed up," he grumbled. He eased himself onto the top of a nearby step ladder, as if the weight of his thoughts made it hard to stand.

"My boyfriend's cousin, Brit," Meg went on, leaning against a nearby post. "She was in the car that hit you. That's how I know."

"What were you doing there?" Kylie pressed, kneeling on the concrete floor to get closer to him. *Now who was being subtle?*

Luckily, he seemed unfazed. "Got a text late at night. One of my friends, Whitney. But from a number I didn't recognize." He paused. Meg eyed Kylie, willing her to stay silent. She did. He continued. "Said her phone had died so she was texting from a friend's phone, and she needed to be picked up. Told me she was at Dante's Ravine."

"Weird."

He nodded at Kylie. "Weirder is that at school the Monday after the incident, I asked her. She says she was home the whole time. Swears she never texted."

"So what happened?" Kylie asked, softer this time.

He lifted a shoulder. "Don't remember much. I was walking through the dark, calling for her. I could hear people, music, so I headed that direction. I came across a pack of them—EastPay High kids—in this clearing by the river. Some preseason party I crashed, I guess. You knew it was them because they were wearing black with these gold helmets like they were all Spartan warriors. I swear those masks all turned as one and looked at me like *what the hell was I doing there*. Whitney texted she could hear me, but I needed to go toward the water tower and near the bend. She said she was close to where the river curves." He pulled his knees to his chest. "I'd heard rumors about that place and Spartans. How they go there—party. Wearing masks and drinking the water so they win. But no one believes it, and you don't think about it—till you're there—how creepy all that shit is." He looked at Meg, dead calm. "You been there, right?"

She shook her head. Finn said he'd gotten an invite for last night, but she hadn't talked to him about it yet. When she'd asked how it was, he'd texted simply that it was "normal."

"Well, you get there," Ryan explained, "and suddenly your heart's pounding like you believe this team has some voodoo power. That place is dark. All thick with branches. Shadows look like dead people. And loud water."

"Things always sound louder in the dark," Kylie said. "One time when we were camping—" But she stopped when she saw Meg shake her head.

"Then I'm standing there," Ryan continued, "calling Whitney's name, and the river's drowning out my voice, swallowing it up, when I see two figures walking out of the shadows all slow-like toward me in their Spartan masks, and I realized they'd followed me from the clearing."

Kylie gasped, and Ryan paused. She covered her mouth, gestured for him to continue.

"Anyway, I took off. Ran back toward what I thought was the highway, and of course I rolled an ankle, but I didn't give a shit. Then one of them tackled me, and I'd bet money he was a football player. Perfect form. Tumbled around with him, we fell into some ditch, I had him, but the other guy jumped in. Thought they were gonna kill me. Then one of them whispered my last name, I think to scare me, but something in me snapped. I got a lucky kick to a guy's face and bit the other one's ankle." He shook his head. "I fucking bit a guy's leg. Not many people can say that."

Kylie, still covering her mouth, stifled a giggle. Meg laughed. Ryan even smiled, though it was brief and rueful. She liked this guy.

"Somehow I got loose. Don't remember much except flying into the road and seeing headlights. Clear jumped in front of a car—that's how amped I was."

Meg remembered Brit's story from here, how Spencer's car had grazed Ryan's shoulder, sent him into the drainage ditch.

"They jumped out of the car—found me. The girl was freaked out. But the guy—his jacket had his football number on it—and after getting jumped, I wasn't about to trust no EastPay football player. Maybe I was paranoid, but I wanted to get the hell outta there. About a mile—"

They were interrupted by a supervisor—someone wearing a green apron instead of the orange employee ones—who passed the aisle, stopping to look at the three on the floor before disappearing. Ryan didn't even glance up.

"About a mile down the road," he repeated, "I called the cops. Cop got there, solo, no partner, and he asks me if I go to EastPay. I say no—Prescott. He looks at his watch, then back at me—had to have seen my bloody nose, my eye swollen shut—then walks away and comes back with his pad of citations. Starts writing me a curfew ticket. Asshole didn't even ask about my face. Finally he asked what I was doing out so late, and I started to tell him these Spartan football players were after me. He asked for proof. I said they were wearing plastic Spartan masks. He laughed. Asked if that was the new uniform. Then he hands me my ticket and says the next time I want to be chased by Spartans, do it on a football field before ten p.m."

"You sure they were football players?" Meg asked.

"It was a textbook tackle. And whoever was whispering my name trying to make me lose my shit—he called me 'Quaid.' Not 'Ryan.' Other teams know you by your last name."

"Wish you got a good look at them."

He grimaced. "Me too."

Kylie said, "Nothing?"

He shook his head, but then thought a moment. "One was Black. Scrappy. Tall but well stacked. Other one was opposite. Shorter and pale, kinda ghostlike. And when I bit him, I saw he had a scar on his knee like the state of Florida."

"You tell the cop that? Their description?"

"Hell no. He'd probably congratulate them on beating the hell outta me. EastPay is messed up."

She had to know if this tied together. "You mentioned text-book tackles. So you play football for Prescott? Varsity?"

"Yeah, why?"

"You ever miss any games?"

He spoke the next words through clenched teeth. "Just one."

"Let me guess, curfew violation?"

He nodded miserably. "Our school has a strict code about that."

She didn't need to ask who his team was playing. She knew.

"I was still gonna go to that game, ya know? It was an away game. I was gonna hang out in the stands. Look for the guys. But how? And hell no. I ain't setting foot in EastPay again. Not until we play them next year. And then it'll be payback."

Meg was already dialing Finn's number before Ryan finished talking.

Chapter 22
FINN

Through the pouring rain outside his car, Finn could barely see the wooden fence that marked the end of Clayton Messler's property, the nearness to the river line. The students' cars would be parked on the far end, away from the highway. But he was about to sneak Meg into an invite-only party, and this was the shortest way to Dante's Ravine.

Meg kissed Finn's shoulder, then rested her cheek there, looking through the blurry windshield into the darkness and rain. "Do we have to leave the car? This is the first time I've had you to myself in three weeks."

Meg was right. Outside of school, all his time was spent watching tape, practicing, and catching up on homework. "I know," he said, playing with a strand of her hair. How long had it been since they'd been alone?

Last night, the Spartans had a bye following a 3–0 start to their season, so he'd asked Meg to dinner. But Meg told him she had plans with their old friends. He knew she wanted him to ask to come along. But part of him was hurt that she didn't straight out invite him. That's the way it'd felt lately. Still talking, sure. But not saying all he wanted. He guessed she was doing the same.

"We good?" he murmured.

"First Friday you guys don't have a game, and of *course*, torrential rain." She half laughed. "You know every EastPay churchgoer is convinced God held off the weather just for them."

"Meg . . ." he started again. He threaded his fingers in hers, but she let them dangle limply.

"Ryan Quaid," Meg said.

A few weeks ago, she'd called Finn to tell him the story. How she and Kylie had cornered Ryan Quaid at work, and it turned out he was a football player—a safety, to be exact—at Prescott High School. Out the week he played EastPay. How the guys who attacked him—one had super-pale skin. Scar on his knee the shape of Florida. Finn told her he'd look into it. But they never talked about it after that. That's what she was really saying. *Why haven't you done anything?*

He had. That Saturday when Meg told him about Ryan Quaid, he'd called Walker. He'd been wary of Walker since his talk with Jamal. Now there was a guy claiming that a football player—two, actually—had jumped him.

Over the phone, Walker denied everything.

Finn also told Walker about the threats on Meg at Jaybee's. Asked him straight up if he was involved.

Walker had answered in typical Walker fashion. "Do I look like a guy who'd be caught dead in a sweater vest?"

Finn mentioned the ballerina figurine rearranged in Meg's room. Walker had laughed. "So I'm breaking and entering to play with dolls?"

"And the players out?" Finn had pressed.

Walker said what he'd expected. "We want the same thing, Finn. Are *you* taking our opponents out?"

Walker was right. It was absurd, and he felt dumb that the rumors had gotten to him. Still, the following Monday, he'd told coaches he studied for a test instead of researched. They'd lectured him on time management and assigned him to field cleanup every day after practice. But it was worth it to prove to himself that his research had nothing to do with absent players. That Friday, there was one starter missing from the Warriors. *See?* Sometimes players just missed games.

He wondered if he told Meg this, it'd change her mind. She seemed dead set on wanting his football program to be corrupt. Still, he should try. The car was awkwardly silent, Meg staring at the rain through the window. "Last game," Finn said. "Mill Creek—only one was out."

"That you know of," Meg said.

He sighed. "I know it doesn't add up. But anyone we bring this to is gonna say Spartans just got a lucky break."

"Nobody has that much luck," Meg mumbled. She turned from the window and looked at him. "That's seven starters not starting against you. We should tell someone."

He felt frustration building, and he fought to speak steadily. "Megs, I agree it looks fishy, but we've got nothing substantial. 'Hi, officer, I heard one guy was out of town, and another had the flu. I think it might be foul play.'"

"Have you talked to the guys who were out?"

Finn let his eyelids close, unable to hide his exasperation. "Have I called my opponents and asked them if their fever's broken? Or how their grades are improving? No."

"Hey, don't be like that." Her voice sounded hurt, and he felt bad. He never talked to Meg like that.

"Sorry." He took a breath. Caressed her wrist with his thumb.

"I think this town's pretty tied to football." He kept his voice gentle. Logical. "If EastPay wins, it's good for everyone. Businesses. Livelihood. So you have individuals—students, adults, whoever— who are intent on keeping things that way." He thought back to the coaches taunting Meg about Finn's *options*. "Makes sense you're a target, Megs." He leaned in for a kiss. "I mean, you know you're everything to me."

She pulled away. "You don't think your football team—"

"No," he cut her off. He handed her his plastic Spartan mask. "But you do. Which is why I'm bringing you to an invite-only party."

He'd been to one party so far, a bunch of students bold from alcohol and disguises of fake Spartan helmets, some with legs dangling over the water's edge. Others, with their helmets off, tucked away in shadowed corners, huddled on towels, passed around beers and joints and stories. Not what adults would want to see, but not a mission control center, either. No secrets to take down the enemy.

"I want you to see it's just kids having a good time." Finn cupped her cheek. "But seriously, don't take the Spartan mask off or the team will have my ass." Megan offered a half smile, but looked down at the gold plastic helmet in her hands. He could tell she was still wary—even after all he'd said—and he could feel his frustration rising again. He swallowed it. "Look, it's a party. Come on. It's fun. It's not football for once."

"It's always football," Meg said. Finn started to pull away, but Meg grabbed his arm. "And I'm fine with that. I just haven't had one moment with you in almost a month. And none of your friends from West Oak have heard from you. You're studying the playbook, staying late for practice, watching tape, waking up before school to run plays. There's no off button with you."

Off button? That stung. He rarely fought with her. But four weeks had put a little distance between them—brought out more of an edge in Meg than he'd seen in the year and a half they'd dated. "Come December, my schedule will free up. We knew it'd be this intense. We talked about it. You know I gotta do this for Grandma. For you."

"I guess I didn't expect you'd go MIA. I told you my dad—"

"Stop." He opened the door. "Your parents aren't buying my way out of or into anything." Now he was annoyed. The mention of her dad could set him off so easily.

"He's not— Fine."

She put the Spartan helmet on. He saw her set jaw, her narrowed eyes on either side of the nose plate. He understood she was the target of overzealous EastPayers. But blaming the football program—

"You're being unfair," he said.

She looked at him incredulously. "Me?"

It was a lousy thing to say, and he knew it. He was on edge.

Meg opened her door and jumped out. She looked back at him through her mask. "We should go. Wouldn't want to be late for *your* party. That would be so unfair of me."

Wow. He'd never heard Meg talk this way. For the first time since they'd started dating, he felt legitimately pissed. How was this his fault? Why was it wrong to work hard—to fight for his grandma's future, not to mention his own future—to be someone different from his mom? *No off button?* She, of anyone, should know the sacrifice it took to be the best at a sport. *She* was the best.

Well, used to be, at least.

"Look," he said. "You didn't want the life you had. And I respected that. But I *want* this."

She whipped her mask off so quickly, it slapped her open car door, and he flinched. "You think *that's* what this is about?" she said, her voice louder than he'd ever heard it. She slammed the door shut and shoved the plastic helmet back over her head, glaring at him through the passenger window. Grabbing his umbrella, he jumped out, landing in a pothole of mud and water. He opened the umbrella, cursing, then started for Meg's side of the car. But instead of waiting for him, she was stomping across the wet earth, sopping wet, making sure to splash behind her as she headed toward Dante's Ravine. *Why'd she have to be so stubborn?*

Once under the opening in the fence, they slogged through the mud and shadows without speaking, the warm rain filling the silence between them. She slowed when she no longer knew the way, allowing him to lead. There was an area near the ravine where the trees grew thicker, formed a canopy along the river. He knew this was where they'd be, tucked away from the rain.

But when they arrived, only a scattering of students were there, all whispering, their masked faces searching like they were going to find the rest of the crowds in the trees. Finn brought down his umbrella and shook it out. The river was louder tonight from the rain, splashing higher up than normal.

Megan searched the darkness with squinted eyes through his helmet. "Did we get the wrong day?"

There was an uneasiness in her voice, and immediately any anger he'd had toward her was gone. Finn shook his head. The team was always here on the first and third Saturday of the month, rain or shine.

"Are we early?"

He looked at his watch: 9:47 p.m. "Barely," he said. The others, still too far to see Meg up close, acknowledged him with a nod or a wave, didn't seem to mind that he wasn't wearing his helmet. Thank God. That's what he was hoping. No one would question whether Finn Geringer had an invitation. And now there were fewer students to wonder. Maybe the downpour had warded off the rest. He wiped the raindrops off his phone screen and quickly pulled up Brit's contact.

> Where r u

His phone buzzed, lighting up the night with Brit's reply.

Did you hear?

"What's going on?" Meg was over his shoulder.

"Nothing," Finn said, but he took her hand. Something *felt* wrong.

He sensed the onlookers' curiosity, the flashlight beams poking at Megan, dancing below her helmet, trying to bring light to this shadow holding Finn's hand. *Didn't Finn have a girlfriend from a rival school? This couldn't be her. So, then, who?*

The excited lights bounced around with the giddiness of gossip, darting to his hand that held the mysterious girl's hand. The silent bobbing flashlights that screamed, *Finn and his girlfriend must've broken up!* And *Who's this new girl? Who is she? Who's he dating now at EastPay?*

Finn felt their curiosity but tuned it out, focusing on texting Brit, but his phone wouldn't respond to his wet fingers. Frustrated, he voice-texted:

> What happened?

Her reply came almost instantly.

> On my way! Get out of dantes.

Something about it all—the shortness of Brit's texts, the emptiness of the party, the night itself with its hollow rain—quickened his heart rate. And then, as if Brit knew he was staring stock-still at her text, his cell lit up again.

> NOW!

He muttered into his phone, "Gimmefive," which thankfully corrected the text.

> Give me five.

Meg, hearing his texts, responded without questioning, a tightened grip and a silent squeeze that said *go*. Finn took off, gripping the closed umbrella and pulling Megan with him, the rushing water and the canopy of trees and bouncing flashlights at his back.

Chapter 23
BRITNEY

Brit winced at the pelting rain. Across the clearing, she saw a faint flashlight beam. She could tell it was Finn and Megan, recognized Meg's graceful gait as they jogged her way. She listened for sirens. Nothing yet. Local law enforcement supposedly always knew about Dante's Ravine—the invite-only parties twice a month—but why break the winning streak by interfering with tradition? Tonight, after the accident, all bets were off. She didn't know if cops would be coming soon, asking questions. Maybe not. Maybe she was the only one who still had questions. But just in case, she didn't need Finn (*or* Megan) getting caught up in something he had nothing to do with. Dante's was the place of rituals and secrets—the last place anyone should be tonight after what had gone down in East Pages.

She galloped hard toward them, twigs slapping her ankles and thighs, reminding herself to breathe through the tears. After closing the distance, she skidded to a stop. She wavered like the wind itself could push her over, and maybe it could. She tried to speak—to tell them the news—but it was like nothing was working. She sputtered something unintelligible, and then her limbs felt tingly, like jelly. She staggered and tipped forward, knees sinking into the wet mud, tears mixing with the rain, her mouth wide like in a horror movie, but sucking in air instead of screaming. *Where had all the oxygen gone?* Finn was at her side. Megan, too, even though she definitely *shouldn't* be here.

They crouched, the wet earth swallowing their knees. They

still hadn't heard the news—she could tell by their confused eyes—but they wrapped themselves around her like a protective covering from the rain, the world, not knowing what had happened, but knowing it was bad, very bad, the bad where no one asked questions, but rather let her catch her breath enough to finally sob.

She'd found out through her cheerleading squad's text thread. She'd Ubered to school, where Tammy was supposed to pick her up for the party. Where a lot of students left their cars so they could either bike there or pile in another car to Dante's. But the student parking lot had been strangely empty tonight. Then Tammy didn't show, so Brit had texted her. Tammy responded through their cheerleading squad's text thread. More texts lit up. Some shocked, others giving more information.

No.

Brit took off running, as if she could leave the reality behind her in the parking lot. The facts repeated and seared into her brain with every beat of her feet as they pounded the two-mile road from the high school to the ravine.

Eli had died.

Eli McGeever was dead.

There had been an accident. A football player named Eli Mc-Geever. Apparently, he was dating a freshman named Leah, who was Spencer's little sister. That's what Meg had gotten through Brit's sobs as they drove her home.

There'd been a fight outside a fast-food joint. Some football player from another school—Cole Martin—recognized a couple of EastPay's football players. Just came in swinging. Got Eli in the temple. Eli lost balance from the blow, fell headfirst and slammed into the concrete. Fractured skull. Bleeding to the brain. Nothing anyone could do.

The rain slapped the windshield. Between the wipers' fast creaking, Brit cried and hiccupped. "Eli was so nice. Only sixteen."

"Was Leah there when it happened?" Meg asked as gently as she could. She had more questions than that, like *Why would this guy Cole Martin want to fight Eli? They were both football players. Did it have to do with football?* But she didn't know what was okay to ask. Brit had just lost a friend.

Brit shook her head. "Thank God, no. She was home with Spencer. Poor Leah," Brit croaked. She turned to Finn. "You know her?"

"Not really," Finn said. He sounded numb. "Spencer drives her to school, and I've seen her with Eli, but that's it."

Brit swallowed between words. "So. Unfair."

Meg took a breath. She had to say it. "Brit, are you sure it was an accident?"

"Are you fucking serious?" Finn snapped. Meg kept her chin high, but the words cut. Tonight he'd proved over and over that he was more worried about protecting his team than her.

But Brit didn't answer. And more than that, she didn't look shocked by Meg's question. Meg could feel Finn's glare. But she also saw the faint shake of Brit's head.

No, Brit wasn't sure it was an accident.

As they pulled into Brit's driveway, Finn tried to focus on Brit. She was broken. But he couldn't shake his anger toward Meg. How could she ask that right now? Maybe he didn't know Eli well, but he saw him every day, and the reality that he had *died* was like this hollow ache in his chest—and then of all things, Meg didn't say, *What can I do to help?* or *Do you need anything?* But instead, a question laced with doubt, hell-bent on proving that every last thing involving EastPay had to be attached to something nefarious.

And now Brit was being seduced by Meg's doubts. Of course she was. She was terrified. She was emotional. It would be easy to assume it wasn't an accident.

The car was quiet. Brit made no move to get out.

"You want us to come in for a little?" he asked.

Brit looked at her hands, kneading one with the other. "At Dante's Ravine," she said, "we do this thing before the first game. We drink the water. Take the lifeblood of the river. It's this ritual for good luck." Brit said this like it was Bible truth. Finn's skin crawled every time superstitions were mentioned, but he kept his mouth shut.

"I've heard about that," said Meg.

"Yeah," Brit said, "but, Finn, remember when Walker drove me home from your house recently? How he thought I knew some secret?"

"What secret?" Meg asked.

"I never told Walker what you said," Finn said defensively, ignoring Meg. "I didn't out you. I swore to you—"

"I know," Brit cut him off. "But I can't shake the feeling that I'm in the dark about something. Until tonight. I remembered the first party of the year." She looked at Finn and Megan through her puffy face, cheeks zigzagged with drippy mascara. "Damarius never drank."

"So?" What did this have to do with Eli?

"Who's Damarius?" Meg piped in.

Brit's eyes widened. "You didn't tell her?"

Shit. He could feel Meg's eyes, but he didn't look her way. "It was irrelevant. What's there to tell? Coaches found out Damarius was thinking of transferring. And if he's not planning on sticking around come State, we needed to figure out our team's rhythm now. *Before* it counts. So, yeah. Coaches were benching him recently. That's called smart coaching."

"Well, at the kickoff party, I saw Damarius," Brit said. "*Not* drink. A few others saw him, too. Recognized him even in his plastic mask. Noticed how he sat back with his beer and watched the rest of us. And now Damarius has been on the bench since—"

"A lot of people are on the bench." Finn kept his words calm, treading carefully. "More on the bench than playing." He couldn't expect his cousin to be rational. She'd just learned that a friend had died, and her mind was going in all sorts of directions. "Think about it, Brit. I never drank from the river."

"That's because you weren't at the first party," Brit said. "We only do the ritual then."

Finn opened his mouth to argue, but she cut him off. "A few weeks ago, I would've thought it was the river. Like it was payback or retaliation or—"

"Stop." Finn had heard enough. "Nothing in the river has the power to—"

"I don't think it's the river," she snapped, but it was full of fear, and she was shaking. "Do you think someone saw he didn't drink, and—"

"*Eli* died tonight!" Finn yelled. "Not Damarius!"

She looked up at him wide-eyed. "That's just it, Finn," she whispered. "It was Damarius. The one Cole came to fight."

Finn grew still.

Fresh tears spilled down Brit's cheeks. "Eli just stepped in."

Chapter 26
MEGAN

Meg sat in the silence of the car, listening to Brit's sniffling. Walker? Eli? Damarius? Names pirouetted, turning in her mind, and she kept hearing Brit's voice: *"You didn't tell her?"*

Finn said it was irrelevant, but there'd never been a filter before with them. She'd told him everything about her encounter at Jaybee's, her run-in with coaches, her worries about Ryan Quaid—even if it was hard. But she also told him about piano practice, and her dentist appointments, and what she had for breakfast. When was relevance their standard for being open and honest?

"What do you mean, he stepped in?" Megan asked.

"I don't know," Brit said. "I kept asking on my cheer thread for more info, but no one's responding. Just that he got in the way. But Eli's that way. Always trying to keep the peace. Doesn't really have any drama with anyone at school."

"Did they say why Cole wanted to fight Damarius?"

"Meg," Finn said tersely.

"Don't you want to know?" Meg shot back.

"Of course I do," he snapped. "But it's not the time. Let her be."

"No one's said," Brit muttered, answering Meg's question. She stared blankly at her dark phone. "I'm sure I'll hear more on Monday." She looked scared.

"You want me to stay over?" Meg asked. Her mom would understand. Maybe.

Brit shook her head, her wet curls floppy. "No, I don't need a sitter. My parents are comin' home later. I think I just wanna be alone for a bit."

"I get that," she said, but part of her was disappointed. Brit looked like she wanted to talk, but no way was Meg going to push the issue in front of Finn.

Finn got out of the car, and Meg followed. They walked Brit to the front door and Finn wrapped his arms around his cousin. "Listen," he said. "I'm not trying to dismiss you. People in this town are shady about football. I'm learning that. But this? A horrible thing happened. And it'd be nice to blame football. But it's no one's fault here except the guy who threw the punch." Meg felt Finn was saying this more for her than Brit, but Brit nodded against his chest, then wiped her tears and went inside.

The rain had stopped, and the dark drive to Megan's was quiet. Finn kept glancing her way. Finally, he asked, "You okay?"

She lifted a shoulder. "As much as expected." She'd say more, but she didn't know where to start. Their argument? Eli's death? Brit's panic? Finn's secrecy?

He pulled up to her house, and instead of getting out, she rubbed her hands on her jeans and leaned over to hug him in the driver's seat. She could feel it in their embrace—how they both wanted to say sorry for earlier. But neither of them did. She wanted to invite him in, talk about things he'd kept from her. They weren't the type to leave things unresolved, but after tonight, she wasn't sure. Maybe they were that type.

She held him. "I'm . . . I'm sorry for pushing Brit, asking her if it was an accident . . ."

He stroked her hair with his fingers. "It was a hard night. Lots of emotions."

"Yeah." She nodded, her head still resting against him. "Why'd she look at you that way? When you hadn't told me something?"

He sighed, the big long sigh, like when someone asked about his mom, how he didn't want to lie but didn't want to share. "I finally talked with Jamal."

What? Meg sat straight up at the mention of Finn's former best friend. "I see him every day at school. He didn't say anything."

"Didn't think he would. I was asking questions. Trying to figure out who was after you." This should make her feel great. Finn *was* looking into things. But instead, she felt hurt. Why had neither Finn nor Jamal mentioned their conversation to her? She'd worked so hard to get them at least to text each other. They'd both been so stubborn, and now they had *talked*?

"Good," she said, swallowing her pride. "Yeah, that's good. So glad. You both okay now?"

He smiled faintly. "We will be."

She wanted to ask "Will *we*?" But that felt selfish tonight with all that had been going on. Accident or not, a football player was dead for a reason she didn't really understand. She kissed him on the cheek. "I better get in before my dad comes out with his Maglite."

She opened the door and started to step out, but he held on to her hand. "Megs?"

"What, Finn?" She didn't mean for it to sound bothered, but it did, because there was so much about tonight that bothered her.

His eyebrows reached for each other, confused at first, then straightened—a resignation. He let go of her hand.

"Nothing. Have a good night." He said it kindly, which made her want to take it back, but also not.

"You too," she said, closing the car door. Only when he'd driven away did she say, "Sorry about Eli."

Chapter 27
BRITNEY

Brit sat against the inside of her front door for over an hour. She couldn't move. It wasn't like she was best friends with Eli. But she saw him every day near her locker. Quiet guy. Arm usually around Leah. Nice. Nice people weren't supposed to die from fist-fights.

On her cheerleading group chat, everyone seemed as clueless as her. After the basic info about Eli, she'd asked follow-up questions, but the few responses were just double-taps with a question mark. Now back at home, she reached out to a couple football players. Nothing. Her text to Walker wasn't showing as delivered. Maybe his phone was off. She sent Jalisa and Dalisa a private text—not on the cheerleading thread.

> Why did Cole want to fight D?

Her phone lit up. Finally! But her shoulders sagged when she read Jalisa's response.

> We were hoping you heard something.

As soon as her parents came home, Brit borrowed their car—promising to be back before midnight—and drove straight to Terrance Walker's house. She needed answers, and she was tired of being on the outside. Walker would know more. He was football captain. Protective of his teammates. If anybody knew something—if there *was* something to all this—it would be Walker.

Maybe she should come clean. Tell him she'd been lying that time he drove her home. That she actually didn't know the "secret"—whatever it was that some students were keeping from her. What did silly high school secrets even matter now that someone was dead? Maybe if she was honest and told him the truth, he'd open up, too. Especially if he knew more about all of this.

The rain had stopped, but the trees still dripped water onto the road, the streetlights bright against the reflection of the wet pavement as Brit looked at the familiar house on Red Sparrow Drive. She remembered where he lived from her freshman year. It was the first house she'd visited with the other girls to hang football jerseys and pictures.

The light to Walker's bedroom was on, and she walked across the grass, avoiding the front door, and tapped on his window. His face appeared, silhouetted behind his lamp. He motioned to the front door and disappeared. On shaky legs, she made it there, and silently, he brought her in, shielding her with his body from the rest of the house and ushering her into his bedroom.

He sat down at his computer and motioned for her to sit on the bed. A knowing look passed between them, the look that said they had lost someone, the same friend, and they didn't need to mention it. "You okay?" he asked.

Tears filled her eyes. "I mean, it's not like we were close, but still." She swallowed. "You see someone in the halls, smiling at you. Or waving. And now. They're *not*." She struggled to form words. "Not there anymore. Monday, he won't be there."

"It's crazy, right?" Walker put his hand to his face, rubbed his eyebrows, swallowed.

Brit fiddled with her lipstick in her pocket. She needed to ask what the secret was that Walker had kept from her, but she didn't know how to begin. "The guy who hit Eli"—she started with what she knew—"name's Cole Martin. Plays for Townsville."

Walker looked out the window. "*Played*. Out for the season. I'm sure manslaughter charges. They wanted Cole out for a game. Not this."

They? Who wanted him out for a game? Like taking him out? On purpose? Brit chewed on a thumbnail.

Walker motioned at his computer. A chat screen was up. Different usernames scrolled up the screen as they chatted live. "Now everybody's freaking out. Wanting to make sure Eli's death was an accident. But it was. You read what they said, right?"

Brit's heart was beating faster. She saw the screen, everyone typing onto the same page. Her mouth went dry, and she swallowed nervously. Her mind went back to ninth grade, when some of the cheer squad showed up at Walker's to hang the signed football jersey of Gronkowski on his wall. Walker's mom had been concerned about its value, that it would attract thieves. To ease her mind, Brit told her it was a fake.

"You know they're real, though, right?" Caitlin had whispered as they walked into Walker's room. *"The autographs on all the swag. Did Marcus try to tell you they were fake? He's always blabbing that to freshmen, trying to see who'll snitch. You watch out for him. He ask for your username?"*

"My what?"

Brit was confused, and Caitlin noticed. *"Never mind. I'm talking all nerves. You keep being our Fearless Flyer."*

"He ask for your username?" It was a meaningless conversation as a freshman, something never revisited, something she'd forgotten until tonight as she sat here in Walker's room on Red Sparrow Drive staring at the conversation on his computer screen. Username.

Oh God. There was a place online where they all talked anonymously? She'd never been told about it. *"I was told they decided not to tell you."* This was what Walker had meant when he drove her home. He'd assumed she knew about the chat room anyway—that she'd figured it out. *"You know more than you let on."* But why hadn't anyone let her in? It made no sense. She was cheer captain. Suddenly she felt it wasn't such a great idea to confess the truth to Walker. He'd be pissed she'd tricked him. Walker was still looking at her, curiously now, because she hadn't answered his question, *"You read what they said, right?"* She fiddled with her lipstick, willed herself to speak. "I, uh—laptop was getting fixed," she lied, but her voice was unsteady. "And parents took my phone last week for"— *Quick, think of something!*—"ditching." *Shoot!* She never ditched class.

He studied her. She knew how her voice squeaked when she lied, but they didn't spend much time together. Maybe he wouldn't notice. She tried to stare without blinking.

He broke their gaze and turned to his computer. "Hold on, let me find it." Her shoulders relaxed as he scrolled up. He'd bought it. "Thursday, Wednesday, hold up, Monday, okay here, Saturday."

Brit read through the chat, reminding herself to breathe.

CH420: Next week. Tigers. Who we looking at?

KLF93: QB not an issue. D-line Steven Farr. O-line Copper Hymen.

OT111: Dude's name is Hymen?

CH420: Stay on topic OT111.

24MBX: Lol, OT111.

PP222: No. Not them. TE Cole Martin. Check his stats. Dangerous.

CH420: Any ideas?

GG135: How about a fight week of? Take Cole out for a game.

STA66: I'll take him. Easy target. Has a gf.

GG135: Just got word, Damarius talking shit again

24MBX: WTF

GG135: Told my friend he's gna stop it all. Think he means us.

STA66: What if Cole hears Damarius is banging his gf.

OT111: He is?

STA66: Who invited this clown? No, idiot. Anyone good at photoshop

GG135: On it

PP222: Yes.

24MBX: Yes. Fuck damarius.

She read to the bottom of the screen. So they were planning to take out Cole for a game and simultaneously send a message to Damarius not to mess with his own team. She was trying to process quickly but appear like she knew this happened all the time. *Steady*, she reminded herself. *Don't blink.* She turned to Walker. "So someone AI-Photoshopped a pic of Cole's girlfriend and Damarius together," she said.

Walker nodded. "Sent a text to Cole from a fake number claiming to be Damarius. Probably saying something crude and asshole-ish. Who knows. But Cole came to fight. Only . . ." He trailed off, shaking his head. "Eli shouldn't have stepped in . . . No one was supposed to die."

She thought back to Finn and Jamal's conversation at the basketball courts. Jamal said Damarius was looking into transferring out of EastPay. "Yeah, well—" She stumbled over her words. "Don't know why Damarius thought he could snitch us all out." She motioned casually to his desktop monitor as if she'd been part of the chat room for years. "There's no proof. It's anonymous." Her voice was shaky. Even she noticed.

"Exactly," he said, but he searched her face again, this time not hiding his suspicion. He noticed, too. *Dangit.*

"I mean," she rattled on. "Everyone thinks I'm clueless, right? But look at me, knowing that The Game's a chat room." She tapped the screen and stopped. She was overdoing it.

"Terrance?" His mother's voice shouted from the other room. "You recognize the car out front?"

Walker's eyes went wide. He put a finger over his lips to urge Brit to stay quiet and crept out of his room, closing the door behind him. Hurriedly, she sat down at his computer and scrolled. She scrolled through the past week's chat—endless scrolling with endless screen names having no relation to anything. One name kept popping up—789TYT—but these names were meant to stay anonymous. Talking about football players. *Other* teams' players.

Oh, God.

All the rumors. She'd seen the crazy coincidences—top players from other schools not present when her team played them. She'd even seen the stats looking odd. She'd calculated them herself freshman year. Originally she thought it was the river. Dante's Ravine. She'd dunked herself in that river and things had never been the same. She became somebody.

But after yesterday and what happened to Eli, she figured it must be a person with a vendetta. It couldn't be so many—

Walker came back, and she spun her chair to him. The jolting movement made Walker stop. *Calm down*, she told herself. He smiled. "Easy. But I feel you. I'm a little jumpy, too. It's strange, yeah? Someone you know dying."

She nodded, but there was something about the way he said it that sounded wrong. Had she given herself away? He sat down on the bed, his knees touching hers. Her knee was bouncing against his. She steadied it, but his eyes flashed. Doubt? He studied her. "What's your username? You and I—we've been in this the longest. They let me in first week sophomore year. Probably same time as you, but you were a freshman. Shoulda recognized you by now."

She didn't know what to say. In a panic, she smiled wide, laid on the same charm she'd offered the policeman at EastPay Day. "No way," she teased, her accent thick. "Anonymous to the end."

He arched an eyebrow. "Just change it. I change my screen name weekly. This week it's GQMAN." He said it slowly. Was he flirting with her? He was.

She rolled her eyes. "Clever." Then she thought about it. "If I can just change it, why's it matter?"

He leaned closer. "'Cause I'll know you trust me. Gimme the

first three." She didn't move away, not wanting to do anything to blow her cover. "I told you mine," he whispered.

She puckered her lips and wiggled her nose like she was debating whether to tell him, but she was desperately trying to remember the screen names she'd scrolled through. She remembered one.

"Seven," she said conspiratorially, clasping her hands together like the start of a cheer. "Eight." She brought her hands together again. "Nine."

He froze. She dropped her hands. *Had she said something wrong?* But then he relaxed. "Oh yeah?" he teased, nuzzling into her ear. "TYT?" he whispered. "789TYT?"

"Mmm-hmm," she murmured, pretending their closeness was no big deal. Part of her loved that Terrance Walker, All-State football player, was interested in her. The other part was wary. She'd always liked the *idea* of Terrance Walker more than she actually liked Terrance Walker.

He pulled back, smiled at her, trailing a finger down her arm. "Listen," he whispered, as if she'd been the one flirting—the one nuzzling. "My mother's here. If she walks in . . ."

She stood. "Totally. As you would say, I feel you."

He grinned. "Let me walk you out."

With the stealth of a spy, he guided her out. "Grabbing my uniform from the car," he yelled over his shoulder to his mother.

In the night that had turned darker, he walked her across the wet lawn, and she noticed something had shifted. He stood stiffly as she climbed into her car, a light drizzle darkening his hoodie. He folded his arms, clearly wanting to say something, because he didn't walk away even when she turned on the ignition. "What's wrong?" she asked, rolling down the window.

"What are you trying to pull over me?"

"I, uh." Brit swallowed. "Nothing. I. Nothing, Walker. I swear."

He looked at her then, really looked. She felt like he could see inside of her. Comprehension dawned on his face, making Brit uneasy.

"Holy shit," he breathed out. "You don't know a damn thing."

"What?" Her palms started to sweat as she gripped the steering wheel.

"789TYT?"

"What about it?"

"That's me, Brit." Brit felt all the air leave her. "Yeah, me."

Of all the hundreds of usernames, she'd picked his.

"And GQMAN?" His voice growled with anger. "The one I said was mine? No such thing."

She knew she couldn't backpedal. "Exactly! Y'think I'd tell you my real screen name? Forget you! Trust no one. Isn't that what they say? Why do you think we're all anonymous? I picked that one at random because I've seen it so much when I'm scrolling through the feed."

"Except that I changed my screen name recently . . . like we all do."

"'Course we do. I was talking about this week, Walker. Duh."

"I thought you weren't online this week."

Dangit. She'd told him she didn't have her phone or laptop.

She felt herself blinking. *Stop!* She reached for her lipstick, but when she pulled the cap off, he stopped her with his hand. Could he feel her hand shaking under his?

"Why are we arguing?" he said. His faced relaxed, and he leaned in. "There's just a lot of unspokens between us."

She nodded. Were there ever.

"Remember your freshman year?" he said softly. She immediately knew what he meant. Not her whole freshman year, but the one night they both got drunk and kissed.

She nodded again, not trusting her voice to stay steady. He leaned in, gauging her response. She met his gaze. They'd always shared this chemistry between them—an unspoken closeness from when they'd both made varsity super young. They'd never revisited their drunken kiss, but now, softly, gently, he kissed her, as if he was picking up where they left off, testing if it would mean anything to her sober. She needed him to trust her. Rather than pulling away, she kissed him back. Maybe she could get out of this if he believed their kiss. Kissing was easier to pull off than talking. More natural. And she needed to be natural. She was Britney Wallace, head cheerleader, who Walker should feel lucky to kiss.

He pulled away from their kiss and grinned.

"Now, *that* was real," he said. "Well, *your* part. Mine wasn't." Confusion flooded her. He was *playing* her? "I mean, that was great, don't get me wrong. But I ain't lookin' for anything long term. However, you, Britney Wallace, can't lie. *That's* why they never told you nothing. You can't do it. Knew it from the first minute you opened your mouth tonight."

She felt her anger rising. She wanted to take down the entire Game for keeping her on the outside.

"You have no idea what I can and can't do," she said. But even as she said it, she felt foolish. He'd just kissed her as a test, and she'd fallen for it.

"You be careful with what you do," he said. "Now that you know more'n you should."

Was that a threat? "You're the only one who knows that."

"Not for long."

A fear, cold and uninvited, penetrated her core. She thought of the hundreds of names. The endless scrolling of gossip and inside information. "You wouldn't."

"I'm in The Game for football, like all of them you spied on tonight," he said, slapping the hood of her car with a palm. "I'm not in it for you."

He turned and left her alone in the dark, alone with the thoughts of the school learning what she'd done tonight, the possessive lovers and relentless protectors of the school, of football, at any cost. There was no magic at Dante's Ravine. There was only a collective hive, a mastermind of many, all protected through their anonymity, all with a singular purpose: winning. She thought back to the key players on other teams she'd noticed missing during her freshman year. How she'd shared her findings with Spencer. He'd been right to worry—to tell people—to bring it to the coaches' attention. She thought of how he'd changed after that. *Had he been threatened?* She fumbled to put the car in reverse and looked into her purse for her lipstick tube. Instead her phone lit up. A text from Walker.

You're probably happy about Eli, aren't you?

He knew she wasn't. It felt calculated. Like he wanted to share her answer with the masses. She typed with furious fingers.

> No! WTH, Walker.

For more than a minute, she willed her phone to light up with another text. He started to write and then stopped multiple times. Finally, a text appeared.

> Been a weird night, sorry. I want to tell you things. Can I trust you?

Again, his text felt forced. He didn't want to tell her things. But he was also her only chance at finding out more. She typed one word.

> Yes.

Somehow, she had to convince him to bring her in. But would he?

He was silent for another five minutes. Brit clicked her fingernails impatiently on her phone. Then her screen lit up.

> Clear our messages. If I can trust you.

She didn't erase anything, but she sent him a thumbs-up emoji.

> Prove it.

Ugh. Seriously. She selected Walker's name. And with one swipe, cleared all texts between them. What difference did it make? She screencapped it and sent it to him.

Done.

He couldn't erase what she knew. And now, she needed to figure out what to do about it. Did Finn know? Was that why he tried to tell her to let it go? No. They were cousins. He'd tell her if he knew anything. Wouldn't he? She thought about how Walker and Finn walked the halls side by side. Walker would be watching. Listening. Maybe it'd be better to keep it to herself for a few days. She needed a plan.

The sky was a dark velvet as Finn drove home from the library Sunday night, his car splashing through the overflowing potholes from two days of rain. He'd tried to get his mind off Eli, focusing on homework or studying plays, but every free moment, thoughts of Eli cropped up again. Somebody from his school had *died*. They weren't close, but still. It was someone on his team. Someone he saw every day. As he drove by EastPay High, a ball sailing through the sky caught his eye. Puddles of rainwater had mixed with gasoline and formed shiny ponds in the empty parking lot, shimmering purple mirages. But the ball was real, soaring above the bleachers. On a Sunday.

Curiosity made him turn his blinker on. The lot was empty, so he drove onto the school campus and across the blacktop, parking at the fence that separated the school from the football field. He scaled the fence, dropping to the inside track. Spencer stood in one end zone, a row of footballs teed up next to him. He couldn't have missed Finn's approach, but he didn't acknowledge him. With water dripping from his clothes and cascading over the top of his trucker hat, Spencer splashed through the flooded grass toward a football and made contact, kicking it high and far. It sailed to the forty-yard marker.

He grunted as he lofted a second one across the field. The moonlight showed it again landing on the opposing side's forty. Spencer shook his head to wick off some of the rain. Beads of water flung away from his cap.

"I didn't know you could kick," Finn said.

Spencer didn't look up. "I can't kick." He lined up for another. Launched it. This one came close to the end zone.

"It's horrible what happened to Eli McGeever." Finn felt like he was shouting over the pelting drops.

Spencer shrugged. "Accident." He pounded a fourth football high across the field.

"Still horrible."

"Accidents happen."

"Did you run here?" Finn couldn't recall seeing Spencer's Blazer in the parking lot. Of course, Spencer didn't reply. No surprise. They weren't exactly big fans of each other. But this wasn't about that. This was about someone they knew dying. Maybe that's why he stayed. Watched Spencer kick two more.

Finally, Spencer strolled over to Finn. His hoodie and sweatpants were like bloated sponges, sagging with the weight. Water dripped from his chin. "You know Eli was my little sister's boyfriend?"

"Leah, right?"

"Yeah. Freshman."

Finn did know that much, and that she probably was taking this hard. "How is she?"

Spencer dipped his head back and opened his mouth to the rain. He laughed loudly. "How is she," he repeated. "How is she."

Spencer took his cap off, dropped it on the ground. Unbuckled his watch and removed his team wristband. Emptied his pockets of his keys, wallet, and phone. Peeled off his drenched hoodie and threw it on top. "Race me."

Finn looked away, toward the locker room through the night air, thick with water. Did Spencer need to blow off steam? Get out his anger that his sister was grieving and he felt helpless? Fine. Finn took off his jacket, wrapped his phone in a pocket to stay dry. Spencer eyed Finn's wristband, irrelevant to his sprinting ability, but Finn dropped it on top of his jacket.

"Go," Spencer said.

They took off. Finn knew he had the fastest forty on the team; however, right now, as much as Finn strained, Spencer stayed with him. As they crossed into the end zone, Spencer finished one stride ahead.

Finn bent over, hands on knees, sucking in mouthfuls of air. "What the fu—"

Spencer stood upright, taking in breaths through gritted teeth. "There's a reason why I made this team as a walk-on freshman. I had speed. But I wasn't a football player. I was never a football player. My sport was soccer." He put his hands on his hips, still steadying his breathing, and walked in circles. "I thought this team was gold. A ticket straight to any college I wanted. I've seen the same look in you."

He felt Spencer's venom at those last words.

"But I learned too late that it's bullshit," he hissed. "And now my sister's suffering because of me."

Whoa. Spencer was feeling guilty? Finn shook his head.

"Spencer, Eli's death was an accident," Finn said. "It's horrible that it involved your sister, but it wasn't to get at you. Is that what you think?"

"You know Dante's Ravine kickoff? First party of the season? I never got an invite."

"So? Neither did I."

Spencer walked up to Finn. There was a break in the rain.

They were so close, he could have whispered, but he spoke, eerily calm. "My little sister did. Yeah. Leah. *Leah* got an invite to go with Brit that night. Fuckin' Spartan mask waiting at our doorstep with *her* name attached. I know it was to spite me. Anyway, she's a freshman. No way in hell I was gonna let her get involved late at night with that. But you can't turn down an invite. Not for that party. You seen how superstitious your cousin is? Most people at our school are like that, only times ten *plus* crazy. So I went in her place. Told her it was fine. Now Leah thinks Eli's death is her fault. That they punished her for not responding to the invite."

"Is that what *you* think?" Finn asked cautiously.

"'Course not. Eli jumped into the fight. It was an accident." He shook his head. "But tell *that* to a paranoid fourteen-year-old."

He grabbed a football and threw a perfect spiral Hail Mary that dropped forty yards downfield.

"Uh." Finn was dumbstruck, looking up as if the ball had left a magical trail of fairy dust. "Can you always do that? Accurately?"

"No." Spencer picked up a ball at his feet. He took a step forward and launched the ball toward the tackling dummy on the sideline thirty yards away. It sailed with little arc, bounced off the center of the pads on the tackling dummy. Square in the chest.

Before Finn could speak, a blue light lit up the sky like a camera flash, followed by a peal of thunder. Fat drops once again splashed down. Both of them were drenched with sweat and rain.

"Lemme drive you home," Finn said, gesturing to the other end zone, to their piles of stuff.

"Fuck you."

"Fuck you back. Let's grab our stuff."

Chapter 29
BRITNEY

Monday morning, Principal Tennessey's somber voice came over the loudspeaker to announce Eli's passing and that counselors would be available. The funeral was private, in a neighborhood church close to Eli's home. Damarius was absent Monday, which Brit expected. She wondered how he was coping, knowing the punch that had killed Eli was meant for him. She doubted Eli's girlfriend would show, either. Poor girl. Brit could barely sleep. She couldn't imagine how Leah must feel.

Following cheerleading practice after school, Brit's teammate Pamela asked if she could stay to help her work on the latest dance for competition. Brit wanted to ask if Pamela was part of the chat room, but she couldn't get Walker's text out of her head. *"Can I trust you?"* If Pamela was in on it, she'd for sure snitch to Walker. Instead, Brit focused on teaching Pamela the dance, which was surprising, given that Pamela was usually quick to learn the counts. She was a stumbly-bumbly mess, but Brit patiently went through the steps.

"Can I record you explaining each count so I can go home and practice?" Pamela asked.

"Like with words?" Brit scrunched her nose. That seemed confusing. "You wanna just film me doing the dance?"

"Sure, but this whole thing with Eli has made my brain all Jell-O," Pamela said. "Can I voice-record you explaining, too?"

"'Course," Brit said. "And I get you. I can't think of much else."

Pamela filmed the dance, and Brit held Pamela's phone close and did her best to explain each count with its individual move. "Might've used all your storage," Brit joked. "That took a million minutes to explain."

"I appreciate it," Pamela said. "It'll give my head something else to focus on."

Maybe I should record one for myself, Brit thought as her mind drifted again to Eli.

On Tuesday, a memorial was set up on one corner of the student lot so students could offer flowers and notes. She could feel the weight of Eli's death in the hallways, muted conversations, pressed down laughter, slowed pace. Still, she couldn't help but wonder if people were ignoring her. Had Walker told The Game what happened between them Saturday night? How she'd tricked him into finding out? *Don't be paranoid. This isn't about you. It's about Eli. People are just sad.*

Friday morning, Amy Jane asked her to meet at Eli's memorial before school. Brit had stopped by every morning, but this morning felt especially sad, in her cheerleading skirt, staring at the photo of Eli set up on the blacktop. Tonight she'd cheer at a game where Eli wouldn't be present. When the first period bell ring, she hardly noticed. Her feet stayed glued to the blacktop, unable to peel her eyes from the photos and candles next to Eli's picture.

"You're late."

Brit jumped. She hadn't heard Amy Jane approach. "So are you," Brit said, smiling ruefully. "It's okay. Feels right to spend a few extra moments here."

Amy Jane adjusted her cheer skirt and crossed her arms.

"Shoulda been Damarius," she said, and Brit felt goose bumps appear. What was Amy talking about? Did she want *Damarius* dead? Or just the one to get hit instead of Eli?

Brit tried to sound casual. "Has Damarius been back? Haven't seen him all week."

"You didn't hear? Transferred. West Oak." Amy Jane grimaced as if West Oak was a bad smell. "Won't be eligible to play." She said it like his decision was absurd.

Britney didn't think he'd care. Not after a friend died breaking up a fight aimed at him. She kept her eyes on one of the many envelopes on the ground. It had Eli's name and football number and a bunch of hearts drawn on it. "Well, I hope he's okay," Brit mumbled.

"Of course he is," Amy Jane snapped. "He's not the one with a shrine set up for him in the parking lot."

Brit's insides jolted at Amy Jane's words, but before she could respond, Amy Jane walked toward the school building without a goodbye.

Brit hurried through the empty hallways, but slowed when she recognized Walker waiting outside her first period class. He was late, too? She'd avoided him all week, but now she approached and stood face-to-face with him in his jersey and a pair of jeans. It was how they all dressed for school on game day. He looked down at her cheer outfit, his mouth lifting in a half smirk. "Doubt you'll need that today." It made her queasy, the easy way he said it, and she pressed her sweaty palms against the pleats of her skirt. Of course she needed her uniform—it was game day. *Relax*, she reminded herself. *You're Britney Wallace.* As an answer, she matched his smirk, and with a flip of her hair, whipped open the classroom door and waltzed in, leaving him in the hallway.

But something had shifted. Maybe it was because she was on high alert already, but she noticed all through first period that students were looking away when she smiled.

When the bell rang, her friends weren't waiting for her at their usual spot during passing period. She could swear she heard murmuring, just barely, like whispers of whispers. She scanned the halls. Students' phone screens were lit. One guy—Randy from her tenth-grade trig class—walked by her and said, "Heartless." *What?* So she wasn't imagining it. So many eyes—not just Randy's— looking at her and then away. Some glared. Others shook their heads, like she was appalling. Her chest tightened, and she started finding it difficult to breathe. She kept her eyes forward and hurried to class.

In second period, she turned on her phone, and a barrage of different texts appeared. A lot of angry and sad faces. A couple gifs of people shaking their heads. Some from unknown numbers. Had someone given her number out? She spotted a text from Hailey, a girl she'd tutored.

I love you, but that was uncool.

Huh? She scanned through them, stopping at a number she didn't recognize.

Why would you send that?

Straight cruel, Brit.

Selfish.

Mrs. Ingham walked by, so Brit was forced to drop her phone into her backpack. She crossed one leg over the other to hold them still. She'd been in on most gossip at school, but not this. People were looking at her funny. *What was going on?* And on top of that, since ninth grade, no one had told her there was a private chat room where students talked anonymously. Those avoiding her must've known she'd been kept on the outside. How many students were part of this? All these years of popularity and friends—was it a facade?

During the middle of class, Brit was handed a hall pass and instructed to go to Principal Tennessey's office. *Why?* As she stood, she saw the number of students suddenly texting, hiding their phones in their laps.

The office was sterile, Principal Tennessey's framed scholarly degrees affixed to the wall in clean columns. On the adjacent wall, a clock hung, its ticking loud and creaky like the springs of her trampoline. She sat opposite him, hands folded in her lap, legs crossed at the ankles. *You've never been in trouble. Relax.* But she couldn't ignore the incessant *tick-tock-tick-tock*, as if a bomb were counting down to detonation.

"I'm at a loss," he began.

"Me too, sir," Brit said.

"Mmm."

Brit shifted, the leather sticky beneath her thighs.

"You were late to first period," he said, and she exhaled audibly.

"Oh. That. Yes. Yes, I was, and I'm so sorry. I was—"

"Sending an audio email to your classmates?" His voice sounded clipped, angry almost.

So *that's* what was sent. "No! I barely use email." *But who recorded her? And when?* "I know I was late. I was standing at Eli's memorial. Paying respects. Anyway, I'm sorry. I can make it up after school." Usually tardiness wasn't a big deal, at least not in the way he was looking at her now.

Principal Tennessey matched his hands, pressing his fingers together to make a teepee. He leaned his forehead against them, thinking. "Britney," he said gravely, "a few students shared the audio file with me." He placed his phone on the desk, unlocked it, and pressed something. Her voice greeted them.

"Hey, all, it's Britney Wallace, head cheerleader."

What? That was *her voice. She recognized it. But she had never recorded that.* Her mouth fell open as she continued to listen to herself—the thick drawl that was unmistakably Britney.

"Thought I'd take this opportunity as your head cheerleader to offer some encouragement. I know y'all are sad about Eli's death, but let's be real, he got in the way. Keep your nose out of other people's asses, that's what I say, unless you want shit on your nose."

Brit gasped. She rarely cussed, and she'd never say something so disgusting. Principal Tennessey looked at the ceiling as if staring at Britney was too painful.

"Anyhoo," Brit's voice drawled, "I mean, sure it's sad, death and all, but Eli dated a loser freshman, Leah, *and* he was buddy-buddy with Damarius, who we all know talked shit about our school every chance he got. You gotta focus on the positives. For one, our cheer team could win the regional dance-off this season! So buck up, buttercups. If you focus on Eli, you could miss out on smelling the roses! Let's keep our glasses half full, not half empty! Here's to the future!"

Principal Tennessey clicked his phone off and slid it back into his pocket. Silence. Britney couldn't move. She pried her mouth open, but no words came out. Finally, she sputtered, "Sir, that wasn't me."

"That was your voice."

"Yes," she stammered. *What was happening?* "It sounds like me, but—"

"The students reported that it was sent when you were missing from first period."

"I was in the parking lot. Amy Jane can verify."

Principal Tennessey licked his lips. "Amy Jane was one of the students who came forward."

Brit was struck mute. *No, not Amy Jane. As snotty as she is, she wouldn't—*

Then like a lead balloon in her abdomen, she remembered how on Monday, Pamela had asked her to stay and record her voice explaining the dance.

"AI, sir," Brit said, and when Tennessey knit his eyebrows together, she clarified. "Artificial intelligence. You just need enough of someone's voice. You enter it in."

"I've heard you're good with technology," he said. *He heard about that? From whom?*

"No, not me, sir. I mean, yes, I'm good with technology, but AI is something anyone can do. Pamela recorded my voice the other day."

"Reciting this speech?" he asked.

"No! Someone else made up that speech—they typed it and then inserted my voice."

It was their words against hers, but she wasn't about to take her exit without a fight. She'd been on the team longer than Pamela. Longer than Amy Jane.

"And yes, I was late, but it wasn't to do nothing inappropriate. There's no proof, just their gossipin'." Her accent grew the way it did when she was nervous, when she needed her sweetness as a weapon.

He buzzed the secretary. "Go ahead."

Walker entered the room, his footsteps padding to the principal's desk. Brit's stomach curled. Walker produced his phone, unlocked the pad, and handed it to Mr. Tennessey. "Sorry about this, Brit," Walker apologized, but it sounded rehearsed.

"Terrance Walker informed me there were some texts exchanged," Principal Tennessey said, sliding her the phone, already open to the texts. There was Walker's appalling question of whether she was happy Eli died. She remembered how, even then, his question felt staged. But her answer of *No!* And *WTH, Walker?* wasn't there. Neither was his second text—something about it being a weird night and asking her if he could trust her. Her answer of *Yes* had not been erased. *Oh, no.* How could she have missed it?

She remembered how long it had taken him to formulate a response. She reread the edited texts, swiping away angry tears.

> You're probably happy about Eli, aren't you?

> Yes.

"Half of my texts are gone!" she cried out. "This isn't what I wrote. I never said I was happy about Eli! I said 'No!'"

"Well, here you say 'Yes,'" Principal Tennessey said, tapping the screen.

"Walker asked if he could trust me!"

"About what?"

"The students—they run this—" And she stopped. Walker held the keys to telling everyone in The Game if she snitched. And if she couldn't figure out a way to shut down the chat room, things could get worse for her if she outed them. She thought of Eli. Damarius. The players from other teams. "Nothing, sir."

"Maybe you could show him the texts on *your* phone," Walker said, his voice gentle, like he was sad for her. Indignation boiled inside her as she remembered the night.

> Clear our messages. If I can trust you.

> 👍

> Prove it.

Principal Tennessey extended a hand, but Brit gripped her phone tighter.

"I can't."

"Miss Walker?"

"I . . . I erased them, sir." She couldn't meet Principal Tennessey's eyes.

"Did you, now." His tone was saturated with doubt. He handed Walker's phone back to him, then weaved his fingers together. "Your speech was extremely callous and insensitive."

"I agree, sir." She nodded. "It's horrible that someone would—"

"Terrance informed me that you're quite the computer expert. That you're an IT girl."

She shook her head. "Cybersecurity." She knew nothing about IT and fixing hardware.

Principal Tennessey nodded. "Also known as hacking. Such as finding the student email distribution list."

It hung in the air until Brit grasped his implication. Her words tripped over each other. "That doesn't prove anything."

"Lying proves a lot. So do multiple testimonies. Pamela. Amy Jane. Mr. Walker's texts."

"Walker and Pam set me up. I didn't do anything!" Her eyes flew wildly to Walker, but he sat like a Boy Scout, hands folded, shoulders back.

Principal Tennessey sighed. "I'm not sure what beef you had with Eli—why a model student such as yourself would send out something so callous to the student body, or be happy about anyone's death."

"I'm not! I didn't—" But he dropped his head, and she stopped. He wasn't going to believe her.

"I was going to suspend you," he started. "Pamela suggested I instead give you a break from extracurriculars. Cheer's not easy, especially given the demands as captain, the difficult personalities. Some of the girls have been concerned. Because this is your first infraction, and because I'm going to believe what Pamela said about your current stress levels, I'm only suspending you two games."

"Sir!" Brit jumped to her feet, searing at the injustice.

"If you'd like, I can extend the suspension to the season and have a meeting with you and Eli's parents."

Angry tears escaped. She had no proof, and the only words that mattered right now were those against hers. No one was listening. Like she wasn't even in the room. Like she could be forgotten again the way she once was. "No, sir. Two games is fine."

"Good. I spoke with your mother. She's requested your sixth period cheerleading elective be spent at home to think about your actions. I've granted you early dismissal."

"Mr. Tennessey, I have to teach the girls our cheers."

He continued. "Your mother will be rearranging her work schedule to pick you up."

"But I—"

"I suggest you think of the ripple effect one transgression can have."

This was backward. She raised her volume, her confidence.

"If I have to miss the game tonight, I will. But I can't miss practices. I'm the one who choreographs their dances. We've been working on a new number." She squared her shoulders. "I'm their captain."

"Do you have a co-captain? What happens if you get injured? Or sick?"

"Well, yes, Tammy, but—"

"I'm sure Tammy would be thrilled to take the reins for two weeks. She'd want the best for you, and I believe this is the best." He smiled at Walker, nodded at Brit. "I thank you both. Mrs. Adams will give you passes to class."

• • •

Brit walked the hallway next to Walker. She was numb. "That was five years ago," she sputtered, recalling her cybersecurity club. A lifetime ago. She'd forgotten the days—blinds closed, curtains drawn, the nights with the blue screen reflecting an eerie glow against her face. "How did you—?"

"Know? I didn't. Tammy commented about that when I informed The Game about how you tried to play me. Pamela confirmed."

So he told the chat room. The school knew.

Before, only an inside crew knew she was kept out. Now everyone knew. Britney Wallace wasn't somebody after all. She felt dizzy. She gulped the air, which stopped Walker, made him look at her. "Why?" she choked out.

He sighed like she was clueless, a naive freshman and not an eleventh-grade cheer captain. "You don't mess with The Game. You were ready to. The moment you found out—I saw your knee shaking. Your eyes all shifty. You were bothered. And what was it you said? *'You have no idea what I can and can't do.'* You'd out every one of us. I had to tell them." He sighed. "But as it turns out, you don't have a lot of enemies. Some even tried to defend you. So a few of us worked on reshaping their views." *The speech.*

Brit jutted her chin out. "They'll know that wasn't me."

He shrugged. "As of this morning, a lot of students bought it. And Principal Tennessey." He turned his back and kept walking. She caught up, her little steps working double to match his long stride.

"Why was I kept out?"

Walker shrugged. "Who knows. But someone with your honesty *and* hacking skills? I wouldn't have let you in either." He kept walking, voice low, head turned toward her so any unsuspecting hall wanderers couldn't eavesdrop. "Second in the National Youth Cybersecurity Championship? That's some serious shit, Britney Wallace."

But it wasn't. The local paper covered it in less than a hundred words without even a photo of her. It was a side of her she'd buried beneath pleated skirts and tumbling mats. She never wanted to relive a day. She'd only been good at it because she had nothing else, no social life, no friends.

"I don't care about that anymore," she said. "Cheerleading's everything."

"No." He stopped at his classroom door. "Football is everything. There are those who know that, who protect that, who work to guard what we've built here. Maybe they didn't think you had what it took."

He started to open the door, but she grasped his arm. "I've protected this school since the first day of ninth grade."

He looked at her curled fingers gripping him. She knew she looked desperate, but she couldn't let go. She was afraid. How many were against her now? He smiled. "Well, let's hope it stays that way. As far as you're concerned, there is no Game. Consider this your warning. And work on your lying. You're shit at it."

He disappeared into the classroom, leaving her alone.

Finn watched Coach Wilkins and Coach Goode huddled in the corner of Townsville's visiting locker room finishing last-minute notes, and they seemed more tense than usual for a Friday night. Wilkins waved at Stockton to give the pregame talk.

The week had been strange. Hallways quiet. Practice subdued. Finn hardly spoke with anyone outside of class. He'd talked with Meg on the phone, but even that took effort. The way they'd left each other the night of Eli's death still hung between them.

Today felt especially off. People were eyeing him weirdly, like they wanted to say something but were afraid. He didn't have the energy to press the issue. Maybe someone had figured out he'd brought Meg to Dante's Ravine. He couldn't care less in light of everything. As he finished suiting up, he could feel the gravity of Eli's absence—the heaviness of locker doors slamming, zippers ripping open, cleats dumping to the concrete, his teammates putting their pads on in silence.

He leaned down to tie his laces, and Reggie Curtis walked by. "Your cousin on drugs?"

Was that a joke? "No, why?"

Reggie's eyebrows lifted as he headed for the bathrooms. "You check your email?"

Of course he hadn't. He never checked his email. Besides, he'd forgotten to charge his phone last night, and it was dead by first period. Before he could ask Reggie more, Coach Stockton and Coach

Hart were gathering the team for a pregame talk. He'd talk to Brit, but he knew she was already on the field. After the game, then. He hadn't seen her in the halls this week, but that happened sometimes. The school was huge. Plus, it had been a hard week for everyone. He'd texted a couple times to check in, but she hadn't responded.

"Take a knee," Coach Hart instructed.

The players knelt, helmets in hand, and bowed their heads. Finn saw Coach Hart, those beady eyes and pinched face, glaring at Spencer, who was the last to take a knee. Finn half listened to the prayer about playing "to the best of our abilities," and God's spirit giving Eli's family "peace in this time," and something about perseverance. Finn overheard Spencer mumble "Bullshit," but it was out of coaches' earshot. Finn believed in God—had no issue with praying—but he was with Spencer on this one. It felt like coaches were using God as a tool to play up the emotion.

The players stood. Coach Stockton's eyes were angry slits. "So they got word that we lost one of our own this week." Coach Hart folded his short fat arms to emphasize Coach Stockton's words. "As sorry as the Townsville Tigers are for our loss, they expect *us* to lose this game because our heads aren't in the right place."

"Would you want that for Eli?" Hart jumped in. He scowled, and the extra skin on his face made folds on his forehead like a shar-pei, poised to attack.

"No, sir," the team mumbled.

"I'm sorry, are you speaking to your coaches?" Stockton hollered. "Would you want that for Eli?"

"No, sir!" the team shouted. Finn mouthed the words but couldn't find his volume. He watched Spencer, who busied himself by tracing a vein on his forearm. In the past, this would've pissed Finn off. Tonight, he could relate.

"No!" Coach yelled. "And would Eli want that for his team?"

"No, sir!"

"And would his family want you to bow out of this game?"

"No, sir!" It felt exploitative. Eli wasn't a prop, and this wasn't a stage.

Walker waved his hands palms up to the team and they followed his direction, jumping up and down, getting psyched. Finn knew this drill, had done it every game, his adrenaline pounding in his ears and through his chest as he shouted and jumped. But not tonight. He stood like a pillar in the midst of a tornado.

Coach Stockton continued his ranting. "You gonna tear into that field and tear into the Tigers like you're fighting for Eli?"

"Yes, sir!" the team responded. Finn felt numb. This wasn't the way he wanted to be inspired.

"He can't hear you!"

"Yes, sir!" Their voices reverberated off the lockers and walls.

Finn stayed quiet while the rest of his team pulsed with emotion.

"Eli on three, one two three!"

"ELI!" As everyone shouted, Finn made eye contact with Spencer, who nodded. For the first time, their look wasn't filled with animosity. They *got* each other.

This wasn't the football they had signed up for.

• • •

It was an easy win after Coach Stockton's speech. The Townsville Tigers' receiver was out on ineligibility, and their six-foot-five tight end had an equipment issue. His cleats were missing, and no one else on the Tigers had a size thirteen. Halfway through the first quarter, he gave up and joined the game in his sneakers, but Finn had to admit the lack of traction was obvious. Again, to Finn this seemed odd, but it wasn't like an EastPay student went around stealing cleats.

The bus ride home was louder than the ride there, amped with victory and sweat. He scanned the bus for Brit, only now noticing his cousin wasn't with the cheerleaders. He couldn't recall if she'd been on the bus there.

"Hey," he shouted to Tammy. "Where's Brit?"

Tammy shrugged. "You didn't hear? Suspended two games."

What? Cheerleading was Brit's whole life. She'd never jeopardize that. She even stretched while she did homework. Before he could say anything, Spencer—two seats up—glared back at Tammy. "Suspended for what? Smiling too much?"

Finn's phone vibrated with a text from Meg.

Are you coming home after?

Jake leaned over the seat and said, "The Eli thing. You know, the email today?"

"I didn't get an email," Finn said, ignoring Meg's text.

"Seriously?" Jake said, pulling out his phone. He showed Finn a bcc email with an audio file attached.

Finn shook his head.

"No shit," Jake said. "No one wanted to bring it up, you being her cousin and all. Kind of embarrassing. But we thought you knew."

He tapped and swiped, then put it to Finn's ear. Finn listened to the voice recording of Brit blowing off Eli's death. *What?* He remembered her sobs, her fear. The voice *sounded* like Brit, but it wasn't Brit. She would never.

"Who made this up?" he snapped.

Jake lifted a shoulder. "Sounds like Brit to me."

"It's bullshit," Spencer said, and a few heads turned, including Finn's. Spencer didn't usually talk to anyone outside of practice. "You know it's bullshit, Jake."

Instead of answering Meg, Finn sent a text to Brit:

> WTF. Jake says this Eli speech was you.

After a long pause—too long for the girl who always had her phone on hand—his phone lit up.

> Yes.

He knew his cousin. When they were children, he unscrewed the saltshakers as a joke one night at dinner, and she yelled at him for disrespecting Grandma *and* Jesus, and then ran outside and flipped on the trampoline until she stopped crying.

This was a setup. No way she made that recording. He'd seen reels of people giving speeches but with celebrity voices coming out of their mouths. A chill shot through him. Not because AI could do this. But because it took work. Someone had to hate Brit enough to premeditate and plan all this.

He tried to catch Spencer's attention, but something told him now wasn't the time. Besides, Spencer had turned his back on them, headphones on and arms crossed.

He had a feeling Brit needed something to make her smile tonight. He texted her, Calling you in 20. Pick up or I'm telling Gma you dont like her banana bread.

On the way to the locker room, he called.

"You alone?" she whispered.

The other players weren't paying attention to him as they walked. "For the most part. Just got back from Townsville. So what's with the Eli speech you *didn't* do?"

He could hear her suck in her breath. "Stop it. If anyone asks, you tell them I told you I did it. And don't get mad if I ignore you at school, okay?"

"Maybe I don't want to talk to you, either," he joked. She didn't laugh. "Look, I'm sorry you got set up with that Eli prank. I know you, Brit. You wouldn't—"

But she clicked the phone off. Then a text came through. All caps. Whispering on the phone and shouting through text.

I DID IT. TELL EVERYONE THAT I SAID I DID IT.

Now Finn was really confused. Brit didn't like to lie. She sounded scared.

Back in the Spartan locker room, Finn showered and waited until most of the team had emptied out, heading to Fourth and Goal to celebrate.

He approached Walker, but before he could say anything,

Walker slapped him on the shoulder. "Solid win, bro. Fourth and Goal. You comin'?"

He wasn't about to be derailed.

"Just spoke with Brit." He had Walker's attention. "She insists she gave that speech about Eli."

"Guess she did then," Walker said.

Why was everyone believing it so easily? People knew Brit. They had to know this didn't match her character. Walker *had* to know.

"You actually believe that?" Finn kept his voice low but steady.

Walker looked over at Eli's empty locker and sighed. "Look, emotions are high," he started, but then Jake emerged from the bathroom, and Walker's demeanor immediately changed. He smiled broadly, put a hand on Finn's shoulder. "Let's go hit up Fourth and Goal. Everyone's goin'."

"Don't feel much like partying," Finn muttered.

"Well, good, then," Jake jumped in, "'cause coaches'll be there." He laughed. "More your speed. Pitchers of root beer—first round's on them."

"No alcohol, no fun," Walker added playfully, and lifted a chin at Finn. "That's your motto, right?"

Finn smiled tightly. "Yeah, yeah," he said, trying to let it roll off.

Everything about Walker's nonchalant reaction to Brit's speech was suspect. He may not be behind the speech. But Finn would bet his jersey Walker knew something. And now, Walker was walking out of the locker room with Jake as if he'd dodged the whole interrogation with ease. Finn threw his duffel over his shoulder. He wasn't letting Walker off that easily.

Chapter 31
FINN

Most of the team was already there when Finn parked at Fourth and Goal, the blue neon sign buzzing and flickering like a mosquito trap.

The team cheered when he walked inside, clapping as if Finn attending a social event was akin to him making an unbelievable catch.

"Well, well, well," Walker greeted him, grinning. "Look who decided to grace us." Finn didn't understand how Walker could juggle doing well in school with leading a football team and showing up to every party. Every free moment, Finn had his face in a textbook, and he still felt so behind.

Finn looked across the restaurant, the air grainy like an old movie. A line of black-and-white signed eight-by-tens of professional athletes ran from ceiling to floor near the pool tables. "Wanna shoot some pool?" Finn asked.

"You know it," Walker said, and clapped him on the back. They stopped at a few tables and said hello to some teammates, eating a couple slices of pizza and recapping the game before heading over to the wall and picking their cue sticks.

Finn leaned over the pool table and racked the balls. He made sure no one was nearby before he spoke.

"Who did it?" Finn asked, keeping his voice low but steady. "Who made up that speech?"

Walker chalked his cue stick. "I'll break." He shook his head sadly, focusing on the cue ball. "Look, like I said, emotions are high right now. People cope in weird ways." He struck the cue ball, and it hit hard, exploding the fifteen balls and pocketing two of them. "Stripes," Walker said. He shot again and banked a few but with no success.

Finn aimed for the four, sank it with a gentle tap, and then smirked. "You can bullshit a lot of people, Walker. But not me. Not about my cousin."

Walker paused. Clenched his jaw tight, his cue stick tighter. "She tell you I was involved?"

Brit had said a while back that Walker was in on some secret. Did Brit find out, and now Walker was getting back at her? It seemed cruel, even for Walker. Either way, Finn wasn't about to narc on his cousin. "No. Brit's a steel trap right now. Won't say a word about who's messing with her." He tried for the six in the middle pocket and missed. "I just find it odd that you'd believe such a load of crap. Took you for smarter."

He could tell his comment pierced Walker's cool exterior. Walker breathed through flared nostrils, his cue stick jutting to and fro like a metronome.

"Hey, boys." A girl sauntered up, smiling in her relaxed, confident way. He recognized her striking features, the green eyes, red hair, but it took a moment.

Tammy Shaw.

She'd replaced her cheerleading uniform with a tank top and jeans. She pulled up a barstool and straddled it. Her presence had a way of helping Walker regain his composure.

"Hey, beautiful," Walker said easily. He leaned toward the

table, aimed, shot, and sank two with one hit. "Must be my good luck charm."

Tammy laughed softly. "That's what they all say." She held a plastic-wrapped plate of cookies up to Finn. "Do you have somewhere you can put these?"

"Ooh, gotta piss," Walker said, winking at both of them as if he was doing them a favor, and then slinking away.

Really? He watched Walker disappearing toward the bathrooms. He eyed the cookies, then Tammy. He could see a note and her phone number peeking out from behind the cookies, scrawled in black Sharpie on the paper plate. He didn't have time for games. "What are you doing, Tamara?"

"Tamara?" Tammy giggled as if calling her by her formal name was funny. She set the plate on the pool table. Stroked the green felt with a manicured finger and then picked up the cue ball. "The cheerleaders all get assigned a player from the starting lineup. I got you! Which means, I'm your girl. We all make something for our guys, only I was running late before the game." She leaned down to set the cue ball back on the table, a totally unnecessary movement that only made her low-cut tank dip lower. "White chocolate chip. They're reaaaaally good." Tammy knew he had a girlfriend. Megan Kaufman, the girl who still made him trip over his words. *Did Tammy actually think this would work?*

"First, you're not my girl," he said, taking the cookies and setting them on the high-top table behind them. "Second, you could've brought them Monday."

"Now, that wouldn't have been any fun," she said, standing tall again, now eye level. Her smile never faltered. "Then we couldn't hang out."

"We're not." He looked at the pool table, then back at her.

She reached for Walker's pool stick, twirled it with her fingers. "I could probably give you a better run for your money than Walker." Again she grinned, all admiration and big eyes. *The way Meg used to look at me*, he thought, and then shook the thought away. "Talked to your cousin lately?" she asked airily. Too airily. She was fishing.

"She's not answering her phone," he said. "For being Brit's co-captain, you don't sound especially concerned. Suspended two games?"

She grimaced, like she was embarrassed for Brit. "You heard her speech about Eli. Everyone did."

"True. But who benefited from that recording? Not Brit. However, coincidentally, her co-captain was suddenly made the only captain."

Tammy crossed her arms. "It was Brit's voice!" she said defensively.

"Impossible." He leaned against the pool table, half sitting on the edge. "I know her. I saw her the night she found out about Eli."

Tammy narrowed her eyes. "What did she tell you?"

"Nothing you don't already know."

They stared at each other, unblinking. She must've realized by his blank face that he wasn't lying, because she relaxed. She walked close, pinning him between her and the pool table with her hips. "You wanna get outta here?" She bit her lower lip. Her hair swept forward, grazing her cheek and covering one eye, so that the other peered longingly at him.

Wow. She was relentless. She was confident, but this felt like too much, even for her. He looked at his body pinned against hers and eased himself away from her. "I'm in the middle of a game."

She reached around him and started rolling the balls on the table toward the pockets. The balls from his and Walker's game. "Oops," she said, but more playful than hurt. She probably didn't get blown off by guys often. "I have a favor." She hooked a finger around one of the loops of his jeans. He looked away, fixed his eyes on the black-and-white photos on the wall.

"I have a girlfriend."

"Maybe I don't mean anything like that." But her voice was sultry, as if she did.

He placed one hand on hers and removed her finger from the loop of his jeans. He turned and began pulling balls out of the pockets to start racking again. "Look. You brought me cookies. Wrecked our game. Now you're asking for favors. Climbing me like Everest. I'm not sure how I'm supposed to respond, but maybe you could tell me."

She smiled again, unruffled by his tone. Leaned against his shoulder. Traced a finger down his arm. "Figured you and your girlfriend broke up."

"Why would you figure that?"

"Heard you brought someone to Dante's."

She let that hang, as if he would respond. He didn't. He knew what she meant. *Couldn't have been your girlfriend. No one would dare.*

"I also heard you've been asking questions."

He narrowed his eyes, and she held up her hands in surrender.

"Walker told me," she said. "Anyway, I get it," and the way she said it made him pause. But then Walker appeared.

"Hey, lovebirds. Looks like you took over my game." He put an arm around Tammy. "Did you win?"

"Always," she said, giggling.

Walker set three cups and a pitcher of root beer on the hightop. He poured them all a glass and lifted his in a toast. "To destroying the Townsville Tigers."

Tammy lifted her glass. "And to all the rest we've yet to destroy."

So that was it, huh? Finn thought. No more talk of his cousin.

He lifted his own glass. "And to the person messing with Brit, who I will *personally* destroy."

He noticed Tammy's and Walker's eyes flicker for a split second. "Come on, man," Walker said. "Let it go. Sometimes people just do stupid shit. Even the people we love."

"Stupid, yes. Heartless, no." He looked from Walker to Tammy. "I know that girl. Closest thing to a sister I got. It's obvious when Brit lies. And she's lying right now. Covering for somebody."

Walker scoffed. "Who?"

Finn paused. "I dunno," he said. "You've got nothing to gain by taking a cheerleader out. Someone's messing with her. And I'm *gonna* figure out who." He took a sip of his root beer, then stopped, his lower lip still on the rim. "And beat the shit out of him."

He could've sworn Walker blinked.

Especially now that he was smiling easily at Finn. *Too easily*, Finn thought.

"Whatever, man. You do you. Just don't get yourself benched. You've got scouts with their eyes on you. And we've got a title to win. You're coming to Dante's tomorrow night, right? We're having a do-over party, since last week's obviously never happened."

"Nah," Finn said. "Told Meg we'd meet up with some of my West Oak friends."

This time Finn didn't mistake Walker's blink. It was slow, deliberate. "I thought you didn't hang out with them anymore."

"I don't. Which is why I need to see them. They were my friends, you know?"

"Yeah, yeah, of course. But you don't want to wait till after the season?"

"Why?"

"Why," he repeated, tilting his head like Finn was missing the obvious. Walker looked at Tammy, who was standing close by, sipping her soda, watching them wide-eyed, drinking it in.

"What're you worried about?" Finn asked, sensing Walker's distrust. He grinned. "I'm just gonna hand over the playbook. Should only take a few minutes." He laughed. "Oh, come on, Walker. You think we talk football?"

Walker didn't crack a smile. "Don't forget why you're here," he said. He shared a knowing look with Finn—a look that carried weight. Spoke of Walker's dad. Finn's grandma. He approached Finn's corner of the table, held up a fist bump, but when Finn didn't respond, he brought it down and added, "All for the game."

Was it?

In the past, this had been their thing. Finn had always repeated, *"All for the game."* But tonight, he didn't.

Walker lifted an eyebrow, handing his pool stick to Tammy. "Go ahead and finish for me. You'll beat him." As he walked away, he said, "His heart ain't in it."

So this was how it was gonna be.

Finn was so over this. He set his pool stick back on the wall and walked out of the restaurant. Halfway to his car, he heard Tammy's voice shouting, "Hey!" He ignored her and kept walking. He heard her feet running behind him on the gravel, but he didn't turn around. She caught up to him just as he reached his door. She set her plate of cookies on his hood, then grabbed his shoulder and spun him around. He didn't resist, but he did say, "What the hell, Tammy." Her face was close and her breath was hot, panting from the run.

"You want answers?"

Her tone was straightforward. Her eyes held an intensity and not an ounce of flirting. He nodded once. Her eyes darted around her.

"There are eyes and ears everywhere," she hissed, "so quit flattering yourself and pull me close."

He froze, only long enough to understand what she meant and make a definitive decision. He leaned his back against the side of the car, pulling her into him the way he would Meg. He wrapped his arms around her lower back, linking his fingers loosely. To any onlookers, their postures might've hinted at something suggestive, but both sets of eyes were steel, all business.

"Stop behaving like such a fool," she whispered. "You aren't gonna get answers by threatening every person you come across."

"What do you suggest? Sit by and do nothing?"

She brought a hand up to his cheek and stroked it softly, but her voice was venom. "No! But the way you're acting is gonna get everyone talking *about* you rather than *to* you."

He threw his head back, but she reached a hand behind his neck and pulled him forward to face her. Their noses were almost touching.

"You gotta play for their team," she said.

He glared. "Is that what you do?"

She leaned close. He could feel her hair brushing softly against his neck. "Play or get played, Finn," she whispered in his ear. "Your choice."

He pulled back so he could look her in the eyes. "How?"

She rested her hands on his shoulders. "Go to Dante's Ravine tomorrow night. Be part of the team." She narrowed her eyes. "*Without* your girlfriend."

"Can't. I promised my friends."

"So, *un*promise them. You want answers?" He knew she could feel him tense. Pretty or not, she wasn't Meg. He didn't appreciate how this made him look. Her hands dropped from his shoulders, down his chest, and then onto his sides. Her tone softened. "East-Pay is about loyalty. You'll get somebody at this school to talk if they trust you."

"Why not you?"

Her eyes looked around at various couples in the parking lot, others on the smoking patio. "I've got too much to lose. But not everyone's as careful. Especially at Dante's. Alcohol and darkness. Trust me. But you keep letting Meg know everything you're in on, people will hear about it, and they won't tell you shit. Also, if you no-show tomorrow night, you think Walker won't tell everyone who you chose over us? Come. To. Dante's."

She made sense, but he hated the idea. "What do I tell Meg? How am I magically gone for the night?"

She licked her lips, thinking. Then her eyes locked with his. An idea. "There's a Longhorns home game tomorrow," she said. "UT is a two-, two-and-a-half-hour drive each way. Tell her you're going with some of the guys. Tell her an assistant wants to meet with you. Tell her whatever."

He wiggled out from under her and crossed his arms. "I don't lie to her."

She crossed her arms, too. "Then I guess you don't really want answers." She backed away, still facing him. "Play or get played. Your choice." She motioned to the plate of cookies on his hood. "You have my number."

• • •

Meg had gone to West Oak's game tonight, so she was likely home by now. He called her on speaker as he drove.

"Hey," she answered. "Where were you?" Her tone was clipped.

"Went to Fourth and Goal with the team."

There was a loud sigh on the other end.

"We won, so . . ." Why was he having to defend himself? "The whole team went."

"Well, I was at *your* house."

"What?"

"I drove straight there after West Oak's game. I texted. You never texted back. So I finally went home."

He thought back to the bus ride. "Aw, Meg. Some stuff happened. It's what I wanted to talk about."

She replied, "I'll just see you tomorrow."

Yeah, she was annoyed. But he kept thinking about what Tammy said, and about getting answers. It pained him to respond, though it was only one word. "Can't."

He pulled into his driveway and parked. Turned his car off. The line was silent, and for a moment, he wondered if the call had dropped. He added, "Something came up. Sunday? You think our friends'll be okay with that?"

"Blowing them off again? You said—"

"I know." He rubbed the back of his neck. Someone had gotten a good tackle on him tonight. He could feel the knot. "Someone's messing with Brit."

Her voice changed to concern. "How?"

"Faked her voice somehow. Got her suspended two games."

"What?" Meg's voice sounded alarmed. "Faked her voice how?"

"I dunno. Pretty sure AI. I think Walker knows something." He didn't need to lie. Meg would understand if he wanted to go to Dante's alone. But so far, he'd figured out nothing substantial. Maybe Tammy was right. Maybe someone out there needed more convincing that he was on their side. Maybe the less Meg was involved, the more he'd find out. He took a breath. "So I'm heading to the UT game tomorrow. With Walker. I figured it would give us some hours in the car, on campus. Maybe he'll talk."

"You want me to come? I'm done in the afternoon. I could—"

"No," he said too quickly.

Meg was quiet. He felt that distance between them, the kind that hadn't left since their big fight at Dante's Ravine.

"There's this assistant who wants to meet with me. We're heading up early. Who knows—scholarships."

"Okay," she said, but it sounded strained.

"Meg?" He waited for her to respond, but she didn't. "You were right. About a lot of things. This school . . ." He thought of Spencer's words about the football helmet invitation for Leah, not him. Eli was dead, but the fight was meant for Damarius—who just happened to be suspicious about the missing players. And now Brit's fake voice recording and Walker's shady behavior tonight. "Something's not right. But none of it connects. It doesn't make sense. And"—he massaged the knot on his neck—"honestly? I'm afraid. My future. I can't lose it."

"I know." She paused, and then, "But Finn, maybe you should—"

"What?" He'd cut her off. He hadn't meant to. Why did he feel on edge?

The line was silent. Finally she said, "Nothing. I miss you."

He sighed, tipped his head back on the headrest. "Same."

"We'll talk Sunday," she said, her voice resigned.

"Sunday," he repeated. "I'm all yours."

They hung up, but she didn't text her usual heart.

Cookies in hand and backpack on shoulder, he didn't bother turning on any lights at home, just tiptoed through the house and flopped onto his mattress. Something crinkled underneath his hand. From under his pillow, he pulled out a folded piece of pink paper, cut in the shape of a heart, the size of his fist. He opened it, and there was Megan's cursive writing visible in the moonlight and spelling one word: *Saturday.*

After he didn't text back on the bus, and after waiting two hours, she still left him a heart-shaped note, a note that didn't say *asshole* or *jerk* but instead, *Saturday.* She'd been looking forward to the very thing he'd just called and canceled. He pushed out the image of Tammy's hair brushing against his cheek. He knew it was just because he missed Meg. He closed his hand over the paper heart, made a fist, clenched it to remember he had the best damn girlfriend on the planet and he better not screw it up.

Chapter 32
MEGAN

Standing in front of her vanity mirror, Meg turned down the volume on her Bluetooth speaker and heard a crack of thunder. The rain was back. She'd love to pretend her music was too loud to hear her mom calling from downstairs, but she'd only get a lecture about volume and premature damage to her hearing. Before, she'd always smile and say okay, but lately, she didn't have the energy to go even one round with her mother.

"Be right down!"

It was the Saturday of the luncheon her mother had arranged with a Harvard colleague. Megan gave herself a final once-over in the mirror. She'd have to pass her mom's inspection, and Mom needed Meg in pristine condition.

"Like you." Meg's fingertips caressed the ballerina figurine on her dresser. "Don't move again," she whispered to the figurine, then closed the door behind her. A text from Finn vibrated her phone.

> Morning. How'd you sleep?

He knew Saturdays were her busy days, and she loved how he always texted to check in. Still, she recalled last night and how she'd waited and waited, but he hadn't bothered to check his phone before heading out. She slid her cell into her back pocket. He could wait, too.

Her mother was standing at the foot of the stairs as she descended.

"Yes on the outfit, no on the shoes."

"Good morning," Meg said through an exhale. *Here we go again.*

"Honey, I'm not pointing out anything new. There is no right outfit with—"

"—with the wrong shoes," Meg finished. "Got it."

"Well, good, then."

They ate breakfast across from each other, one slice of toast each that crunched in their silence. Meg busied herself with pushing the scrambled eggs around her plate. She could hear it raining again. "Where's Dad?"

"Work. Early meeting today." She watched her mother stare at her food, and in these brief moments, Meg felt bad for her. Her mom had grown up in a big family with small paychecks. Single parent. Constant noise, chaos, and financial stress. And then she fell in love with a lawyer while catering a New Year's party. Years later, she had no noise or chaos. Even when her husband was home, Meg knew her mom saw more of his bent neck than his eyes, his body hunched over the daily stocks on his iPad or an open suitcase for a business trip. Meg saw how hard she tried to play the part of happy housewife.

Her mother scooted out her chair, her fork clattering on the plate, and she disappeared while Meg turned her banana end over end, not peeling it. A moment later, she returned with a Kate Spade necklace, a dainty diamond in the center.

"Mom, I really don't need—"

"Your blouse is off the shoulders. If you're going to show your collarbone, you need this. Otherwise, you look indecent and suggestive."

Meg started to protest, but then clamped her mouth closed. She'd never spoken back to her mom, but recently it was getting harder. "You're right," she said, and her mom smiled and handed her an umbrella.

Halfway to the car, her mother called from the doorway, "I heard about that football player. This morning."

Meg stopped and turned. *What had she heard?*

"Eli McGeever," her mother added.

Meg nodded.

"The same team as your boyfriend."

Meg tried to keep her voice calm. "Finn. You mean Finn." As frustrated as she was with him, she was instantly protective.

"Maybe you need space until things settle. Become less dangerous."

"Eli was punched, Mom. By a guy from another school. Not EastPay. He didn't start the fight."

"Still. If things are heated around that school, I think it's best you're not involved."

Meg breathed deeply. "I'll think about it." She definitely wouldn't, but her mother didn't need to know that.

Meg had forty-five minutes before she had to meet Dr. Florence Strohman at Café République. It was past East Pages in the neighboring suburb Trussels, which meant she'd have to stop and get gas, but she'd given herself plenty of time.

•   •   •

Through the windshield wipers wicking away the fat drops, she could see a hanging banner of a Spartan helmet draped down the side of a building. She definitely wasn't in West Oak anymore. As she slowed at a stoplight, the sign above the banner came into focus: "East Pages Community Church."

Seriously? The church was a Spartan fan?

A sudden familiarity flashed into her head. She'd seen the name of this church somewhere.

The building was so white that it stood out against the pale gray of the stormy sky. It looked like a one-story house with a single spire above and a small cross on top. The cross seemed tiny to Meg, like an afterthought, like something added only after they got the building right. But the banner. The banner was huge.

Meg glanced at the car clock and then pulled into the parking lot, which was empty except for a single car. A woman emerged from the car, her white hair teased out and paralyzed with hair spray, shielding herself with an umbrella while reaching into her car for a flower basket.

Meg jumped out and splashed across the lot in her boots, the rain plastering her hair to her cheeks and soaking her tight jeans. "Can I help?"

"Why, thank you!" came a sweet southern drawl, but when the woman looked up, she froze. "Megan Kaufman."

Meg's heart thumped. "Yes?"

Then she relaxed and smiled broadly. "Oh! Sorry, how rude, just a bit of a shocker seeing you this side of town. I know your mama from Women's League. And book club, of course. I'm Ms. Tristan."

Meg exhaled in relief. "Sorry. You looked at me so strangely, I thought maybe—you know East Pages—and . . ."

"Girl, do I ever!" Ms. Tristan laughed. "Help me with this, will you, doll?"

Meg lifted the huge flower basket, probably for the altar at the Sunday service, from the car. Ms. Tristan held the umbrella over both of their heads but mostly her own, so that the edges of the umbrella dripped water onto Meg's neck and shoulders as they walked to the church entrance.

"So what brings you *here*"—at *here*, Ms. Tristan motioned to the church doors—"'specially on Saturday? In this weather?"

"I had a few minutes. Just passing through on my way to Trussels."

"So you stopped here?"

"Thought I recognized something about the church," Meg said. "Couldn't remember what." Again, the name was so familiar. *What was it?*

"That so, now?" Ms. Tristan paused, wiggled her nose as if it itched. She collapsed her umbrella, shook it out. "Well, then, you'll have to come back on the Lord's day. No one but me around setting up for services tomorrow."

"Mind if I look around?" Meg asked as Ms. Tristan unlocked the doors. She didn't really have time, but something gnawed at her gut. Harvard could wait.

"Ooh! Afraid I can't, darling. Pastor Mike wouldn't approve." With her foot wedged between the double doors, she took the flower basket from Meg's hands. "Policy. Church is closed. It's a liability thing. I'm sure you understand."

Meg wasn't sure she did, but she nodded.

"You get on with your day and be blessed."

"Sure," Meg said.

"Bye-bye now." She closed the glass doors, her face on the inside looking out, and, through the glass, blew Meg a saccharine kiss that matched her thick makeup and poufed-out hair.

Ugh, Texas, Meg thought. Not all Texans were that way, but those who were made it hard to break the stereotype.

She followed the church's perimeter, stopping in back—the parking lot now blocked by the building—and walked onto the wet grass. She imagined the small back meadow would be better groomed during the spring for Easter egg hunts and after-service barbecues, but now it was up to her calves, and lawn mushrooms grew in fairy circles the size of parachutes.

She scanned the perimeter, some of the grass flattened from kids playing tag or rolling through it after sitting for an hour of worship. What was she looking for? She felt the rain dampening her clothes, dripping off her chin, but her thoughts kept her feet planted. She couldn't pinpoint what felt *unsettling* about her conversation with Ms. Tristan. She read the sign, the marquee for the church, like a billboard on the west side of the road.

"I'll be damned," she whispered.

"What's that."

Meg jumped and whirled to face Ms. Tristan, who was now soaked, the rain matting her hair in two flat white sheets of paper. She no longer cared about the umbrella.

"Your sign." Meg pointed to the marquee, where the sign announced Executive Pastor Michael Menke along with his photo. She recognized the silver slicked-back hair and sweater vest. The stranger from Jaybee's. The one who'd tried to intimidate her. Underneath the photo, the marquee read "Come worship with us!" And underneath that, a Bible verse: *"Gal. 5:9 'A little yeast works through the whole batch of dough.'"* She thought of his parting words to her as he left the restaurant that night. "I believe Pastor Mike said that to me."

Ms. Tristan's lips formed a thin pencil line. "Did he now. Can't imagine why." She stared at Meg like she could imagine *every* reason why.

Meg smiled without blinking. "Me neither."

"I think it's best you be finding your way home now." Her tone was curt, not a trace of sweetness left.

"Gladly."

Meg stopped at a gas station to fill up, gave the cashier forty dollars, then called Finn, but his phone went straight to voicemail. "Hey, it's me. Figured out who harassed me at Jaybee's. Call me." With her tank filled at $27.02, she went back inside to retrieve her change. The cashier looked at her blankly. He had a rigid posture and a lined face that hinted at years of hard living.

"May I have my change for pump number five?"

"No change."

"I filled up at twenty-seven dollars. I gave you forty."

"You gave me twenty-seven."

"No, sir. There were two twenties."

He turned his back and started organizing packs of cigarettes.

"Sir."

The digital clock on the wall blinked at her. She was going to be late for her meeting with Dr. Strohman.

"Sir!"

He kept his back to her when he said, "Maybe in West Oak, they'll count your change better."

Her body felt that familiar fear. This town knew her and hated her. The enemy was dating one of their own. Did they *all* know her? Was she being paranoid? She turned and raced out to her car, her heart thrumming louder with each step, and floored the gas pedal, leaving thirteen dollars and East Pages behind. She called Finn again, and his phone again went to voicemail. "Finn? I hate that your phone's off. Where are you? You okay? I need to talk to you. This guy at the gas station, he— Just call me."

· · ·

The luncheon was a welcome distraction, although Dr. Strohman did look at her watch when Meg showed up late and sopping wet. Meg blamed the rain, which seemed to placate her, and for the next hour, they nibbled on crepes while discussing Meg's six-month, one-year, and five-year goals. She returned home to find her mother at the foot of the stairs, as if she hadn't left her post since morning.

"I spoke with Dr. Strohman. She called when you hadn't showed for lunch."

"I showed," Meg answered. She kept her voice steady, like ballet. *Plié. Breathe.*

"Fifteen minutes late."

"I was held up." She made sure to sound nonchalant. Nothing to give her mom reason to worry.

"Dr. Strohman said you mentioned trying out for volleyball next year."

Shoot. She'd forgotten about that. Dr. Strohman asked for her six-month plan. She'd blurted it out without thinking, just spitballing ideas, but once she said it, she liked the idea. Volleyball sounded fun. Different. Kylie was on the team. "I just thought—"

"Trying out as a senior? There's no future in that," her mother quipped. "It'll take time away from excelling in other areas. Volleyball, really? And fifteen minutes late? This isn't an opportunity to take for granted."

"I didn't. I was held up."

"By what?"

"It doesn't matter." She hadn't thought that far, and saying that was a misstep. That's not how she spoke to her mom, ever, and Mrs. Kaufman's raised eyebrow was further proof of that. It was always a delicate dance, but today, it was like she couldn't find her footing. Her mom held out her hand, and Meg reluctantly unlocked her phone and handed it over.

She scanned Meg's recent calls. "Finn?"

Meg had no answer because she hadn't made any other calls that morning. Just to Finn. Twice. Her mother didn't return the phone.

"This is uncharacteristic of you."

"Is it?" Meg asked. She wasn't sure what *was* her and what *wasn't* anymore. "I stopped at a couple places in East Pages, and—"

"Why?"

"Gas!" She threw her hands up, feeling her self-control going. The dance was over. "Does it matter? And the guy shortchanged me, so I called Finn because—"

"You didn't get gas last night?"

"Are you even listening?" The ballet slippers were off. She really didn't care how she sounded.

"I'm hearing that tone of voice. Megan, you've known about this meeting for weeks. We even rescheduled your piano lesson. You had ample time to—"

"You're right. How irresponsible of me." She held out her hand for her phone. "I've got to go soon. Key Club volunteer work in fifteen."

"You'll be fine without your phone. I need to speak with your father."

"He's not home until tonight."

"It'll give you time to think. In the meantime, you don't need any distractions from your obligations. You can iMessage your friends from your laptop. Once you're back home."

Her mom knew Finn had an Android.

Megan was simmering, but the boil was intensifying. "Great. If there's an emergency, I'll travel to the nineties and then Rollerblade to the nearest pay phone."

"Megan!" her mom called out, but Meg was out the front door and slamming it behind her.

Chapter 33
FINN

That morning in the kitchen, Finn saw Tammy's cookies, her name in her loopy handwriting on the paper plate smiling up at him. He glared at the name and texted Meg. She didn't text back, which wasn't like her. So many unanswered questions, each one wedging more distance between him and Meg.

This had to stop.

He looked back at the cookies and texted the number on the plate.

> Ok, I'm in.

Tammy immediately responded.

> EastPay 10 pm? Drive together?

He texted a thumbs-up, packed a lunch, and grabbed his backpack. He told his grandma he was heading to UT and wouldn't be back until late, and with a kiss, she shooed him out the door. He felt guilty lying to her, but he'd rather not drag her into all this. It was pouring, so it was the perfect day to spend at the Crestview Library. He was dangerously behind on schoolwork, so he locked himself in a study room to catch up on assignments, his phone off so he wouldn't have to answer anyone.

He hadn't expected to hear from Meg today, but when he

turned his phone back on at five p.m., it showed two missed calls from earlier. Usually her Saturdays were packed: piano, Key Club, home hospice visits, but maybe she'd called to share about the Harvard lunch her mom had planned. The reception in the study room was garbage. He tried texting out by the second-floor restrooms, but it didn't deliver. Part of him didn't want to talk to her today. She thought he was at UT, which meant she might ask about it, and then he'd have to add to his lie. Lies upon lies. If he found out anything tonight, he'd tell her everything. Maybe Tammy was right. Maybe the reason he knew so little was that students figured he was more loyal to Megan Kaufman than EastPay.

They wouldn't be wrong.

Chapter 34

BRITNEY

Saturday evening, Brit heard the light knock at her front door, but she didn't move from her spot in the corner of her bedroom. She sat tucked into a ball, chin on her knees, staring at her perfectly hanging cheer outfit from the game she didn't attend last night. Downstairs, there was some conversation—a familiar guy's voice and her mother's—and then the door closing and someone padding up the stairs, down the hallway toward her room.

She glanced up. *Spencer?* He stood tentatively in her doorway, wearing a tucked-in button-down shirt. Well, half tucked in, like he was either in a hurry or hadn't worn one very often. Caution narrowed her eyes. *Why was he here?*

"I didn't text because I didn't think you'd respond," he said.

He was probably right. She lifted a shoulder.

"Didn't see you in the stands last night," he said.

"Parents." She was grounded, in addition to everything else.

"How long?"

"Long as my suspension from cheer." She pressed on her eyebrows with the heels of her hands. Her temples throbbed. "Two weeks. Time to *think*," she said, spitting out the last word.

"You didn't tell your mom the truth?"

She looked up again. A new fear shot through her like a quad espresso. Was Spencer sent by Walker or Tammy to check on her? "Course I told her. After all, I did it."

"No, you didn't," he said.

"Look, if they sent you to see if you can crack me, you ain't doin' it, so you can pack your Marlboro-carrying ass up and leave. I told you I did it. You can tell them I said so."

"Will do. I'll tell 'em you said it proud like a six-year-old Texan recitin' the Pledge of Allegiance."

If this was his way of getting a reaction from her, forget it. She gave a curt nod, then turned toward the wall, a muted dismissal. She tucked herself back into a ball, her arms hugging her shins, her hands gripping a cheerleading trophy. Spencer was watching her intently, like he actually cared. She wasn't falling for it.

Finally, he took in her room. She followed his gaze as he looked at her trophies. Taller ones stood on her dresser, giants that stood over even Spencer. He rubbed a thumb over one—the shiny fake-gold girl atop with arms outstretched and holding gold-covered pom-poms. A real set of pom-poms hung, one on each side of her mirror, plastic strings dangling red and black and tattered from overuse. He trailed a hand across her wall, his fingers grazing the littered pictures of dance competitions, cheer camps, and football games—group photos, solo photos, selfies, and some faraway shots, taken of her from the stands. Framed on one wall, set apart from all the others, was a poster-size photo of the varsity cheer squad, the girls doing the splits, pom-poms overhead and smiling like they sat that way all the time.

"Damn," Spencer whispered.

"What?" Brit remained as still as one of her trophies.

"It's like a cheer museum in here." He grinned at Brit, but she didn't smile back. She used to think she could trust Spencer, but she also thought she could trust Walker, once.

She watched him approach her the way one would a wounded animal, not lifting his socked feet, but sliding them across the carpet. He crouched next to her, drew his knees in the way she had hers, wrapped his arms around his legs. Something was different about Spencer's demeanor. She'd seen him soft around his sister. But never with her. Not since ninth-grade tutoring.

For minutes, neither of them spoke.

"They're using my sister against me," he finally said, "as collateral."

She felt it then—the raw honesty—and relaxed.

He rested his chin on his knee. "You remember what you told me in ninth grade, the last day you tutored me?" Brit's eyes met his. "You remember that day—yeah, you do. You showed me how the football stats were skewed."

Brit nodded.

"Well, I looked stuff up, after you told me those numbers," Spencer continued. "And you were right. I compared our team with other teams. We were winning by three-point-five points more than them against teams with better records."

"You didn't tell on me," Brit said, smiling shyly, remembering why she always trusted Spence even when he played the jerk.

"'Course not—you thought it was Dante's Ravine. You swore the river changed your life the night you dunked in it."

She felt foolish, thinking of how much faith she'd placed in superstition.

Spencer continued, "Only I didn't believe in all that river garbage, so I started asking questions. I couldn't keep my damn mouth shut, that was my stupidity. That's on me." He untucked his legs, leaned back against the wall, as if he needed support for his next words.

"Shortly after, I was sent an anonymous email, some two-minute foreign movie clip of a bunch of people beating the bloody hell out of someone in the street. The person was barely recognizable. The subject line was simply 'Leah.' So, yeah. My little sister's my Achilles' heel, and they know it. So that's what they use. Haven't said a word since, and they've let her be. But I hate that she's unsafe because I started digging. Even the coaches told me to shut up and play football."

He inhaled, tightened his fists and then released.

"I'm sorry," she croaked. "That's horrible. I never should've confided in you."

"No," he said. "I'm glad you did. That's why I'm confiding in you now. I don't know what you did to piss 'em off, but it's good that you're laying low. We don't know where it's coming from, and we can't stop it. So don't give 'em a reason to look your way."

"I found out." She chewed on her lip. "Where it's coming from." Spencer's head snapped up, and she knew for sure he wasn't on Walker's side. "That's why I pissed 'em off. And it ain't no magic river."

"What?"

"A chat room," she blurted.

Spencer cocked his head. His eyebrows reached for each other.

"Yeah," she continued, her trust in him growing. "It's the most basic elementary rubbish of a tactic any moronic fourth grader could set up. And because I found out, that's why all this shit is happening to me."

The corner of Spencer's mouth lifted.

"What? What's funny?" Brit said, but Spencer shook his head. "Tell me," she demanded. She was tired of secrets.

He waved a hand to calm her down. "When you cuss, it's cute." He smiled, and her irritation dissipated. "Like you're not used to saying curse words and don't know how to give them the hard edge. It sounds like 'shet,' like the Shetland ponies down near Clayton Messler's property, all small and soft." She glared at him, and he coughed, erasing his grin. "Sorry."

"It was an accident, how I found out," she said. "Walker thought I knew. Then he realized I didn't. So he ratted me out."

"Chat room," Spencer repeated. He was still processing. "What does a chat room—"

"It's how they communicate," said Brit, reading his confusion. "Anonymous. No tracing. They come up with ideas to take out certain players from other teams. And when their best players aren't there—"

"We have a better shot at winning."

"Hence the higher winning percentage." Brit couldn't believe how clueless she'd been.

Spencer closed his eyes, absorbing it all. "A chat room. The Game's a chat room. And Walker made the mistake of thinking you were in on it."

"Exactly."

"So he needed to take you down in front of everybody. In case you'd out him later. Too risky for him."

She nodded miserably. "Pretty sure the captains decide your freshman year who to bring in. Someone musta told the captain to keep me out. Pamela, maybe? She's a year older. She's the one who got me to record my voice."

"Wait, if the captains decide, how'd Walker not know?"

"He was only a sophomore that year. Not captain yet. I think he assumed I'd know. It's safer if you never talk about the chat room, so he probably thought *I* started the rumor that I didn't know anything."

"So Pamela felt threatened by a fourteen-year-old?"

"Thirteen," Brit corrected. "I was thirteen starting ninth grade."

"Ha. Never find a football player saying that."

Brit recalled how many guys in East Pages were held back in fourth, fifth, and sixth grade. Funny how the ones who weren't socially "ready" were also coincidentally the bigger kids, taller than the rest, more fit, who could catch like Velcro and outrun their older siblings. If they could have one more year, think how much bigger they'd be by junior and senior year, the year of recruitment, the year of scholarships and dollar signs and championships. It had never bothered her before.

But now, it made sense. Britney sat up. Since the football stadium was the only Friday night social outing during the fall, those two years could raise these parents to the top of the East Pages social ladder. Status, status, status. Yes, they'd hold their bigger children back. *They'd be idiots not to.* The thought made Brit's jaw clench.

"I know why they felt threatened," Brit admitted. "My sixth-grade award. I didn't think anyone remembered."

"In what? Tumbling?"

"Cybersecurity."

Spencer laughed, and it was gentle, like he thought she was

making fun of herself. Brit stared at him soberly. "Cybersecurity," he repeated. "No, really. Look, you tutored me in math, I get it, but . . ."

She didn't say anything.

"You," he repeated.

Part of her was grateful she'd done such a good job disguising her past computer skills behind all the tumbles and Russian splits. She stood, opened her closet door, and rummaged through a box until she retrieved a plaque and walked it over to him. He silently read the three lines etched on the brass plate: "National Youth Cybersecurity Championship. Second Place—Individual Category. Britney Wallace."

"You gotta be shitting me."

She wished she was. "Since I found out about their secret," she said, "I been racking my brains trying to figure out why they kept me sidelined. Walker flat-out told me. This dang award's a death sentence. Whatever they're doing or not doing, it's all funneled through a website that hosts a chat room. To them, *this*"—she waved the plaque over her head before burying it again in the closet—"means I know how to hack. To get in the way. To add my own agenda, if I need to. Too much risk to let me in—'specially an honest girl fighting her nation's cyber wars."

Spencer coughed out a one-syllable laugh. Even Brit knew how ridiculous it sounded.

"How the hell did you get involved in homeland security?"

She smiled ruefully as she sat again next to Spencer. "Turns out I have a photographic memory, like, in a weird way. Sequences. Configurations. Pattern recognition, mostly. Probably wouldn't have discovered it, but, well . . . I guess loneliness has its benefits."

God, she hated thinking back to junior high. "They don't realize that I don't know a thing anymore. Do they have a pie hole clue how far technology's advanced since then? I'd be looking at a foreign language if I tried to do anything. Doesn't matter to them, though. Stupid award got me hog-tied five years ago."

Again the corners of Spencer's mouth lifted. *"Pie hole clue?"*

"Oh, stuff it, Spence!" But she offered a weak smile. "How'd you break into my house?"

"You're tutoring me for my math test."

"'Course I am." She stood and retrieved her calc book and laptop. "In case Mom walks in." She looked at her laptop, sitting down at her desk. "There's more. About Eli."

Spencer stiffened. "Do I wanna know?"

"There was talk of Damarius in the chat room," she said. "Before. Someone said they'd 'take care of it' or something like that."

Spencer remained stoic. "My sister has to believe Eli's death was an accident."

"It wasn't Leah's fault. But I don't think it was an accident, either." Brit flipped through the pages of her calc book. "Eli accidentally got in the way, but the fight was planned. Damarius was asking questions. I think they wanted to teach him a lesson. Pretty sure he found out things he wasn't supposed to."

"Kind of like you did?"

She swallowed. She hadn't thought about that. She recalled the stream of hateful words about Damarius she scrolled through that night. Was she next on their list?

He stood and leaned over her chair, tapping the laptop. "Any chance you can use that cyber award to break into that chat room?"

She grimaced. "I wish. It's all password protected, invite only, blah blah blah. I'd need the administrator to shut it down, and God knows who that is. Tammy? Walker? Pamela?" She stopped. There was that grin again. "What?"

"Your accent," he said. "You dropped it." She started to argue, but he set a hand on her shoulder. "It's okay. Makes me feel kinda good you forgot."

Her face flushed, realizing how real she actually was being with him. *Was that a compliment?* Their eyes met, but he removed his hand and looked away.

"So how do we find that guy?" His voice was all business again.

"We don't. Could be some unknown nerd who sits in the second row of our Gov class, for all we know."

"Could you break in using someone's username?"

"Then what? Watch and play defense? And then when that person tries to log on and can't because they're already logged on, who they gonna suspect first?" Brit drummed her fingers on her desk. "What if I showed it to the police?"

Spencer guffawed as if Brit had told a joke. "The police. Good, Brit. Real good."

"What."

"You ever wonder why the cop dismissed me after hitting someone with a car? I *hit* someone. You ever wonder why the guy I hit—Ryan Quaid—was nailed for a curfew violation? Why I never filled out a stitch of paperwork?"

Britney's face turned paper white. "You think the cops are part of it? That they're in on the chat room?"

"No! 'Course not! This whole fucked-up operation is student-run, like you said. I doubt cops are in on it. But did you know that cop played for EastPay in '87? Tom Clarke, tight end. He's a perfect example of this godforsaken town, how there's at least one in every group just like him, someone who can't let go of his glory days or who doesn't like outsiders in our business. And you're an *insider*. Word gets out that you're trying to snitch? Cops'll take one look at that chat room and declare it's an online study hall. Then threaten to fine you for false incrimination."

"What do I do?" Brit felt her world collapsing.

"Same thing I do. Stay off their radar. They're watching you. And they'll ruin you if you so much as whisper a word of what you know. And I'd avoid Finn."

She scrunched her nose. "He's my cousin!"

"Yeah, well, they think he doesn't know jack, and there're eyes everywhere. He already knows more than he's lettin' on, and if they figure that out, who they gonna blame?"

Brit's hands squeezed the sides of the desk. Her breathing gained volume, and she sucked in gasps. Her eyes widened and she looked around the room wildly. Where was the air? Spencer wrapped his arm around her, gently held the back of her neck, eased it toward her knees.

"Whoa, Brit. Breathe. It's okay. You're okay. Everything's going to be fine."

Her head stayed tucked between her legs, and she began to cry, heaving sobs that shook her shoulders.

"Shh." He spoke to her tenderly, the way she imagined he would with his sister. "It's just two years. I've been laying low for two. What's two more?"

"I don't know if I can," she choked out.

"Sure you can. You're the Fearless Flyer."

She laughed a hiccupping sob.

A text came through on Spencer's phone. Brit peeked up at him. Maybe he sensed her fear, because he showed her. It was from his sister. Where are you?

On my way, he texted back so that Brit could see.

He stood. "Listen, I gotta go. Nights are hard on Leah."

She nodded and took a deep, trembling breath. She was a mess of curls—her face smudged and puffy for sure. And where was her lipstick tube? He turned to leave, but as he reached the door, she offered a barely audible "Spence?"

He turned.

"Why you bein' so nice? I only seen you once this way, and that was to Leah."

He cocked his head, taking in her words, but maybe it was to take in her accent, which she'd brought back in full force. It was thick and "Brit," but also—now he knew—full of the girl who worried what everyone thought. It made her feel naked, exposed, and she wished he'd stop looking at her that way.

"Yeah, well, don't get used to it," he said with his typical hardened tone, but then he smiled warmly and closed the door.

Chapter 35
MEGAN

That afternoon, since Finn had canceled, Meg came home after Key Club, avoided her mom, and went straight to homework. By nine, she was itching to tell Kylie everything. She hadn't messaged about her run-in at the church and the gas station, partly because Kylie would have a million follow-up questions. She'd wait until they were alone. Meg's mom had held on to her phone, so she flipped open her laptop and iMessaged Kylie.

Jaybee's?

Ugh can't. Family game night. But tmrw!

Meg had convinced the gang to meet for lunch in West Oak, even though they told her they'd bet money Finn would cancel again. *Not a chance*, she wanted to say. But lately, she couldn't predict him. She didn't know if it was a different version of him or a different version of her evolving, but the gap between them was growing. She hugged a pillow. She could use a friend right now. As if Kylie could read her mind, a message appeared on her screen.

Come to family game night! Dad said ok!

Meg snatched her keys and bounded out the front door. The night was dark, moonless, as Meg rushed to her car. She looked each direction like she was crossing the street, which had become her habit these past few days. Look to the side, look behind. Every time she drove, she'd check her rearview mirror, wondering if it was coincidence anytime a car switched lanes with her. Was she overreacting?

It dawned on her that she'd turned her key now three times to a coughing, sputtering response.

Back inside, she found her father in the office, his usual hideout from his wife. "Hey, Dad." He looked up from his papers. "I was heading to Kylie's, but something's wrong with the Audi. Won't start."

He gave her a funny look. "Keys?"

Together they walked to the car. He eased into the driver's seat and tried the ignition.

The car sputtered. He looked at the gauges, tapped the glass in front of the steering wheel, turned the key again. Then came the disappointed drawn-out tone. "Megan . . ."

Meg lifted her hands. *What?*

Keys in hand, and with a swift closing of the door, he returned to the house. Meg followed at his heels.

Her mother was now at the front door. "What is it?"

Mr. Kaufman reached for the keys to his BMW. "Take my car to the local Chevron on the corner of Hamilton. Buy a gallon of gas."

"You let your car run out of gas?" Her mom had now invaded the conversation.

"No!" Meg argued, as her father said, "Yes."

"No," she said again. "Remember? I had errands. I told you I stopped for gas in East Pages."

Her mother placed a hand to her hip, her elbow jutting out like an accusing finger. "That's right. On your way to showing up late for your lunch."

"You were late for the lunch with Mrs. Strohman?" her father asked.

"*Dr.* Strohman," her mother corrected, and added, "Did you maybe forget to put in gas because you were running errands to Finn's house?"

Her father's eyes narrowed. "You went to Finn's house?"

"No," she said.

"Then where were you? What made you late? What errands?" Her father's volume was growing.

Meg didn't know what to say. "Errands."

Her mom crossed her arms. "Around *here*? Ms. Tristan from Women's League phoned to tell me you were in East Pages that morning. Snooping on private property, she says."

"That's not private property." She couldn't believe that woman had snitched on her. And why should her mom care what Ms. Tristan said?

"So you *were* there." Disappointment creased her dad's eyes. "Instead of filling up on gas before your meeting."

"Look, I told Mom I got sidetracked. But I know I got gas, because the guy shortchanged me."

Her mother crossed her arms. "Then why would it be empty?"

"If you want to see Finn," her father said, "I have no problem with that. But not at the expense of your primary obligations. I heard your mom took your phone away."

He gave no offer to return it, so Megan said, "The phone wasn't the problem."

He shook his head as if he hadn't heard her. "Running out of gas, Megan? Really?"

• • •

Meg walked out into the night. She heard the screen door swing open and her mother's clunky footsteps behind her.

"Megan," said Mrs. Kaufman when Meg hadn't slowed. "Listen to me," she hissed, and Meg stopped.

"If this is about my phone—" she started, but her mother cut her off.

"This thing with Finn has gone far enough," said Mrs. Kaufman evenly.

"Thing?"

Mrs. Kaufman drew her shoulders back and crossed her arms. "Your relationship isn't helping either of you. You're not focusing on your opportunities. Sounds like he isn't, either. East Pages is not the place to mess—" She faltered. "I think it's best if you both took a step back to reevaluate."

Megan chuckled darkly. "Are you ordering us to break up?"

Mrs. Kaufman looked daggers at her. When she spoke, it was slow and deliberate, an eerie calm to her. "You know that Finn's mom, Kat, isn't related to Finn's grandmother?"

Meg wasn't sure what this had to do with anything. "Stepdaughter. Yeah, I know."

"Not even that, technically. Finn's grandparents never married."

The quiet confidence in her mother's voice unnerved her. "Okay."

"Kat—Finn's mom—was the daughter of a previous marriage and ten years old when her father started dating Mrs. Callahan. Mrs. Callahan also had a daughter around Kat's age."

Brit's mom, Meg thought.

"Well, little Kat did *not* take well to a sister who—rumor has it—did everything better. She was convinced that the only reason her always-absent father was suddenly in the picture was that he loved his new girlfriend and daughter more than her. Rather than appreciate the new family, she resented them. Started *rebelling*."

She knew what her mom meant by "rebelling." Drug use.

"Mrs. Callahan did her best with Kat. Splendid job, really." Meg hated how her mother used words like *splendid*. It was a happy word. It meant Meg's mom felt that she had the upper hand. Meg couldn't figure out her angle. "But when Kat's dad died shortly after . . ."

Meg tried to stay stone-faced, but her eye twitched. She knew Finn's grandfather had died before Finn was born. But how'd her mom know?

"Well, he died in the midst of Kat's teenage drug issues," said Meg's mom. "And talk about a snowball effect. Strung out by fifteen. Pregnant at sixteen. Finn was a miracle, totally normal, but Kat didn't care. When Mrs. Callahan took over caring for Finn, Kat was probably relieved. I'm sure she came back less and less, right? Maybe for money?"

Meg knew that her silence would be an admission, but she couldn't find the words. Her mouth felt dry as sandpaper. She squeezed the car keys until her knuckles cramped. *Steady.*

"I'm sure you know," said Mrs. Kaufman.

Meg swallowed. "Then why are you telling me?"

"I can't have you in the dark. What happens when the State

finds out the truth? You know our county process. He'd be placed in a group home that day."

Meg felt relief. "No, he wouldn't. His grandma's taken care of him his whole life."

"She forgot one detail."

Meg rubbed her sweaty palms with her fingers.

"Adoption," her mother said. "Legality. She's never filed for legal guardianship. Finn's just some kid living in her house."

"They can fix that." Meg tried to say it confidently, but her voice wavered.

"Sure, they'll sort it out. It'll take a year or so, but they'll figure it out. Maybe toward the end of his senior year?"

Suddenly she felt dizzy. She knew where her mother was going with this. She placed a hand on the hood of the car to steady herself. "You wouldn't."

"Like I said, I think it's time you took a break. Let him focus on his future. Wouldn't want an anonymous call to ruin all that."

Meg could barely find words. "Who else knows?"

"Not many people. I had to do some digging."

"So you could break us up? Control my life? Take my phone?"

"This is so much bigger than your phone," Mrs. Kaufman hissed, and she looked furtively around, then straightened. "I trust you'll make a wise decision." And she swiftly turned and headed for the house.

• • •

In a daze, Meg drove her dad's BMW to the Chevron and bought the plastic canister and a gallon of gas. She poured the gallon into her Audi's tank, then returned her dad's keys and announced to a quiet house that she was going back out to fill up her car.

"Ten minutes, and no Kylie tonight," was all her dad said before closing his office door. From the kitchen, she could hear her mother shuffling around, the clinking of ice cubes.

Of course.

She ran upstairs and opened her laptop to iChat.

> Can't make it. I'll explain later.

· · ·

After the gas station, she looked at the car clock. Her gas had been siphoned. There was no other explanation. But why? Did her mom not know that Finn was out of town, and was it her attempt to keep Meg from seeing him? She almost laughed, imagining her mother siphoning a car. Not a chance. Then who? And why?

Her dad's "ten-minute rule" tugged at her, but she shoved it aside. Without a second thought, she was creaking through Finn's front door, not pausing to wonder what her parents would do if they found out.

Mrs. Callahan lay on the couch, the cushions half enveloping her, and Meg rushed to her side. She stirred as Meg knelt beside her. "Hi, sweetheart. Finn back?"

Meg blew out her breath. Had she been holding it? "No, just me."

"I hope you weren't wasting gas money on me. Told Finn I'd be fine."

Meg leaned over and kissed Mrs. Callahan on the forehead. "It's no bother. I was in the neighborhood."

Mrs. Callahan squeezed her hand. "Sure you were. You be careful this hour. People are very"—she paused to find the right word—"*enthusiastic* about this town."

"No kidding." She thought back to Ms. Tristan's look of indignation at Meg as she "trespassed" among the high grass and the fairy circles of lawn mushrooms, reading marquees and walking the church grounds. Did Ms. Tristan know about Meg's run-in with Pastor Mike at Jaybee's? Was that why she went out of her way to call her mom about it? A new fear curled through her.

"Mrs. Callahan . . ."

"Hmm."

Mrs. Callahan adjusted the cushions. She looked at her with a no-nonsense expression. "What is it?"

"Nothing." Inside, a knot twisted deep in her stomach. "You lock your doors, right?"

She yawned and nodded, then turned off the TV with the remote. Pushing herself up from the couch, she ambled toward her bedroom. "Well, when you want to tell me what's really on your mind, come on back. I'm fine. I hope Finn didn't tell you to check on me."

"Told you," Meg called after her. "I was in the neighborhood."

At the end of the hallway, Mrs. Callahan waved a dismissive hand. "You keep telling yourself that. Night, sweetie."

Meg blurted, "I think my gas was siphoned."

Mrs. Callahan turned to her, lifted an eyebrow.

"I had gas. And then I didn't have gas. But Finn's away, so I thought—"

"Ah." Mrs. Callahan rubbed her knuckles together. "You thought someone from your school put a hit on Finn's grandma?"

Meg barked a laugh, her wound-up nerves relaxing. "No. Gosh, no. Not West Oak. I thought maybe EastPay . . ." But as she said it, she realized how preposterous it sounded. Finn was their golden ticket. Why would they harm his grandma? That reminded her. "Does Finn know he's not technically related to you?"

Mrs. Callahan looked up at the towering photo of Gale Sayers, framed and smiling, hovering above Meg.

"'Course he does." She scrutinized Meg. "Let's talk outside, dear. I need to stretch my legs."

They stepped onto the porch, the mosquito light buzzing above them, and walked toward the garden.

Mrs. Callahan circled her arm around Meg's as Meg muttered, "My mom said I have to break up with Finn or she's going to tell the State that Finn isn't legally yours."

"Mmm." They stopped midway between the house and the garden. "Yes, he knows. Was never a concern, really."

"But now it is. What if they send him away? If I don't break up with him, I could ruin his football career."

Mrs. Callahan sighed. "That does put you in a pickle."

Meg chuckled. She loved how this woman could find the humor in what looked dire. "What do I do?"

"Can't tell you that. But let me worry about the legal side of things. You worry about Finn. There are colleges who would take him even if he didn't play for EastPay, but he's not convinced. He's gotta figure out what he wants—I ain't gonna do that for him—and if you stick around through all that, then, like I said before, he better put a ring on you before he gets hit in the head too much. Your parents know you're in East Pages this time of night?"

"Heck no."

"Then I suggest you make your way back. This neighborhood isn't great to West Oakers in the daytime, much less at this hour."

"Good thing I don't have a bumper sticker that says 'West Oak Honor Roll.'"

Mrs. Callahan laughed. "Don't need that. Everyone here knows who Megan Kaufman is, the Achilles' heel of their favorite running back."

A chill ran through her. Still, it felt comforting to be near someone who understood her fear and anxiety—and didn't make her feel like a paranoid lunatic. She had more questions, but Mrs. Callahan was right. She was on borrowed time.

● ● ●

Meg drove back onto the highway, checking her rearview mirror for anything suspicious. For miles, the inky blackness stared back. About a mile before West Oak, flashing lights appeared. She moved to the right to get out of his way, but the cop drove up next to her, matching her speed, and waved her to pull to the side of the highway.

Great, Meg thought. *Now what?*

The cop approached her window once she stopped. "Thought I recognized you," he said, friendly enough.

She didn't recognize him. "You know my parents?"

He tilted his head. "Met you the day of the parade."

He was the cop who'd questioned Brit. She smiled, but her leg was twitching. "Oh, right. Sorry. It's late."

"It *is* pretty late. That's why I pulled you over. What brings you to these parts so late?"

These parts? She was a block from West Oak.

"Visiting someone's grandma. She's alone tonight."

He nodded. "That's right kind of you. However, mighta started that earlier. Curfew's ten p.m. in East Pages for underagers."

Her clock read 9:57. But it wasn't the time to argue. "Sorry. I meant to get there earlier."

"And then head home later—against the law?"

"No. Originally, no. I would've been back before—" She stopped. This was strange. She'd never heard of the curfew law being enforced to drivers. Mostly it was for kids who loitered, who lingered in shadowed alleys, who smoked outside convenience stores waiting for someone to buy liquor for them. The understood rule was if you were en route somewhere, no problem. She and Finn had driven countless times dropping friends off after curfew.

She felt a prickle, her clothes sticking to her like wet Saran wrap. Her gas had been siphoned. Now she was being pulled over for a curfew violation.

He started writing a ticket.

"Please, sir. I'm heading home. My parents wouldn't appreciate—"

"I suppose they wouldn't. I'll escort you there."

"That's really not necessary."

"It's most necessary. I'm obligated by law to make sure you get home safe. You're a minor. People in East Pages aren't always fond of foreigners, minor or not. What if something happened?"

Foreigners? Was he referring to her hometown? Or her race? Being mixed, she'd felt judgment before from both sides. A new fear rippled through her and split her confidence. Her fingers trembled against the steering wheel. He wasn't concerned that something might happen. He was threatening that something *would* happen if she kept coming to East Pages. Indignation welled up in her, but she shoved it down. Defying him would only get her in more trouble.

"Yessir," she mumbled. "I'd be most appreciative."

He handed her the ticket, tipped his hat, and strolled back to his car, no longer worrying about the time or keeping her out later. They drove in tandem, his red-and-blue flashing lights igniting the dark highway. Near the edge of town, they drove by a car on the shoulder of the other side of the highway, smoking from the hood. The situation across the highway looked much more severe than Meg's, but of course, there was no cop there, none that Meg could see as she craned her neck. She was seething, anger coursing through her, adrenaline making her fingers shake. She balled her fists.

Her parents were proper and poised throughout the whole exchange. The cop, Officer Tom Clarke, explained the dangers of the dark highway in East Pages. "No place for a young girl," he said. "Lots of travelers come through those parts. Truck drivers. Vagabonds."

"Thank you for keeping her safe," her mother said, her voice rigid. She looked visibly nervous, and Meg noticed the way she stood closer to her husband than Meg had seen in months. "We respect the law. Don't we, Megan?"

"Absolutely." Her words were swallowed in the back of her throat.

Officer Clarke smiled tightly. "It might be more advisable if she planned her visits to her boyfriend during daylight hours. No reason to put herself in harm's way."

Meg stared at Officer Clarke, unblinking. She'd told him she was checking on someone's grandmother. This was the first mention of Finn, of Officer Clarke's knowledge of Finn and Meg's relationship, and the clear evidence that he didn't like it. His message was clear.

"Of course," her mother agreed, speaking politely through a locked jaw and thin lips. "I appreciate your concern."

He only offered Meg's mom a cursory glance. Instead, he focused on Meg's father as he tipped his hat. "You all have a good night. Gotta get back to my neck of the woods. I'm on duty."

• • •

"I don't know where to begin," her mother started the moment he exited, but her father was strangely quiet, watching until Officer Clarke drove away before he closed the front door.

"Dad," Meg pleaded.

"Don't turn to him about this. He's as upset as I am."

Her father still didn't say anything.

"First the gas, and now sneaking out?" her mother fumed.

"I wasn't sneaking out! My curfew's eleven! And I was checking on Finn's grandmother."

At this, Mr. Kaufman looked at Meg. Their eyes met, and she couldn't tell whether he believed her or he was trying to expose lies.

Meg's mother didn't seem to hear her. "Do you have any idea

the earful I'm going to get when the Doheny sisters hear about this? I don't even want to show my face at the club come Monday."

"Then don't," Mr. Kaufman said dryly, and it shocked her mother into silence. "I think Meg's had a trying day. Perhaps we should offer her a break."

Mrs. Kaufman was incredulous. "The only break she needs is from Finn."

"Maybe until we get this sorted out," he said, "I can drive you when you want to visit your boyfriend."

Mrs. Kaufman protested, "Lee!"

Megan didn't like this idea either. He was on business trips half the week. "Speaking of my boyfriend, did Mom tell you I have to break up with Finn or she'll send him to a group home?"

Her dad turned slowly to her mom, and Meg was relieved to see that this wasn't a joint effort. He was silent.

Mrs. Kaufman put both her hands on her hips. "You've seen how lax she's been about her commitments. And Finn isn't focusing on his football, either."

"Since when do you care about Finn's well-being?" Meg quipped.

"Enough," said Mr. Kaufman. "Meg, do *not* run out of gas or be late anymore. For anything. Understood?"

"Yes, sir," said Meg. She wondered what he thought about the group home comment, but this wasn't the time to ask. This was a yessir moment unless she wanted to make things worse.

Mrs. Kaufman huffed upstairs and slammed her bedroom door. Mr. Kaufman retreated to the office, and Megan was left alone at the foot of the stairs.

Chapter 36
FINN

The lights of Crestview Library flashed that they were closing in fifteen minutes. Finn packed up and, once he got back to his car, turned on his phone. 9:50. A voicemail from Meg appeared, but it was from hours ago. Her voice was worried and cryptic, and as much as he'd rather not call her before Dante's, he immediately did.

Straight to voicemail. Her phone must be off. He could FaceTime with his Android if she sent a link from her iPhone. But she hadn't. He texted.

> Driving home. You ok?

She didn't respond, and with his Android, he couldn't tell if she'd even read it.

He tried to lose himself in music as he drove the ten miles to EastPay High, but thoughts churned in his head. What if he found actual proof that EastPay football was cheating somehow? Would he keep quiet? If he didn't play for EastPay, what was the point of everything? Moving his grandma. Losing his friends. Struggling with his relationship. If he wasn't recruited by a legitimate four-year, he'd have to work his way up through community college. The thought made his heart sink like a heavy stone. His whole life, he'd worked to have the best shot. Now he finally had it.

Finn's hands trembled on the steering wheel as he pulled into the EastPay High parking lot. A few empty cars sat, their passengers already piled into other cars and gone. He knew students carpooled. Designated drivers. Some even walked from the school to Dante's Ravine. It was a dark two-lane highway, but it was only a couple miles. He spotted Tammy leaning against her blue Honda, Spartan mask in hand, the only one left in the parking lot. He rolled up, and without a word, she climbed into the passenger seat, secured her seat belt, and stared out the window.

"Hey," he said.

She didn't answer but took a sip from her Nalgene bottle, wincing in a way that told him it wasn't water. Something high in proof and low in expectations, no doubt.

"Rough day?" he said as he drove.

She scowled at him, definitely not the flirty Tammy of last night.

They drove in silence until the dark shoulder near Clayton Messler's property. He parked in the dirt behind two other cars, and she took another gulp from her Nalgene bottle. She made no move to get out of the car. He couldn't figure out if she was angry with him or wanted to talk.

"I liked your cookies," he said. "I mean, if this"—he made a circular gesture in the air referring to her anger—"is what it's about."

She laughed and put her face in her hands, mumbling something like "not over." Suddenly, her shoulders shook and he could hear her muffled sobs.

"Heyyyyy." Instinctively he put his arm around her, and, without pretense, she burrowed her face into his chest. He ignored the softness of her hair, tried to think of her as a sister. "What's not over?"

She lifted her head, and he noticed how pretty she was, even with wet eyes and a mess of mascara. He quickly warded off the thought—focused instead on the tears crisscrossing her face, how they reminded him of play #32: spread formation, two wideouts each side running slants across the middle of the field.

She looked around furtively, then placed a hand on his and gripped it. "There's this tradition. Drink the water at Dante's Ravine. First party. Stupid, right?" He remembered Brit mentioning this. How Damarius and Eli didn't drink. Tammy grimaced. "How do I know there's not some parasite in it?"

She watched him, waited for his reaction.

"Probably ten parasites," he said gently.

"Got a text from an unknown number tonight," she said. She fiddled with her phone, showed him the message.

Drink the lifeblood. You missed once.
Don't miss again.

"Someone knows I didn't drink from Dante's that night," she whispered, even though they were alone.

Annoyance rose in him. Superstitions were real in this part of Texas, fueled by adrenaline and gossip until they became gospel, making folks believe in the power to sway the outcomes of games or the health of players—using *fear* to convince others of that power. Others like Brit. And now Tammy, too.

"This is *them*," she said. "I think I'm in control, calling the shots, staying loyal to EastPay, and then someone sees one misstep, and suddenly I don't know if I'm about to lose everything." She dropped her face in her hands and choked back a sob.

Her fear crept into him, the hair on his arms lifting, touching against the inside of his jacket. Was this true? Was someone going to make Tammy's life worse if she didn't comply with the superstitions of EastPay football?

"Okay," he said. "Listen. Let's start over. Can we do that first?"

She nodded into her sleeve.

"Do you have any idea who might be behind it? Any suspicions? Anyone who's threatened you before? Maybe Walker?"

She laughed mirthlessly and took another sip.

"Hey, at the end of the night, can I drive you home?" He motioned at her Nalgene bottle.

"I'll manage." She took a big breath, snapped her Spartan mask over her head, and opened the passenger door. "Uber. You'll probably Uber, too."

He wouldn't need to. The truth was, he wanted to be in bed already, dreaming of the NFL and future Super Bowls. He was exhausted and frustrated. He wanted football to be football, but until he figured out this mess, it would never be that. The truth of the underhanded goings-on lay somewhere between Tammy's tears and Walker's lack of concern.

Finn used his flashlight app to illuminate the path as he and Tammy headed for the riverbank. He adjusted his mask, thankful for the extra protection. The moon wasn't as bright as the last time he was here, and at certain places, they walked through total darkness, slapping through spiderwebbed fingers of tangled brush.

They continued toward the distant sound of rushing water and the faint echo of music. The voices grew louder as they ducked through a corridor of low-hanging branches and emerged in a clearing. Around the banks and under dark trees, shadows of students gathered in tufts of three or four—dancing, drinking, laughing. Finn could see the tops of the Spartan masks adorning their heads, the nose plates cascading down their faces. Some lounged on the river's edge, their bare feet lazily swinging over the dark water. The music and laughter somehow made it less ominous, even with the muted moon.

Kneeling down on the soft earth near the edge of the bank, Tammy scooped a handful of water and drank.

"There!" she shouted to the sky. A few shadowed figures stopped and looked her way, then resumed whatever they were doing.

"Over here," Tammy whispered, sitting and patting the ground next to her. He sat, rested his elbows on the earth. It was incredibly dark under this particular tree, and Tammy removed her mask. The wind whistled through the leaves like a distant cry. And the cicadas screamed along.

His phone flashlight revealed the side of Tammy's face. She looked miserable. "Kill the light," she muttered. He turned it off and removed his mask. She sipped from her bottle. Offered him some. He shook his head.

"You don't drink?"

He didn't answer.

"Ever?"

He lifted a shoulder. He'd had a beer on occasion. Not during the season, though. And he never wanted to get used to it. His mom started drugs that way. Just fun. No big deal.

"Walker told me about your mom," Tammy said, like she was in his thoughts. Before he could react, she said, "Don't be mad at him. He only told me because my older sister's an addict." She lifted her bottle like she was toasting. "I'm my parents' last hope."

"That's a lot of pressure." He could relate. He felt like he was his grandma's *only* hope.

She offered him the water bottle again. "We're not gonna end up like them. My sister. Your mom. We're different."

He felt connected to her—the way she said it like she truly understood his fear. He took the bottle and sipped tentatively. It was strong and sweet, and it burned going down.

"That text I got? Wasn't Walker," she said, and Finn tensed at Walker's name. "I know some EastPay things," she admitted. "And Walker and I? We're on the same side. But what if there's more going on?" She looked down at her hands. "And you're afraid to ask. Or say anything. Afraid to lose what you've worked so hard for. You ever think that?" She bit her lip, peered at Finn.

"All the time." He couldn't have said it better. Maybe he'd misjudged her. Maybe they were more alike than he thought.

"I'll tell you what I know. But first, what do *you* know?" she asked, taking a drink again.

"Nothing," he confessed. "That's why I'm here with you. I know someone made a fake recording of Brit's voice. Someone wanted Damarius to fight." He looked around, made sure no one was within earshot. "I don't know how it ties together, or if it even does. There's been some players from other teams missing on game day, but I'm afraid to find out more. What if we're legit cheating somehow? How will that affect my future? Reflect on me as a player? I been thinking all day," he said. "What would I do, ya know, if I found out something that could jeopardize my plans?"

"And?"

"I think I'd have to do the right thing."

"Isn't the right thing protecting your future? At all costs?"

He laughed halfheartedly. "That's something Walker would say. All for the game." He drank again, this time a solid gulp. It was calming. Reckless. It felt good to release. "I dunno."

"What if it escalates? If they go after who you love?"

He thought of the people he loved—not many. His dad he'd never known. Mom showed up every five years, but he no longer missed her. It was his grandmother on the sidelines of every football practice, talent show, science project. Grandma. Megan. Brit. Jamal. The thought of someone threatening them didn't make him fearful. It made him angry. He felt distant from Meg lately, but that wasn't her fault. It would get better once the season ended. It had to. Doubt crept in, and he took another drink to swallow it.

Tammy stood abruptly, reached down a hand to help him up, and he took it. "Come on," she said. "Let's do a lap."

She linked her fingers with his, and he stopped. "Don't flatter yourself," she grumbled. "You wanted to do this. Convince them you're on their side."

"Who?" he said.

"If we knew that, we wouldn't be holding hands now, would we?" She squeezed tighter. "Let's go, Geringer. We got a game to play."

Together they worked the crowds. They approached Jake and Reggie dancing with a couple of girls Tammy knew from the cheer squad. The guys slapped him on the back. The six of them danced. A short while later, they found Walker sitting along the bank with some girl from Finn's sixth period. They sat with him, and Finn introduced himself. Liv was her name. Student Council vice pres. Finn took a swig from Tammy's Nalgene bottle and offered it to Walker. Walker sniffed it before drinking and wincing. He laughed heartily. "Well, well, Geringer, look who's evolving and shit!" Finn made sure they approached each and every crowd of silhouettes, and that he subtly lifted and adjusted his mask to make sure people saw Finn Geringer was at Dante's, he was holding hands with Tammy Shaw, and he was having a good time.

They circled back to their spot under the darkness of the oak tree.

He flung himself down, leaned against a log, and rested his arms on his knees. No one had talked about secrets or lies. Cheating or scandals. It was all surface level—TikToks, newest songs, who was crushing on who. It's not like he was expecting a canon event, but he felt like he'd sacrificed a lot to show up tonight. He took a drink and raked a frustrated hand through his hair. "I didn't hear anything," he muttered.

"You will. Give it time."

He thought of Meg and the growing distance between them.

"Don't look, but Pamela's over at the next tree," Tammy whispered. "She's watching us." She leaned into him, nuzzled herself into his chest, laced her fingers into his.

"Tammy . . ." he started, uncomfortable.

"It's just for show," she hissed.

How could he explain that as a guy, this wasn't something that was easy to disengage from physically?

"Sorry, it's just—" This was nothing, he told himself. He ignored her, focused on the bottle. Drank. And then drank again. It no longer burned going down. She wasn't forcing him to drink, he knew that. This was him. All him. Wanting to forget the stress he didn't even recognize until the alcohol started taking it away. Football. Meg. His future.

Meg.

Would she understand this random girl cozying up to him? He felt lighter and so did the bottle, and when Tammy got up and returned with two beer cans and leaned back into him, he suddenly didn't mind. He cracked open the beer. Meg would be fine with this, he reasoned. Everyone would be fine with everything.

Thirty minutes later, the silence now comfortable between them as they drank and waited—for what, neither of them knew—Tammy nudged him. It felt good. He was feeling the buzz heavily.

"I don't come from a lot," she said. "Everyone seems to have more. More money, more choices, more future. I've got one shot. Cheerleading. I can't go to college without a scholarship. That's my ticket."

Finn found it comforting to hear that someone else understood the stakes. He felt closer to her somehow.

"It's my ticket out of this wasteland," she continued. "If that ticket's taken away from me? I don't know what I'd do. Does that make sense?"

It made total sense.

Tammy scowled at him and rested her head against his shoulder. "What do you know? Everyone loves Finn Geringer. You must've always had everything, too."

"No, actually." His words felt thick. Was he slurring? He took another drink. "Actually I haven't. Grandma's sacrificed everything"—he waved a sweeping hand—"to get me to this point. If it falls through?" He threw his hand down dramatically. "Whoosh," he said. It felt good to say it out loud, to be near someone who understood.

"You know what it's like . . ." she said, almost a purr. His senses heightened. ". . . To only have one way out?"

He did.

She pressed her cheek against his neck, as if seeking reassurance. Comfort. Closeness. He felt her, the connection of knowing she knew what he felt. A branch snapped behind them, the sound triggering a warning in him, faint, that he had a girlfriend, and her name was Megan. He squinted at the inky blackness behind him. "Hello?" he called. Words were hard. He struggled to his knees and shook his dizzy head. "I should go." The alcohol was pulling Finn under, he could feel it, and he was willing himself to tread water. He was only here to find answers.

His head fell straight back, and he whipped it back up. He felt Tammy's soft hand turning his chin toward her. "You shouldn't—" he started, but couldn't remember the rest.

"I know," she murmured, but her voice felt nice, like common dreams, like how she understood, and he should stop but he couldn't remember why. "Megan," he murmured, but he couldn't remember what her face looked like, and his body desired this more than he'd ever desired anything. He let her fingers run down his shoulder to his biceps down to his forearm and back up again. And this girl—Tammy—so soft and gentle and just like him, leaned in to kiss him. In the moment just before her lips touched his, he recoiled.

"No," he said, and stumbled to his feet. "No," he said again, his word chalky but firm.

She looked hurt and then embarrassed and then angry. "Don't flatter yourself," she snapped. "Nothing happened." And she stomped off into the darkness. Finn couldn't remember much, only that he needed to get out of this place, this was wrong, completely wrong, and he needed to be anywhere else. He stumbled away, fumbling with his phone—swiping around for his Uber app—and heading in the basic direction of the highway.

Meg couldn't sleep. After sending an iMessage to Kylie explaining why she'd been a no-show, and answering Kylie's multiple *WTF*s, she had crawled into bed. But her mind kept spinning. Her own mom was blackmailing her to dump Finn. What had her mom said? *"This is so much bigger . . ."* What did she mean by that?

When she and Kylie spoke with Ryan Quaid at the hardware store, he'd said his curfew ticket had kept him out of the game against EastPay. It seemed obvious to her that he was lured to East Pages precisely for that, but she had no proof.

Other opposing players were out here and there during games against EastPay. The average person would never notice. Student athletes missed games. It happened.

The week Finn played EastPay last year, his grandma was ill. Food poisoning. Had it been meant for Finn?

It was a long shot, but maybe Google would know. She moved her pile of pillows and opened her laptop. 2:43 a.m. Yikes. She typed in the search bar: *EastPay illness football players*. But it spit back out articles on NFL players with chronic traumatic encephalopathy. She tried multiple searches. Nothing showed about food poisoning or stomach flu with local players. She messaged Jamal.

> You awake?

She was about to give up when her laptop pinged.

> Am now. What's up.

> Heard you and Finn talked

> Was wondering when he'd spill

She rolled her eyes. Bro code. Her fingers flew across the keyboard with the speed of a *petit jeté*—a quick leap in ballet she'd perfected at age six.

> Listen, do you know anyone from ANY team who was out for illness against EastPay?

> No sorry maybe Damarius knows he was asking questions but hes laying low rn

> Kk. Thx. Night.

> U woke me up for that lol jk cu tmrw

Closing her laptop, she flung herself back on her pillows. Church was going to be rough tomorrow if she didn't get to sleep. In desperation, she shot a prayer up.

God, what should I do?

God was into exposing the truth. Maybe He'd know. And then it hit her, and she scrambled up and flipped open her laptop.

"Come on, come on."

Searching the PDFs of local church bulletins, she located last season. Two hours later, in the prayer requests for Sun River Church, she saw it:

Please pray for James Jackson and his grandson Rondell, a twelfth grader at Mountainview. Both suffered illness, and James was hospitalized for dehydration. Pray for his recovery, as well as full restoration of health for his grandson Rondell.

She searched the Mountainview High School website and found Rondell Jackson on the Eagles football roster.

"Bingo." She looked at the thumbnail pic of him and searched Instagram until she found him. She sent him a DM and prayed he'd read it, then shut her laptop and prayed for sleep.

• • •

When her phone alarm chimed at seven a.m., she checked her Instagram. Rondell had written her back.

> Hi, Meg. Lol. I've had stranger DMs no worries. I've always thought it was strange too. Our meal that night was spaghetti. I'm guessing bad meatballs. Sucked for both of us but more my grandpa. Thanks for checking in.

At seven thirty, Meg tiptoed out the front door. Church would be starting soon, the one place she could escape without interrogation. No parent in Texas would object. As she drove, the Sunday morning stillness hung on the trees, the closed stores, the quiet houses. She loved her church in West Oak—loved the pastor and his family—and she'd need to be back in time to attend with her parents. A two-service day for her, but she didn't mind. After checking her mirrors, she made a U-turn and headed north instead of south.

After parking at East Pages Community Church, Meg walked the lawn where she'd last talked to Ms. Tristan about Pastor Mike Menke—the stranger who'd spoken to her and Kylie at Jaybee's. She knelt down and examined the fairy circle of mushrooms. She plucked one, examined it closely, comparing it with the photos from the internet on her phone. These were the ones, and there were even more filling the lawn than the last time she was here.

When Meg walked inside, she did her best to stay inconspicuous, but unfamiliar faces glanced her way. Shoulders nudged others. And more strangers turned. Pastor Mike Menke was dressed in a suit, tie, and jacket. He saw her and blinked a few times as if he could blink her away. His sermon had the cadence of a carnival ride announcer, half shouting, half singing—waving his arms like an overly enthusiastic orchestra conductor. The collection plate was passed around three times.

After the service, she waited on the back lawn as cars filtered out, the damp blades of grass brushing her feet as she paced, following the arcs of mushrooms. She knew he'd find her eventually.

Sure enough, her back to the chapel doors, she heard the familiar drawl over her shoulder. "Well, well. What good acts did our church do to receive your presence this morning?" She turned to face Pastor Mike, his smile matching his gelled hair, plastered and stiff. Before she could answer, he added, "The Lord meets in West Oak, too. There a reason you needed to find Him here?"

"My understanding is the Lord welcomes all, Jew or Gentile, woman or man, East Pages or West Oak."

"Indeed." He squinted, though the cloudy day didn't require it. He waited for her to say more, and when she didn't, he added, still smiling, "Why are you here, Miss Kaufman?"

She walked over to him. "The night you paid me and my friend Kylie a visit? I was studying a certain Pioneers player. Watching film from last year. Turns out he missed playing the Spartans this season. Out sick that night. Flu symptoms."

"Terribly unlucky." Pastor Mike sighed with painful exaggeration, already bored with her.

"Right? Then there's Rondell Jackson. Quarterback for Mountainview High. Seen any tape of him yet? Twenty-two completions the game before the Spartans last year."

"You know a lot of football for a girl."

She ignored his sexist attempt to derail her. She'd held her tongue with far more difficult people at her parents' parties. "Strangely, he told me he got a nasty bout of food poisoning from spaghetti. And guess who they played that week? I mean, crazy coincidence, but how could the Spartans have anything to do with that? *Just*—as you would say—*unlucky*, right?"

Meg could see beads of sweat prickling his forehead. He licked his lips.

"I thought I'd come to the man of God in East Pages to see if he had any spiritual insight."

"Is that right," he said. "Seems to me you have a student illness. And a kid who ordered the wrong thing at a restaurant. Not sure the correlation you're aiming for."

"Correlation! Thank you." She reached down to the fairy ring and plucked a mushroom. Tossed it to him, and he caught it with one hand, his smile fading. He didn't say anything, but he pressed his lips together, stone-faced.

"*Chlorophyllum molybdites*," Meg informed him. "It grows on the lawn. Looks a lot like the kind you buy at the grocery, the kind you throw in salads and on pizza—*spaghetti*—sauce, but this one has a different effect. Takes a few hours, but it catches up. Vomiting, diarrhea, severe cramping."

"Is that right," he repeated, and Meg noted that he looked perplexed. Was he *this* good at faking it?

"Found it on the internet," she went on. "Mostly you're okay again once your body kicks out those angry amino acids, but in severe cases—like if you're old?—hospitalization might be needed to maintain that electrolyte balance. Did you know Rondell's grandfather ate the same bad food that day, but he got dehydrated from the vomiting? Had to go to the hospital and get his fluids replenished. Wild, right?"

"I'm sorry to hear that." But the words felt detached, hollow echoes in a grass field. "You implyin'—"

"No, no." She waved a hand dismissively. "Just brainstorming. Throwing it out there. Shootin' the shit." Her hand swatted her mouth. "Oh, sorry, Pastor. Unladylike language. How about we talk facts? In one night of research, I've found two players who've come down with some sort of stomach virus or food poisoning, right before they play good ol' Sparty. I find that . . . *unlucky*."

He folded his arms, dropping the mushroom.

"Right," she went on. "Then last season my very own boy-friend, the infamous Finn Geringer, the only one who could poke holes in Sparty's lineup, magically got a pizza delivered the same week West Oak was set to play EastPay. Delivery guy said it was a mistaken order and to keep it."

"He played that week—" Pastor Mike snapped.

"Funny you remember. Yes, and beat you handily. Probably because I fed him my own home-cooked anniversary meal. However, his *grandmother*, who enjoyed the delivered pizza, almost went to the hospital. Can you guess the pizza toppings?" She motioned at the fairy circle on the grass at their feet.

He licked his lips and stepped toward her. "As ingenious as that is, I can't take the credit."

"Really. Strange how the church lawn happens to be over-grown with them."

"You gonna round up every house that's got rampant lawn mushrooms? Gonna get half the town arrested." His eyes twinkled, like he thought her theory was cute.

"With all the money coming in for the Lord's work, the land-scaping looks neglected. Wouldn't hurt to share that with the authorities." She ruffled a few mushrooms with the toe of her sneaker. "Might be a danger to children."

His mouth formed a thin line. "Before you go blabbing empty accusations," he said through gritted teeth, "you be careful what else might come out. Not everything's on Wikipedia." He pressed the mushroom in her hands as they locked eyes. "I'd keep this little conspiracy theory tucked in your palm, unless you're ready to end a lot more besides your boyfriend's football career. I have a few secrets I could make public, too. But your mother may not appreciate you ruining her reputation."

My mother? Meg thought.

He stepped away from her, returned his plastered smile to his face. "Enlightening as always, Miss Kaufman. Go on and have a blessed day."

With a shaky foot on the accelerator, Meg drove to Finn's house. She waved to Mrs. Callahan out in the garden and let herself inside, the steam from the recent shower wafting over her as she hurried to his room. Finn, in a pair of jeans, was slipping a shirt over his head as she entered, and he jumped when he saw her.

"Hey," she said. "Just me. You okay?"

It had been days since they'd last seen each other. He wrapped all of himself around her, like he couldn't get closer to her in that moment. She felt the same and collapsed into him, the heat from the shower still emanating from his skin. She could smell alcohol faintly. *Had he— No, he wouldn't.* He hardly drank, and never to the point where she'd smell it on him the next day. They hadn't had a moment this close in a month. She knew both of them felt it—the heaviness of their separation lately—and neither wanted to let go.

"I have to tell you something," he mumbled. "Something I did. I can't remember it too clearly, but . . ."

So he *did* drink last night. "Don't beat yourself up." Her heart beat faster when she thought about this morning. "I have to tell you something, too." She pulled away so she could close and lock his door. "They tried to poison you."

His forehead crinkled. "What? Who?"

"I don't know. This whole town? Last year. The week before you played the Spartans. Did you get anything out of Walker?"

She was removing the mushroom from her pocket when his expression changed. He raked a hand through his hair. "Megan . . ."

"I know it sounds crazy. But so much has happened, and I haven't had a moment to tell you. By the way, UT has horrible reception. And Mom took my phone." Finn pulled away and sat down on his bed. She tucked the mushroom back into her pocket and continued. "Anyway, I looked up church bulletins last night."

"Yeah?" Finn looked exhausted. He didn't look like he'd found out anything from Walker. She'd figured as much. Urgency and fear propelled her words.

"I spoke with a football player who was out last year because of food poisoning."

"Mmm." Finn traced invisible lines on his jeans with his finger. Why wasn't he looking at her?

"And your grandma ate pizza that was *mistakenly* delivered," she rattled on. "I'd bet it was lawn mushrooms. Finn?"

"Mmm," he said again. Something was distracting him, the way his eyelids dragged heavy with more than lack of sleep.

She wanted to tell him everything, about the players' illnesses, the cop who pulled her over, the chance that someone siphoned her gas to keep her home last night. She hadn't had the chance without her phone.

But now, she couldn't shake Finn's expression. He looked *pained*.

"What is it?" She'd never seen him so wrecked. *What happened?* "What did you want to tell me?"

"I . . . Last night . . ." He dropped his head. "I . . . I don't know why this is so hard to say . . ."

Last night, Meg told Finn's grandma how her mom said they had to break up. Had Mrs. Callahan told him? Or was it that he had drunk too much? He closed his eyes.

"Aw, Meg . . ." He trailed off.

He opened his mouth to say something, but nothing came out. Tears filled his eyes. Meg reached her arms around him, letting go of all she wanted to say.

"We don't have to talk about it," she whispered.

He buried his cheek into the cleft of her neck, and she let her hair fall loosely over his face. His tears soaked her ear and chin. She knew him. Knew there was more he wasn't saying.

"Look, I don't care what people say," she said. "I love you." She could've sworn she heard a small muffled sob against her. His grandma must've told him about her mom's ultimatum. Nothing else would make him this miserable.

How do you choose between the person you love and your future? It wasn't just football he'd lose. If they didn't break up, would he be separated from his grandma?

She saw the locked door over his broad shoulder, wished she could lock out everything that invaded their life together. Right now, there was only the two of them. Not her parents, or EastPay High, or Pastor Mike. Not a town who hated them being together.

She lifted his bowed head and kissed him in a way she hoped would make them both forget what awaited them outside these walls.

He pulled away. "I can't—"

His distance felt weird. "Can't what?"

He blew out a breath—"Nothing." His words sounded tired. She'd assumed this was about her mom's ultimatum. Was there more?

"Is this about you drinking?"

"No." He swallowed. "Yes." Then he settled for "I don't know."

Whatever it was, she felt his inner wrestling match. She took his hands into hers, but his wrists hung limp.

"Hey," she said. "Want to talk about normal stuff? Like—*not* football stuff?"

He lifted and dropped a shoulder.

For months, there was nothing she'd wanted more. She missed him so much, felt like she hadn't spoken with him in weeks. But the possibility of players being poisoned—it *all* had to do with football. She also knew the only thing Finn wanted was a future in football. Even if her mom was bluffing and would never send Finn to a group home, Meg had discovered something that could implicate his school's football program. Could he transfer back? What would colleges think if he'd been associated with EastPay? She felt the weight of it all. Maybe they could wait a morning before tackling those thoughts.

She squeezed his hands. "Did you hear about Kylie and Tara?"

He smiled weakly. "Nuh-uh."

She linked his fingers with hers and sat on the bed next to him. He stayed quiet, but she sensed a tension in him lessen, just barely.

They spent the next hour side by side on pillows, rehashing old memories of Kylie and Tara, friends from his old school, and how much they used to hate each other but were now secretly dating ("Really?" Finn had said, but they both agreed they'd seen it coming), which unleashed a list of other memories from their old school together. She didn't mention how bummed their friends were he never texted anymore. She knew their friends. They'd let it go the second they all met up again later today. Besides, even as he smiled and joked with her, she could see a pained expression cross his face from time to time, like he was recalling something that weighed him down.

She knew how that felt.

Once back home, and all through church with her parents, she couldn't stop thinking about the unspoken words between her and Finn, but she didn't know what to do with those thoughts.

After church, before heading out with her friends, she opened her laptop to message Kylie that she was on her way, and that's when she saw the Instagram message from Finn: Not feeling well. Gonna have to raincheck.

Chapter 38

BRITNEY

Brit's mom had allowed her to take two mental health days, but insisted on Wednesday that it was time to "face the music." Spencer had said to lay low, but Brit was going for invisibility. In class, she kept her head buried in her books. During passing period, she walked with the briskness of a lawyer late for court, eyes straight ahead. Britney Wallace, Fearless Flyer.

What a joke. She was terrified.

"Brit!"

The second time, Finn's shout was clipped. Every student in the math wing turned. Finn caught up to her, and the close space between them made her back up against a locker. She faced him, trying to look unfazed to any onlookers.

"What's going on." It was a command, not a question. "You're never absent. You've ignored my texts. And calls."

"If you'd care for a duplicate of my notes for Calc, I suggest after-school tutoring on—"

"What the hell, Brit—" His voice rose and she shifted uncomfortably. Walker had ears and eyes everywhere. "Somebody's messing with you. And the way you're acting, you know who."

She leaned into her accent and spoke for all to hear. "Did you get tackled too much Friday?"

"Quit bullshitting. I'm your cousin." She shrank away from his volume and pushed a loose curl behind her ear to steady her shaking hand. She didn't need Finn making this worse. Who knew what else the chat room could do?

"I'd rather not hear that type of language, thank you," she said, but her voice squeaked.

She pressed on her tucked-in dress shirt, smoothing out creases, wrinkles, anything. She looked out of the corners of her eyes. She didn't see anyone recording; still, she no longer trusted anything. She ducked to dismiss herself, but he planted a hand against the locker, blocking her.

"We need to talk."

No! she wanted to scream. *Stop making a scene, Finn!*

With hands on hips, she said, "Sorry, Charlie!" She increased her accent in case anyone was watching. Smiled big and clueless. "I'm departin' after fifth period. No time for after-school fun. I'll have my face in my schoolbooks till Mama gets home from work." She knew she was laying it on too thick. She could tell by Finn's raised eyebrow.

He put his cheek next to hers, his lips close to her ear. "Look, I know you didn't do the Eli thing, so cut the crap."

She dropped her forehead to his shoulder, relieved that Finn believed in her innocence no matter what. "Please leave it alone," she whispered.

"I won't say anything," he promised. "You have my word. But I ain't leaving this alone. Did you piss off some cheerleader? Was it Tammy? Pamela? Amy Jane? The twins? Who?"

She knew Finn wouldn't snitch her out, but he also wouldn't stop until he knew. She pulled away, retreated a step. "Would you excuse me a moment?" she spoke in a heightened volume. "I left my planner at home. Just remembered a meeting with Ms. Ricky. Gotta write myself a reminder." She rummaged through her leather sack for a pen, clicked it open, and began scribbling on the palm of her hand. She made sure it was dark and wet, shiny with excess ink and thick as a tattoo. He leaned in, but she covered it.

"Listen," she said while scribbling hard against her skin. "I leave campus before sixth period, as you know, for the email I sent. That silly recording about Eli." She made sure to say that part extra loud. "I'm on house restriction, and Mom doesn't want anyone visiting, cousins included, for two weeks. I'm sure you understand. I need my cheerleading spot. There's no time to talk, especially with your schedule and mine. But thank you."

"You're welcome."

She knew her words sounded forced, but he played along. When she held out her hand to shake his, he took hold, and she gripped tight. She squeezed and locked eyes with him, and that's when she saw something click. He knew. Knew it before she felt the inky writing sticking their palms together as he peeled his hand away from hers. She tried to relax, hoping he wouldn't look down and read the transferred message until later, much later, when he was alone in a bathroom stall or his driver's seat and could safely read the faded copy of what she'd written, only right-side up and not backward across his sweaty palm: *62*.

Walker's number.

"Best of luck." She hoped no one else saw the way he wavered on his feet as he glanced down, how his nostrils flared. She did her best to distract anyone by curtsying goodbye elaborately, smiling the way people smiled when they run for office, all teeth and gums and promises, the smile of someone who knows the world's judging her every move.

Chapter 39
FINN

By Wednesday, the memory of Tammy was already dim, like those dreams you can't quite remember the minute you wake up. She hadn't spoken to him since, which was both worrisome and a relief. He'd tried to approach her once in the halls, just to check on her, but she gave a quick head shake and said coolly, "Not interested."

When he had his chance Sunday morning to tell Meg everything, he'd cowered. How do you confess something like *that* to the person you love? *"I lied. I went to Dante's Ravine. I wanted answers. I thought maybe people would talk if they thought you were out of the picture. I drank. A cheerleader named Tammy tried to kiss me. I left."* Technically they hadn't done anything, but he'd let himself get into a compromising position. Wasn't that just as bad?

Meg had been focused on telling him something about poisoning players, and he wanted to ask more, but how could he? How could he have a real conversation about anything else until he confessed?

As soon as Meg had left that morning, he'd collapsed onto his bed, wanting to shut out the world from his thoughts—what he'd done the previous night. Meg had said her mom took her phone, so he messaged her on Insta, canceling meeting up with their friends. No way he could act normal in front of them while keeping this secret. Of course, he'd gotten no response. What was there to say? He'd let them down. *Again.*

Monday night he'd driven to her house after practice—he

needed to do this in person—but the driveway was empty, and the curtains were closed. He'd left her a note in the mailbox, but still, nothing. Part of him was thankful. He knew once he told her, they might be over. As much as he owed her the truth, he dreaded thinking about what life would be like without her.

Then this thing with his cousin today. Walker's football number inked on his palm like a branded steer. He had dismissed his earlier suspicions of Walker because he couldn't imagine Walker gaining anything from making a false recording of Brit. He thought for sure it was some girl jealous of her popularity or position. But now that he knew Walker was tied up in a cheerleading prank, it made Finn wonder what else Walker could be tied up in. Was Walker the common bond?

Finn had promised he wouldn't say anything. Because of this and only this, he held it together until the final bell.

His anger was simmering, and when he walked into the locker room, Walker nodded a hello, bringing his anger to a full boil. As Finn laced up his cleats, Walker approached. "You okay, man?"

"Fine," he growled. "Just a lot on my mind."

"I'll bet," Walker said.

"Can we take a walk?"

"Sure, sure," Walker said agreeably.

Finn fumed but led the way outside through the doors. Walker followed, and they stopped next to the track, the sun beating down without warmth.

Finn folded his arms. "You wanna tell me what's going on?"

"What's . . . *going on?*"

"Oh, get off it! I'm not out here for your bullshit."

Walker raised an eyebrow.

"Here's it straight," Finn said. "Some of my toughest matchups aren't there on game night. My girlfriend's talking about poison, and not all those missing players were sick, but *some* were. And now Brit's suspended from cheer, which makes as much sense as a wide receiver becoming a nose tackle. You keep claiming you have no clue, yet you're hands down the most popular and connected guy at our school. I don't buy it. Be. Straight. With. Me."

Finn glared at Walker, daring him to look away. Walker broke first, sighed like a resignation, and nodded. He gestured with his head to help him line up the tackling dummies. Finn stood with his feet planted. Walker shrugged and started pulling one into place by himself. "We have a chat room," Walker said. "We call it 'The Game.' Invite-only. All anonymous. All students. We discuss football, that's it. We kept Brit out for obvious reasons."

A chat room? Why was that such a big deal?

"Why? She cheers for the team. She loves this school."

"Not as much as she loves telling the truth."

Finn followed Walker to the next dummy. Watched as Walker maneuvered it into place. *Why would that be a problem?* Walker said the chat room *discussed* football, that's it. "You rigging games?" Finn asked.

"What?" Walker placed a hand on his heart in mock insult. "No! Never. Come on, Finn. That's cheating. We just might *help* ourselves play a little better."

Finn felt the air leave him as if he'd been sacked from behind. "You set Ryan Quaid up that night Spencer hit him."

Walker bobbed his head side to side. "Not me, per se. Getting hit by the car was a bonus. But we were just going for the curfew violation."

It was one thing to have hunches, suspicions. It was another to know it as truth. Finn's throat felt like sandpaper. "Who's in on it?"

Walker searched the sky like he was trying to recall names. "Nobody. Everybody. I know certain people who have access, but we don't share screen names. Safer that way. More effective."

Effective?

"So who was behind Brit's suspension?" Finn pressed. "What the hell does that have to do with football and taking out our opponents?"

Walker smiled. "Do you know how Texas executions are done?" He grabbed the water bottle carrier. Walked to the filling station. Finn followed and watched as Walker filled the bottles. "A team of executioners stands behind a curtain. At the warden's signal, they all inject the lethal doses into the IV bag. But only one is pentobarbital, and the team members don't know which one. Saves them from feeling like they're killing someone, even if that someone deserved it." He closed one of the lids and pointed the bottle in Finn's direction. "But here's the interesting thing. Some of the executioners wear a hood so not even their own team knows their identity. If word ever gets back, and it only takes one, they could receive a lot of backlash from people who found out. But behind a curtain and under a hood, they can be bold."

Finn knew what he meant. He'd seen it on social media. People who created fake accounts just to troll. Say things they'd never say in person.

"We need people who protect our team to be bold," Walker

said with conviction while returning the full bottles to the carrier. "So we need to make sure they feel safe. Safety first. You feel me?"

"No."

Walker strolled back to the benches with the water bottles, talking over his shoulder as Finn followed. "Brit found out about the chat room recently, and she wasn't a fan. She would've snitched. You know she can't help herself. Plus, apparently she's some computer genius. No one knows what she can do with her hacking skills, so we needed to help her stay quiet. Make sure everyone who was part of The Game could continue feeling safe."

"The AI recording of her."

Walker set the bottle carrier with the bottles on the player bench and clapped. "He's smart on *and* off the field, folks."

How could he have been blind to all this?

He felt awful for the ways he had doubted Meg. *Oh, Meg.* He had to tell her the truth about what he'd done. And soon.

"Look," Walker continued, "you were bound to find out. I've been debating when to tell you since the start of the season. Just surprised to see what side of the fence you landed on. Especially after our talk that first night over beers. What happened to 'all for the game'?"

Finn felt sick. "This isn't what I signed up for."

"Sure it is. You signed up for the best chance at your future. We're giving you the best chance. Making sure that you shine. That I shine."

"This has to stop. I'll tell someone if Brit doesn't."

"Good luck." Walker shrugged. "You can't prove it. Nobody's names are on there. You can't find it. And even if you could, you couldn't take it down. It's the internet. We could just start another, and you'd never know. Come on, Finn. You told me what keeps you up at night. Think of your grandma."

Finn shook his head vehemently. "No. Not like this. I want my future the honest way."

A text buzzed on his phone.

Meg. Finally.

His last text had been,

> Seriously. You ok? You've been dark.

Her response?

> We need to talk.

On Sunday, she'd said there was more she needed to share with him. He'd said, "Me too"—understatement of the year—but neither of them had said anything. And now this text: *We need to talk.* No apology for ghosting him the past three days. He didn't blame her. He'd canceled Saturday. Then he'd canceled Sunday.

"Always the honest guy," Walker said, who was looking over his shoulder at Finn's text. Finn pulled his phone away from Walker's line of sight. Walker smiled. "I'm sure your girlfriend loves your honesty," Walker said. "How you don't lie. You know what else doesn't lie? Photos."

Finn felt the blood drain from his face. He thought of Tammy at Dante's, the way she'd leaned into him, linked fingers, said it was to get people on his side. To give him a chance at hearing gossip. Apparent secrets.

Then he remembered Tammy's words: *"Walker and I, we're on the same side."* Finn's rage pulsed through every part of him. "You son of a bitch." Everything she'd done that night had been calculated for the perfect camera angle. "Is Tammy's sister even an addict?"

Walker grinned. "Nah. Only child. And filthy rich." He shrugged, unapologetic. "Safety first. Like I said, if people feel safe, they're bolder. We need our fans to be bold. We have a championship to clinch." He headed for the locker room, leaving Finn stunned. Halfway across the track, he turned and gestured to the field around them. "All for the game," Walker said, smiling. "You feel me?" He winked, aimed his finger and thumb at Finn like a fake gun. "Yeah, you feel me."

Walker was gone by the time Finn could breathe normally again. His talk with Meg would have to be today, the moment football practice got out. He wouldn't chance her finding out from anyone else. Did someone really take photos? There was no way . . . It had to be just a threat.

Finn spoke a text to Meg as he headed inside to suit up.

Talk later today. Not over the phone

What time does practice start?

3:15

K

He walked into the bathroom, washed his hands, scrubbing the 62 off with his chewed-down fingernails. Jake approached him. "You and Walker cool?" he asked. Finn shrugged, grabbed a paper towel. Brit's faded writing was no longer visible on his palm, but he could still see the fear in her eyes as she scribbled. He walked outside and called her. It went straight to voicemail. Her phone must be off. He looked at his phone: 2:40. If he hurried, he could make it back before practice started.

Brit gazed blankly at Finn, one hand resting on the open front door of her house, her head tilted with her braid flopping over her shoulder. This new, quiet Brit unnerved him. No hello. No emotion. She looked past him to see if he'd driven with someone.

"Just me."

"Aren't you supposed to be at practice?"

"I heard," he said. "About the chat room. Walker told me how you found out."

Brit's eyes went wide. She spoke slowly. "Tell me you didn't say anything."

"I didn't tell him we talked."

She looked unconvinced. "How much did he tell you?"

"That you were gonna snitch. That they kept you out because they were worried you were too honest—that you wouldn't approve. They knew your hacking skills, were afraid you could mess with the site if you found out."

"Hardly." She laughed mirthlessly, then paused, confusion knitting her eyebrows. "Why was he so willing to tell *you*?"

"They have something over me." He recalled a moment of his night with Tammy—the snapping of the twig behind them. Someone *had* been there. "Something I've kept from Meg."

Brit looked at him funny, like he'd just claimed to have never seen a football. "Since when do you keep things from Meg?"

The comment wasn't meant to dig, but he winced.

Brit looked tired, resigned. "Whatever boneheaded thing you did, tell her before they do. They'll have nothing over you once she knows everything."

Finn dropped his head. "It'll break us up."

Brit didn't argue. He wished she'd say something like he and Meg could weather anything. But her mind seemed elsewhere. She kept looking over his shoulder into the street. "You should go," she croaked. "You're late."

He buried her in a hug, but she was right. Getting here had taken longer than he'd expected. Every red light. "I'll just have to run bleachers. It's fine."

His cell phone buzzed. He kept Brit in an embrace with one arm, pulling the phone from his pocket with his free hand. It was Meg:

Where are you?

"Please don't tell her you're here," Brit said, reading his text. "She'll want to know why."

"So?"

"Please," Brit repeated, her voice full of desperation in a way that tugged at Finn's heart.

He wrote back:

@practice

Really?

Can't talk now. I'll call later.

He shoved the phone into his back pocket and hugged Brit tighter. She mumbled into him, her tears soaking his shirt, "If they find out you were late to practice because of me—"

"Hey!" He lifted her chin and caught her glossy eyes. "Nothing's gonna happen to you. Not on my watch."

She smiled ruefully. "Please go."

He nodded, turned to leave, but stopped. "If you found out that the sport you loved was being run by a bunch of cheaters, would you still want to play?"

She thought for a moment. "That depends."

"On?"

"Can you get rid of the cheaters?"

He felt the look on his face go vacant, defeated. "I don't know how."

She looked at him sadly. "Yeah, me neither."

He squeezed her hand, then drove back to school. Brit was right. He needed to tell Meg before someone else did. Tonight. He voice-texted her as he drove.

> Dinner my house after practice?

It showed as delivered, but she didn't respond.

Finn could only remember flashes of his night with Tammy, like a strobe light of fuzzy, out-of-focus memory pictures. That alcohol had wrecked him. He remembered the rushing water, Tammy's eyes—worried, comforting—her fingers tracing his biceps, her body leaning. Closer. Closer. He slammed a hand against his steering wheel.

He'd done this. He'd gotten wasted in the arms of a girl he barely knew—for what? *"Play or get played,"* she'd told him, and then by convincing him to play others, she'd played him. He slammed his hand against the steering wheel again. He tried to get his mind on something else—but every thought drifted back to Meg and a dark undefined night with someone who wasn't her.

Fifteen minutes later but still wound tight, he entered the empty locker room. The team was already on the field practicing.

"Geringer." Coach Goode's voice echoed against the lockers.

Here we go, Finn thought. He walked into the office, the freezing air-conditioning blasting its arctic cold against his bare arms. Wilkins and the other coaches were on the field, but Coach Goode busily worked at a computer.

"Hey, son. Heard UT's recruiters are interested in you."

Finn cleared his throat. "That the rumor?"

"That's what I'm hearing." Goode reached down, slipped his cleats on, and began tying the laces. "Ohio and TCU reps are coming next weekend. You go out to a meal, you pay for your own, you hear me? We do this by the books. Nothin' to jeopardize our titles."

"Yessir."

"Oh, son." Goode placed a whistle around his neck, reached for his phone and his playbook. "You left your backpack earlier. Running errands?"

Finn scanned the office and found his backpack under a chair.

"Your girlfriend offered to bring it to you," Goode continued. "But I said we didn't mind."

Finn's body stiffened. "Girlfriend?"

"Oh, your girlfriend stopped by. Didn't see you on the field, so poked her nose right into the guys' locker room. Second time, I might add. Luckily it was only me."

Finn couldn't move. The words crawled out of his mouth. "What'd you tell her?"

"Practice was canceled."

"But—" Finn gestured toward the direction of the stadium where his team was running plays and hitting tackling dummies.

"For *you*. Practice was canceled for you." Goode reached for Finn's backpack and handed it to him.

"It was?"

"No. But you seemed to think so. You got something more important than football today?"

"No," he said with finality. "Which is why I needed to take care of some things."

Coach Goode sighed. "I spoke with Walker. Was wondering when you'd find out."

Finn's heartbeat quickened. "You know about the chat room?" he said, his anger surging. "Why don't you stop it?"

Coach Goode looked at him, a sad expression in his pale eyes. "Easier said than done. You think anyone's gonna tell me everything? I just hear rumors, but I hear enough. Play like I coach. Keep your head down. Focus on your talent. Stay out of that garbage."

"But it's cheating," Finn said. "Those students—that chat room—they're trying to mess with the integrity of the game." All along, Coach Goode *knew* about his players rigging the game? "I need to talk to Coach Wilkins."

Coach Goode flew to his feet and closed the distance between them so quickly, Finn flinched. "You think he doesn't know?" Coach whispered, even though no one was around.

Finn recalled the one time during a game when he'd asked Coach Wilkins about the missing players. How Wilkins had told him not to waste his halftime.

"How do you think he's kept his position?" Coach Goode shook his head, and his eyes pleaded with Finn. "Do *not* talk to him about this. You have such a future, Finn. Don't mess with that."

"Then why don't *you* talk to him?"

He hesitated, then admitted, "I need this job." His next words were slow. Deliberate. "And you don't know who he knows."

Finn understood Coach Goode then, the way he implied that his safety, not just his job, was on the line. They stayed silent, until Coach Goode cleared his throat and sat back down at the computer. "Your girl insisted you texted that you were here," he said, "so I told her I sent you home."

Coach had covered for him?

"Thank you, Coach."

"Now, get changed and give me fifty bleachers. I'll tell Wilkins you were making up an assignment."

• • •

Finn's quads burned. Running fifty sets of bleachers was no joke. By the last ten, his legs were cramping, but he welcomed the pain, drove into it as if he could erase what he had done if he suffered enough.

The pain resurfaced when he parked in his empty driveway. No Meg waiting for him. He called her, tapping his steering wheel and waiting. It rang and rang, eventually going to voicemail. He pulled nervously at his shirt, pressed against him from the max AC blowing. His sweat had formed the shape of a heart across his chest down to his stomach, caked and dried now, stiff as cardboard.

He texted her.

> Sorry I wasn't at practice.

She responded.

> You lied.

> Went to Brit's. Had to check on her.

> Why

He called again. Voicemail.

> Will you plz pick up?!

She started to write, then stopped. He saw the interminable three dots. Thinking. Thinking. They disappeared. Reappeared. He killed the engine and reached for his backpack. As he opened his car door, his phone lit up.

> Finn, we have to break up.
> I found out some things.

His phone tumbled out of his hand onto the ground. He

retrieved it, a single damp leaf clinging to the screen, and his mind flashed to that night—damp leaves, the river, Tammy's eyes. He redialed, and again—voicemail.

Pick up, he wrote as fast as his heart was beating. This was not how he wanted her to hear about it, by someone sending her compromising photos of him at night with another girl. Please, Megs. I'm so sorry. Can I explain?

This is hard enough. Don't call or text.

Shit. Walker must have sent her the pictures.

Chapter 41

MEGAN

Meg had gone to bed hours ago, but she couldn't sleep. She'd done it. She'd actually done it. *I broke up with Finn Geringer.* The day kept replaying in her head.

That morning, her mom had returned her phone, on the condition it would be used to break things off with Finn. She'd had no intention of doing so.

She'd caught her dad on the way to his car.

"Dad, I need your help."

He'd offered help so many times throughout her life. From calculus and APUSH down to middle school math. She'd never once taken him up on it. It was a game they'd play. He'd offer. She'd refuse. Say no problem was too hard for her. He'd respond, "That's my girl." And he'd say something about real winners seeing the world as a puzzle, not an obstacle. She sort of believed he took pride in how she refused his help.

Her dad paused, maybe thinking the same thing. He tucked his keys in his pocket. It was a sweet gesture for a father always on the move, never home. He was listening.

Meg took a breath and forged ahead. "Can you make a call to Mrs. Callahan and help file whatever papers are required for guardianship?"

He waited a beat. "Can't guarantee the expediency."

"It's okay," Meg said. "It's something."

He nodded. She nodded.

"Why's Finn having you ask?"

And there it was. The subtle jab at Finn's character.

"He's not," she said. "*I'm* asking. Finn would rather be shipped off to a group home than ask you for help. Or admit that he can't take care of things himself. But I'm admitting that we *need* your help."

Her dad, the lawyer, was rarely at a loss for words, but he stood still, the way he'd listen to Berlin's Philharmonic when she used to practice her *Swan Lake* at home. Like he was trying to discern each instrument.

He yanked his keys from his pocket. "Tell Finn I'll see what I can do."

She closed the distance between them and hugged him, not like the polite hugs that she respectfully gave her parents but the ones she gave when she was little, all arms and legs squeezing. He chuckled. "All right," he said. "Go on, or you're gonna be late to school."

Hours later, she'd had early dismissal, so she'd driven to East-Pay to catch Finn before practice. She didn't want to do this behind his back. His car wasn't in his usual spot, so she'd texted. He said he was here, so she went to the bleachers and scanned the field. She couldn't find him in the mix of players. One of the coaches headed toward the locker room. He gave a small jerk of the head, beckoning her to follow. She stepped down and made her way around the concession building to the side entrance.

The door was ajar. Her voice echoed in the empty locker room. "Hello?" Silence, so she tiptoed inside. "Hello?"

The coach was in his office, his back to her, talking to someone on the phone. "Yes, okay. Thought you should know. Will do." He hung up. Still didn't acknowledge her.

She knocked on an empty locker to catch his attention. "Excuse me, sir? Finn texted he was at practice, but he's not out there. Is he okay?"

The coach cleared his throat and swiveled his chair to face her. He'd beckoned her—she was sure of it—but now he looked at her as if she'd intruded and trespassed.

"I canceled practice for Finn today."

Finn had never texted that. "Why?" She hoped he wasn't in trouble.

"Something you need, Miss Kaufman?"

It unnerved her, how everyone in East Pages seemed to know her first and last name and enjoyed pointing it out, as if by calling her by name, they held some power over her. She glanced away, and that's when she saw Finn's backpack on a bench, lopsided with textbooks. "Oh," she said. "Want me to take that home for him then?"

The coach cleared his throat again, and rubbed one of his nostrils with a knuckle. "Not allowed. I'll take it." He walked over and lifted the backpack, then stopped in front of her. "Just got off the phone with your mama before you barged in."

Meg kept quiet. He *had* motioned for her to come. And now he'd called her mom? How'd he even have her number?

"She says she didn't know you were paying us a visit today," he said. "Says there would be no reason, considering you no longer had a boyfriend here."

Meg felt shaky. She didn't know what to say, so she settled on "Sounds like something she'd say."

"Hmm." He walked back into his office, dropped the backpack next to a filing cabinet. Meg could feel the air-conditioning of his office seeping out, the draft of freezing air against her bare arms. "She suggested you head straight home. I think that's wise."

Twenty minutes later, Meg opened her front door, a hollow pounding in her rib cage that hadn't stopped since she'd left EastPay.

Her mother was sitting on the entryway bench, her mouth a pencil line of disapproval, her body ramrod straight with anger. There was a wall clock, but she looked at her watch for emphasis.

"We had early dismissal, so I went to talk with Finn in person," Meg said, holding her poise and control.

"This has to stop."

"You told Finn's coach it already did."

Mrs. Kaufman stood. "That's because we gave you boundaries. Since when do you blatantly disregard—"

"What's this really about?" Meg quipped.

"You used to be better before Finn."

Hearing his name rubbed Meg raw. "You never had a problem with Finn until he transferred."

"That's not true."

Meg was so sick of people lying. Cops, coaches, her parents. Her mom's words sent her over the edge. She was done with watching her every move, as if she were on stage. She wasn't a ballerina anymore.

"It's totally true! When Finn played football at our school, you came to the games, invited him for dinner. Suddenly, since he's transferred, he's the enemy. You're no better than anyone in East Pages, trying to break us up for your own self-interest!"

The slap came hard and quick. Meg's hand touched her cheek, the tender redness already throbbing. Her mother had never hit her, and she looked as shocked by it as Meg. With a shaky hand, she lifted her drink from the side table. "Don't you dare align me with that town." Mrs. Kaufman steadied her breathing. "People are talking. Saying you're snooping where you don't belong. Ms. Tristan mentioned you've been acting paranoid—"

"Wait." Something struck Meg, sent a shot of adrenaline coursing through her. "The night I was out. You had book club. She was here."

"Of course, but that has nothing to do—"

"I think she's the one who went through my room."

"No one went through your room!"

"Someone was there that night!"

"Please, Megan." Her mother looked desperate. She spoke low, her voice catching like she was ready to cry. "That lady has contacts. People who could ruin our family's good name." Meg rolled her eyes. All she cared about was her reputation. "She saw you at her church."

"Is that a crime? I was only there because of you!"

Her mother cocked her head, set her drink down. "What?"

"Something was familiar about it, so I pulled in. I didn't realize it until later. The logo on the building. The same logo was on the envelope you tore up. Remember? East Pages Community Church? You said it was junk mail." Mrs. Kaufman's eyes flickered with recognition—Meg was right.

Meg reached into the pocket of her hoodie, tossed the shriveled mushroom she'd shown Finn onto the table. It rolled, banking against her mother's empty vodka glass.

Meg waited for a response, but her mom looked lost.

"Chlorophyllum molybdites." Her mother shook her head. "Lawn mushrooms," Meg explained. "Toss 'em on salads, in a stir-fry, grind 'em up and sprinkle in a Gatorade." She noticed how she had far less fear speaking up recently. Was her mom changing, getting smaller the more she drank? Or was Meg changing, stirred up by these injustices she was discovering? "Not sure how it's being delivered, but players are being poisoned, Mom. Other players. Not EastPay. And I think your pastor's supplying it."

"He's *not* my pastor." Her mother's words were ice.

"So you know him."

She blinked.

"You're involved in this?"

"No!" she yelled.

"Then what do you know?"

Mrs. Kaufman's mouth clamped shut.

Meg was furious, but she spoke calmly. "Fine. Dad should be home from work in an hour. I'll ask him about it."

Her mother's eyes went wild with fear. "Do *not* involve your father."

"What? He's a lawyer. It's his job to do research. And if you know nothing . . ." She trailed off.

"Please. Believe me, I'm not involved. But you can't bring this up to him." Her mom's breathing sounded labored.

"Then tell me the truth. Tell me how you're connected. And don't lie, because I'm so over this town's bullshit."

Her mother reached for the empty glass with unsteady fingers, walked to the living room, and poured herself another vodka tonic before sitting down.

Meg followed, and her mom scooted over, made space for Meg on the couch. Mrs. Kaufman took a sip, and with eyes cast downward, she began. "This summer, your father started working a DUI case, going for hard sentencing, working late hours." Her voice was quiet, defeated. "I was out one night with some ladies from the club—one of them was launching a cosmetic line, anyway, that's no matter—and, well, it was like he was waiting for us as we left the bar."

"Who? Dad?"

"A cop. I didn't do anything, didn't run a stop sign, nothing like that, but I saw the blue lights as soon as I turned the corner."

Meg was piecing this together. A cop. A bar.

Mrs. Kaufman bowed her head. Didn't look up as she said, "He pulled me over and I panicked. You don't know what it's like with the way the police treat people like us. Being pulled over by a cop late at night. Anyway, I was afraid—wasn't sure he'd recognize me—or know I was respected in this town—and I—" She stopped, then mumbled, "I offered him money."

"Are you crazy?"

"No crazier than a lawyer fighting the hardest DUI case in the state and having a wife getting a DUI midcase."

"You drove *drunk*?"

"Don't say it like it's a strange thing around here."

But it was. It was for Megan Kaufman, daughter of the pristine and exemplary parents, who kept their bad habits within the house walls like a good Texas couple. Outside they were metaphorically linked arm in arm in enviously perfect matrimony, head attorney and community outreach socialite, regal in reputation among the three towns of West Oak, East Pages, and Trussels.

Mrs. Kaufman continued, an outpouring of unfiltered honesty, a confession expelling from her like a breath held too long.

"He refused, saying that bribing an officer was illegal. I, in turn, refused the Breathalyzer test, so I was taken to the station."

"Holy shit, Mom."

"Language," she corrected.

Meg found herself apologizing despite the irony of the moment.

"Before I could call your father," Mrs. Kaufman continued, "a man I didn't recognize came into the station. I guess the cop phoned him about me. He said an arrangement could be made."

"What *kind* of arrangement?" Meg's stomach churned. "Do you mean . . ."

"God, no! Not that. He heard I'd offered money. And for the right price, he'd make it 'go away.' So we waited the three hours until I could safely take the Breathalyzer. I passed, Ubered to my car, and was home before your father got back from work."

"So this guy still takes your money?"

"It has to be funneled."

Funneled? Meg channeled her party posture, stayed poised and steady while her confusion boiled inside. "Like through a business?"

Her mom paused. "Or a church."

It was all becoming clear.

"East Pages Community," Meg said.

"My monthly donations are tax deductible. Your father leaves me alone about that kind of spending. I thought it would be enough." Tears welled, her eyes suddenly wild with fear. "But if you don't stay away from Finn—"

Meg flew to her feet. "That's extortion!" She clenched her

fists. Blew out a long breath and spoke calmly. "What does Finn have to do with Pastor Mike blackmailing you?"

"Pastor Mike?" Mrs. Kaufman tilted her head. "No, no. He just takes a cut. I'm sure the officer does, too."

"But the guy you didn't recognize. The one who made the arrangement."

"At the station that night?" She chuckled darkly. "That's Finn's coach. He conveniently ran into me at the grocery store shortly after. Introduced himself. Reminded me with a smile how EastPay fans don't love their players dating anyone from rival schools."

Meg's head was spinning. "Why does it matter?"

"Oh, come on, Meg! You know how tightly football programs hold their secrets. You're a direct threat to that. The way you're digging. Showing up where you shouldn't." Mrs. Kaufman quieted, then searched Meg pleadingly. "You have to break up with Finn."

"Or what?"

Mrs. Kaufman drew her eyebrows together, like she couldn't believe her daughter didn't see it plain as day. "It'll come out that I bribed an officer after a DUI. A cop camera caught it all."

Meg shook her head like she could shake away her crashing reality. "So? Won't the officer get busted, too?"

"He never took the bribe! And there's no trail linking him to my money. It's me donating every month out of the goodness of my heart. It matches my reputation of generosity toward the church, God, and the people of every town in the county." She spat those words like she couldn't get the poison off her tongue fast enough.

"But there was no DUI."

"Don't you know where you live? Reputation's far more

important than innocence or guilt. You think people won't be told that I stayed the night at the station? That I couldn't pass the Breathalyzer test? You know that a good name in this ridiculous town is everything." She pleaded softly, "Please."

"So the pastor then? Did you know about him poisoning students?"

Mrs. Kaufman harrumphed. "No. Never heard anything even close. But if you haven't noticed yet, a few adults in EastPay like to play sheriff and mayor. And in his case, God. Mike Menke's pockets are lined with people's love of God and football. A winning team means God's on their side and they're doing something right." Her voice had the mocking cadence of someone giving a sermon in a pulpit. "The better the record, the bigger the tithes to thank God for His favor toward East Pages. So, no. I wouldn't be surprised if he was behind that. But if you don't have proof, don't expect to find it." She turned to Meg, tears in her eyes. "I swear to you, on the state of Texas, I knew nothing about it. You have to break up with Finn. Please. I know I'm thinking of myself for once, but—"

"For once?" Meg barked out a laugh. "When have you ever thought of me?"

She stood to face Meg. "Everything I've done since the day you were born has been—"

"To control me."

"To give you opportunities! You don't get it because all you've experienced is privilege. We live in a white county, Megan. I'm not just representing you in this. I'm a respected Black woman in a county where we make up less than ten percent of the entire population. And we live in the South. Do you understand how hard I've worked to give you the opportunities you have?"

Meg felt her mom's hot breath, smelled the alcohol creeping through her nasal passages. She winced. "No. It was to give *you* every opportunity. You said it yourself—reputation is more important than anything. The better you look, the more attention you get. And the better I look, the better you look."

"It's not like that."

"It's exactly like that!" Finn's ringtone blared. She clawed her phone out of her back pocket. She stared at it, let it ring. She wanted to answer, but she was full of fury. He immediately texted:

Sorry I wasn't at practice.

With fast and angry fingers, she typed a text to Finn.

You lied.

His next text took her off guard. He'd gone to Brit's. Before practice? Was she okay?

"Meg—" her mom started, but Meg ignored her. Why, Meg texted.

Her phone blared Finn's ringtone again. Meg sent it straight to voicemail. She wasn't going to discuss this in front of her mother. She needed to finish this conversation.

Will you plz pick up?!

Finn's desperation ripped at her. She started to type again. "Megan!"

Meg stopped typing long enough to hold up her palm. Not now.

A hand gripped Meg's wrist. Not angrily. When she looked up, tears were chasing down her mother's cheeks, dripping off her chin like the fat drops of last week's rain. "Megan," she whispered. She dropped her hands limply at her sides. "If you stay with him, you know they'll ruin me. We'll lose everything."

Meg faltered. She knew what her mom meant by everything. Irene Kaufman was a recipient of multiple awards from several Black business organizations for her example, leadership, and service. This was more than just EastPay, West Oak, and Trussels. She thought back to her ballet idol, Annabelle Chang, when news came out that she'd tested positive for PEDs. Annabelle had insisted it was just acne medication. But it didn't matter—anything on the World Anti-Doping Agency's list was illegal, performance-enhancing or not. All her sponsorships dropped. Praise recanted. Awards stripped. Scholarships retracted. An award had even been started because of her and named after her—the Annabelle Chang Award for Young Female Minority Athletes. Her name was removed, and it was renamed simply the Award for Female Minority Athletes. Meg was eight at the time. She hadn't heard anything about her since, but that's all anyone in the ballet community remembered of Annabelle Chang. Not her talent.

Meg took a deep breath and typed before she could take it back.

> Finn, we have to break up.
> I found out some things.

Again her phone rang. Again she sent it to voicemail.

A series of pleading messages appeared on her screen, but her eyes blurred from tears, and she couldn't read them all.

She typed one last message.

> This is hard enough. Don't call or text.

Then she blocked him and turned her phone off.

"Done." Her words felt empty. Her mother took a quivering breath, her whole body exhaling, sinking into itself in relief. They stood quietly for minutes. Meg couldn't cry. She felt hollowed out. Finally she turned, and without any limp—she wasn't sure if her dad had told her mom she'd been faking her injury, but either way, she was done with lies and cover-ups—she walked upstairs and closed herself in, turning her lights off and crawling onto her bed, curling up with a pillow and not moving a muscle, though sleep never came.

Chapter 42
FINN

Finn's head rattled like a western diamondback's tail.

He was flat on his back looking at the blurry Friday night lights of the Cedar Park Ducks' stadium, waiting for the air to return to his lungs. He'd been mowed down, bruised, and knocked flat. He'd love to blame the guards and tackles for not sealing their players in, but he knew this was on him. His mind was elsewhere. On Meg. On the chat room. On the fact that he couldn't talk with Meg about the chat room. Who was involved? To what extent? Was his team winning only because it wasn't a fair game? He wished the two of them could sit down and talk.

Them.

There was no more "them." He'd ruined that.

He was actually thinking this when the Ducks' cornerback read the play and killed his chance of a clean catch, ripping him down to the turf. Finn stood, shook himself like a wet dog, and ran back to the huddle with his ears ringing.

Thomas White called the play: "Offset Right Near Syracuse on two!" *Syracuse*, Finn reminded himself as he ran into position. Stretch right. *Stanford* meant stretch left. *Syracuse*, stretch right. So much harder to think after a knock to the head. The center snapped the ball. The tight end held the outside linebacker and Finn cut wide to block, but the corner read him and darted around to tackle the receiver. The play was dead. Again.

Halftime came. Scoreless and down by ten, the team jogged to the locker room, but Coach Wilkins stiff-armed Finn across his chest. "What the hell's happening out there, Geringer?"

"Uh"—Finn fumbled his words—"dunno. O-line isn't directionally blocking to open up the holes."

"You know damn well they're doing their job. You got no threats out there. Where's your head?"

"I— Sorry, Coach. There's a lot on my mind."

"You're gonna let girl problems get you decapitated every play?"

Finn swallowed. So his coaches had heard. Which meant everyone had heard. "No, Coach."

"You wanna meet a bench for a quarter? That what you're saying?"

"No, Coach."

"Then remember why you play for EastPay." He stepped to the side. Allowed Finn to pass. Finn nodded and jogged to the locker room.

Spencer came up alongside him. Made sure no one was within earshot before he muttered, "Whatever you found out, lock it up."

Finn slowed to a walk. Did Spencer know about the chat room? He felt relieved he might not be alone. Still, he had to tread cautiously.

"What do you know?"

"Not the time." Spence gave a quick shake of his head. "And get over your girl quick."

Meg was all Finn had thought about since their breakup, but he hadn't spoken a word to anyone about it.

"So you heard, too?"

Spencer lifted an eyebrow. "This *is* EastPay. Look, don't assume you get a pass just because of a bad breakup. They'll come after you if you keep playing like garbage. You have no idea what you're up against. You need to play like you're playing for your grandma's well-being. Because you *are*." Finn whipped his head toward Spencer, but Spencer jogged off before anyone could suspect them of talking too long.

Coach yelled a lot during the halftime talk, but Finn hardly paid attention. Harassing Meg was one thing. But there were students out there who would threaten his *grandma*? For football?

Surprisingly, he was put back in at the start of second half. Spencer's words repeated in his head, lighting a fire in his belly.

Some play-calling came from the sidelines, and Thomas White nodded. In the huddle, he shouted, "Offset Right Near, Power O Strong on two!" They'd run this play only twice in practice. Finn had to zone in.

They ran through the middle with Finn kicking out the outside linebacker, the tight end releasing to seal the inside linebacker, and the guard leading the way like a bowling ball knocking over pins, plowing through any guards trying to fill the hole.

It worked.

In five minutes, they'd scored their first touchdown of the game, and the Spartan crowd roared and pounded their shoes on the aluminum stands of the guest section.

The rest of the game was evenly matched, leaving them with the ball in the last minute on their own forty-yard line, still down by three. "I right, twenty-nine sweep!" Thomas shouted over the Ducks' fans, who were trying to drown out the quarterback's voice.

"No!" Finn shouted. Ten sets of eyes turned to him. Nobody

ever disagreed with the quarterback. "The corner's expecting that!" Finn continued. "He reads it every time." He pictured his grandmother, and it kept him bold. "Remember Edelman against the Ravens in 2015?" Every player knew the Patriots' wide receiver who'd been quarterback in college, and the trick play that secured the AFC divisional playoff game. "Line up for the twenty-nine sweep to sell the defense. White, you audible a Wildcat spread option. Take the snap, backward pass to Collins wide. Collins, make the throw. By the time their D seals the lane—closes in on you—I'll be halfway to the end zone." Finn knew he had the speed and Collins had the arm to pull this off.

"You callin' plays now?" White shouted.

He ignored him and said, "ON TWO!"

They lined up stretched left. On the second "hut!" Finn took off like the day he raced Spencer neck and neck, like he was trying to outrun his grandmother's arthritic future, or beat the feeling seeping into his peripheral vision, creeping in on the edges, that his team was far from golden.

He willed his quads to reach farther, his arms to pump faster. Every muscle burned and begged for oxygen as he strained forward.

He didn't have time to make sure the ball was snapped cleanly to White and that a backward pass made it into Spencer's hands, or if Spencer could deliver under pressure and launch the ball. But when Finn looked over his shoulder, a perfect forty-five-yard spiral was soaring straight for him. He reached up and nabbed the ball, beyond his defender and too far for the safety to reach Finn before he crossed into the end zone, making it 13–10 as the clock ran out.

No time and no need for the extra point, and the crowd of

Spartans whooped and danced in their red hoodies and blue jeans like a waving Texas flag. Finn's team dogpiled while the Ducks walked off the field. Finn wasn't sure whether the coaches would be pissed or elated as he headed toward the sidelines.

Coach Wilkins approached Finn. Coach Stockton and Coach Goode flanked Wilkins on either side. "White says it was your idea."

Finn shrugged. "Not really. All the plays I've learned. Studying the other teams. I knew it would work. I'd say it was your coaching."

The coaches' eyes pinballed between one another, unsure how to respond.

A local news crew interrupted, shoving bright lights and a microphone at him and Spencer. "We're here with Spencer Collins and Finn Geringer, the playmakers who sealed the victory against the divisional rivals, the Cedar Park Ducks. Had you practiced this route? Were you planning to use it?"

Finn motioned to Coach Wilkins. "There's a reason Coach has us memorize so many plays. Like he says, 'Gotta be ready for everything, so you can make sure they're ready for nothing.' I followed his coaching." The cameras and lights turned to the three coaches, who stood, arms crossed, jaws clenched, forcing tight smiles as they nodded along.

Finn and Spencer headed toward the buses. New beads of sweat prickled the back of Finn's neck. His shoulders dropped as he exhaled the stress from facing the coaches. "Stand tall," Spencer whispered. "You handled that well. Walk away like you don't know a thing."

He so badly wished he didn't.

Chapter 43

BRITNEY

Damn, Britney Wallace can fly!
The most amazing gymnast on the team.
Have you seen her walk? It's like her feet have springs.
I heard she doesn't drink alcohol during the season.
Is she dating anyone? She should date so-and-so.
Even her curls bounce, just look!

Rumors about Brit had always been fun, but now there were narrowed eyes, whisperings like trees rustling every time she passed a group of girls in the halls. No one could believe she was behind her insensitive speech about Eli, but everyone did because it was bubbly, bouncy Britney—*Yes, her! Can you believe it?*—and Brit knew it was more fun to gossip about the unthinkable.

Not knowing which students were part of the chat room, she watched her every move, made sure she was perfect and pristine in every class. She kept her shoulders back and eyes unblinking during every passing period, walking with purpose. If she stopped, she might collapse. Inside, she was terrified. Even her two closest friends, Dalisa and Jalisa, were acting distant. They still texted each other funny gifs and still sat together during lunch, laughing about boys and classes, but their eyes darted around a lot. When the bell rang after lunch today, Dalisa squeezed her hand under the table and whispered in a rush of words, "Be careful, love you, 'kay."

As she walked the student parking lot to head home after fifth period, she heard sniffling one row over. She paused midstride and peeked around the corner of a car to find Emma Li, a tenth grader on JV cheer. She never talked to Emma, but she'd recognize that closely cropped dark hair anywhere. Strange. Emma wasn't in the locker room dressing for practice. She was sitting on the asphalt, her head resting against the back of an old minivan, the bumper dwarfing her body. She raked her hands through her hair, the gelled spiky pieces poking out between her fingers. Her eyes were red-rimmed and swollen from crying.

Brit's fingers tightened around her keys. *This isn't your problem.* Her mom had lent her the car today for the first time since her cheer suspension, but what if someone spotted her "wasting time"? Not getting home to her sixth period restricted environment? Would Walker hear about it? Find a way to extend her suspension?

Emma's head snapped up, and Brit jumped like she'd been caught spying. She smiled weakly. "Hey." Emma didn't respond. "You okay?" She was met with silence.

Brit searched the lot. Nobody would see them from where Emma was tucked behind the minivan. She walked closer and knelt beside her. "Well, I know a thing or two about rough days." Emma's eyes flitted to her and then away. Brit crouched, waiting.

She'd learned during cheer camp team building that sometimes it was best to sit and "be" rather than sit and "solve." She focused on Emma's eyebrow ring, wondering if it hurt. Emma's jacket was draped over one of the back tires. Her backpack lay open beside her. Some textbooks and a binder peeked out.

Emma gurgled. "It's . . . I'm . . . aghhh." She stopped. "Ugh," she exhaled. Her face was wet with tears. A stream of snot, like pulled taffy, made its way toward the asphalt.

Brit removed a Kleenex from her purse and reached across the backpack, handing it to her. Emma exhaled into the Kleenex.

"Don't tell anyone," Emma whispered.

"'Course not," Brit promised, sighing inwardly with relief that Emma wouldn't snitch on her either for being here. "Besides, can't tell anyone what I don't know."

Emma chewed her bottom lip. "But what if I tell you?"

Brit kept her voice calm, like at the end of cheer practice, when they listened to yoga music and she led the girls through stretches and breathing exercises. "I'm not sure. Are you planning to hurt yourself?"

Emma swallowed hard. Shook her head. "I talked crap about one of the football players," she whispered. "In English class. Next day, this." She removed her jacket from where it was draped over the tire. Underneath, the tire was slashed. She motioned to the side of the minivan, and Brit peeked around to see the bright white of the word *bitch* sloppily painted across the side of the tire. Brit sucked in her breath. "They trashed my PE locker, too," Emma said, her voice cracking. "Wrote awful things. But now someone's spreading the rumor that I did this to myself to get attention."

Brit's heart broke for Emma. "I know how you feel."

"How would *you* know? You're the Fearless Flyer of EastPay. You get away with everything. After that speech you gave about Eli's death? I would've been kicked out of school. But you," she spat. "You get a slap on the wrist."

"That wasn't me," Brit blurted. Emma looked at her, eyes doubtful. "Someone set me up."

"Who?"

Brit licked her lips. She checked under the cars. No one was in the lot, at least not nearby. "Who knows. There's a chat room of all the die-hard EastPayers. Coulda been any of them."

"Did you tell anybody?"

"What good would it do?"

"But you told *me*."

"Well." Brit smiled warmly. "I made an exception."

Something shifted in Emma's expression. "Is that what you told Finn, too?"

Brit felt her eyes go wide as she registered Emma's words. "How did you—" But Emma cut her off with an annoyed wave, then typed on her phone with fast fingers. Her phone vibrated in response.

Emma stood and stretched, swiped at her face with the back of her sleeve. The red-rimmed eyes smeared a light pink. It was *eyeliner*? "My time's up," she said.

Something thumped wildly in Brit's chest. "Your time?"

Emma answered the phone. Her voice was crisp, not broken like a few moments before. "Hi, Kymberlin. No, let me call you back."

"Kymberlin?" *Kymberlin from cheer?* They never hung out. It had to be a different Kim. But Emma didn't say "Kim." She said "Kymberlin."

Emma produced an envelope and extended it toward Brit. Brit's heart lurched into her throat, but she fought back with a steady glare. "So what? You set me up?" She pressed her lips together and jutted her chin out. Refused to stand or take the envelope.

Emma smirked. Brit hated that smirk. It made her feel like a child. "Tammy wants the best shot at a scholarship. For her, that means not sharing her titles. She never wanted a *co*-captain." She gathered her Kleenex and balled it in a tight fist. "But Ms. Ricky insisted. You've always been the favorite. The cheer coach's darling that she personally discovered. So Tammy and I made a trade."

Anger coursed through Brit. She felt blood rushing to her face. "You slashed your own tire?"

Emma shrugged, gathering her things. "Small price to pay." She pulled a switchblade out of her backpack before tucking it into her back pocket. "If I got you to snitch, I was guaranteed flyer my senior year. They'd even try to pull me up from JV this year."

"They can't," Brit said. "The roster's full."

Emma eyed the envelope, still extended toward Brit. "Not for long."

"Well, then, I'm reporting you." Brit folded her arms. "The vandalism."

Emma barked a laugh. "You're not reporting me. It's my car. I can do whatever I want to my own car."

"I'm not taking your envelope."

Emma stepped over Brit, who was still kneeling on the asphalt. "I thought it was strange seeing you shake hands with your cousin. Then one of the football players saw Finn washing his hands in the locker room. Noticed the sixty-two. Kinda genius, kinda stupid."

Brit felt dizzy. How closely was she being watched?

"This doesn't even have to do with the chat room," Brit sputtered.

"Oh, it does." Emma looked at the envelope. "It gave us the perfect opportunity." She dropped the envelope to the ground in front of Brit. "I'm out. I gotta go call Triple A."

Brit sat, slumped over her knees, listening to the sound of Emma's Doc Martens as they faded into the distance.

She grabbed her phone, began to text with shaky fingers, and then stopped. What if someone found the text? She called Spencer.

In one ring he answered, "S'up?"

"They know."

"Who?"

Her head felt dizzy and she took a deep breath, blew it out through puffed-out cheeks.

"Know what— Brit?"

"That I told Finn," she managed, and then quickly added, "Not about the chat room. I told him about Walker. How he got me suspended."

Spencer groaned. "You have a death wish? Why'd you admit that?"

"I din't just offer it!" she screamed back. "You think with my"—she lowered her voice—"you think with cheer on the line I'd say anything? He's my cousin. He knew I was lying. I had to say something."

"So, what, he hold a gun to your head?"

"No," she said. She eyed the envelope.

"Don't talk to anyone. Lay low." She knew he was waiting for her to say okay, but she couldn't. Brit hadn't become who she was in high school by *laying low*. "Britney. Brit, listen, you're at their mercy. Do your suspension. Do your homework. Ignore Finn. You can't win this. They know cheerleading's everything to you. Be careful."

She hung up, snatched the envelope off the pavement, and

sprinted to her car, feeling watched the whole time. What could they threaten her with? A picture from elementary school when she had glasses? In middle school when she'd sit solo during lunch? She'd had a drunken kiss with Walker freshman year. That was the worst dirt on her. She opened the envelope and read the typed letter inside.

No.

She'd have to be home late today. There would be no *laying low* about this.

In less than five minutes, she was tearing through the double doors of the girls' locker room, the letter crumpled in her tight fist. The cheerleaders looked up in surprise, but then continued chatting with one another as if she'd never entered. Sweat trickled down Brit's neck. The lockers with their open locks dangling, the girls changing into their practice clothes, and Brit, invisible. She bounced against them, their shoulders like pillars in a pinball machine, and headed for Ms. Ricky's office. One girl gasped an angry "Ouch!" and another "What're you—" but Brit ignored them, entered Ms. Ricky's office, and closed the door behind her.

"Miss Wallace!" Ms. Ricky exclaimed. Brit set the wrinkled letter in front of her.

"Did you know about this?" Brit asked.

Her face fell as she skimmed the note. "Is this what you want?"

And just like that, Brit knew Ms. Ricky wasn't in on it. Thank God.

Brit snatched up the letter and backed out of the office. The girls watched her, their faces revealing nothing. Maybe they'd been told to ignore her, but surely they didn't all know why. They couldn't *all* be part of the chat room. Dalisa and Jalisa avoided eye contact. *Oh no. Not them, too.*

"Brit?" Amy Jane said. She put an arm around her and led her away from the other girls. Out of earshot, Amy Jane asked, "You okay?"

Brit nodded. At least Amy Jane wasn't afraid to be seen with her. She felt like she had a mark on her, like if students talked to her, they'd be ostracized, too.

"It's really too bad," Amy Jane said. "I'm sorry about your decision. The team will miss you."

Brit's stomach clenched. *Amy Jane wasn't on her side.* "I never— I haven't decided— I—" She waved the envelope with a flimsy hand. The confidence she'd built over the last three years felt zapped.

"Oh, you held on to it?" Amy Jane said, looking at the wrinkled letter in Brit's hand. "You won't. I mean, you're a flyer. Tammy's your back base in your stunting unit. She says you haven't been tight lately—hitting your skill. And you know she has that one *vital* responsibility—"

Amy Jane didn't need to explain the obvious. Brit knew Tammy's responsibility: catching the flyer's head and back. They were threatening her safety. Brit's body went cold. "I'd hate to see her be a fraction off," Amy Jane continued. Brit stood frozen, locked in, like her opening position in a dance number, right before the music started.

Kymberlin approached, the sound of her bleached tennis shoes padding down the hallway.

"We've been talking," Kymberlin said. "Tammy and me." Amy

Jane nodded. Tammy appeared. Placed a hand on Amy Jane's and Kymberlin's shoulders in solidarity.

"We're thinking Emma Li might be a better option for third flyer while you take some time to get back up to par," Tammy said. "We were thinking of talking to Ms. Ricky about pulling her up from JV. I mean, one person, she might not believe. But if a few of us are concerned . . . If your main base and secondary base are noticing, too . . ."

Kymberlin spoke sweetly. "It's your safety we're concerned with."

"I'm sure Ms. Ricky would understand," Amy Jane said.

Brit was speechless. They were threatening to drop her during a skill? She was their captain! "I haven't done anything! You're the ones who kept me out of the chat room."

"Never heard of it," Tammy said. "But if there is such a place, it's a good thing. The first chance you got, you told not one but two people."

"Emma already knew—"

"But you didn't know that," Kymberlin interrupted. "And snitching out Walker to Finn? That was one of the worst things you could've done."

"He's family!" Brit heard her voice getting squeaky.

"*Football* is family. You know nothing comes before that."

Brit's whole body shook. "This doesn't even have to do with football! It's you using the chat room as an excuse to get what you want."

"Again with this chat room," Amy Jane said, sweet as sugar. "Listen, you're under a lot of stress. Maybe you could go back to playing computer games for a while. We hear you're good at that."

Brit's mouth went dry. The reality was setting in. "You're kicking me off?"

"Of course not," Amy Jane said.

"But the letter—" Brit sputtered.

"That's your decision, of course," Kymberlin said sadly. "But *we* want you to stay."

Amy Jane put a hand on Brit's shoulder. "Desperately," Amy Jane added. "But it's your decision. We wouldn't take that from you. That would be unfair. Take the weekend. Think it over."

Brit had come here to fight, but she'd had no idea what she'd be up against. She turned and walked out slowly, afraid that if she sped up, she'd collapse or fall over. She held on to the crumpled paper, the letter supposedly typed by Brit, the letter saying she needed to take the remainder of the season off for rest and recuperation, that she would love to cheer again, maybe once basketball started, but right now she felt overwhelmed.

In the letter, "Brit" suggested the pressure from the upcoming regional cheer competition in December had led to her breakdown and her appalling email recording after Eli died, and that maybe taking three months off would let her reflect and regroup. Be a better team player. She wanted what was best for the team and school. It was typed and printed in business letter format, twelve-point font, and double-spaced, dated this coming Monday, with one blank line at the bottom awaiting the only finishing touch to make it official: her signature.

Chapter 44
MEGAN

"You're gonna need to rewind," Kylie said, flipping on her turn signal. "So Finn's grandma is his grandma. But also not his grandma."

It was Sunday night, and Kylie was driving Meg to Brit's house. In the back seat was a box of Finn's things: letterman jacket, oversize hoodie, extra pair of flip-flops he'd left at her house, two books, and a pair of board shorts from their trip to the lake this summer. Inside one of the books, Meg had slipped a note: "I'm sorry. You're probably so confused. One day I'll explain. There's so much more to this. Please know I love you and that nothing's changed." If anyone found this note, they wouldn't learn anything incriminating, so no repercussions.

Meg pinched the bridge of her nose, still trying to figure out how this was all pieced together. "Finn would kill me if he knew I was telling you this."

"Well, then, good thing you're broken up."

Meg gave her a look. "Too soon."

"You saved him jail time at least." Kylie grinned, but Megan stayed straight-faced. "Because if he killed you, then . . ." She trailed off. "Oh, never mind." She motioned to the back seat. "Did you pack up your sense of humor in that box, too? Okay, back to Grandma. Go on."

They were already close to Brit's house. Meg would have to give the brief version. "Finn's mom—" she started.

"Name?"

"Kat."

"Got it. Kat."

"Kat was ten years old when her dad started dating Mrs. Callahan."

"Finn's grandma-not-grandma?"

"Yes."

"Ooh! Was he having an affair?"

"What? No! He was single. But Mrs. Callahan and Kat's dad never married. Just dated. Five years later, he died. That same year, when Kat was barely sixteen, she got pregnant with Finn and, well, she was already messing with meth. Started disappearing more and more, and Mrs. Callahan took over raising Finn. Full grandma duties."

"Only she never signed the legal shit to make that legal."

Meg nodded. "And my mom said she'd call Child Protective Services if I didn't break up with him." She swallowed. Left out that her mom was being blackmailed over the DUI. She felt ashamed somehow to say it out loud.

"Damn," Kylie said. "Why's she hate Finn so much?"

She doesn't, Meg wanted to say with a pang in her chest. *My mother's blackmail is now my blackmail.* But instead, she said, "I'm slacking off on my commitments. Ruining the future she's helped me to build."

Kylie made a raspberry sound.

"She'd do it, too," Meg said. "Report him. I've lived with her long enough to know you don't call her bluff. Closest group home is in Winchester County. Zoned for Hyde Park—a team with a one and nine record last year and the 'one' was a forfeit. Their line-backers are, like, five foot three. And that's *if* the school lets him play. Transfer rules."

Meg glanced nervously out the windows, her eyes ricocheting between the motion sensor lights and bug zappers flashing across the dark houses they passed. "God, I've become so jumpy."

"No one's eavesdropping from their porches." Kylie grinned. "And besides, we're here."

She parked along the curb in front of Brit's house. Meg reached into the back and grabbed the box, only hesitating briefly. It was best this way. Brit could return Finn's things.

Brit opened the front door, and before Meg could even say hello, Brit wrapped her in a hug, squeezing the box painfully between them. "I'm so sorry you broke up," she said, her voice full of emotion. "That's like if Adam and Eve called it quits."

"Blasphemy," Kylie said.

"Right?" Brit said.

Megan giggled and a single tear escaped. She let Brit take the box and set it down, then lead her and Kylie upstairs. Kylie skidded to a stop and did a full circle the way anyone did when they walked into Brit's room. A funny gasp-sort-of-choke escaped Kylie's mouth. Meg remembered the first time she'd come here. Such a stark difference from her elegant and shabby chic bedroom. Brit's walls were floor-to-ceiling photos—friends, dance competitions, high school football games. Three poster-size team photos of cheer— one for each varsity year—dwarfed all the others. First-place ribbons and decorations from school dances were strewn across her dresser. And the cheerleading trophies.

So.

Many.

Meg thought back to the early days of her own dance recitals and ballet company performances. Her mother would neatly frame all the awards and place them on the awards wall in the downstairs hallway. None of Meg's ribbons ever made it to her bedroom walls. That would not fit the decor.

"Okay, spill," Brit said. "Finn won't talk. Asked him why you broke up and he would only say that he messed up."

"He didn't."

"You wanna talk about it?"

"Not really. Not much I can do."

Kylie interrupted: "Brit, how'd you even fit this in your car?" She was holding Brit's six-foot cheerleading trophy from nationals last year. "How'd you fly home with this?"

Brit visibly sagged, her face frowning, her head dropping. "You want it?" she mumbled. "I don't need it anymore."

What?

"No thanks," Kylie said. "Already have a coat rack."

"What's that mean?" Meg asked Brit.

"Seriously?" Kylie looked at the monstrosity. "That was funny. Coat rack?"

"Not you," Meg said. "Brit."

Brit looked up, then away. She put a hand on her dresser for support. "I'm quitting the squad tomorrow." She closed her eyes as she said the words.

"What?" That sounded absurd coming from Brit. "Why?"

"I'm a liability," Brit said evenly, swallowing. Not making eye contact. "Lost my confidence as a flyer. It's for my own safety."

Meg tilted her head. Brit wasn't telling everything. She wanted to ask, but she also knew there was no chance she'd tell Kylie about her mom's DUI. Maybe Brit had a secret like that. Maybe Brit, like Meg, was scared of something that felt bigger than herself. Still, her heart broke for Brit. Meg couldn't care less about losing out on her ballet career. But for Brit, cheerleading was her joy.

This time it was Meg wrapping her arms around Brit, squeezing tightly. "Well, we both know that's bullshit, but you're smart as hell. You'll figure this out." Brit collapsed in her arms. She could feel the desperate way Brit clung to her. How she fought to keep her face neutral. The girl was so honest. So easy to read.

Brit reached into her pocket for her lipstick and applied the bright red to her lips, round and round—a nervous rhythm Meg knew well. Brit rubbed her lips together, the ritual seeming to steady her.

Kylie eyed her weirdly but said nothing.

"There's a chat room," Brit finally said. "It's anonymous. There's no way of tracing. I'm already in trouble for snitching, so what does it matter if I tell two more people? Besides, once I quit the squad, there's nothing else they can take away."

"Chat room," Kylie repeated, processing. Brit tucked her lipstick back into her pocket and pressed her sweaty hands against her cheer sweats.

Meg felt lightheaded. She made a fist, kneading her sweaty palms with her fingers.

A chat room.

A *chat* room?

Of course. That was the thread. The seemingly disparate goings-on weren't disparate at all. The chat room was the single line connecting anyone who wanted to "help" EastPay. Why hadn't she thought of that? Absent players. Curfew violations. Ineligibilities. Even the poisonings. A safe space where they could brainstorm who and how. Meg had seen how powerful a team of eleven could be on a field. She could only imagine how powerfully an anonymous group of fanatics could work as one if they weren't afraid of consequences. Eli's accidental death. She suddenly had a sick feeling that the fight meant for Damarius had been set up in this chat room. Had a student died because of it?

"How do we stop it?" Meg asked.

"We don't," said Brit flatly.

"But can't you do your computer wizard magic and shut that whole thing down?"

"You're a *coder*?" Kylie looked like she'd just been told Britney was part walrus.

"I don't know the administrator's password," Brit said, ignoring Kylie. She laughed, but it was empty, void of feeling. "Heck, forget the password. I don't even know the administrator."

"So, then," Meg said, "what's that mean?"

Without looking at them, she said, "I think it means I'm quitting cheer tomorrow."

Chapter 45
BRITNEY

Brit awoke Monday morning to the sound of thunder. It was still dark, spiderwebs of raindrops against her window. So much rain these past few weeks. *Fitting*.

There was no way she was bringing the box of Finn's things to school and handing it over in the parking lot, where someone would see—she was sure of it—and there would be more talk. Always more talk. She got up and drove to Finn's house two hours before school. She'd barely slept anyway, so why not make good use of the time?

When Brit let herself in with her spare key, the lights were all off. She turned on the living room lamp, set Meg's box down, and sat on the couch, her resignation letter in hand. She read it over and over, as if by reading it enough, she'd make the words disappear. Her eyes were heavy from lack of sleep.

She let the paper slip from her fingers onto the coffee table. Curling up in a ball, she wrapped a throw blanket around herself and stared into the dark. She thought of all the dance moves, the choreography she loved to plan, the giggly moments with the girls as they did their makeup before games in front of the locker room mirrors. Had any of them ever liked her?

She must've dozed, because when she woke up, the kitchen light was set to dim, and the coffee was brewing. Grandma must be up. A glass of orange juice sat on the coffee table beside her. She turned to the hallway and saw Finn exiting his bedroom, clothes and towel in hand. He did a double take at seeing her there so early, but offered a nodding hello, and then skulked to the bathroom and closed the door. The breakup had obviously been hard on him. She looked down at her resignation letter, staring back at her from the coffee table. She wasn't exactly feeling festive, either.

She rose and rapped gently on the door. He cracked it open, toothbrush in mouth, and looked at her with eyes that were tired or sad or maybe both.

She hated this part. She could see how awful he already felt. "Look, I don't mean to spit in your cornflakes, but Meg gave me a box of your things to return to you."

"I'm sure she had some choice words for me," he mumbled, and resumed brushing.

She shook her head. "She didn't tell me anything either."

He chewed on his toothbrush, like he was thinking of sharing more, but then said, "Thanks, Brit. You can set it on my bed."

"Look, I don't know what went on—you say you messed up, she says you didn't, but—"

"She says I didn't?" His eyes were incredulous.

"Sure as day. So why don't you just apologize? It's not like you hooked up with another girl or something."

He gnawed on his toothbrush some more, and then spit in the sink. His neck stayed bent, and Brit saw the underlying look of guilt. Her stomach twisted.

"Aw, no, Finn, tell me you didn't."

"I didn't," he said. "You need a ride to school?"

She shook her head. "I have my mom's car."

"Okay, well, then, I should shower."

He held on to the doorknob, twisting it absently. She thought of telling him how she was quitting cheer, but it felt out of place in this conversation. Maybe later. He tapped the door twice with an open hand—a quiet resignation—before closing it and turning on the shower.

Aside from the sounds of the water, the house was quiet now without the usual shuffling of her grandma's slippered feet. Brit opened the refrigerator. Nothing. She nibbled from a plate of cookies on the counter until she saw the note on the paper plate. She and Tammy had made enough pep rally posters for her to recognize those extra-curly letters. Of course. Finn was Tammy's "assignment," the same way Jake had been hers. She took the whole paper plate, cookies and all, and dropped it into the trash can.

Through the kitchen window—dawn finally breaking through—she saw Grandma in her raincoat in the garden. She must've walked out while Brit was asleep on the couch. As if Grandma could sense Brit peering from afar, she looked up and squinted, then beckoned her outside with a wave. Brit held up one finger, downed her orange juice, and slung her backpack over her shoulder. She snatched the envelope from the coffee table on the way out.

Outside the air was cool and damp from the previous night's rain. There were pockets of leftover summer every few steps, but autumn had definitely taken over. A light mist wafted down. Mrs. Callahan was pruning her tomato plant as Brit leaned in to kiss her cheek. "Morning, Grams," she greeted. "You're up early."

"Couldn't sleep. Indigestion. Not enough Tums in the world for this stomach." She cut a stem with pruning shears. Peeling off the dead leaves, she said, "I noticed you're up early, too. Drove here before the roosters got up." She twisted a ripe tomato at the stem until it popped off and then placed it in a wicker basket at her feet. "And from the looks of your tired eyes, you didn't sleep much either."

Brit readjusted her backpack. "Yeah," she admitted.

Last night, long after her parents had gone to sleep, Brit had stared at the resignation letter—wondering who had written it, if the chat room assigned the letter to a person, or worse yet, whether the person had volunteered. Did someone stay up late making corrections and proofreading? Or did a group come together like a school project, meeting at a coffee shop and discussing the best way to ruin her? At around three a.m., pulled under by fatigue, she'd decided it was pointless and she should take Spencer's advice—forget it all and give in to them. They'd won.

"I had a lot on my mind," she finally said as her grandma plucked a weed. "You know, cheer."

Mrs. Callahan made a noise, a kind of "humph" layered in doubt, and then knelt onto the wet earth to get at the bottom leaves. "You know why a tomato's considered a fruit and not a vegetable?"

"Seeds," Brit responded.

Mrs. Callahan nodded and held a yellow bud in Brit's direction. "It's also the part of the plant that grows from the flower."

Brit waited, not sure where this was going.

"Back in 1887, U.S. tariff laws put a duty on vegetables, but not fruits. So this family got all disgruntled for having to pay taxes on their tomatoes, and they wanted money back. Case went all the way to the Supreme Court."

"How do you know all this?"

Mrs. Callahan tapped her head with a finger. "You gather a lot of useless cow dung in this trap if you live long enough." She fished around a tuft of leaves. "Also I dated a botanist before your time." Her gloved hands emerged with a long, fat zucchini. "Anyway, they lost. The family that didn't want to pay. The judge actually ruled it a vegetable. He said that when words haven't gained a special meaning from trade, then the ordinary dictionary definition works. But in this case, because of commerce, or maybe popularity, he decided that since a tomato was usually served at dinner and never as a dessert, it was a vegetable."

"Okay?" Brit shook her head, lost.

"But it's two different things." She handed Brit a plump tomato so Brit could examine it. "Legally, the Supreme Court made it a vegetable. Why? It helped the economy. But botanically, it remained a fruit. The courts didn't change it botanically. Do you get what I'm saying?"

"No."

Brit's grandma looked at the house, the road, and then back at the tomato. "People will do anything for money. Even change definitions of right and wrong, definitions that were considered unchanging truth. That is, until money becomes involved. Tomatoes were popular. Because they were *popular*, they were worth more." She looked at Brit then. "No one ever went to court to fight over okra."

"Does this have to do with me somehow?"

Mrs. Callahan wiped her hands on her pants. "I don't know, does it?" She used Brit's hand to pull herself to standing position. She was creaky. Slow. She looked at Brit. Really looked.

All Brit could say was "I think you're taking some medical marijuana on the side for those bones."

Mrs. Callahan leaned in for a hug, patted Brit on the back. "Maybe I am. Why, you want some? Might help you sleep."

Brit smiled. "I gotta get, Grams. Gotta go over some new steps with Tammy so she can teach the girls."

"*You* teach the girls. You're a tomato, Brit. Not okra."

It was like Grandma knew. Knew without Brit saying, but she couldn't imagine how Grandma would. Unless . . . She *had* left the letter on the coffee table while she slept. She thought of asking, but instead, she joked, "Does that mean I'm a fruit or a vegetable?"

"Depends. Does nature decide? Or money?"

Brit climbed into her car and slammed the door. The ignition roared in her ears, the air suffocating. Even though it was drizzling, she rolled down the windows as she backed out.

She waved at her grandma through her rearview mirror, and Mrs. Callahan waved back, like they had chatted about the weather or the price of gas. Her basket of vegetables (*or were they fruits?*) tottered in her hands. As Brit drove away, she heard her grandma calling out the way the captain of the squad calls out the counts, projecting over the crowds so that no one would miss it. No option for an offbeat misstep, not on her watch. "Remember who you are!"

Her grandmother said it twice more as she drove away.

It unnerved her. Before she'd even gone a mile, she U-turned back to Finn's, and without a word, raced past her grandma and into the kitchen. Finn was most likely in his room, getting dressed, but she didn't have time to check. She dug through the trash for the paper plate with Tammy's writing.

She thought of Finn's question the day he'd shown up at her door: *"If you found out that the sport you loved was being run by a bunch of cheaters, would you still want to play?"*

"That depends," she'd said. *"Can you get rid of the cheaters?"*

They'd both admitted that they didn't know how.

But now. She lifted the paper plate from the trash, Tammy's loopy letters across grease stains.

Her grandmother's words echoed in her mind: *"Remember who you are."*

Paper plate in hand, she raced outside, jumped back into her car, and then drove above the speed limit, passing the high school, going the extra five miles back to her own house, where she sprinted to her room.

Brit's bedroom was a shrine built through hours of sweat and bruises, tumbles and stunts, water bottles rolled on her exhausted shoulders. She weaved around three standing trophies and stopped, facing the far wall. Photos overlapped from floor to ceiling like wallpaper, most every picture in her cheer outfit, leaping or high-kicking, arms up and fingers splayed. She stood in front of the poster-size photo of her varsity cheer squad all in the splits with their pom-poms overhead, her friends. Friends. She turned from them, her pinkie trailing across Tammy's plastic smile, and moved in front of her vanity, looking at herself in the mirror. She reached up and twirled a plastic string from the pom-poms around her finger.

"Remember who you are."

Her grandmother's words taunted her like those songs that would get stuck in her head after she had to replay them ad nauseam to learn a dance. Who was she? She used to think she was a cheer-leader, and without that, she'd be nobody. But she didn't *feel* like a nobody. Sure, she was good at tumbling. But she was also fun. Confident. Honest. She liked people. God. Animals. Coding, too.

She reached into her backpack, pushed aside the greasy paper plate, and removed the resignation letter, waiting to be signed in her own hand. Signed because Amy Jane had told her that if she didn't, Tammy might be a *fraction off* in catching Brit's head and neck. It all was so unfair.

She remembered Amy Jane's parting words. *"Maybe you could go back to playing computer games."* She thought back to her middle school days of cybersecurity. She'd felt like a nobody back then, but the truth was, she kicked butt at what she did. Systems would attack, and she'd have to think *around* the problem.

But this was different. There was no getting around it.

Or was there? Maybe she hadn't ever been *just* a computer geek. Maybe she hadn't been *just* a cheerleader, either. Maybe she'd been a Fearless Flyer all along.

In cybersecurity competitions, if stopping the hacker looked impossible, it was because she was going about it from the wrong direction. She removed the paper plate from her bag and walked back to the photo of the team, the exact replica of the one hanging in the girls' locker room. She checked her phone. If she left right now, she might still have time. She crossed her fingers and hoped her grandmother was right. *You're not okra.* Sitting down at her desk, she removed her resignation letter from the envelope, and carefully began to sign.

Chapter 46

BRITNEY

Brit waited until cheerleading practice was well underway before she walked into the gymnasium sixth period. She watched the girls bouncing through their hugs and hellos as Tammy set up the music and then taught the team the first two eight-counts. One girl, Gwen Stevens, saw her and offered a shy wave, her eyes darting around to see if anyone noticed. Another, Keisha Isaacs, gave Brit an apologetic look before she resumed stretching. Jalisa and Dalisa jogged over and gave her hugs. Dalisa whispered, "Sorry." Jalisa whispered, "We're not part of this nonsense." It was just the extra bit of courage she needed. Not everyone hated her. They were just afraid. She understood. It was what had kept her quiet the past couple weeks, too.

Everyone else pretended they hadn't heard her enter. She tucked herself into a ball on the second-row bleachers, holding her resignation letter in hand, signed this morning with her signature.

After practice, she followed the girls into the locker room.

Amy Jane and Tammy approached her, looked down at the envelope in her fist. "Have you thought it over?" Amy Jane asked with fake tender eyes.

Brit swallowed and hoped she looked scared.

She walked past the girls to her locker and tried her combination. It didn't work. "Hey," she said, loud enough for others to look. She spun the numbers, tried again. Stopped on 4, past 19 once, then back to 6. She wiggled it. Nothing. She looked at all the locks.

"Who did this?" She whirled. The girls shook their heads. "Who did this!" she screamed.

"Did what?" Tammy asked, looking genuinely perplexed.

"Oh, don't act like you don't know."

She started to march to Ms. Ricky's office, then stopped. She turned to the wall. Looking at the mounted ten-by-fourteen photo of the cheer squad, she tilted her head and peered closer. *Here goes nothing*, she thought. She let out a bloodcurdling scream that made the girls jump in unison. Ms. Ricky rocketed out of the office, probably imagining a girl needing an EpiPen.

"Jesus, Brit!" Amy Jane yelled. "What the hell!"

Brit ripped the framed picture off the wall. "Really?!" she screamed.

They looked at her, confusion clouding their usually bright faces.

Alarm flooded Ms. Ricky's voice. "What's wrong?"

"This." Brit handed Ms. Ricky the portrait. "Notice anything missing?"

Ms. Ricky scanned the photograph. "Well—"

"Me," Brit exploded. "*I'm* missing from that photo. Amy Jane Photoshopped me out in computer class."

"Don't be insane," Amy Jane said.

"She sits at computer number twenty-two during third period."

Amy Jane glared. "We don't even use Photoshop."

Brit folded her arms, glared back. "But all the computers have it loaded."

Ms. Ricky jumped in. "Is this true?"

"No!" Amy Jane yelled. She seemed unnerved by Brit's confidence. "I don't even know how to use Photoshop!"

"Doubtful," Brit said. "Ms. Ricky, have someone check her computer. Open Photoshop and see what's saved."

Amy Jane looked at her, and the look was pure death. "Ms. Ricky," Amy Jane started, keeping her eyes fixed on Brit the whole time, "we've been meaning to speak with you about Brit."

"We? You mean you and Tammy, right?" Brit said.

"That's right," Tammy answered, stepping forward. "She's been struggling on the flies. It's just not safe for—"

"Because that's funny," Brit interrupted. "Today I walked into the locker room and my lock wouldn't work. I'm pretty sure Tammy locked her lock on mine."

"I did not, loser."

"Tammy!" Ms. Ricky chided.

Brit threw her hands up in surrender. "Why would I make that up?"

Jalisa stepped forward. "Brit doesn't lie."

"Yeah, she doesn't," her twin, Dalisa, echoed, and it felt so good that these girls weren't going to let the chat room intimidate them, if they even knew it was out there.

"Enough!" Ms. Ricky said. She stomped back into her office and returned with a piece of paper. She walked over to Brit's locker, and, looking at the paper, tried a combination. The lock snapped open. "This is a list of all the girls' locks. This was your lock, Tamara."

"But I didn't do that," Tammy argued, her eyes going wide.

"She wants my spot," Brit blurted. "She and Amy Jane and some of the others have been threatening to drop me on the stunts."

"What!" Ms. Ricky was appalled.

"And then I found this." She pulled out the resignation letter from cheer squad. "Remember how I brought it to you asking if you knew about it?"

Ms. Ricky nodded.

"Well, when I refused to sign it, they signed it for me. Look." She riffled through her backpack and pulled out the letter written to Finn on the paper plate of cookies. She held it next to her resignation letter. There was Britney Wallace's name signed in the same curly writing that was on the paper plate, the one signed by Tammy, both signatures complete with hearts over the *i*'s. "That's not my signature," Brit said. "But it's obvious who forged my name."

Ms. Ricky looked at Tammy. "Well, I never!"

Tammy shook her head, eyes wide bulges of fear. "No. Ms. Ricky, I didn't—that's not my writing."

Ms. Ricky looked around the room, seething. "Who else is in on this? This 'bullying'?"

Dalisa and Jalisa looked at each other and said in perfect twin unison, "Kymberlin."

Kymberlin, jolted from the accusation, shrieked, "Lies!"

Dalisa said, "We have a text from her."

Jalisa handed Ms. Ricky her phone, and Ms. Ricky scanned the text. She read it aloud. "'FYI, keep talking with Brit and you can go where she's headed.'"

Brit had no idea. It explained their darting eyes in the cafeteria. Their recent radio silence on the phone. They'd been scared. She loved them so much for having her back right now.

Kymberlin's lips pursed tightly, her face turning an angry beet red.

"How long has this been going on?" Ms. Ricky demanded. Eyes looked anywhere but at her—down at their pom-pom socks and at the concrete walls. "Well, then," she said, "since you all want to jeopardize your championships by losing your best flyer, we'll start with *this* for team unity: Tammy, you're relegated to JV for the remainder of the season."

"What?" Tammy's mouth fell open.

"Kymberlin, suspended two games. And I'm walking this minute to the computer room with the custodian. If I find this picture on Computer 22, Amy Jane, I will erase you from this team the way you erased Brit."

"She's setting us up!" Amy Jane screeched.

"And if I so much as see any of you even *looking* disrespectfully at another teammate, I will kick you off this team farther than our punter can. This isn't football. I don't need championships. I need respect. As of today, I'm putting our team on hold for state competition until we learn what the word *team* means. We'll see. I'm not taking individuals to State. Understood? Fifty sets of bleachers. All of you except Brit." She strode into her office long enough to grab her walkie-talkie. She called the custodian on her way out, telling him to meet her in the B-wing.

Silence.

Brit turned to face the horseshoe of girls surrounding her.

"You did this—" Tammy started.

"Careful," Brit warned. "You're on JV. You don't want to be demoted to the frosh squad."

Tammy's eyes crinkled, furious. "Your accent's gone," she said, noticing Brit's pronunciation.

"It's just disposable." She smiled. "Like you."

"I didn't erase you from the picture!" Amy Jane screamed. She actually stomped a foot, fists curled, like a child. "I don't even know Photoshop!"

Brit turned to Amy Jane. "I do. And lucky for me, someone warned me to go back to playing with computers. So I did! And now that Ms. Ricky knows I've been threatened, she's got my back. And thanks to Tammy's lock and Amy Jane's Photoshopping, I have proof." She addressed all the girls, looking at each one individually. Made sure there wasn't even the hint of a twang. She wanted this to be all Brit, the *real* Brit, the one who didn't hide behind an accent or anything else—who was proud of every part of herself. "I'm honest. Usually. But today I played like you. From here on out, if I get so much as a sprained ankle, there'll be a lawsuit. So if you're one of my bases, you better lock it in." She put her shoulders back, riding on the words of her grandmother. "I'm your captain. This is *my* team."

"Yes, girl," Dalisa said.

"Go on," Jalisa added.

She looked at Tammy and Amy Jane. "I've gotten rid of two. Didn't even need a chat room." She looked at Kymberlin, and then the rest of the squad, many of whom avoided her eyes. "I'll get rid of more of you. So you better know what you're doing." She reached down to tie her shoes. "Amy Jane, you can stay here. I know what Ms. Ricky's going to find. And Tammy, JV's in the gym today. But the rest of you, let's go run some bleachers."

"That's my Fearless Flyer," Dalisa cheered.

"But Ms. Ricky said you don't have to run bleachers," Gwen said.

"Yes, I know," Brit said. "But we're a team."

Gwen smiled at that, and there was a look of relief that Brit had won this, like the fear had been keeping Gwen quiet even though she'd never wanted to be part of it. Brit was sure Gwen wasn't the only girl who felt that way.

Chapter 47
FINN

Finn needed a moment to talk to Spencer when no one else was listening. It came toward the end of practice Tuesday as they were jogging back to the team after a play. "Hey, you free tonight?"

"If you're trying to win Megan back, I assure you, dating me won't work."

As crummy as Finn felt, Spencer's humor almost made him crack a smile. *Almost.*

They didn't have much time, so Finn cut right to it. "Brit wants to meet with us."

"Us?"

"Yeah, she specifically asked for you." Finn saw Spencer grin and then catch himself. But then they were back in the huddle, and all talk ceased. Walker hadn't spoken to Finn since their confrontation, but Finn could sense him watching, wondering if their chat was enough to keep Finn in line. The offense ran two more routes and finished the practice with a speed drill, which Finn made sure to finish first.

Back in the locker room, Spencer shoved a calc book into Finn's chest.

"I need it back tonight," he growled, loud enough for other players to hear. "Can you drop it off?"

Spencer was good. No one would question them getting together if it was to return a textbook. "Yeah, yeah," Finn said, improvising. "Just need it for an hour or two."

"Don't make me hunt you down for it!" he hollered before pushing through the double doors.

Just past sunset, Finn pulled into Spencer's trailer park. He walked to Spencer's place, calc book in hand—their prop so they could have an excuse to talk. Spencer opened the screen door. "Have a beer," he said, and disappeared inside, so Finn followed through the door of his double-wide. He set the book down, his eyes locked on the framed picture of quarterback Peyton Manning above their stove.

"Yeah," Spencer said. He held a beer to the side of his kitchen counter and popped the cap off. It clattered and bounced on the linoleum floor. "We all get them. The gift to the football players." He held the bottle up in a mock "cheers," then handed it to Finn.

"I'm good," Finn said. He and alcohol weren't on speaking terms.

"Suit yourself," Spencer said, and took a sip. "You live with anyone?"

"Grandma. You?"

"Dad. He works nights. Sleeps days. He's in back." He motioned down a narrow hallway toward a door at the end.

Another door opened and Leah walked out in a T-shirt and jeans, normal except for the dark undereye circles and greasy hair. She slid to a stop in her socks, her lips pursing when she saw Finn. He felt like he'd barged in rather than been invited. She glared at Spencer.

"A word?" she said, then pushed past him outside, swinging the screen door so that it smacked the back of the trailer.

"Be right back," Spencer muttered.

Finn watched as Spencer crouched outside next to Leah's slouching body on the wet trailer steps. He listened, uncomfortable, through the screen door. It felt like he was accidentally reading someone's diary, but he couldn't look away.

"Hey," Spencer said gently. "Thought you hated the dark."

"I do." A limp cigarette dangled from her fingers. She pressed her lips around it and flicked the lighter on, breathing in and instantly coughing. It was obviously a foreign action, like she was mimicking Spencer, hoping it looked the same. Her chapped lips hung on to the filter while she hacked.

Spencer set his beer down on the step and pulled the cigarette from her lips. "You shouldn't smoke." He re-lit the cigarette with another lighter, shielding the flame with his hand. He sucked in a deep breath, blew the smoke away from her.

She looked away.

"I'm serious," he said. "It's a horrible habit. Listen to your brother." He pushed his shoulder against hers once, softly.

"Why's he here?"

"Geringer? I asked him to stop by."

"Interesting."

"Come on, Leah."

She flicked the lighter absently.

Spencer sipped his beer. "Why don't you invite a friend over. Dawn? Morgan?"

"Sure, okay. Maybe I'll do that."

Her tone said she wouldn't. Finn listened to the crickets. Spencer stood, stepped down the stairs, and turned to face her. Finn wondered if Spencer could see his outline, a couple feet away, facing him from the other side of the screen.

Spencer took a drag of his cigarette and exhaled, the smoke blending into the dark sky. "Stay in tonight, y'hear me?"

"Where're you heading?"

"Going to take care of some things."

"Right now?"

"Soon."

She looked away. He squatted and placed his hands on her knees. "I'm gonna fix this, Leah. I swear to you."

"And then?"

"I don't know. But it'll all be okay."

He went back inside and tipped his beer to Finn.

"One sec," he said, swirling the beer around in his bottle. He left half his beer on the counter and disappeared into a bedroom, emerging in a hoodie. He removed his wristband and set it on the counter, then grabbed his keys and motioned with his chin outside. Finn opened the screen door, and they stepped around Leah, who had lain down on the concrete step.

Finn paused. "Nice to meet you," he said awkwardly, and then followed Spencer.

"So where to?" Spencer asked.

"Dante's Ravine," Finn said, the words like sandpaper.

Spencer cocked his head. "Why?"

"No clue," Finn said. He was hoping Spencer might know. "She said seven thirty. She's too jumpy lately for me to press her with questions. Not sure why it has to be at Dante's Ravine, but she insisted." He hated even the thought of that place.

They stopped in front of their cars. Spencer nodded to himself. "Bad luck to go there on Tuesday nights, if you believe that bullshit, which most people in this town do."

The drowning from several years ago—it had happened on a Tuesday. That part Finn knew. So whatever Brit wanted, she wanted to make sure they were miles away from listening ears. Still, there were other places. Maybe Brit was just being Brit.

"Did you know there was a chat room?" Finn said.

Spencer looked surprised that Finn knew. "As of a few days ago. Your cousin told me."

Brit? Really? She'd warned Finn about Walker, so maybe she'd known of the chat room all along. But it wasn't like her to hide anything from him. "Brit *knew?*"

"*Discovered* is the better word."

That made more sense. If she'd recently found out something bad, she wouldn't keep it from Finn. Not for long. Finn had a feeling that's why she wanted to meet. He wasn't sure how Spencer fit into all this, except that he held a general disdain for EastPay, and therefore, Brit trusted him.

Spencer said, "I'll drive. Get your invitation helmet from your car. If we run into someone, we can fake a reason for visiting—paying tribute, whatever other garbage people go there for." He motioned to Finn's red-and-black team wristband. "And maybe leave that?"

Before Finn could ask, Spencer said, "For all the things you pick up on, you're pretty slow to the obvious. You saw me leave mine on the counter."

"Yeah, but—"

"GPS tracker," Spencer said.

Finn slowly peered down at his wrist like he was wearing a grenade.

"It's no secret," said Spencer. "You can ask the coaches. According to them, it's their way of making sure we stay out of trouble and respect our curfews. After all, we're an *honorable* team." He said it with irony through every syllable, then climbed into his car and started the ignition.

Finn's head was dizzy with the new information. *They could track him?* Finn retrieved the plastic helmet from his back seat and dumped his wristband. No chance he was putting that back on anytime soon.

As he got into Spencer's Blazer, he held up his plastic invitation helmet. "You really think we need to wear these?"

Spencer shrugged. "Never be too sure. Ever. Not in EastPay."

Finn was understanding that more and more.

"Walker told you?" Spencer said as he turned the key in the ignition. He whistled low. "Pretty bold move. What's he *got* on you?"

Finn thought about Tammy. Gritted his teeth. "Enough. He has enough."

Chapter 48
BRITNEY

Brit had parked her car behind a cluster of oak trees near Clayton Messler's property, well off the main road. She waited in the shadows near the clearing of Dante's, wearing dark clothing, her own plastic Spartan helmet in hand. No one had asked her to return it . . . yet. She saw Finn and Spencer in the distance. She smiled. *Thank God.* Then she looked at her watch and frowned. *About time.* They donned their plastic helmets, and as they came into the clearing, Brit emerged from the darkness. Both of them jumped like startled cats, which made her giggle.

"Boo!" she whispered.

Finn and Spencer collectively exhaled, then took off their helmets.

"Let's go," she said, wasting no time. She ducked under some trees and headed along the river. "Took you two long enough. I'm guessing my timed forty is faster than you slowpokes."

Spencer laughed at her joke, which caught her off guard. She felt her face flush with heat, and she was grateful for the dark. On the side of the clearing, they broke off into a wooded area, lit by a muted moon. Damp leaves stuck to the bottoms of their feet as they walked. It wasn't really a path. More like an indentation from erosion and the treads of shoes tamping the ground through the years. The desperate quest for popularity. Victory. Invincibility.

She'd been part of this path.

For this reason, she needed tonight to happen here. So much of who she'd become was tied to this place. She now knew there was no magic in the river making their football team's wins outnumber their losses. Which meant there was also no magic water that had "knighted her" Fearless Flyer.

How long had she protected the honor of this place? In doing so, she'd unknowingly protected the chat room. The higher the superstitions about Dante's Ravine, the lower the suspicions about the chat room. If this place acted as a solid cover for any nefarious ideas hatched by The Game, then she wanted this place to be where she hatched her plan to disarm and destroy The Game.

She also knew that most EastPayers wouldn't dare come here on a Tuesday unless they wanted to guarantee a loss the following Friday. Bad luck. Sean Lloyd died in the river on a Tuesday. No one drank the water on Tuesdays.

"So . . ." Spencer said. "We're here because . . ."

"I have an idea," Brit said. "But first." She turned to Spencer. "Did you tell him? About the chat room?"

Spencer lifted a hand. "Walker beat me to it."

What? She looked at Finn wide-eyed. "How much did he tell you?"

Finn rubbed his temples. "Enough for me to feel dumb that I didn't see it sooner."

"It's okay," Brit said. "I think we all feel that way a little." She remembered when she had discovered the chat room on Walker's computer. The swirling thoughts in her head begging for her eyes to be mistaken.

"Sean Lloyd dies when we're kids," Spencer said, "at *Dante's Ravine*, supposedly for threatening to reveal some secret about our team. You guys never wondered?"

Finn lifted a shoulder. "They found alcohol in Sean Lloyd's system—I just figured he fell in . . ."

"Same," Brit admitted. "Until freshman year. My whole life changed the night I dunked in the river. Then I thought back to Sean, and I seriously believed it was the magic of the river." She snorted derisively at herself. "It could bless, it could curse, and all that nonsense. So, Finn, do *not* feel bad for missing the obvious. It's not obvious. Love and loyalty are fierce blinders."

"I missed it, too," Spencer admitted. "I may have wondered about Sean when I was a kid, but once I made the team, I had the same stupid stars in my eyes as both of you. Didn't suspect a thing. Not until your cousin started throwing numbers at me." He gently nudged Brit, and she thought she might fall over from his touch. When had he become so attractive?

"Numbers?" Finn shook his head.

"Her freshman year. I went to her for tutoring—to keep me eligible. She knew I played. Somehow she'd noticed that the football team's winning percentage was bent all out of whack from normal statistics." He swatted absently at a mosquito on his neck. "So she did some math. Said scores were higher by three and a half points against teams with better records."

"Three point five *three*," Brit corrected.

Spencer smiled at her. It was such an inappropriate time for her to be so distracted by that smile. He sat, and she crawled onto the wet earth next to him. He continued. "Brit wanted to know why. Totally innocently. I told her to stick to cheerleading."

"Yes!" Brit said suddenly. "I remember you saying that! So rude!"

He chuckled. "But I checked it out later and—"

"And let me guess," Finn said. "You discovered our games are stacked."

Spencer nodded. "In every single game against a team with a winning record," he said, "two to three key players from the other teams are missing that night. Ineligibility, illness, family emergency, surprise injury, missing uniform. You name it. I just never tied it to a chat room."

"Yeah," Finn agreed, resigned. He sat down with them, rested his elbows on his knees. "Walker basically told me as much. And it stays under the radar because it doesn't give us the win—"

"But it always gives us the advantage," Brit finished.

Finn drew absently in the dirt with a finger. "If you weren't looking for it, it's not something you'd notice."

"Exactly," Spencer said. "It seems random, unrelated, but it's not. I know it, you know it."

"Damarius knew it?" Finn asked weakly.

Spencer nodded. "And when he started asking questions, it led to people swinging at him but accidentally hitting Eli."

"Killing Eli," Brit corrected, sadly. "And it's why I got suspended from cheer. Oh, and kicked off."

Finn snapped his head up at Brit.

"I was gonna tell you," Brit said, "only you were neck-deep in a breakup." Finn's head fell forward again in his hands, maybe guilty he hadn't noticed. "But don't worry," Brit said cheerily. "I'm back on. Small hiccup. They're not messing with me anymore, not if I can help it." She still could see the look of shock on her teammates' faces. There was a new strength she felt deep inside of her. Now she was truly fearless, not just as a flyer.

Spencer said, "And I can't prove it, but I have a sick feeling it's what got Sean Lloyd strained in the river debris and washed up downstream."

Finn squeezed the bridge of his nose. "You think the chat room offed him?"

"Inadvertently, yes. And because it's anonymous," Spencer said, "they can hide behind their screens."

"No one gets caught," Finn said, marveling at the simplicity.

Brit groaned just thinking about the AI voice of her. "People can get ruthless when they don't have to answer to anyone. Look at what was done to me with the fake recording. I'm not *that* hated at school. But if the few who are jealous of me are given a free pass— no consequences—no chance of getting caught?"

"You ever been to a concert?" Spencer asked. "Kids who won't raise their hands in class are suddenly jumping with the masses. Putting their arms around sweaty strangers, feeling closer than family, all because they're quoting the same lyrics." Brit had felt that at the last Taylor Swift concert. Closing her eyes, swaying, losing herself in a weird euphoria.

"Group hysteria," Finn said.

Spencer nodded. "Chat room works the same. A place to get students hyped and angry. Make them feel like they're the chosen ones for the greater good." He pulled out a cigarette. "Just takes one to suggest a player to take out, and you have others clawing to figure out a way to make it happen."

He lit the end, took a drag. Brit waited for him to calm down a little. He looked ready to fight someone.

Finn kept shaking his head, then looking out into the water and squinting as if there was an answer somewhere in the dark, a way to fix it or wipe it all away.

"If anybody gets in the way," Spencer continued, blowing out the smoke, "and believe me, they'll know, eyes are everywhere, that student's threatened. With what, who knows? But enough to keep them quiet. For those who are moral enough, who are bent on doing the right thing, well, they knew Brit would be."

Brit thought back to the night she had accidentally found out about the chat room. She grabbed fistfuls of wet earth recalling Walker's smugness as he manipulatively kissed her. She assumed the fake recording was all his idea, but he might've just outed her name and waited for the ideas to flood the chat.

"And sure, Eli was an accident," Spencer continued, "but only because Damarius was ready to go to the authorities. He knew better than to go to the local ones."

"Are you saying—"

"No, I doubt policemen are in the chat room," Brit said, thinking of her squad, the hive mentality, how they'd almost gotten her to quit. "Pretty sure it's entirely student-run."

"But." Spencer took another drag of his cigarette. "EastPay football is the heartbeat of East Pages. And the people who live here will fight to keep that heart pumping, at whatever cost. Yes, adults. And yes, police officers."

"If Officer Clarke saw something instigated by the chat room," Finn said, "you think he wouldn't intervene?"

Spencer tapped his cigarette, flicking ash off the end. "Can't prove it, but I wouldn't test it with the ten-yard chains, either."

"I told Meg," Brit said to Finn, and his eyes dropped at her name. "Figured you'd want her to know."

He nodded humbly. "Thanks." He added tentatively, "She said my grandmother was poisoned—some mushrooms on a pizza meant for me last year."

Brit felt her stomach dip. "What? She didn't say anything to me about that."

"It was a theory," Finn said. "She had a run-in with Pastor Mike Menke. Thought he might be behind some players getting sick."

"Wouldn't be a shocker," Spencer said.

Players had been poisoned? By adults? Brit's head fell back. She looked up at the sky. *The idolatry for this sport knew no bounds . . .* She laughed at the wildness of it all. "A month ago, I would've said this was so far-fetched. But it's simple. Texas loves a small-town team that can't seem to lose." She stood, wiped the dirt off her backside. "Football is our town's paycheck. Without it, how many local businesses could still support their families?"

"And I get it," Spencer said. "And so do you." He pointed his cigarette at Finn. "How far would we go for our families?"

The weight of that pulled Finn's head down. Brit had grown up with Finn. She knew the loyalty he had for his grandma. "So, what?" he mumbled. "We just stay quiet?"

"Hell, no," Spencer said. "That's why Brit brought us out here. Right?"

She loved that he assumed she'd have a plan. He reached out and took her hands.

"Listen," he said softly. "Before I left tonight, I told my sister I'd fix this. And I believe it. But only because of you. I know you're a shit-ton smarter than any of them. And us. And I know you haven't let this rest since you found out about it." He slowly switched her grip and linked their fingers. She could feel the electricity—this tension between them—and she again couldn't believe these feelings. Falling for a football player, one thing. But Spencer Collins? She swallowed. "So tell us, brainiac," he said. "How are we taking down the football program?"

Wait, what? "We're not," Brit said. His hands released from hers, dropped at his sides. She could feel his immediate anger and suspicion.

"Why not?" He glared. "I could cheat on purpose. Get caught. Say the coaches planned it."

Brit shook her head. "Won't work. You still have the garbage."

"What?"

She'd thought about this a lot in the past few days. It reminded her of Sunday's sermon. Something about trying to get rid of bad actions rather than first dealing with inner hurt. "You think you can solve it all by getting rid of the rats. But there's still the garbage. So, it'll attract more rats. Backward. You gotta get rid of the garbage. Then the rats got nothing to eat."

"What in hell are you talking about?" Spencer asked.

She rolled her eyes. "You can't get rid of the football program. Town won't have it. You fire the coaches and get new ones? You still have The Game. What if I can get rid of The Game? The chat room. Get rid of the mass access to names, ideas, threats?"

"They could just start another one," Spencer said.

"What if I can stop that, too?"

"I'm in," Finn said. "If you can do it—"

"You know there's nothing else I'd want for Leah." Spencer folded his arms. "But didn't you tell me it was impossible?"

"Look, you want to mess with The Game, right? What if I can hack into Walker's account?"

"And then what?"

"Take note of every screen name on there. Go one by one. Break into each of their accounts. Change their passwords. Lock them out. Eventually I'll find the administrator, be able to shut the whole thing down."

"*That's* your plan?" Spencer said, his doubt obvious. "Sounds like it's gonna take a hella long time."

She nodded. Which was why she needed their help on the field. She needed them to buy her time. "You've gotta convince them we've given up and we're all in." She looked at Finn. "Make Walker think EastPay's your new girlfriend—that Megan never held a candle to this team. I'm not locking him out. I need to use his account."

Finn said, "I can do that," but Spencer remained unresponsive, looking out at the river, and whether he was doubtful or just thinking it through, she couldn't tell. She bobbed her head around until she broke his concentration and he looked at her. He stared into her eyes, unblinking.

"Please," was all she said. Honest. Raw. She was holding her breath, waiting for him to break his gaze but hoping he wouldn't. She knew Finn was next to them, seeing it all, but she no longer cared who saw what or whether they approved.

Spencer sighed, and there it was—the slight break in his steel demeanor—which was all she needed. She wrapped her arms around him and kissed his cheek. His body stiffened again. "What are you doing?"

"Thanking you," she said, squeezing him warmly.

"I never said okay."

She smiled, looked up at him through her eyelashes. "Yes, you did." And then she clapped, bouncing up and down as if they'd made a two-point conversion, forgetting briefly that this wasn't the time or the place. Spencer shushed her, but he smirked. She allowed the boys to usher her out of the ravine, ducking low and hurrying back to their cars, dodging moonlight that darted down through openings between trees and branches.

Finn had left his car at Spencer's, so the two guys told her to text when she was home safe. Both cars kept their lights off until they were far from Clayton Messler's property, but Brit blasted her Spotify pump-up list on the way home. She had work to do, but she wasn't working alone. She had a team now. Or, as she would call it: a squad.

Chapter 49
FINN

On Friday night, the Spartans were held to a tie until the third quarter when Finn thought, *Here goes nothing*, and made a quick trip to the referee for a chat. He ran back to the huddle while the ref waved one of the Broncos' players to the sidelines. While the ref conferred with the player, Thomas White asked, "What's that about?"

Spencer said, "Coach complained his athletic tape is illegal."

"Illegal tape?"

Spencer motioned to Finn. "Geringer pointed it out."

Finn lifted a shoulder as the Broncos' coach called a time-out. "Tape's supposed to be white, black, or their colors," Finn said. "Red's *our* color." The guy jogged to a teammate, who riffled through a nearby bag and handed him white athletic tape. He sat and began unwrapping the red athletic tape around his foot.

Thomas said, "Nice. Didn't know you had it in you, Geringer."

Finn felt Walker's stare but avoided eye contact. Just shrugged and mumbled, "All for the game," a private admission of defeat just for Walker. He hoped Walker bought it.

The player eventually subbed in, but by that time, the Spartans had been on a drive down the middle, gaining three or four yards each play until their kicker made an easy field goal. Two minutes later the Spartans defense intercepted a pass and the offense was back on the field. White threw long for three downs and then hammered a short five-yard bullet into the hands of Finn, who ran for a touchdown. The Spartans kept their momentum until the final seconds ticked down, sealing a smooth victory.

As they walked off the field, Finn lagged behind, stacking a few cones and handing them to the team of volunteers who cleaned up every week. Nearby, Spencer threw a bag of footballs over his shoulder. Neither acknowledged the other.

"That was a good move," Spencer said when no one was within earshot. He didn't look at Finn. "All our players saw it."

"They didn't ask for my input this week," Finn muttered.

"Yet you still pulled a key player out. That says a lot."

Finn grabbed some water bottles and put them back in the carrier. "Somebody was out, though. I could feel it."

Spencer smirked. "Just their key D. Cornerback and safety. Ineligibility."

"Grades?"

"Nah," Spencer replied. "Some outside-of-school tutor confessed to writing some papers for them. Wonder how much the Booster Club paid him."

Suddenly, the guy who subbed out third quarter to rewrap his foot sprinted down the sidelines and cut off Finn. "What the hell, man? You were the one who came to me pregame. Asked if you could use my white tape, but you used it all, so you gave me your red. Then you complain about it?"

Finn held up his hands in surrender. "That was my coach."

"My teammate saw you point it out to the coach."

"Did he? Well, I didn't know the color would be so distracting."

"That's messed up." He turned and walked back toward his bus.

As Finn was about to climb aboard, Walker blocked his path,

faced him. Suspicion creased his eyes. "What gives?" His shoulders were back. Tense. Poised for attack.

"Coach didn't ask me to research this week." Finn kept his voice calm. "So, I thought I'd do my own." He looked around, checking for nosy eavesdroppers. "And." Finn channeled the laser focus he used on the field. Eyes only for the end zone. "Been thinking about what I want." He lowered his voice. "What I really want. If I play my cards right. The doors that might open . . ."

Walker stood still, maybe weighing his words. A slow grin spread across his face. Finn knew why. Walker believed the chat room was invincible with or without Finn, but it stroked his ego that he'd won a convert. Walker clapped Finn once on the shoulder. "So, what? You pay off the refs?"

Finn shook his head. "NFL rules—thought you knew that," he said, even though he'd been up half the night Googling obscure rules and ineligibility offenses. "DeSean Jackson got fined six thousand dollars when he wore police tape on his shoes to protest brutality."

"Solid work," was all Walker said, and he moved out of the way for Finn to enter the bus.

• • •

When Finn came home that night, he found his grandma near the side of the house pruning a thick vine of flowers on a trellis. "Hey, Grams," he said. "We won tonight."

"That's nice, dear." She snipped a few dead leaves and flowers. He'd told her earlier this week that he and Meg broke up. Said he didn't want to talk about it. She'd frowned, started to speak, but then patted his hand and said she'd be right here when he did.

He set down his duffel, his energy suddenly zapped. "What are you, night gardening or something?" From the dim porch light, he could make out her faint smile.

"Mmm, it's technically called moon gardening, but the clouds are making me a liar tonight."

"This your moon garden?" He motioned to the new pots full of bright white flowers.

She nodded. "Only bloom at night. All white or light colored so they reflect the moonlight. Even planted some white pumpkins."

"Sorry you didn't get to go to the game tonight," he said. She paused and then resumed pruning. He sat down on a freestanding bench swing near a row of large potted plants. "I know Meg's usually your ride, but—"

"Oh, I went to the game." She picked up a hose and turned it on. Finn stopped swinging, digging his heels into the soft earth. She fanned the pots with a misty spray of water. "Megan still picked me up. She stayed, too. Your drive third quarter was strong, but they pulled out the one who kept tackling you in the second, so who knows if you just got lucky."

The red athletic tape.

"Meg was there?" His words sounded far away to him, full of wonder or disbelief or maybe both.

His grandma lifted some leaves so the water hit the soil. "I don't think she wanted you to know, so we left in the middle of the fourth—but she's like this one here." She motioned to a potted plant. "Look at these beauties."

Finn looked at the white flowers, how they drooped rather than opened up to the sky. "They look like bells."

"Angel's trumpets," she said. "Brugmansia. When it gets too cold, you tuck the pot away in a closet and bring it out when winter's over. It'll look dead, but it's dormant. That's like Meg. And to her, you feel like winter right now."

"It's complicated." He thought of the night at Dante's Ravine, the fuzzy memory of sweet alcohol, damp earth, Tammy's behavior, the way he let her draw him in . . .

"She's a strong girl. She can handle it. Why don't you pay a visit to your old school? Show her you care enough to talk through things." Mrs. Callahan snipped a bud off the brugmansia and held it under Finn's nose.

He tilted his head away. "Whoa. Strong. Like perfume." He took it, twirled the bell-shaped flower in his hand. "Nothing to talk about. I messed up. She knows."

He handed her the bloom, and their hands touched. "She's hearing rumors from her side"—she sat down next to him on the bench swing—"wondering how I'm your guardian if we're not related."

"That a big deal?"

"It's fixable. But." She sighed and set down her pruning shears. The cicadas screamed over the sounds of crickets. The swing creaked as they rocked back and forth. "Might take more time than I'd like."

Her gaze drifted to her hands, and she wrung them like old sponges, one over the other. "I gave him my word—your grandfather—before he died that I'd do everything I could for his daughter. But Kat—"

"Not your fault. Mom's an addict."

His grandma sighed. "Your mom *has an addiction*," she corrected, and he marveled at how Grandma still protected her. "And she didn't always. Anyway . . . she didn't want anything from me." He'd heard this story before, but it felt weightier tonight—more like a confession, an apology. "But you. You came along and . . ." She trailed off, then looked at him. "You enabled me to keep my word." She touched his cheek. "I never felt like you *weren't* mine."

His throat tightened. His words came out as a hoarse whisper. "Same. Who cares about stupid paperwork?" He reached his arm around her bony shoulders.

"*I* should've cared," she mumbled, then leaned down to grab a potted rosebush underneath the swing. "See this?" She pointed to a swollen area in the middle of a thick stem. "This stem was originally cut from a yellow rosebush. But this"—she shook the potted plant—"is a red rosebush. See?"

She peeled back the leaves, and tucked underneath was a dark red bud. He touched the stem again, the one with the swollen middle, making sure to avoid the thorns. At the top was a yellow rose, bright as the sun. Red and yellow roses. On the same plant.

"It fused," he said. He'd never seen this before. Didn't know it was possible.

She smiled. "Once it fuses, it's not separate. It's the same plant now. Like us."

Fused. He reached for her delicate hand, brittle yet soft with wrinkles, and held it in his lap.

Chapter 50
MEGAN

"What are you doing here?"

Meg knew she sounded mean, but she had to. It was the only way to keep Finn at bay. It was hard enough letting him go. She'd already made the mistake of showing up at his football game, but thank God he never found out. She hoped any witnesses would understand she was a chauffeur—nothing more. Just there to help Finn's grandma get to the game. But now he was *here*, at her school in the middle of the day? She couldn't do this. Not on a Monday. Not any day. His eyes pleaded with her, but she turned away and said, "I'm going to be late for fifth."

"No, wait. I'm sorry."

The words slapped Meg to attention. She shifted her notebooks from one arm to the other, kept her focus downward. Why was he apologizing? She was the one who'd cut him off.

"Meg, look at me. I messed up." Her eyes turned to him, confused. Was this about him saying he was at practice when he really was at Brit's? Or the excessive drinking at UT? She could hear his voice cracking—see the tears in his eyes. Oh no. He thought this breakup was all his fault, and it wasn't. Something softened inside her—there was no way she could keep up this mean front. They both leaned against a locker, heads tilted close, "If I could"—he searched for the right word—"take it back, do it differently, I know I can't, but—" His eyes darted, afraid of who might be watching. She didn't know why. This was West Oak, not EastPay. There couldn't possibly be people involved here. She covered his mouth with a gentle hand, two fingers pressed against his lips. He kissed them on instinct.

"It's okay," was all she could say, her throat constricted.

"It's not." She could feel his lips as they spoke through her fingers. "It's so far from okay." He tugged at her wrist. Her fingers dropped to his chest. "Whatever you saw, it wasn't—"

"What I saw?" Now she was confused, but he barreled on.

"I know it's no excuse, but I couldn't figure out a way to tell you, and I was so afraid—"

"I've kept stuff from you, too." She held his hands, but he peeled them away. He studied her, like he was trying to understand. "Your grandma talked to you, right?"

He nodded. "She's the reason I'm here."

So he knew—his grandma had told him—how Meg was blackmailed to break up. How she could ruin the chances of him being seen by scouts.

But he was still here, willing to jeopardize that.

All the locked-up emotion inside her unfurled at once, and she reached for his face. In response, he threaded his fingers through her hair and kissed her, his lips hungry as they pressed into hers. She trembled under his mouth, drinking it in, feeling his wet tears spread from his cheek to hers. When they parted, both gasping, the air rushing in, she rested her forehead on his chest, felt the way his arms tentatively wrapped around her. She pulled back, took his hands in hers, and set them at his sides. "I shouldn't have gone to the football game."

"I'm glad you did."

"Look, they know I care about you," she said. "You've gotta stay away. This is bigger than us."

"I know." He squeezed her hands. "Which is why Brit's gonna break into the chat room, shut down the whole thing."

"What? How?"

"We're working on it. I—" Finn's phone buzzed. She saw the light bloom on his screen with the caller's name: BRIT WALLACE.

He answered tentatively, "Yeah?" And then, "That works. I'm already out of class. Yeah, I can meet you. You at your house?"

Her house? Brit was home during school?

"Why would you ask Spencer to do that? He needs to get out of there," he hissed. "Because, Brit! It's *one p.m.*" He rubbed his forehead with the heel of his hand. "On a *Monday*. So coaches are in meetings all day. They only leave for bathroom breaks. Everyone knows that." It was true. Even Meg knew EastPay's drill. All day Monday, different players came to the office to discuss strategy, or, in some players' cases, "research." Then on Wednesdays, coaches discussed all their findings, watched more tape, went through the game plan, never left their room. "Sixth period, Brit. I told you that. Coaches take their lunch before practice. Yeah, on my way."

He clicked off the phone and met Meg's searching eyes. Clasping both her hands, he said, "Do you wanna come?"

She shook her head. Even if they shut the chat room down, it wouldn't fix her and Finn. Meg's mom would make sure of that. "The less I know, the better. Also, I can't skip class."

He shook his head stubbornly. "Come with me."

She dropped her head, pulled her hands out of his. "No." She rubbed her arms as if the fear and frustration was crawling through her skin, spreading like a rash. "I can't."

He persisted, "Your dad's a lawyer. Offing you would be a bad move. They want you out of the picture, not dead. They're not gonna hurt you."

He held out his hand, looked solidly into her eyes, trying to anchor her with his gaze, but she looked away. "Finn, it's not me I'm worried about."

"What if I'm willing to risk that?" he said, but she was already shaking her head. No way. At best, he wouldn't get to play football. At worst, he could be separated from his grandma until they sorted everything out. Finn cut off her thoughts. "Look, I've spent a week learning what it's like to do life apart from you, and I mean, I can do it, but it's shit." Meg laughed despite her sadness. "I realized," he continued, "that no matter how things turn out, *whatever* my future looks like, I"—his voice cracked again, and he cleared his throat, swallowed—"I want you in it." Something broke in her right then. Maybe he knew it—he always read her so well—because he tentatively reached a hand toward her and tucked a piece of hair behind her ear. "So." He laced his fingers into hers. "Follow me in your car?"

She nodded miserably. Classes could wait. She grabbed her keys and let herself be led toward the parking lot.

Chapter 51
MEGAN

"Hey, Meg," Brit chirped. "'Bout time the two of you stopped your nonsense."

Meg was immediately swaddled with an octopus hug from Brit, all legs and arms, as she and Finn walked into Brit's room. Even though Meg was missing school, nothing felt more right than this moment. If her parents found out, she'd pull the lawyer card on her dad—he should understand about making sacrifices to right the wrongs.

Brit sat at her desk and woke up her computer. "Spencer got into the computer lab at school. And sixth period's conference, so no one's there."

Meg folded her arms. "*Spencer's* part of this?"

"How'd he break in?" Finn asked, as if he and Spencer were old friends. *What was happening?* Meg looked to Finn for an answer, but he leaned back on Brit's cheerleading box and said, "Computer lab's always locked."

"I know!" Brit waved a box of Kleenex over her head like a pom-pom. "I stuffed tissues in the doorjamb last week when I had to sneak in and alter a few things to get back on the cheerleading squad."

"You're back on?" Meg swelled with joy. "I knew you'd figure it out." She threw her arms around Brit, and Finn wrapped an arm around them both. She loved being part of this family. Loved feeling Finn's warmth against her—the unique way it made her feel secure, calm, protected. She pulled away reluctantly. "So, *Spencer?*"

"I know, right?" Brit said, swiveling in her computer chair. "Who'd a thunk it?" She smiled in a giddy schoolgirl way. *Wait. Spencer and Brit?* It had only been a couple weeks, and already Meg felt so out of the loop. She plopped on the ottoman next to Brit.

Brit motioned to the screen. "Spencer's searching the browser histories of all the student computers. In the meantime, look at what I found. I don't know what it proves, but it's eerie." She typed a web address. A black screen came up with two white rectangular boxes, one for a username, and one for a password. "Welcome to The Game," she said.

"This is the chat room?" Meg said. "But how'd you even find—"

"I saw the web address at Walker's," Brit said. "Memorized it."

Meg looked at the web address. It was long. It had symbols and numbers and zero order to it. *"Really?"*

"You say that like it'd be a strange thing for me."

Brit pointed at the trophy—the one she had dug out from the back of her closet the other night—now standing tall on her desk. Announcing her second-place victory in the individual category for the National Youth Cybersecurity Championship.

"But still. How?" Meg asked. She touched the trophy, marveling at how proud Brit had become of her past in such a short time.

Brit shrugged. "I just remember things. Like my brain takes a screenshot. That's how I stumbled across Walker's username. It was all over the chat that night." She typed *789TYT* in the prompt for the username and then entered the password.

Meg was dumbfounded. "He told you his password?"

Brit laughed. "He'd just as easily drink rooster pee. No, I have a program. Had it since sixth grade. My computer coach at the time had to sign papers to get approval. It runs every combination of password until finding a match with the username." She tapped on the screen. "This one took about two days."

Meg was starting to understand. If they found the administrator, Brit could figure out the password and shut the whole thing down. Which was why Spencer was looking for clues on the school computers.

Meg scooted closer. The chat room looked like a long scrolling conversation between people with cryptic names. Brit clicked on a tab on top titled "Yearbook" and typed her name in the search icon. An info sheet appeared with "Britney L. Wallace" across the header in bold font, and a thumbnail photo of her in the top left corner. It was a PDF of a typed form, the blanks filled in with cursive.

"Who wrote that?" Finn asked.

Brit shrugged. "Me."

Meg raised an eyebrow.

Brit continued, "Advisory class. Homeroom? The detailed bio we filled out the first day? Remember?"

"Mine was three pages," Finn said. "They said it was for emergency purposes."

"And here it is, every page scanned and entered. ASB started it years ago, for teachers to have on file. Your file only has this year's because you transferred. But they still have mine from ninth and tenth, too."

Meg's head reeled. *These students had access to other students' bios?*

"I remember that day," Finn said, his face slightly paler. "Some student from leadership collected them. Supposedly to alphabetize them."

"Supposedly." Brit pointed at her answers. "So it's all the basics. Residence. Email. Cell. Addresses. But then all my favorites too. Best friends. Pets. Foods. Allergies. College choices. Parents' income for 'FAFSA purposes.' Five-year plans. Likes and dislikes."

"So every student who has a password has access to all your school gossip," Meg said. "Secrets. Weaknesses." The truth left her breathless. She whispered, "That's how they know."

"It's so basic." Brit winced. "And we hand it all to them. Wrapped in a perfect bow." She clicked forward to a grainy photo of her walking out of cheerleading practice from the gym. *Click.* Another at school laughing with her friends.

It was obvious, but Meg needed to say it aloud. "So it's for blackmail." Meg's stomach knotted. "Just like your coach is doing with my mom."

Finn halted at her words like they were playing freeze tag. She gulped, finally ready to tell him the *whole* truth.

"Your coach caught my mom in a DUI years ago," she continued slowly, "and she's been paying him off to keep quiet."

"The football coach?" Brit squeaked, grabbing her phone. "I'm texting Spence."

There was no going back once Meg admitted it. But Finn deserved the truth. He'd always been honest with her. "So that's why my mom threatened to call CPS on your grandma if I didn't break up with you."

"Wait. What? CPS?" Finn said in a high-pitched sort of way, the tone that said he had no clue. Now Meg was lost.

"You said your grandma told you that part already," Meg replied, but Finn's brow furrowed. "You said that's why you showed up today."

Brit's eyes popped wide. "Like, hush money? For real, Meg?"

Meg turned to Brit. "It's funneled through East Pages Community Church, but I'm sure it's going to the football program. Which means the police, the church, and the football program are getting a cut."

"What if she's not the only one 'donating'?" Brit asked.

Meg nodded. "I wondered that, too."

She was about to ask Finn *what* his grandma had told him, but Brit tapped the desktop monitor. "Speaking of blackmail, look at this." She typed Spencer's name, and his page popped up.

Meg grinned. Some of his answers were jokes. Finn read out loud, "'Favorite hangout spot: *on your mom.*'"

Brit giggled. "God bless his socks, he knew. They're aware he knows, too. But like he'd snitch . . ." She clicked forward. All the pictures were candid photos of Spencer and his sister. Sitting. Walking. Laughing. "They know his Achilles' heel."

A chill shot through Meg as she recalled the words of Finn's grandma the night Meg checked on her. *"Everyone here knows who Megan Kaufman is, the Achilles' heel of their favorite running back."* Meg touched Finn's arm. "And they know I'm yours."

Brit looked nervously at Finn, and Finn looked away. It made Meg uncomfortable—*Had Brit looked at his file? What pictures had been snapped of Meg?*—but Brit immediately said, "Look at

Walker's." She clicked on Walker's bio. It was more generic, sparse—just the emergency info, college choices, his basic likes. Food allergies: *none*. Five-year plan: *NFL*. Favorite hangout spot: *football field*. She tried to click forward to the photos, but it wouldn't let her. "Because I'm logged in to Walker's account," she started to explain.

"—you can't access your own photos," Finn finished.

"Clever," Meg said. That way, players could see everyone else's dirt but their own, keeping them constantly unsure if anyone had documented any missteps. *Ugh, the fear.*

"There's more. You're not gonna like this." Brit clicked out of the "Yearbook" tab and onto the "Players" tab. It had fifty or so hyperlinked numbers.

"What's your football number?" Brit asked.

"Seriously?" Finn said.

She laughed and said, "Keeping you humble, twenty-five."

Brit scrolled to the "25." There were two links: 25a and 25b. She clicked on one. There was one of those "sound" emojis, and she tapped it. It was silent. Brit clicked on 25b. More silence. But then—scratchy but clear—someone taking slow deep breaths. Someone sleeping. Finn shook his head, confused.

"Gram . . ." Brit started. "She always naps on the couch."

"Yeah, so?" Finn said.

"Right under the portrait of Gale Sayers," Brit said, her voice steel.

Meg clapped a hand over her mouth. Her heart rate quickened. *His house was bugged?*

"Oh my God," Finn said.

"Twenty-five A must be your bedroom," Brit said. "Twenty-five B, Gale Sayers."

"Wait," Finn started. "But you—"

"Hung most of those pictures?" Brit answered quickly. "Yup. I had no darned idea. Must be in the frames."

"Wow." Meg couldn't say anything else. "Wow," she said again, this time at a whisper. These students. She understood deep love for a sport. She could relate to sacrifice and drive. Passion for one's future. But this went beyond. This was obsession—the need to win and control the victory at all costs.

She couldn't speak for a minute. No one could. The only sound was the light breathing of Finn's grandma.

Unaware.

Meg thought about the private conversations they had had in his room. *Nothing had been private?*

"That seems way over your pay grade," Meg finally said, trying to keep her voice steady. Finn's nostrils flared. He was taking deep breaths. Processing it all.

Brit pointed at the hyperlinked numbers. "It's wireless. Way simpler than TV spy stuff. If someone clicks on it, and if the internet's working on both sides, they can listen."

Finn was angrier than Meg had ever recalled seeing him. She could feel his hot breath next to her. He rose, paced the room, walked away from them and over to Brit's closet. He steadied himself, a hand against the door.

"But what about Walker?" he pressed, his voice tight and clipped. "What about other players who know? They all have memorabilia in their houses."

Brit threw a hand up. "They probably disconnect it. It's not rocket science."

It sounded like rocket science to Meg. It seemed like so much trouble. For what? For a championship football team? Or was it more than that? Was this the way anyone would act if they were given free rein? No consequences? Anonymous access and no accountability?

Meg reached across Brit and canceled out of the "Players" tab. She clicked again on the "Yearbook" tab and typed in Finn's name. She felt Brit's hand on hers. A warning.

But why?

She scrolled down. No. This couldn't be right. "Finn?" The word caught in the back of her throat. She didn't look over her shoulder to see if he responded. Her arms hung limp and she stared at the screen.

"Oh, God," Meg murmured. She heard Finn rush across the room, instantly behind her. There, in front of them, was a photo taken at Fourth and Goal. She recognized the pool tables. A girl with red hair leaning into Finn. Her hand on his arm.

She clicked on the next photo. The parking lot of Fourth and Goal, Finn's arms looped around the same girl, her body pressing his against the car, her face close to his ear.

She clicked. Dante's Ravine. Finn laughing with a group, holding hands with the same girl. *Click.* Finn drinking with her.

Click. His arm around her. Her head on his chest.

Click. Her hands on his waist. Their faces close. Too close.

"Meg," he breathed out. "I tried to tell you. It's nothing close to what it looks like."

What?

"It's time-stamped," she croaked. "At Dante's. That was the night you canceled on our friends."

He didn't speak at first. "Yes," he finally managed, and it made her angry that he sounded like he might cry. He wasn't allowed to be sad about this, to share her grief.

"Did you even visit UT?" she asked.

"No." She could barely hear him. His voice was thick with something. Sadness? Grief? "Meg, I apologized. I told you—"

"You told me you were sorry about going to Brit's."

"I told you I was sorry that I lied to you. That there were photos—you saw these." His face looked pained, but also confused. "It's why you broke things off!"

Her mouth fell open. "I broke things off because my mom told me if I didn't, she'd end your football career." She couldn't breathe. The world was blurry around her, the room too small. "Tell me this is some Photoshopped garbage—tell me." She turned to him. He put his head down.

Why couldn't he just lie? She wouldn't know the difference, and right now, she needed him to lie.

"You really—?" Tears of unbelief filled her eyes. "Who?" she whispered. Then she screamed, "Who!"

"Her name's Tammy," Finn mumbled, and she could hear the misery in his words. It made her angrier. "Tammy Shaw. She's varsity captain with Brit. I thought you knew. Megs, I didn't do anything. I stopped. It meant nothing."

"Which night?" she cried. "Which night meant nothing? These were different nights. Same girl."

Finn's eyes pleaded with her. "She tried to convince me that if people believed you were out of the picture, they'd talk."

"You didn't think to run this by me?" They'd never kept things from each other. Secrets were only if you had something to hide. "I need to go."

"Please don't."

But she'd grabbed her keys. Brit didn't move, didn't follow. Meg ran down the stairs to the front door, not even bothering to shut it. She could hear his footsteps behind her as she reached her car. Everything in her was about to break, but she breathed. Stayed calm. "Finn, you need to let me be."

"Meg," he started.

"Please," she pleaded. Tears dripped freely off her chin. "Please," she whispered.

She saw his Adam's apple bob. Tears filled his eyes, too. "Okay," he managed.

Meg crawled into her car, eyes straight ahead, not looking once at Finn, who stood to the side, unmoving. Meg respected herself too much to be in a relationship with someone she couldn't trust. She wouldn't be back. She couldn't. This was it, and for a moment, she felt paralyzed.

This was really it.

Then she put the car in reverse, and as soon as she knew the car was out of Finn's sight, she burst into heaving sobs.

Chapter 52
BRITNEY

Brit found Finn standing in her driveway, Megan's car gone.

"You want to go after her?" she asked.

He shook his head and sighed in a way that seemed to breathe sadness.

"Look, I'm sorry," Brit started. "I feel like cow dung saying this, but your breakup is real bad timing. Just heard from Spence. After my text, he somehow broke into the coaches' office."

Finn whipped his head in her direction, momentarily pulled from his stupor. "Really?"

She couldn't believe it, either. Finn turned back to the empty road, as if he could still see Meg in the distance. He closed his eyes like he was fighting off physical pain. When he opened them, they were glazed over, the same focus he had right before kickoff. "You're right. Let's go."

She hurried back inside and up the stairs to her room, Finn in tow. She opened the screen-sharing program she'd downloaded earlier, swiveling in her chair while she waited. Her phone lit up with Spencer's name, and she answered it on speaker. "Okay, Houdini," Brit said. "How'd you break into a locked office?"

"I didn't," Spencer said. "I clogged one of the johns with paper towels, enough that coaches came out to check. Then I had about thirty seconds to use your breaking and entering skills."

"Ohmigosh, you stuffed Kleenex in the doorjamb?" Brit couldn't hide her excitement.

"Yeah, don't let it go to your head. But okay, it worked. Door swung right open."

Brit giggled. "Brilliant. And coaches?"

"Just left in their cars for lunch."

"Okay, let's move," Brit said. "Hey, Finn's with me."

"What a treat."

Usually that would get a half laugh from Finn, but it was as if he didn't even hear. She noticed his face, a blank sheet of paper, and hoped he was up for this.

She clicked to a web address. "Spence?"

"Still here."

"Shush. I'm gonna text you this address. I need you to download the screen-sharing program."

"Aye, aye, Captain."

Brit grinned but covered it up with a cough. Finn sat slumped in the chair next to her. He stayed zoned in on the screen, eyes unblinking. Her cousin still felt like crap, she could tell, but at least he knew how to shut everything out and focus on the task. God bless football.

The program went through on her end.

"Great," she instructed. "Now I need you to tell me the number code it gave you on your screen."

Spencer recited a list of numbers and letters that she typed into her program. She pushed send.

"Look at that," Spencer's voice echoed through her phone speaker, and she could hear him smiling through his words. "It says *r20431 would like permission to share your screen. Accept?*"

"That's me," Brit confirmed.

"Damn, you're hot."

Brit felt her face grow warm, but thankfully, Spencer was miles away and Finn's eyes were glued to the screen.

"Okay," Spencer continued. "Clicking *yes*."

Brit's screen dwarfed and another screen appeared with a second cursor moving around.

"I'm in," Brit said. She clicked on the search box and typed, *Can you see this?*

Another cursor moved across her screen, highlighted her text, and deleted it. In its place, Spencer typed, *R20431, what are you wearing?*

Brit gasped, half laughing.

"Uh, I'm still here, guys," Finn said.

Brit cleared her throat, immediately sobering. Spencer didn't know Finn was heartbroken. But she did. Not the best time to be flirting.

"Okay, Brit," Spencer said, his voice tinny from the phone speaker. "You see anything funny on here?"

She clicked on various files, but they were a lot of what any coach would have on his computer. Football plays. Itineraries. Phone lists. Scheduled meetings. She could hear a lot of rustling in the background. "What're you doing, Spence?"

"Looking through their backpacks. Nothin'. Wait. Found a flash drive. Stand by."

He must've inserted it, because a folder appeared on her screen titled "EPCC." She quickly saved a copy to her own desktop, then clicked it.

Finn leaned in. "What is it?"

But he could see for himself. It was a spreadsheet of income and expenditures. A list of names and donations.

"Oh my," Brit breathed out, and it came as a whoosh. "EPCC. East Pages Community Church."

"So?" Spencer sounded confused.

Brit said in a rushed voice, "Meg told us the pastor there is taking her mom's money. Well, she said Coach was taking it, technically, but funneling it through the church and probably the pastor. She thinks it's going to the football program."

Spencer asked, "Pastor Mike Menke? He's an asshat. He'd keep it for himself—no way he'd give it to football."

Brit squinted at the screen. "Then what's a church finance ledger doing in the briefcase of a football coach?"

Spencer sighed through the phone. "Could mean a lot of things. One of our coaches could volunteer there. Be a deacon. Treasurer. Who knows. It's not surprising. Not in this town."

"But after what Meg said—" It seemed too close a coincidence. Brit searched for Megan's mom, scrolling until she found "Kaufman, Irene." It was an obscene amount, but the next day, it showed the same amount going back out to A&F Contracting. She looked at other costs, then scribbled some quick math on a piece of paper.

"What's going on over there?" Spencer said.

Brit felt Finn leaning on her as he looked over her shoulder. "Brit's getting all Rain Man on us," Finn said.

"Hot."

Brit would've blushed, but she was too disappointed. "Spencer's right," she said. "It's nothing." She sighed. "Nothing's illegal here. It's current records." She put her elbows on the table and dropped her forehead into her open hands. "Shit."

Spencer spoke through the phone. "Shet? There you go again with the Shetland ponies."

"Oh, shut up," she said, but it was playful.

"Shet up," he mimicked.

"Everything that's going in is going out," she concluded, dropping her pen. "It's clean."

"Or not," Finn said. She'd forgotten for a moment he was in the conversation. "What if people are paying extra so nothing happens to them? Like the Mafia does to businesses."

"I dunno," she said. "Even if our Booster Fund's overflowing from quote-unquote *donations*, it doesn't matter, Finn. Everything checks out."

"Well, shet," Spencer piped in, and Brit glared at the phone.

"What about what Meg said right before we broke up?" Finn asked.

"You guys broke up?" Spencer said, and Brit could hear his shock. "Why?"

"Doesn't matter," Finn said.

"So . . . she's available?"

"Fuck you." But it was the first time Brit had seen the hint of a smile cracking through Finn's despondent face.

Spencer laughed through the phone, then sobered. "Seriously, though. You okay?"

Brit was used to guy humor but she would never understand it.

"Guys!" Brit shouted. "We're on limited time." She opened the coaches' search engine and scrolled the history, clicking on a familiar address. And what popped up made all three collectively gasp.

"Well, well," Brit said, grinning.

The familiar black home screen was open with the same two white rectangular boxes for username and password. The chat room. Only the username was auto-filled.

On the coaches' office computer.

She took a screenshot and focused on her breathing, her adrenaline starting to surge. An *adult* was part of this? "You think one of them's the admin?"

"Maybe Coach Wilkins," Finn said. "Meg *just* said he's blackmailing her mom. Coach Goode even admitted he knew Wilkins was shady."

Brit felt her heart racing. "What? Why doesn't he say something?"

"Needs his job. He warned me to stay off Wilkins's radar. Said, 'You don't know who he knows.' If there's a coach involved, it's gotta be Wilkins."

The head coach? She looked at the time. "Okay, Spence," she said. "End the sharing session. Put the flash drive back and get out of there. Now."

"All right, kids," came Spencer's voice. "Finn, get your ass to practice. You got twenty minutes. I ain't covering for you."

Everything on the screen canceled out one by one, and then the whole screen disappeared and was again replaced by her own desktop background.

Finn's breath was shallow, like he was trying to recover from a wind sprint. "How long will it take?"

"To figure out his password?" She tapped her desk with her fingers. "Couple hours, couple days? But technically, we don't know if he's the admin. Once I'm in, I'll try to delete the site. But, if he's not the admin . . ." She didn't finish her thought, but he understood. His shoulders sagged.

"Listen," she said. "Right now, I'm going through every screen name in the chat room—I've written them down—and running them through my program. Every time it spits out a correct password, I'm checking to see if that one's the admin. If not, I change the password so they can't get back in. I'm shutting it down one by one."

Finn didn't buy it, she could tell. "Can't the admin just give them another screen name and password?" he asked.

"Absolutely," she said. "It's gonna be two steps forward, three steps back. Which is why I'm going through every single screen name. One of them's gotta be the admin."

Finn nodded slowly. "And when you find him—"

"Or *her*," Brit added. "Then yes, it's over. And I know they could make a copycat site. But I'm compiling IP addresses. A whole list. I think we might have some collateral."

"Still," Finn said. He rubbed his forehead like he had a headache. "That sounds like it could take a while. To get everybody?"

He was right. It would be weeks. And students would start to know someone was interfering. "Which is why"—she looked pointedly at him—"you and Spencer have GOT to play it cool. And every chance you get, you convince them that I've rolled over and waved the white flag. That I'm just here to cheer."

It took a moment, but something seemed to shift in Finn. The sadness of football and Meg still filled his eyes, but there was something else, too. Pride.

"You've got an incredible mind, Brit," he said, smiling faintly. "Always have."

She reached her arms around his neck and squeezed. "You'll be okay. You know that, right? In a few months, this stupid website will just be a bad memory."

Finn mumbled into her shoulder, "It won't be the only one."

Chapter 53
MEGAN

"It's late." Meg didn't know what else to say Wednesday night when she opened her front door to Spencer.

"Well, you sure as hell don't make things easy."

Since when did she have to? And what was he doing here?

"We're working on it," he said matter-of-factly. "Kicking people out of the chat room one by one."

She nodded. "I'm glad." And she meant it.

"Homecoming's Friday," he said.

"And?" Did he know what had transpired? Was he here for Finn, to try to make amends? Or for himself? If he thought for one second that—

"I have an idea," he said. "But I need your help."

Her mother padded down the stairs. "Who's here?"

"No one, Mom." She realized how lousy that sounded. "A friend. It's fine." Her mother eyed Spencer from his face down to his shoes, like his choice in brand might've given him a pass, but he failed.

"It's after ten," Mrs. Kaufman said, moving into the living room, out of sight but not out of earshot.

"I'm sorry," Meg whispered. "I can't. I'm glad you're working on it. Truly. But—I'm done. Finn and I—"

"I know." Great. So he knew what Finn had done. Maybe he knew before. Had Finn been flirting with Tammy all along, in front of the team, in front of Spencer? Leading to that night?

"I'm not sticking around," he said, and she knew he didn't mean her house. He meant East Pages. "I don't want to look around every corner wondering if my sister's gonna be okay." He traced the wallpaper, a slight smile creasing his face. "But I don't wanna go quietly."

"I told you. Whatever it is, I can't."

"Tomorrow. Five p.m.," he said as if she'd agreed. "Meet me in Weaver—the fields over by Old Town."

"No," she said, not angry. Just defeated. She could feel the exhaustion in her voice as she said, "I'm done."

"You don't have to be there." He held out a flash drive. "But I think you'll want to be." He nudged the drive into Meg's palm. "Brit gave me a copy."

Apprehensively, she took it, turned it over as if there might be a secret message written on the other side. "East Pages Community Church," he said. "The income and expenditures."

Her eyes went wide. *How'd they get—*

"According to Brit, it all checked out," he said. "The donations from your mom matched perfectly with the costs of the renovations for the grounds, not the gardening but the landscaping, and the new flooring, parking expansion, new roofing—"

She barked an angry laugh. "Really? Crappy job if it's a new roof." She thought of how it sagged, dripped on her head even under the awning while Ms. Tristan glared at her.

"Funny you say that. Because A&F Contracting isn't just crappy." He scratched behind his ear. "It doesn't exist."

Meg felt her mouth opening, an invisible pry bar wedging itself in. She was making sense of it all, getting a glimpse of why he was telling her this, when her mom appeared from around the corner.

Her slippers no longer shuffled. It was more of a silent stomp.

"If you'd like to come back," her mom said, "maybe there's a better time. We're about to turn in."

Meg's hand closed around the flash drive, indicating to him that she understood.

"I'll text you," Spencer said, backed out and closed the door, leaving Meg and her mother alone, the ticking of the grandfather clock echoing in their ears.

"No," was all her mother said before turning for the living room, clearly having listened to their entire conversation.

"Mom, this is the proof." She followed her mom to the couch by the bar. Meg held up the flash drive. "You said we didn't have proof. You can finally make this stop."

"How?" Her mom's voice was clipped.

"What do you mean *how*? Your money is being funneled through a church to a false company! That's embezzlement. And you can get them on extortion, too."

Her mother extended an open hand to Meg, her palm facing up.

Waited for Meg to hand over the flash drive.

Meg tightened her fist around it. "I'm giving this to Dad. Tomorrow."

Her mother pursed her lips. "Do you want to ruin us?" she hissed. "Is that what you want?"

"No." Meg wanted to yell, but she steadied the urge, stayed at a low volume. "I want to do the right thing. And I will. I'm just giving you the chance to do it first."

They stood there, a standoff between strong wills, but Meg had been taught by the best, and today, she was stronger than her teacher. Her mother fell into a crumpled heap onto the sofa. "Please don't do this, Megan."

Meg stood over her mom, who looked like a child, folded over on herself.

"He'll be home in an hour. You can let him know. Or I will."

• • •

Thursday after Key Club, Meg drove twenty-three miles to the town of Weaver and the wide-open fields of its public park across from Old Town. The soccer nets had been removed and chalk lines added every ten yards. Even though the field was only eighty yards long, it still packed twenty-two six-year-old boys. The stadium lights glared on Meg like a spotlight. She pulled her baseball cap down to shield her face, doing her best to blend in with the packed sidelines. Even though Spencer had texted her what they were about to do, she was still jittery. She had a pen in her hand, and she clicked it open and closed.

"Hey." Spencer's voice in her ear made her jump, but she was instantly relieved that he found her first. The sidelines were packed two rows deep with parents sitting on lawn chairs or ice chests, some standing and pacing with the coaches, yelling at their sons to collide and tackle. She heard one father yell, "Go for the kill shot!"

"Come on." Spencer led the way, weaving through a few parents into an open space where he stopped next to Pastor Mike

Menke, in street clothes, arms folded, staring at the field. She knew they had driven here specifically to find him, but still she startled, stopping a full step behind them, her heart jumping and then settling. Pastor Mike couldn't see her from where he stood. Still, she tucked her head down at her phone, busied herself with it.

"So this is where it all begins, huh?" Spencer said to Pastor Mike, who glanced at Spencer, then back at the field.

"For some," he answered good-naturedly, as if Spencer could've been anyone.

"Not for me," Spencer said. "But I bet you've heard. Small towns and all." Pastor Mike side-eyed him. "Just like I heard your nephew practiced here Thursday nights." Pastor Mike turned his entire body to Spencer, curious. Wary. But Spencer kept his eyes on the field. "EastPay rumors."

Pastor Mike slowly turned back to face the field, but he stood a little more stiffly.

"There's a girl out there." Spencer motioned at the field. "Number twenty-four. She's holding her own." A deafening cheer broke out as a five-yard pass was caught.

Pastor Mike licked his lips, probably trying to stay quiet, but he couldn't help himself. "Shouldn't be out there," he said, but then offered no more.

Spencer nodded. "Heard a lotta talk about that, too. Like, what happens"—here he paused for dramatic effect, his tone incredulous but over the top—"if the guys start focusing on protecting *her* more'n their quarterback?" He shook his head. "It's a shame. Takin' away the purity of the sport. Don't you agree, Meg?"

Meg's heart was in her throat, but she almost laughed at the shock in Pastor Mike's face as he looked over his shoulder. She stepped forward—her adrenaline making her bold—to stand on Spencer's other side. Pastor Mike's eyes went from wide to narrow real quick.

"I do," Meg said. "That girl ends up interfering with *everything*." Her voice was melodramatic, and she shook her head like Spencer, more times than necessary, like she was replaying the thought and getting appalled all over again. "What is it I heard one time? *A little yeast works through the whole batch of dough.*'"

The ball snapped, and the teams slammed into each other, but with all their forty-five inches and forty-five pounds, it was much more pushing than knocking over. The referee blew the whistle and called a penalty. Some parents cheered. Others booed and hissed. "Let 'em play!" one yelled. Another hollered, "This is football, not a tea party!"

Spencer said, "You'd think it was a championship game, not a six-year-old peewee scrimmage."

Meg said in mock reverence, "When you love the sport, it's a championship game every time." Both of them stayed facing forward, toes to the chalk, but Meg added, "Isn't that right, Pastor?"

"Why are y'all here?" Pastor Mike was clearly tired of the small talk.

Spencer nodded at Meg, who pulled out a Post-it from her pocket. She clicked the pen and wrote a number on it and stuck it to Pastor Mike's arm. "We're gonna need this from you."

A coach shouted to a small boy, "Donaldson! Which way are we going?" Donaldson pointed a tiny finger toward an end zone. "Good job, son! Don't forget!"

Spencer chuckled to himself. "Sounds like he has a history of scoring for the other team."

Pastor Mike peeled the Post-it from his arm, examined the yellow paper.

"Is this a joke?"

Meg tipped her head side to side. "More like an even exchange. My mom's been *donating* to your church every month. That's just the lump sum."

A smug smile crept across Pastor Mike's face. He crumpled the Post-it and let it flutter to the ground.

"Donations are powerful." He clucked his tongue. "We recently redid the flooring." He looked up at the sky. "We are renovating God's house, after all." He spoke like a televangelist, a twisted musical cadence that made Meg cringe.

"The pastor at my church is a good man," Meg said. "Honest. Hardworking. Humble."

"Happy to hear it," Pastor Mike said disinterestedly.

Meg was undone. "There are good pastors out there. And there's also good football out there. And you're giving a bad name to both."

Pastor Mike rolled his eyes, didn't give her the dignity of a response.

"I'm going to need my mom's donations back," Meg said evenly.

Pastor Mike took a satisfied breath. Inhaled the smell of wet grass. It unnerved her how unaffected he was by her words. He smiled at the noise of scattered applause and whistling parents. "I love the sound of a crowd on a football field," he said. "So much joy. Passion. It's like you can hear the angels rejoicing with you."

Spencer said, "Or a bunch of dads living out the careers they never had."

Pastor Mike laughed good-naturedly. "Let's go, QB!" He clapped his hands. "It's what keeps football going. Those fans have more passion than some of the players." Meg knew this was pointed at Spencer. "I'm afraid I can't do that, Megan. Construction isn't cheap these days. And I doubt your mom would want to ruin her marriage. Or her reputation."

That was meant to be a threat, but Meg nodded at Spencer, who patted Pastor Mike on the back. "Shame," Spencer said. "I thought you might say that."

The kids' coach shouted, "Donaldson! Other way!"

Spencer removed a flash drive from his pocket. "You can have this one if you'd like. It's just a copy. But I've been looking at your church's ledgers." Pastor Mike blanched. "You're not the only one who can dig up secrets."

Pastor Mike didn't hide his volume. "How about you beg me not to contact the local newspaper and by tomorrow, have a front-page story about you as a lowlife—not a far stretch—caught stealing from my church and trespassing. Breaking and entering? Robbery? Trespassing? I'm sure Officer Clarke would love to contribute a quote about your altercations with the cops."

"I've never had any."

"Your word against his." The corner of his mouth lifted. "And he's the law, remember?"

Spencer looked at Pastor Mike with an amused expression, which only goaded him on.

"If they find it false later," Pastor Mike continued, "even if there's a reprint, your name is already out there. Why? Because technology's a bitch. I only have to push a button once to infect the masses. Copied and pasted, forwarded and shared with every football lover in America. Spreads like a disease. Your reputation? Done. People will always label you as a violent kid—not as a talented running back."

"You should save that speech for Finn," Spencer said with an easygoing drawl. "You forget. I don't care, Mikey. Not about my reputation. Definitely not about football. Even less about you."

"It's Pastor Mike, you little shit. And you may not care about your reputation, but I bet you care about your sister's. Rumors don't have to be true to be hurtful."

Spencer remained cool, but his jaw clenched and his nostrils flared. Meg had heard enough. "Michael Menke?"

"It's *Pastor* Michael Menke," he snapped. Meg was looking for a yes, but that was a small bonus.

"Excuse me." Meg pulled her phone out. Pushed play on her voice recording app. Pastor Mike's voice, hollow and tinny, came through the phone's speaker. "—How about you beg me not to contact the local newspaper"—Meg scrolled the playback forward with a finger—"Your word against his. And he's the law, remember?"—she moved it forward again—"It's Pastor Mike, you little shit. And you may not care about your reputation, but I bet you care about your sister's. Rumors don't have to be true to be hurtful."

Meg closed the app, then looked steadily at Pastor Mike and said, "I'm sure your congregation would love to hear your thoughts."

"How dare you—" Pastor Mike swiped a hand for Meg's phone, but Spencer stood between them with a firm arm extended.

"Careful," Spencer said. "She only has to push a button once, remember? You know, she could feed this through the speakers during the middle of your Sunday sermon. As someone once said, 'Technology's a bitch.'"

Pastor Mike's mouth clamped shut, but his eyes bulged with rage.

Spencer motioned with his eyes to the sky. "You don't strike me as a praying man. But you better pray no one says a word about my sister."

"I've gotta get Spencer home," Meg said. "Big game tomorrow. Homecoming. Oh, I almost forgot." She swiped the crumpled Post-it from the grass and slapped it against Pastor Mike's puffed-out chest. It barely clung to his shirt. "I'm guessing it'll be cash. Not sure you want a paper trail. You know where to find me. And don't be too slow." She looked up at the sky, a silent nod to the God she wished Pastor Mike actually honored. "Sunday's coming."

As he and Meg walked away, she looked over her shoulder and smiled. "You have a blessed day now."

Chapter 54
FINN

It had been a nerve-racking week, waiting on Brit to find the admin. Students were starting to wonder. Finn had seen it in the halls. The slight shift. Not everyone knew about the chat room, but even the clueless ones felt it—the darting eyes, extra whispers. The atmosphere was charged. Maybe it was fear—if accounts were getting blocked one by one, who would be next? And did that mean it wasn't as anonymous as everyone thought? Students tried to keep their faces neutral—laughing harder, talking louder— looking guilty by trying too hard *not* to look guilty.

On Friday night, Finn charged onto the field with his team, the turf shaking from the pounding drums and the feet stomping in the stands. Homecoming was a sold-out crowd, a sea of bodies spilling over the bleachers and onto the asphalt. The Greenville Bengals warmed up opposite the Spartans. Finn hoped no one was missing, but he wouldn't even glance at the other end of the field.

At the entrance to the track, the student-made floats for all four classes were ready to go for halftime. He spotted Brit on the track with the cheerleaders and jogged over to her. "Any luck today?" he asked.

She pulled him away from her squad so they could chat privately. "No admin yet. But twenty-two accounts shut down," she said through a plastered smile, just in case anyone was watching. "Only a matter of time before they start looking my way." And then, as if she was suddenly aware of that, she covered by pointing out their grandmother in the stands. Finn waved, but his stomach knotted when he remembered that Megan would be nowhere tonight, not sitting next to his grandma, not hiding somewhere else in the stands.

"Just keep playing your part," he said. "We'll find the admin soon. In the meantime, tonight should provide some interesting *distractions*." She crossed her fingers for only him to see and then quickly uncrossed them and bounded back to her team.

He took his sadness for Meg and his nerves about getting caught and drove it into his legs, running back to the field and sprinting a forty. As Finn was running his warm-up pass plays, Coach Goode flagged down Walker. He was shouting something indecipherable. Walker scanned the opposite sidelines, his eyes landing on a Bengals player before looking back at Goode and shrugging. Finn watched Goode head off the field toward Coach Wilkins. He read his lips: "—the hell's he doing here?" Finn double-knotted his cleats, busied himself with stretching.

A few days ago, Brit had told Finn and Spencer about two Bengals players being mentioned in the chat room that week as targets. That night, Finn sent them an anonymous note—warned the guys to run a printout of their grades before anything could be switched, to avoid eating food they hadn't made themselves, to watch their cars, their family, their football gear. Finn toyed with the idea of also having Brit get on the chat and mention other players who weren't a threat, just to throw people off. But he didn't want to be responsible for making anyone a target for something potentially bad.

The two Bengal players were both present and accounted for, and the coaches noticed.

"Collins!" Wilkins yelled. Spencer jogged over. "You're in for James," Wilkins said. "Warm up."

This was exactly what Finn was hoping for. It meant Wilkins had seen it, the way Spencer had played his heart out at practice this week, impressing everyone. Finn knew Spencer was good, but he had no idea the amount of athleticism Spencer had been holding back until he saw him this week in action. Their hope was that if they were both on the field and playing well, it would deflect suspicion as Brit continued to disable accounts. They hadn't known if it would work, but they'd banked on Coach pulling out all the stops for the win. And he had. When the other team showed up with all their biggest threats, Wilkins made the last-minute decision to start Spencer.

Spartans won the toss and deferred. At the kickoff return, the Bengals were tackled at their own ten-yard line. A great start for the Spartan defense, and when the Bengals threw long, the Spartans cornerback Smith intercepted the lobbed ball at the forty-five and was taken down at the fifty. Finn and Spencer snapped their helmets on. As Finn jogged onto the field, he felt the rush of a pure game, one unadulterated by outside influences.

On the first down, Finn gained eight yards on a simple hand-off. In the second play, they tried creating a lane up the middle, but the Bengals' linebacker—the one Finn had warned—broke through the O-line, and Finn felt himself cracked against the ground, the wind knocked out of him. He shook it off, but third down was an incomplete pass to Spencer, and they went three and out.

They remained scoreless through the first quarter. In the second, Finn was on the sidelines during a defensive play when a frenzy erupted in the crowd behind him. He turned to see people shoving to get out of the way, clearing a space in the stands. He caught a glimpse of Tara, Kylie's girlfriend, trying to blend into those backing away. He grinned. When the play was dead, the referees walked over to make sure the commotion wasn't a safety concern. "What the hell—" Finn overheard Coach Wilkins say.

Goode looked at the crowd and grumbled, "Ammonium sulfide."

"What?" Wilkins asked.

"Stink bomb," Goode muttered, crossing his arms. "You know about this?" he said to Finn and Jake, who happened to be standing nearby.

"Never heard of someone dropping one during football," Jake said.

Finn shook his head. "That's, like, sacrilege." He turned back to the field. He didn't dare look at Spencer, and Spencer never looked at him. They couldn't risk any connection. Not tonight.

Even if anyone discovered the instigators were from West Oak and used to walk in Finn's best-friend circle, they wouldn't ever assume he'd told them to do such a thing.

Or that he'd pulled all his old friends together—minus Meg, of course—and told them the full story. The plan was to give East-Pay coaches and players a taste of what it would be like to be "played," the way they'd "played" other teams for so long. It was Spencer's idea, really. He was moving away, but before he did, he wanted to have the last word. To tell them all they hadn't won by making him fearful for his sister's safety. There were caveats, however. No harming of players. No vandalism. Nothing illegal. All of Finn's friends had said *absolutely*.

Of course they had. Meg had said they'd stick by him even when he was MIA. His gut twisted again as he thought of how amazing she'd always been. Continued to be. Always would be, but now without him.

Across the track, Brit caught his eye, motioned to her phone. As the referees resettled, he reached into his duffel and glanced at his texts. One from Brit to Spencer and Finn.

> Notification came thru. Found admin.
> Disabled it.

She shut down the chat room? He looked over, but she was typing on her phone.

Her text appeared.

> It's over.

It's over.

He stared at those two words, his eyes blurring in disbelief.

"What's over?" Goode said, looking over his shoulder.

He dropped his phone back into his bag.

"You got something better to do?" Wilkins growled.

"No, sir," Finn said. "Sorry."

Wilkins stomped off, but Goode stayed. He lifted an eyebrow at him and asked, "What're you doing, Geringer?"

Wilkins was looking their way, and it made Finn uncomfortable.

"Nothin' to you, Coach," he said to Goode under his breath. He tried to move away, but Goode put a hand on his shoulder.

"We need this game."

"I know," Finn said quietly. "And we can win without outside help. Which is why we're shutting that down." On the field, the defense made a quick tackle to end the play. The Spartan bleachers erupted in cheers and stomps.

He wanted to tell Goode everything. To tell him that he didn't have to be Wilkins's puppet anymore. He remembered Goode's words warning Finn about Wilkins: *You don't know who he knows.* He wanted to tell Goode that they had put an end to the chat room Wilkins had access to—the chat room that had manipulated games, intimidated those who questioned, perpetuated fears. But he didn't know who would overhear. Instead, Finn shook his head, a sad smile on his face. "The irony is, Wilkins's a good coach. He just needs to be one."

The ball sailed over them, the fourth-down kick to the thirty-yard line. The offense was up. Finn shook Goode off and ran back onto the field.

On the third down, Finn caught a twenty-yard pass and spun around one Bengal while kicking his foot out of the grasp of another. He bolted toward the end zone, but the lights of the field suddenly shut off, and the entire stadium went dark. Finn kept sprinting to the end zone, the moonlight so dim, it barely illuminated his way, but the crowd still saw and cheered for him when he made the touchdown. Finn, his arms raised in victory, saw movement in the dark corner of the asphalt near the basketball courts. There, where the electricity box for the stadium was housed, he watched a shadowed figure in a dark hoodie scamper away. He noticed a few of her dreads flopping loosely out of her hood. *Kylie?*

He looked over at the bench. Goode was on his phone, texting with angry fingers, probably already working on a solution. Sure enough, in less than two minutes, a maintenance worker was at the box turning the main breaker back on, but the damage was done. The play was called dead because of the lighting issue: no touchdown, and they had to redo third down. This time, the Bengals read the play, and the pass to Finn was incomplete, forcing the kick, the Bengals now amped at their stroke of luck.

Whoa. He hadn't expected his friends to do something so elaborate, and he actually hadn't wanted anything that could affect EastPay's possibility of a clean victory.

But still, he was impressed.

Chapter 55
BRITNEY

At halftime, Finn was too far ahead in the line of players heading to the locker room, but Brit found Spencer trailing in the back. She yanked him by the shoulder away from the team, not even caring if people were watching. "There's a problem," she whispered. Her heart was in her throat, and she breathed slowly to calm it down. "I texted you how I disabled the admin. Shut down all access to the chat room."

"Look, if people assume it's you," Spencer said, bouncing his helmet against his thigh, "then let 'em assume. They can't prove anything."

"That's not it," she snapped. Her eyes swept her surroundings and then returned to him. "It's back on."

He tilted his head. "How's that even possible?"

"It's not," she said. "Unless—"

"Unless what?"

Brit scanned the field. The marching band started up, a sea of rows and columns, bouncing and stepping as they played. Next to them, the color guard tossed and twirled in unison.

She bit her lip, rubbing off a strip of lipstick under her teeth. "Unless there's another admin."

"There can be more than one?"

She grimaced. The class floats began their slow lap around the track. Four classic cars lined up to enter the track, the royal court perched on the back seats in their crowns. She didn't have much time until she had to perform.

"Technically, yes," she admitted. "I just figured there wouldn't be."

Spencer threw his head back. "So what does that mean?"

Brit sighed. She hated saying this out loud. "Whoever the second admin is, they rebooted it. Which means the first admin probably talked to the second after he was shut down, and they know we're trying to shut them down. They'll just assign more usernames. Get everyone back on. Start changing the admin password too frequently for me to crack it."

Spencer raked a hand through his hair in frustration. She felt it, too. The hopelessness. "There's no chance you can kill it some other way?"

She dropped her head. "Not unless we can destroy the server." She thought of all the students. So many houses. So many hiding places. "And who even knows where to start looking."

"I might know," came a voice behind them.

Meg hadn't planned to go to Finn's game. But here she was, at halftime, facing a very shocked Brit and Spencer, hoping to God Finn was already in the locker room and wouldn't see her. "Look, I could be wrong," Meg said, "but I've been going over all the possible places the server could be. At first I thought Dante's. It was such a sacred spot; wouldn't that be ideal?"

"There's no way," Brit interrupted. "Not enough power, service, connection . . ."

"Security," Spencer added. "They wouldn't risk it."

"Exactly," Meg said, then prompted, "But even if it had all those things . . ."

"It's not temperature controlled," Brit finished for her. "You don't put servers outside."

Meg nodded, her words quickening. "You know the day I accidentally ran into the coaches in the locker room?" She thought back to how the freezing air from their office had hit her like a tidal wave. "No one questions why their office feels like Alaska?"

Brit's eyes widened. "For reals?"

"Sure, we notice it," Spencer said. "But the players joke it's to keep us out. I think we all just assume coaches do it to keep themselves alert—planning plays, designing formations."

"Or to match their cold hearts," Meg added.

"Good one," Spencer said.

Meg could see Brit's wheels turning. "You don't think . . ." Brit started, her voice breathy.

Meg nodded. "What better place to hide than in plain sight? And if Coach Wilkins is so in love with football that he'd exploit my mom for it, why *wouldn't* he keep the server in his sights? The single thing that protects his winning percentage?"

"Also not traceable at his house. No higher AC bills," Spencer added.

"Dang!" Brit said. "I'm as useful as a dead skunk. How'd I not put that together?" She slapped her forehead, buried her face in her hands, groaning. "The coaches are always in hoodies, too!"

Meg laughed. She hadn't really thought about that point, but it was valid.

"There's a file cabinet," Spencer said. "Lots of AV equipment on top. DVD player. Books. Things like that. It'd be easy to hide it there—blend right in with all the other junk."

"Spence, you gotta get in there tonight," Brit urged. "You could find it."

Spencer shook his head. "They're already gonna have my ass." He motioned to the locker room. "I need to go. We can try next week."

"It's too late next week!" Brit said. "If he knows we're trying to shut it down, he'll move it."

"She's right," Meg said. They had to do this *now*. Which was the only reason Meg found herself at the last place she'd wanted to be tonight, near the ex-boyfriend she'd intended to avoid the most. She opened her fist to reveal two shriveled mushrooms in her palm and looked at Spencer. "You wanted to go out with a bang."

Brit gasped. "No way," she said. "Absolutely not. That put Grandma in the hospital last year."

"Because she's old," Meg said, her voice steady. "EastPay has been doing it to opponents because it works. It doesn't kill them. Too mild. Just disables them as a player."

Brit shook her head fiercely. This wasn't going to be an easy sell. "Brit," Meg pleaded. "You said it has to be tonight. If he could get in there alone, then—"

"I'll do it." Spencer snatched the mushrooms from Meg's hand. "That is, if I don't get benched for being late to the halftime talk." Brit started to protest, but Spencer gently cupped a hand on her face and kissed her cheek. "I got this," he said, leaving her stunned as he took off for the locker room.

Meg saw Brit swallow. "He'll pull through," she said, trying to reassure her. "He'll just be hating life for a while."

Brit still looked unconvinced. "What's that mean?"

Meg smirked. "It means he'll be seeing his lunch in reverse. But don't worry, the only GoFundMe you'll have to start is for his dignity."

"Brit, you're up," a girl's voice said, snapping Meg to attention.

Standing next to them was the girl from the photos. Tammy Shaw. She flicked a nervous glance at Meg and then quickly looked away. Rage shot through Meg, sharp and immediate. Her fingers twitched, ready to tear into Tammy, to say something, do something—make her pay for even daring to stand here. But she couldn't. Not now. Not tonight.

Her eyes landed on Tammy's uniform. JV? That didn't make sense. Hadn't Tammy been varsity captain with Brit?

"You want someone else to fly for you?" Tammy asked, a timid request, not a threat. She seemed rattled by Meg's presence, maybe wondering how much Meg knew. Meg wanted to yell that she knew everything. She wanted to glare at Tammy with laser eyes that burned holes right through her. But the curtain was up and she couldn't break character.

"No," Brit said. "I'm coming. Good to see you, Meg." Brit gave Meg an innocent smile.

Meg couldn't let on. She couldn't. She couldn't. Tonight depended on nobody interfering with what they needed to do. She fought back angry tears and channeled the poise she'd held through every ballet performance.

"I was just dropping off Finn's things," Meg said to Brit evenly. "I gave them to your grandma. I'll be leaving now. Good to see you, too, Brit."

She waited until they jogged onto the field before she squeezed her eyes tight with rage and hurt.

Chapter 57

FINN

Finn was practically pacing by the time Spencer entered the locker room. *What was he thinking?* They had to lay low tonight and play by the rules. Disappearing at halftime was no way to stay inconspicuous. Miraculously, the coaches were still piled into the office, the echo of angry conversation bouncing against the closed door. Some players glanced up at Spencer as he entered, but no one said anything. It was the first time this season they weren't leading at half, and the mood was somber. Many sat on benches retaping, stretching. Even Walker was keeping to himself.

"Where've you been?" Finn said quietly.

Suddenly, the office door flung open, a rush of cold air sweeping into the sweaty room, and Coach Goode rushed Finn, backing him up against the lockers. "This all a big joke to you?"

Finn, in total shock, held up his hands in surrender. The team stood around them, stock-still.

"You're sabotaging the football game?" Coach Goode yelled. "That what you're doing?"

Finn's mind was reeling. He'd never seen this side of Goode—the way his eyes bulged. "I'm on the field," Finn stammered. "I can't help it if—"

"Who's doing it?" Goode's mouth twisted with fury. Finn's heartbeat quickened.

"Doing what, Coach?"

Coach Goode leaned close. Whispered in his ear so only Finn could hear, "You wanna go the way of Sean Lloyd?"

Sean Lloyd, who had drowned in Dante's Ravine. Sean Lloyd, whose death was deemed an *accident*.

"Goode!" Coach Wilkins yelled. "Enough!"

Finn could feel Coach Goode's hot breath as he stood inches from his face, glaring, not moving.

Coach Wilkins turned to the team. "Let's talk about our running game." There was uncomfortable shifting of cleats and shoulder pads as the team refocused on Coach Wilkins. "Goode, take a walk. Cool off."

Coach Goode smirked, holding Finn's gaze longer than necessary, backed away slowly, and then pushed through the double doors. Wilkins cleared his throat. "Stockton, take the defense, go over adjustments. Offense and special teams, with me. Now." Players rearranged and gathered in different corners of the locker room. Finn's head was spinning. *Goode had always defended him.*

"What's with Goode?" Spencer muttered, filling up his water bottle from the giant water cooler that always rested on the corner bench for the players. He straddled the bench and sat.

"I don't get it," Finn said more to himself than Spencer. "Goode always had my back—"

"'Course he did," Spencer growled under his breath. "You're his chance at a title. You know that scar's from the play that ended his career? He's been obsessed with winning a championship since the year he never did."

Finn's skin prickled. "What scar?"

"His knee."

Finn wanted to vomit. He'd seen the scar many times, the boot-shaped puffy line against Goode's pale skin, but only now remembered Megan's words. *"He says one of them had a scar on his knee the shape of Florida."*

Across the room, Coach Wilkins was talking plays, sketching *x*'s and *o*'s on a whiteboard, but the drawing blurred and his voice became a fog.

Finn sat down next to Spencer. "The guy you hit with your car," he whispered. "Ryan Quaid?"

"What about him?"

"Meg talked with Ryan. He said two guys were chasing him. One with a scar the shape of Florida on his knee."

"Are you shittin' me? But I thought Meg said Coach *Wilkins*—"

"Meg just said 'Coach.'" He was struggling to keep up with his own thoughts. "Her mom said the guy blackmailing her was my *coach*. We just assumed she meant Wilkins. It's Goode."

"But there's no way either of them are the admins. They were busy on the field when the chat room rebooted," Spencer said.

"What?" Finn could barely speak. *But Brit said it was over!*

"That's why I was late. Chat room's back up. Brit found the admin account, shut it down. But it started back up again, middle of the second quarter. Which means—"

"There's a second admin." Finn balled his fists. He thought back to the stadium blackout—how he'd looked over and seen Goode frantically texting. He'd assumed it was to maintenance. But the texts had come immediately after he confided in Goode—telling Goode not to worry about Wilkins anymore because they had shut down "outside help"—the chat room. Goode wasn't texting maintenance. He was rebooting the chat room. *Goode was an admin.*

Well, at least one of them.

"It's okay, though," Spencer said. "We found the server. It's in Coach's office."

Finn looked at the office. The blinds were closed, along with the door. All this time, it'd been *there*? *How did Spencer know?* The coaches continued to talk to the team, but if they saw Spencer and Finn mumbling to each other, no one acknowledged it. Maybe since Finn had just been accosted by Goode, they were letting him slide.

"You sure?"

"I'll find out second half."

"Okay, genius," Finn said, "how are we supposed to leave midgame and break into *their* office . . . midgame . . . when we're on the field?"

Spencer uncurled his fist to reveal something brown with thin stems and little bell tops. "With this." Finn cocked his head. "Lawn mushrooms," Spencer said.

Were these the same kind Meg said were being used to poison players? Did Spencer think Finn would actually poison himself? "What the hell?"

"Collins," Wilkins called. "Geringer!" Their time was up. They gathered in with the players, and Wilkins briefly reviewed a couple plays before hyping the team up with a reminder of big comebacks in NFL history. Again, Finn only heard pieces. His mind was a flurry of panic, trying to figure out an alternative to poison.

"Here goes nothing," Spencer said quietly, popping the mushrooms into his mouth.

"Don't," Finn said, but Spencer drank from the water bottle, and in one gulp, swallowed them whole.

"Quickest way to the locker room when it's empty?" Spencer whispered, grinning. "Injury or illness. As soon as I'm in, I'll break into the office and find the server." He motioned to the water cooler. "And I will drench that fucking thing until it swims."

Chapter 58
BRITNEY

Brit had thrown herself into her halftime routine with such vigor that her mind didn't have any space to worry about Spencer. But now the third quarter had started, and she was jiggling a leg nervously as she stood on her cheerleading box watching the game.

"Brit," Dalisa called, waving her to start a series of defense cheers. She turned her back to the field and faced the stands. At least the offense would be on the bench for a few minutes, which meant she didn't have to keep an eye on Spencer. This was such a dumb-as-rocks idea. Why couldn't he just *pretend* to be sick and head to the locker room?

She smiled wide. "*T-A-K-E*, take that ball away!" *Clap clap.*

Her squad joined her. "*T-A-K-E*, take that ball—"

The crowd roared, stopping them midcheer.

Interception.

Shoot. Brit turned around and waved her pom-poms as Spencer and Finn again took the field. They were ten minutes in, and Spencer still looked okay. He caught a pass for a five-yard gain. She focused on her breath, willing herself to relax. Maybe the mushrooms wouldn't hit him badly. Maybe he could just exaggerate the severity of it.

As if he could read her mind, the next play when he was brought down, he pushed himself to his feet and then curled back down, clutching his stomach. *A little dramatic*, Brit thought, *but nice touch.* He rose again slowly and staggered to the sidelines, barely making it to the trash can.

Where he promptly threw up.

Gross. So much for exaggerating.

Brit jumped off her box and ran toward the bench. It wasn't far from where the cheerleaders stood on their boxes, and she could hear Dalisa's voice calling after her.

Spencer was quickly replaced by a sophomore, but Brit overheard Coach Hart ask him, "You have the flu?"

Spencer shook his head and groaned.

When the defense was back on the field, Brit crouched next to him. She didn't care if cheerleaders weren't supposed to stand with the players. She was worried. Spencer's face, the color of paste, dripped with sweat. She couldn't believe he'd done this to himself, just to get into the locker room. Finn came up beside them, put a gentle hand on her, but she pushed it off. "What did you eat today?" she said, loud enough for coaches to hear.

Spencer tried to speak, but he gurgled. Shook his head.

She knew it would make her queasy, but she willed herself to look into the trash can. She screwed up her face in disgust. "Pizza," she announced loudly, and then glanced at Finn, who nodded slightly. Just enough to tell her he knew where she was going with this. Thank God for cousins who knew you well enough that you didn't have to spell everything out.

Spencer lifted himself to his knees, gripped the trash can. She stepped away as he disposed the contents of his stomach again. *Ew.* She hated vomit.

"Hart!" Wilkins bellowed, and Coach Hart trotted over. "Get an athletic trainer to take him to the locker room. I'll take special teams for a minute."

"That pizza have mushrooms on it?" Brit asked loudly.

Spencer looked at her, then Finn. Even violently ill, he picked up on his cue and nodded miserably.

"Huh." Brit looked down at him, his face a pale green as Hart helped him start toward the locker room.

She walked over to Walker, who was sitting on the players' bench, retying a cleat. "Someone knows," she said, putting on her best concerned face. Crinkled brow. Eyes big like a fawn's.

"I don't think you're allowed to be here," he said coldly, keeping his eyes on the field.

She did her best to look unfazed. Like she cared more about him than herself. "Look, it's called *Chlorophyllum molybdites*. Lawn mushrooms. I only thought of it because of our grandma last year." She motioned to Finn. "Happened to her with pizza, too. The night Finn was playing against us. Pretty sure it was meant for Finn."

Out of the corner of her eye, she saw a security guard approaching swiftly.

"Haven't you seen what's going on tonight?" she rushed on. "Someone's paying us back! Things are *happening*. Too many things. Lights going out. Stink bombs stopping the game. And now, Spencer!" She gulped, not really having to fake how awful she felt for him. She knelt down in front of Walker. "The Game doesn't hurt their own players."

He gave her a cursory glance. "What Game? Only 'game' I know is football."

She thought back to his threatening words: *"As far as you're concerned, there is no Game."* She wasn't allowed in, and he'd hold to that. No discussions about it. He wouldn't give her the satisfaction.

He stood and snapped on his helmet. Behind her, she knew that the Bengals had run through the Spartans' soft defense and were now in the red zone.

She stayed crouched, hoping that her upward gaze would look more contrite. "Look, I'm sorry you kept me out of The Game. You had your reasons." She stood up. Addressed the whole bench. "You all did. But I love this school. EastPay's everything. I love cheering for you guys. So I'm telling you, guard the chat room." For the first time, Walker's eyes shifted to her, then flitted away, but she saw it. He believed her. The security guard, now next to Brit, reached out an arm to usher her off the sideline, but she waved him off. "Guard it!" she shouted as she backed away. "Someone's onto us!"

The whistle blew, indicating that the Bengals had just scored a touchdown. Brit hopped back up on her box, and Dalisa, one box over, said, "What was that?"

Defense, she wanted to say.

Instead, she said, "Just doing my part." And then she said, "Dalisa, I gotta pee. Can you take over for five?" Before Dalisa could answer, she hopped off her box and made a beeline for the women's locker room, which happened to be opposite the men's locker room.

Which was always unlocked during games.

Chapter 59
FINN

Something was wrong.

In the fourth quarter, Brit caught Finn's eye from her cheer-leading box. She was gnawing on her lip. That was never good.

"What is it?" he mouthed.

"Locked," she mouthed back.

The office was *locked*? But what about the toilet paper they'd stuffed in the doorjamb? They'd gotten in easily the other day. Had it been removed? He glanced over at the coaches to make sure they weren't watching. Goode hadn't even looked at him since their confrontation at halftime. All four of their faces were grim, eyes locked on the field as if their victory depended on it. He turned back to Brit.

"Spencer?" he mouthed. Was he working on another way in?

"So. Sick." She exaggerated her syllables so he could read her lips. She looked terribly worried, not just for Spencer, but for their plan. She'd purposely warned the whole football bench about the chat room, assuming the server would be destroyed before the end of the game. If it went down when they were all present and accounted for, no one would suspect her. And even if someone did, there'd be no proof. But if they didn't get to it before the final whistle, the admin no doubt would put up extra firewalls or pass-word protection to ensure it stayed up.

They'd be done for.

There had to be another way in. Couldn't Spencer knock down

the office door with enough force? Maybe. But not in this state. *So sick.* That's what Brit had said of him. It was doubtful he could stand, much less knock a door down.

Offense was called out onto the field, and Finn followed the play-calling like he was on autopilot. Handoff. Lateral. Block for the receiver. Quick pass to space. Through the slot. To the sideline.

Four of the last eight plays were directed at him, and he gained yards on each one. There was little time, and he needed to get off the field quickly, so he'd have time to think. Thomas White called a touchdown play for Finn, but the Bengals blitzed White and sacked him before he could release the ball.

Come on!

In the huddle, Thomas called an iso slant, which was the perfect play for both the touchdown and for what Finn needed to do. He lined up on one side with the receivers, and the tight end lined up on the opposite end, which ideally would force the Bengals' safety to try to take away the slant.

It worked.

The ball was set, and Finn ran. He ran like he'd never run before. He ran alongside his teammates, his hopes, his future dreams, the cheers, the accolades, and his willingness to risk leaving it all—his friends, his girlfriend, his life in West Oak—all for the game.

It used to be enough.

But as they charged into the end zone, and he heard the echo of the bleachers—the shouts, the stomps and claps, knowing that their tight end had caught the pass and broken free—he knew there was more than this.

He kept running, past the end zone, pass the field goal posts, past the track, and onto the baseball fields toward the locker room. No one would follow. Not during the game. He'd have questions to answer afterward, but he'd face whatever came his way. He had a job to do. A bigger role than being an entire town's star running back.

He pumped his arms and drove hard, his lungs burning and his leg muscles taut with anxiety. His cleats dug into the ground, spat chunks of dirt behind him. He had no time to think, to wonder what the best approach would be.

As Finn skidded to a stop inside the locker room, he could see Spencer's legs sticking out of a bathroom stall as he lay sprawled out. "Hey, man," Finn said, gasping. "You wanna help me end this thing?"

From under the stall, Spencer groaned, "Don't move me."

Finn ran to the coaches' office, jiggled the door handle. It *was* locked. He shoved a shoulder against it. It didn't open, but it rattled. Maybe with enough power . . . God, he could use Spencer's help about now. He rammed a shoulder against it again, harder. His body absorbed the blow like a tackle. He rammed it again. And again. And then . . .

A body collided into him, knocking him sideways. He skidded stomach-down, his face inches from the concrete, a heavy body on his back. He wriggled madly to turn around, and his face connected with the hard swing of a fist. He felt the pain rip through his cheek, the warmth as it swelled. Through his one good eye, he saw Coach Goode straddling him, swinging at him. Finn drove his strength upward and propelled Goode off him. He stood and crouched, the two circling each other.

"Don't make this worse," Finn said.

"You're missing the fourth quarter," Goode snapped.

"So are you. Unlock the door."

Goode spoke calmly, but his eyes were filled with venom. "Was it fun for you tonight? Ruining things for me?"

"For *you*?"

"A year ago, they were worried we were going to start slipping. We graduated eight All-District players and two of those were All-State. But I said no. Not if we had *you*, I said."

Could Spencer hear this from the stalls?

"Don't you get it?" Goode continued. "I'm the whole reason you got recruited. I gave you your shot at a future."

"You also stole a future from Eli," Finn said.

Goode swept Finn's feet from under him, toppling him to the ground. Finn scrabbled to his knees before Goode was on him again, pushing Finn onto his back, his forearm across Finn's neck, Goode's bulging eyes looking derisively down at him.

"Eli was an accident," he barked, flecks of spittle hitting Finn as he spoke. "Damarius needed to learn you don't snitch on a legacy. And he moved away, so . . ." Goode's lip curled into a grin. "Lesson learned. The Game's not going anywhere, by the way. Why fix something that ain't broken? Students, nonathletes, nobodies—they all feel like they're part of it. The victory. It's not just the team's victory. It's theirs, too. And you feel that energy when you're out there. We all do. The whole community's invested."

"You gonna kill me?" Finn sputtered through gasps. Goode pushed his arm harder against Finn's neck.

"Kill you?" Goode laughed. "I'm not a murderer, Finn. Just a businessman. As much as I'd like to dispose of your worthless ass, your running game is our ticket. And part of my hefty paycheck.

We can still salvage this season if we make playoffs. Even take State."

Finn's body jerked with rage, but Goode kept him pinned. *Where was Spencer?*

"You know if I hadn't been injured senior year, it would've happened for me," Goode said. "My whole future would've turned out differently. Instead, I'm stuck coaching ungrateful babies who have no clue how lucky they are." He sneered. "However, the money's nice. I just have to keep enough collateral to ensure you're playing your best."

Finn's body bucked, convulsing from lack of air. His thoughts were getting muddy.

Goode smiled. "So in case you ever feel like snitching, remember that if anything happens to your ex, people will just assume she was depressed, and that's why she showed up at Dante's Ravine one night, thinking about what you did there, with another girl. It won't even look suspicious if she's found swept under the current. Dante's Ravine, the symbol of Spartan football, the sport that stole you away from her. Suicidal and tragic, sure. But kind of poetic. And your grandma, well, people die of old age all the time."

Finn felt himself blacking out, the lines of dizziness squiggling down his vision. But he saw another vision, a picture of Megan's eyes, the ones who saw him the way he wished he was, a picture of his grandma showing him the yellow and red roses fused on one stem, telling him that they were the same—they were family. Saturated in that thought, he agonizingly pushed Goode's arm up to release his throat. His muscles strained. Somewhere deep inside of him, he found more, drove himself harder, yelling and groaning as he rolled Goode off him. They both clambered to their feet, circling again. Finn could barely see, barely breathe, and Goode charged, but Finn ducked low and drove a leg at Goode's scarred knee, striking hard. Goode howled, his whole body buckling underneath him.

From somewhere behind Finn, a football torpedoed and sailed into the office window, causing it to shatter inward. Finn didn't look to see who threw it—just used the moment when Goode was caught off guard to pin Goode underneath his body, both on the floor again. He gagged to find his breath but still punched Goode in the face. He held his forearm in the same position Goode had done to him. Goode thrashed, but Finn held until Goode slackened and passed out. Finn staggered to his feet, coughing again.

He turned to where the football had been thrown. Spencer had crawled out from under the stall and now sat leaning against a nearby bench, crumpled and woozy.

His face was still sickly pale from the mushrooms.

Finn wiped a trickle of blood from his eyes. "Nice throw."

Spencer shrugged. "I was aiming for *you*." He crawled over to Finn, and they both looked down at Goode, passed out cold against the locker room floor.

"You know we could do a little more damage," Spencer said. "It would look like self-defense."

Finn chuckled. "Don't tempt me. You think he killed Sean Lloyd?"

Spencer rose to one knee and breathed slowly. He looked like he still might puke. "I don't think he touched Lloyd," he said. "Gossip is the killer in this town. Get enough people talking, that's all you gotta do. Eventually somebody gets caught up in the mass hysteria. Helps an *unfortunate circumstance* to occur. Goode knew that. That's what made him so good."

Finn approached the office and put an arm through the shattered window, taking care to avoid any shards as he reached around to unlock the door from the inside. He stepped inside the cold room, the broken glass crunching under his cleats. On top of the back file cabinet, underneath a stack of papers and hidden behind three DVDs, a couple of green and yellow lights blinked at him from a black rectangular box. It was bigger than he'd imagined. Nothing he could carry out of here easily or unseen.

He stepped out of the office and walked to the corner locker bench where the giant water cooler sat. He unscrewed the top. "Can you do this?"

Spencer hobbled over and grabbed one of the handles. As they lifted, Spencer winced, clutching his stomach with his free hand. "God, these mushrooms are death."

Together, they walked the cooler around Goode and into the office. It sloshed sloppily, leaving a healthy trail of water behind them. With one swift heave up to their shoulders, they tipped it over and onto the file cabinet, the torrential splash soaking the DVDs, the books, the loose papers, the folders, and, finally, the server. It sparked and smoked and sizzled, the lights blinking from green to yellow to red and then finally, with one last wink goodbye, going dark.

Finn felt the freedom immediately, even as it continued to sizzle, a small plume of smoke still seeping out. Not a word between them, Spencer kicked the plug from the outlet, and they exited the office, Finn still holding the empty cooler by one handle, dragging it behind him like an oversize rag doll.

"We should take that out with us," Spencer said. "Dump it on the lawn somewhere obscure."

Finn nodded. Looked down at a still sleeping Goode. "So we've shut it down?" he asked.

"The chat room? Yes," Spencer said. "The obsession with winning? Not as simple. Not in this town."

Finn hovered over the crumpled figure responsible for so much manipulation and fear. "We should call someone."

"I will once we get out of here." Spencer indicated the exit door.

Finn thought of Officer Clarke, and every muscle tightened. "Local?"

"Hell no. Someone outside jurisdiction. We're on county line anyway." Spencer motioned down at Goode. "We'll get him on assault."

Finn looked out toward the double doors. His face was throbbing, swollen with pain. He touched his lip, split and double in size. "Thanks, by the way."

Spencer leaned his neck to the left. Cracked it. "I still don't like you, Geringer."

"Well, good. You still saved my ass."

"Fuck you."

But Spencer grinned, reached for Finn's hand, and shook it. They retrieved the water cooler and headed for the exit door, only pausing once to look over their shoulders at Goode before slapping the Spartan on the wall as they passed by.

Chapter 60
BRITNEY

After the fourth quarter ended, Brit loaded her cheer equipment into her car and waited. Even there, she could see the scoreboard's lights glaring down at everyone 34–17, an embarrassing loss. She watched the stands empty out, fans dragging their foam fingers behind them, feet clopping heavily down the bleacher steps as if their sneakers were sticking more than usual to the dried soda and open mustard packets. There was sure to be talk about why Finn had gone MIA fourth quarter, and why sirens and lights appeared and disappeared before the game ended.

But for now, it was eerily quiet.

Finn texted in the fourth the only word she needed to hear: *Done.*

Under a lamppost, an orange water cooler lay sideways, its top open, a little trickle of water on the pavement shimmering from the light. It was the kind of Gatorade cooler from the TV shows—the ones that players dumped on their coaches after a victory. Tonight it looked more like a sad sort of symbol of defeat.

Brit imagined that later, some people might second-guess why there was only a trickle, not a puddle. Maybe the Spartan football players would remember the water covering the floor during the postgame talk, how they shuffled through it in cleats, their loss heavy in the air as they removed shoulder pads, dumped gear in their lockers. Maybe if their defeat wasn't the only thing on their minds, they'd think it was strange that the cooler was missing from its spot on the corner bench.

Later they might wonder. But tonight, Brit sighed thankfully, it would mean nothing.

"I bet you think you're clever."

Brit closed her trunk and found Terrance Walker glaring at her.

"Hey, Walker," she said airily.

"I got the email," he said, crossing his arms. "Is it true?"

The email she had anonymously sent to everyone. Telling them how The Game was over.

"I wouldn't know," Brit said. "I hear it was only sent to people who had access."

"Don't play dumb," he said, his voice taking on a threatening tone. But there were plenty of crowds still milling around.

"Okay," she said, offering him a flash drive. "Here's me not playing dumb."

He uncrossed his arms and took it. "What's this?"

"Enough to let you and whoever else needs to know"—Brit looked at Walker pointedly—"that *someone* made copies of every thread. Every PDF. Every chat."

He laughed silently, the kind of laugh that implied she was a total idiot. "How you gonna prove that?" he asked. "All you got is a bunch of fictional conversations with random screen names." He sneered at her. "You can't pull up the chat room anymore. You killed the server, remember?"

"I didn't kill it," she said, "but thanks for the credit!" Brit steeled her expression. "However, someone *might've* traced every IP address and created a list of first and last names."

Walker stood there, stunned.

She raised her hand and smiled. "Guilty!" She was no longer afraid of Walker, of what he knew. He'd been led by fear, just like everyone else. She'd heard how he had a father in prison. He, too, wanted a way out. From his father. From this town. But this wasn't the way.

"Oh, and in that mass email," she said, "I think it said that if anyone tries to start some lousy counterfeit version, every one of those IP addresses will be made public. All of them. One for all and all for one!" She retied the red bow on her ponytail. "Also, you better hope to the football gods that none of our opponents' players gets sick or ineligible before they play us. You better be sending them tutors and vitamins."

He stepped closer. "You saw what I did before to you," he said. "You think I won't do more?"

"That's why I made copies and delivered them to 'sources.' If anything happens to me, they take it public. I don't doubt what you can do, Walker. You're smart that way. Using AI to fake a speech about Eli was low. And pretty crafty." She hopped onto the hood of her trunk and sat. "Which is why I sent Principal Tennessey an AI recording of *his* voice reciting the same speech I gave about Eli. Just to clear the air."

Walker went limp and slack-jawed.

"Don't get me wrong, Walker," Brit said. "You're a great player. Absolute magic on the field. And smart as hell. But you overlooked one teensy thing."

She propped her feet on the bumper and offered her best Crest White smile.

"I'm smarter."

434

Chapter 61
MEGAN

Meg had waited in the baseball dugout for Brit's text. Only a couple cars were left in the parking lot when her phone finally buzzed the okay. She emerged from the dugout and made her way to Brit. The parking lot was dark and empty. It felt good to see Brit's friendly wave—to know that the worst was over.

Meg joined Brit sitting on her trunk hood. She rested her feet on the back bumper and her head on Brit's shoulder.

"Well?" she asked.

"Finn texted it was done." Brit motioned to the water cooler on the grassy hill near the curb.

"Done," Meg repeated. "We did it." She was so relieved, but she could only think of who she'd lost along the way. She'd miss Finn so much. But there was no turning back. She'd never looked back at ballet. And she wouldn't look back at Finn.

Brit nudged Meg to indicate Coach Wilkins finally emerging from the locker room. He paused at the water cooler, whether out of anger or reverence, she couldn't tell. They watched him stroll to his van before they climbed down and crossed the parking lot.

When they approached him out of the shadows, he didn't even flinch.

"Thought I might run into you," he said to Brit.

"Why me?" Brit asked. "Coulda been anyone."

He smiled, but sadness touched the edges of it. "I hope my daughter grows up to be as smart as you."

Meg hadn't expected this side of Coach Wilkins. Defeated. Soft-spoken. They had just destroyed his office and the chat room.

"It was actually Meg who tipped us off about the server," Brit said.

Coach Wilkins lifted an eyebrow at Meg. "Surprised to see you here. I thought you—"

"Broke up?" God, the rumors. Even the coaches knew. "Yeah. But I had some . . . unfinished business here. Finn didn't even know I showed up."

Wilkins sighed, again not looking remotely angry. He opened the back sliding door to his van. Inside was a contraption Meg had never seen, but she could tell it was some sort of wheelchair lift.

"Why'd you blackmail my mom?" she blurted.

He turned, looked at her funny.

"Please don't try to lie. I'm so over lying," she said, thinking again of Pastor Mike, Ms. Tristan at the church, the clerk at the gas station shortchanging her, Finn . . . "Just. Why'd you do it?"

He shook his head.

"Oh, come off it." She was tired. Her nerves were taut. "Pastor Mike Menke already admitted it. My mom said Finn's coach came into the station."

"Which coach?" His words sounded tired, too.

Meg paused. "I just—"

"Four paid coaches. Eight assistants. Two volunteers."

She never considered anyone other than the head coach. Coach Wilkins was *in charge*. He had to be a part of it. "I—"

"Coach Goode," he said, eliminating any chance of her deliberating between all fourteen. "Pretty sure of it. He and Officer

Clarke played for EastPay. Best friends and teammates. If anyone's cutting deals and showing up at the station, I'd bet money it was Coach Goode."

"I'm sorry. I just assumed—"

"Most people do."

"So Coach Goode was the second admin," Brit said, a dawning comprehension. "Musta got word of it midgame and rebooted from his phone."

Meg tried piecing it together. "Was it you, then?" she asked Coach Wilkins. "Did you tell him after you noticed you were locked out?"

As Coach Wilkins loaded his van with his duffel and backpack, he said, "No. No idea how he found out. But . . . Goode was both admins. I was never one. I've never even seen the site. But I knew about it, which is just as bad. Anyway, I fired him tonight."

"For the chat room?" Meg asked.

Wilkins shook his head. "No proof of that. No, he gave Finn quite a halftime speech. Verbally attacked him in front of the team. And, apparently, according to a phone call from the authorities, attacked him physically when he ran off the field in the fourth." Meg's stomach tightened. *Finn was beat up?*

It still felt muddy to Meg. "But if you knew," she said. "You *knew* about The Game. You *knew* Coach Goode wasn't playing fair. Why . . ." So many *why*s. Why would he pretend he didn't? Why wouldn't he stop it? Confront it? At least bring it into the light?

Coach rearranged the duffel, moved a little pink sweater from underneath the seat. He gripped it, but said nothing.

"I think I know why," Brit said. Meg looked to her, curious. "I had the same questions. So I did some digging this week," she continued. "Your daughter."

"Daughter?" Meg asked.

Coach Wilkins still said nothing.

"She's eight," Brit said. "Seventeen surgeries since she was born."

The weight of that closed Meg's eyes momentarily. She couldn't imagine.

The sweater dangled in his hand, its pink sleeves peeking out through his knuckles. "Four more scheduled this year," he added quietly.

"Four," Meg repeated, the number echoing in her head. She looked back at the wheelchair lift.

"It gets more complicated as she grows." Wilkins's voice cracked, and he cleared his throat. Swallowed. "Medical costs," he continued, his eyes looking up toward the silhouette of the distant mountain. "They're covered. Every penny. But there are rules. I didn't have a choice to break them."

"Who was making those rules?" Meg asked, matching his quiet voice.

He shook his head. "I never asked."

"Didn't you want out?"

Wilkins pushed a gust of air out of his lungs, a single-syllable laugh that found nothing funny. "There was no way out," he said, still not looking at the girls. "My wife was—is—her full-time caregiver. Who was gonna cover her expenses while I was out looking for a job? I did what I had to."

She thought back to when she felt she had no way out of ballet, until the injury. How she exacerbated her injury nightly behind closed doors, rather than let it heal, so that she could make a way out for herself. A way out rather than being honest. *I did what I had to.*

"Anyway, I'm resigning." Coach Wilkins's voice was soft but it jolted her.

Meg shook her head. Resigning? "We killed the server. We gave you your way out. You can keep coaching. Why would you—"

"Eli."

The word hung in the darkness like the mist under the streetlamp.

He kneaded the pink sweater in his hands. Tugged and kneaded. "I didn't know—never looked at that chat room. Hive mind is a dangerous thing. But I heard things. Heard threats thrown around. I kept quiet." He threw the pink sweater on top of the duffel. "Might not have changed anything. But to stay silent when you *know* the right thing to do is to speak up—because you're more worried about what it'll cost you—sometimes that's just as bad as if I'd hit him with my own fist."

Meg didn't think Coach Wilkins's hands were clean in this, but she also didn't like the idea of one man taking on all the culpability. "Lots of people stood around and did nothing," she said.

Brit nodded. "You know those deer off East Pages Highway— how they just stand there stuck in the headlights? Fear's like your high beams. Makes us all roadkill if we're not careful."

"I'm hardly innocent," Coach Wilkins mumbled.

"I know," Meg said. She looked up at the night sky like she was acknowledging Someone—because she *was*—then smiled back. "None of us are."

Chapter 62
FINN

It was late and Finn was exhausted. He lay on his bed, freshly showered, his face raw and red. When he heard a car approaching, crunching on their gravel driveway, he didn't bother to look out the window. He'd given his statements to the police. He wasn't ready for more questioning. Not tonight.

"Finn!" his grandmother called.

He reluctantly pulled himself off his bed and caught his reflection in the mirror. His eye was swollen shut, his lower lip puffy and scabbed. He exited his room, cradling one arm gingerly, and froze. Mr. Kaufman was in his living room. Finn was always stiffer around Meg's father—his words, his posture—and it was no different now. As sore as he was, he felt himself straighten, standing tall and on alert.

"Grandma?" Finn said, looking to her, then back to Mr. Kaufman. "What's going on?"

Mr. Kaufman blurted, "Damn, son."

"Just a little *scuffle,*" Grandma said, lifting an eyebrow, "according to Finn."

"Got word from the county about your scuffle," Mr. Kaufman said.

"We gave our statements," Finn said tentatively.

"You're not in trouble," Mr. Kaufman said. "Goode's in custody. Whatever you and Spencer need, I'll walk you through that process."

"Thank you." Finn paused, still unclear about why Meg's dad was in his living room at this hour. "Is Meg okay?"

"Of course. Yes, she's fine," Mr. Kaufman said. "But your illegal grandmother has informed me of a few issues she hasn't dealt with."

At the word *illegal*, Finn's whole body sagged. "Look, I know she's not technically, I mean"—he faltered—"she *is*." He looked at his grandma. Swallowed. "You're *Grandma*." He faced Mr. Kaufman. His whole body ached, but he stood with his shoulders back. "If your wife told on us, that's fine. I won't play football if that's what this is about. But you're gonna break my grandmother's heart if you send me off to a group home. I can start working on the papers, but you—"

"Papers!" Mr. Kaufman said. "Ah, yes." He produced a manila folder from his coat pocket. "I have some papers—court approved, as a lawyer would say—but I seem to be missing an autograph from a certain Finn Christopher Geringer."

Finn cocked his head. Mr. Kaufman handed him the papers. He scrutinized them in the dim living room light, flipping through the fine writing. "Are these—"

"Emancipation papers? We could go that route, but no, they're not. Definitely not." Mr. Kaufman pointed at them. "They are, however, papers that declare you *are*, without a doubt, by the powers vested in the state of Texas, Mrs. Ruth Callahan's grandson."

He looked at his grandma, who was smiling and quietly blinking away tears.

"Adoption papers?" Finn whispered.

"I should have done it years ago," Mrs. Callahan confessed. "That was my mistake. Just didn't think it mattered much. You were always mine."

"My daughter luckily was honest pretty early on," Mr. Kaufman told him.

Something in Finn sank at the mention of Meg, Meg who Finn had adored since fifth grade, Meg who wouldn't ever be with him again. He remembered the way Meg's big eyes had scrunched closed with hurt when she saw the images of him and Tammy.

"Finn? You okay, son?"

Finn swallowed the lump in his throat and nodded.

"Meg told me her concern that she was being followed," Mr. Kaufman continued. "I've been around East Pages long enough."

"But did you—"

"Know who? Or what? No. Thought someone was just mad that she was 'dating the enemy.' But then your grandmother called me, asking for help. She suspected something foul. Kept telling me it was bigger. The football games tipped her off."

"You kept playing against nincompoops," she said.

"She brought it to my attention that you were matched against backups. Never the best. And she noticed Brit looking haggard. Like someone in trouble. At first I told her it was just the students," Mr. Kaufman said. "Hazing, bullying, I mean, this *is* Texas football. But then I found out one of the coaches was involved when my wife"—at this, he faltered, and Finn saw the look of sadness and hurt darken Mr. Kaufman's face—"my wife." He didn't finish the thought but, instead, cleared his throat. "Anyway, when Meg mentioned to your grandma that people were questioning her guardianship, she called again. Said it had to be connected. And, well? That was at least one thing I could help with."

Finn opened his mouth, but he had trouble forming words. "I

don't— I— It's—" He felt like he was recovering from a tackle, not even sure which end zone was his. He was at a loss. No man besides a coach had ever stepped in. He thought he'd hate it.

He didn't.

"Why are you suddenly being so nice?" he asked.

Mr. Kaufman sighed. "My daughter's got a good head on her shoulders. I've known that, but I . . ." He trailed off. "Parents just want the best for their kids." Mr. Kaufman nodded to himself, like he was working up the courage to say his next words. "But maybe the best is what they choose. She chose you."

"But we—"

"Broke up. I know. If that was in any way my fault—"

"No," Finn answered quickly. "It wasn't you."

Mr. Kaufman paused, taking it in, doubt creasing his forehead, but he finally accepted it with a "Well, then. If you say so." He clicked the back of a ballpoint pen and handed it to Finn. "Now, if you'll just sign here. We'll have a few more court-appointed meetings, but most of the legwork is done."

For the first time, Finn felt the weight of what he was about to do. He looked at his grandma, who beamed at him with glassy eyes. He gripped the pen like it could hold the tears in.

It didn't.

"Looks like you're stuck with me," Grandma said over his shoulder.

"Fused," Finn murmured, and with a shaky hand, signed the paper.

Chapter 63
BRITNEY

On Monday, November 13, the halls were quiet, the students' attitudes still damp from the playoff game they never had against Centennial last Friday night. After their homecoming loss, Coach Wilkins resigned, and an investigation was opened on Coach Goode, not just for his assault on Finn Geringer, but for extortion. Multiple people had come forward, but until there was a verdict, the team was allowed to play. They'd won the final three games, including the game against Finn's old team, the West Oak Brahmas. But the ruling came out three days before their first postseason game. No playoffs. Two years. They were still allowed to play the regular season next year, but again, there would be no playoffs. No chance at State. It made national news. Brit swore she could feel the glares from students she didn't even know, students who believed the rumors.

It was her fault, after all.

But Brit was cheerleading captain, and she continued to bounce and smile through the hallways, and as much as students wanted to hate her, she knew that most of them couldn't for very long. And if they did, she no longer minded.

She stood, ready for practice in her bright white cheerleading skirt—basketball season would be starting soon—leaning next to Spencer's locker as he cleaned it out. She tried to pretend it was no big deal. In the past four weeks, he'd gone back to being his aloof self. Stopped checking on her. Stopped calling. She was too proud to say anything. But now. Now it was real.

"So where're ya going?"

Spencer shrugged. "Away. There's a tract home complex about an hour outside of Houston we can afford. Dad's new retail job can transfer him there. Leah just needs a fresh start. Found a charter school with an art focus. No sports program." He laughed more to himself than for her. "And now, thanks to Richard Sherman, I got our first and last month's rent covered." Word got out quickly that Coach Goode had been arrested on charges—assault, fraud, embezzlement, conspiracy, extortion, the list was long. And the chat room Brit had shut down—there were rumors about that, too. The cheerleaders' donated photos—the ones strategically placed at every player's house as "gifts" for the duration they played at EastPay—were all taken back to be sold at auction to pay for the general football fund. Without an accurate inventory, the school could only do a general sweep of the players' houses over the weekend after the news. Spencer made sure to sell his two signed prints and jersey online and ship them out before they were picked up that Saturday afternoon.

Brit leaned against the neighboring locker. "Sometimes students look at me like they're still in the chat room talking. I know it's just me bein' paranoid. Emma looks at me like she's ready to bore a hole in my stomach."

Spencer laughed, and it made Brit's stomach flutter.

"And Walker . . ." Her voice disappeared.

"I assured him his dad ain't gettin' out." Everyone knew his dad had been incarcerated for five years. Still had ten to go. But she was sure Walker worried that someone might find a way to release him early.

"He dun' believe you." She noticed how fear made her slip back into her accent. She fought against it. "He hates me, Spence. For what I did."

"So let him," Spencer said. "People are always gonna have their games. You don't have to play them." He closed his empty locker, dumped the papers in the hallway trash bin.

"You know, some students still think The Game's around. Anytime something bad happens, they wonder if it's the chat room."

Spencer lifted an eyebrow but said nothing. Together they walked out of the school and into the parking lot toward Spencer's Blazer. Most of the cars had left for the day.

Brit didn't really know how to say goodbye. He'd pretty much ignored her since everything had gone down with Coach Goode, but every time she was at a pep rally and found him in the bleachers, he was looking at her with that mocking smile. Or was he charmed? She could never tell.

"So when all this high school crap is over in two years," Spencer said, "you gonna call me? Cheer girl?"

Brit stopped. Looked at him open-mouthed. "Cheer girl? And seriously? You've barely said a peep to me in a month!"

"That's because I don't *peep*." They reached his car, and he turned, leaned against his window. The back of the SUV was stacked with boxes. Leah, already in the passenger seat, waved shyly at Brit.

"Britney," he started, and his sincerity made her knees buckle, "it's a lot easier for me to call you 'cheer girl.' You get that, right? Look, I knew I was leaving. Why start something?"

She blushed. He was thinking of starting something?

"So," he tried again. "You wanna look me up in two years?"

"That's a long time."

"Maybe, maybe not. I hear the town I'm moving to is pretty nice in the summers. Near a lake. I'll make sure Pastor Mike flies you out on his dime."

She grinned. Although most of what Meg gave Spencer would be spent on his family's move and on Leah's new start, there was also sweet justice in spending Mike Menke's money on something frivolous.

"You can always spend his money and visit in the fall," she said. "First and third Saturdays. I hear there's this party by the river. Can't break tradition."

"I thought it was invite only," he said.

"Well, then, I'm Britney Wallace, cheer captain, and I'm inviting everybody."

He laughed. "I hope you do."

"Anyway." She held out her hand to shake Spencer's. "Safe travels."

Spencer cocked his head in disbelief. "Really, Britney?"

She didn't know what he meant, but he didn't give her enough time to think. He pulled her in and kissed her, his tongue finding its way into her parted lips, exploring, and without thought or pretense, she explored back. Spencer pulled away and got in the driver's seat, slamming the door so loudly, Brit jumped. He turned the key in the ignition and rolled down the window.

A cigarette dangled from his lips as he fumbled in the car for a lighter. He lit it, pressed his lips around it, and sucked through the filter, crackling the embers, before saying, "You be careful. A lot of people at this school think it was you. Some people would be pretty pissed off that you ruined their chances at a championship. Not the players, either. The fans."

Brit thought about that. The greed. The desire to be number one. The demeaning and drunken shouts from the parents in the stands. How far so many of them would go if pressed against the wall. She shook her head. "Their love for the game. It's . . . *I don't even know the word for it.*"

Spencer laughed. "I do." He drew a deep drag and blew the smoke in Brit's face. "Texas."

Was he right? She lived in a state that did everything big, and at times, that was a good thing. They loved big. They fought big. They believed big. And because they never did anything small, they were proud of what they stood for, what they fought for. Their loyalty was big. But there was a flip side to that, and sometimes, loyalty was bigger than honor. That's when it could get ugly. But she was here to stay, and she'd fight to keep honor above loyalty, because she believed that the love of the game could be pure and beautiful. Could unite families. Build community. Create amazing memories. Give hope.

She shook her head defiantly. "*Texas* ain't a bad word," she said.

"Neither is *shet,*" he said, grinning, the warmth between them palpable. And with that, Brit watched as the Blazer drove away and out of her life, Spencer's middle finger hanging out the window as a sentimental goodbye.

"Megan." Her mother poked her head into Meg's bedroom. Meg looked up from her piano book. "Someone's at the door for you."

Meg smiled a thank-you, which had been happening a lot lately. In the past four weeks, her mother hadn't suddenly become a super parent, but she was attending meetings. Meetings where everyone was honest about who they were. Where accolades and benefit dinners held little value. Her mother fiddled with a crochet needle, her new hobby, one she didn't like as much as holding a glass, but she was trying.

On the night when Mrs. Kaufman confessed everything to her husband, Meg heard muffled arguing through the walls of her bedroom into the early hours, until maybe her mom had run out of words. At least it felt like that, because in the morning, she had no words left for Meg. Her eyes were puffy, swollen shut with too many tears, but it didn't matter. She wouldn't have looked at Meg anyway. She didn't speak to her for two days.

Meg's dad, however, showed up at Finn's house with adoption papers, and she and her dad been talking ever since. She said she wanted to try volleyball. A total pivot from ballet, but her dad (and shockingly, her mom) told her to "go for it," which was something she never would've heard from them even a year ago. West Oak's volleyball team, the Brahmanettes, or the "Nettes," as they were known, had made it to regional playoffs every year she'd been at West Oak. Although Meg had natural athleticism, she'd never played. But she'd always loved the sport, and now, she was finally chasing after what she loved rather than what her parents felt was best. Plus, she'd get to hang with Kylie every day.

Women's volleyball was a fall sport, so they were almost done, but she had her sights set on next year. She didn't want her parents to pay for private lessons or connect her to professional volleyball players. She wanted to do this her way. Kylie said she'd work with her. She'd also talked to the men's volleyball coach—their season didn't start until spring—and he'd agreed to let her practice with them.

Something shifted in their house, too. Mr. Kaufman was home more. At first, it was like three roommates sharing space, but at least they were there, uncomfortable and quiet, but there. Slowly, they adjusted. Her dad no longer brought a newspaper or his iPad to the table. It was a lot of eyes and no words, and sometimes you could only hear someone chewing, but it felt real. Megan could handle real. This morning, her dad had actually touched her mom on the waist before he left. A small squeeze, barely noticeable, but as soon as the door closed, Mrs. Kaufman went straight for her yarn and crochet needle with a new determination, like she was telling her husband—and herself—that a fresh start was possible. At least that's what Meg imagined as she headed upstairs to study her piano theory. Ballet was done—no one mentioned it anymore—but Meg loved piano. She didn't have to give up everything that her parents pushed onto her. Compromise. Everyone else was doing it in the household. And as Finn taught her—the sadness of losing him was still so real even after a month—you should be willing to sacrifice a lot for your family.

Meg took the steps down two at a time—no more limping, no

more secrets—and opened the front door to someone who looked like he'd aged years in just one month. Stubble covered his chin, an even distribution that somehow softened him, made him look less angry. "Spencer," she greeted.

"Hello, Megan."

They stood like two people who'd been through a war, who felt the same emotions but had no words to place with them.

Spencer shifted to his other foot. "I'm moving." Dug his hands into his pockets. "Today, actually. My sister's waiting in the car."

She knew this was coming, had known it for weeks. "Where?"

"Away. Found a good district for Leah. New start. She needs it."

"Do *you*?"

"Nah. Well, who knows. Maybe."

Meg nudged him with her foot. "So you're quite the celebrity in this town. Bad boy does good. Puts a football coach behind bars."

A corner of his mouth lifted. "Not for football. Just white collar stuff."

"Made for a better story, anyway. Extortion? Plus, you also got him for assault."

She didn't mention who was assaulted. She was trying to move on, create a new life, one that didn't involve Finn Geringer, and it wasn't easy. It had been four weeks, and she still felt shaky, a dry leaf that could crumble if she thought about him too much.

Spencer looked up at her high ceilings.

"Sorry, by the way," she offered, filling the empty space in conversation. "I already apologized to Brit—assuming she told you by now. But I misled you guys—I just assumed it was Coach Wilkins.

Head coach. He was the meanest. At least I thought. I had no idea Coach Goode—"

He waved her off. "No one did. Doesn't matter. We figured it out. And everyone lived happily ever after."

He was being sarcastic, but it still stung. "Yep. Happily ever after." Meg shook her head, switched the focus before her emotions betrayed her. "I also heard that you were secretly working with Coach Goode," she said, smiling at the crazy gossip that was circulating. "And that you paid the Mafia thousands of dollars to keep you out of jail."

He grinned. "That the rumor?"

"That's the rumor."

He bit his lip, like he wanted to say more.

She couldn't believe all that Spencer had done to help her, Finn, and Brit. She thought back to their first meeting—the way he'd taunted Finn, kissing her hand in front of him.

"Brit talked to me," he said. "Told me how Pastor Mike came through. Paid you back every last penny in cash. And that you turned around and gave it to Wilkins to help with his little girl's medical bills. Fifty grand? Bold move. Giving away your mom's money."

She shrugged. "Mom already had given it away. Dad hadn't even noticed. I told her, though, after the fact. Thought she'd be mad." She chuckled. "She ended up sending him more. We'll be fine. Besides, I didn't give it *all* to Coach Wilkins."

His face reddened. She'd also given ten grand to Brit to give to Spencer.

"About that," he started.

"No," she said. "I already talked this over with Brit. She said if you try to give it back, I should spend all of it on a billboard of your face and the caption 'I sing Taylor Swift songs in my underwear.'"

He laughed. "Promise?"

She smiled warmly. "Leah needs a new start. You all do. It'll help."

He nodded. They stood there for a few awkward beats.

"Listen," he said, tapping the screen door he was holding open, "I know you're trying to move on from Finn. And I know you can call Brit if you want any updates. Brit knows a lot, but"—he paused—"she doesn't know everything." He raked his fingers through his hair. "Can we talk outside for a minute?"

• • •

Old Clayton Messler's property was an overgrown mass of weeds and "No Trespassing" signs. The chain-link fence that lined his property was gnarled like arthritic fingers, curled down from the top metal bar in some areas and lifted back from the dirt in the low spots. Meg found the hole in the fence—the one hidden behind a tree where someone had used pliers. She bent it back and weaseled her way under, snagging her shirt only once.

She kept her eye on the water tower and followed the faint sound of splashing against rocks. At the river's edge, she continued north, the bottoms of her shoes plastered with damp leaves. Finally, she saw the river's elbow, the sharp corner where the course was redirected. Dante's Ravine. And just like Spencer had told her, there was Finn in his hoodie and sweatpants, sitting on the edge, his legs dangling over.

She approached tentatively, and he looked up. His eyes tracked her like he wasn't sure if she was an apparition. Behind him was a huge mound of dirt, like an upturned grave, a four-foot volcano of loose dirt.

She sat down next to him and leaned against it. She could feel his body heat emanating. "I was told I'd find you here."

His eyes were curious yet confused. He said nothing.

"I spoke with Spencer," she said, running her fingers through the dirt. "He told me about the sanctions on EastPay."

He turned toward the water, the whitewash gurgling and gushing along the rocks.

"No playoffs," she continued. "No championships. Two years."

He nodded. Sighed.

"But you guys still get to play the season. You still can be seen. I hear coaches are still looking at you."

He lifted a shoulder and dropped it.

"Jamal mentioned you got him a meeting with one of the UT coaches." She swallowed. "Maybe you'll get to play together after all." He still didn't look at her. "Anyway, it's good you two are back to talking."

They sat quietly, the sound of the water filling the silence. A bird chirped from a nearby tree. She tried again. "Heard you come here a lot," she said gently. Spencer had said Finn hated his memory with Tammy, so he was determined to keep coming and creating more memories until it dulled into the background. But looking at him now, staring off at nothing in particular, she thought maybe it was more to make himself suffer. "Spencer says you asked Cedric Wilkins to stay."

"He resigned anyway."

Megan felt her stomach drop at hearing Finn's voice again. It was rich, deep. Sincere. But there was also a gravelly thickness to it, and he coughed to clear his throat.

"Supposedly he had nothing to do with the sabotaging of other players," she said.

"He didn't." His voice sounded scratchy. Was he sick? Her shoulders slumped at the thought. She was no longer in his life enough to know even if he had a cold.

She couldn't handle this anymore. She reached out, touched his shoulder. He flinched. She caressed his cheek, but he pulled back, turned his eyes down at the river. He pulled his knees to his chest.

"Meg . . ." he started, but he choked on his words. Tears filled his eyes, and he didn't even try to hold them back. "Tammy— I'm so sorry—"

"I know you are." Her eyes filled, too, her tears turning Finn blurry. "She wasn't playing fair. Spencer said she purposely put herself in multiple locations to implicate you."

He shook his head. "Doesn't matter." He put his forehead on his knees, burying his face from her. "I shouldn't have put myself in that position."

"No, you shouldn't have." She avoided looking at Finn's shoulders, how they shook with tears and regret. Looked instead at his cleats. "I'm not the same girl you started dating back at West Oak."

"I know." His words were low. Ashamed. He brought his head up and stared at the river. "You deserve everything. So much more than me."

"I could never compete with her, you know."

He shook his head fiercely, opened his mouth to protest.

She said hurriedly, "Not Tammy." She paused. "Football."

He didn't speak, so she peered at him. His eyes were red-rimmed and tired.

"Football was your first girlfriend," she said. "Spent all your time with her. And I get it. She was beautiful. Smart. Taught you how to plan, think, look at life. How every moment was a possible play, a chance at something if you fought hard enough, lived hard enough." She thought back to how she used to pour everything into ballet. "It wasn't all bad. But life's so much bigger than a football field. And I'm not a sidelines girl."

"I know," he said miserably. "You never were."

"This might be—what do teams call it? A 'rebuilding year' for us. But we could try." She linked her index finger with his. "As friends?"

He swallowed. "I'd like that."

She wrapped her arms around his waist. She felt him instantly tense, unsure how to respond. She rested her cheek on his shoulder, drinking in the scent of him—sweat and grass and something else—not soap or laundry—just that soft and familiar scent that was undeniably *Finn*. She sighed deeply, breathing it in.

He reached a hand tentatively around her, looked at her as if to ask, *Is this okay?*

She pulled him close as an answer, and they embraced. She could feel the wetness of his tears on her cheek, and although it was nothing more than a hug, Meg felt a deeper and more powerful emotion than she'd ever felt with him before. It was longing, betrayal, regret, deep anger, and an even deeper sadness, but over that there was a love that looked straight in the face of it all and was up for the fight. She didn't know if it would win—the odds were against them—but she was willing to suit up and see what they were made of.

ACKNOWLEDGMENTS

All right, team, gather round. We've reached the end of a long, hard-fought season, and now it's time to look back at everyone who played a part in getting us here, to the end zone of this book.

First and foremost, I want to thank the One who's truly in charge of it all, the ultimate Commissioner—God. Nothing happens without Your blessing, and I'm in awe that You believe in a knucklehead like me. You've gifted me with creativity and the chance to bring stories to life, and I'm beyond grateful for Your kindness.

Next, a big shout-out to our quarterback, Michael Bourret, more commonly known as my agent. You believed in the play enough to make me run it again, and again—until I got it just right. Thanks for seeing the potential in this story and pushing me to be better than my best effort.

To Elizabeth Lee, our offensive coordinator, thank you for your patience and positivity as an editor. Even when I got stuck on the sidelines or slowed down with an edit, you were there to brainstorm a different angle or strategy . . . and to share my giddy love for Kristen Bell and Dax Shepard.

Laurel Robinson, our trusty copy editor and referee, you kept me in check, reminding me that I'm not British and to leave off the *s* at the end of *toward*. You made sure the game stayed clean, throwing the flag when I veered offside with *on to* versus *onto* or had twelve men on the field—too many words!

Now, the Critique Mafia—AnneLise Wilhelmson, Tim Burke,

and Lorian Steider-Brady—you were my defensive line, dissecting every chapter, page, and word. Your relentless pursuit of excellence pushed me to dig deeper to get the win.

Phil Blyth, my MVP, you were always there to help me cut down the field, add some yards, give me that crucial male perspective, tell me to "lock it up" when I got discouraged by the score, and send me to Texas for those research trips. On and off the field, you're the play that keeps me going. Forever my touchdown.

Nate Morton, our team's very own Texas high-school-football alum and NFL veteran, you were the fact-checking, lingo-slinging guru that made sure I didn't fumble. Thanks for keeping me on track and making sure this book had the authenticity it needed to score big.

Ronni Davis, our defensive coach (aka our sensitivity reader), you had my back, keeping the game clean and respectful. Your insight was invaluable in making sure our portrayal was accurate, thoughtful, and kind. I'm deeply grateful for your support in helping this book shine and resonate with so many.

Octogenarians Kenneth and Jo Kucan, you're the smartest Hall of Famers (aka ex-teachers) I know—intimidating in the best way, on the sidelines pushing me for quality over quantity. Knowing you'd eventually read this book made me sweat and put in the hours, never settling for mediocrity. Whatever the outcome of this manuscript, I can walk off the field knowing one thing for sure: I gave it everything I had and left it all out there.

And to those tough scouts—the editors who initially passed on this manuscript (you know who you are)—thank you for your feedback. I am grateful for you, truly. I took your words to heart, and I hope this final version is something you'd be proud to acquire now.

Finally, to my family, my biggest cheerleaders—thank you for always being in the stands, cheering me on, no matter the score. Your belief in me is often the driving force behind every page.

We've put in the work, we've left it all on the field, and now it's time to celebrate this victory together. Here's to all of you, my team—couldn't have done it without you.